MAKING FRIENDS

Awalmir asked, "Are you here to destroy the poppy crops?"

Brannigan shook his head. "No. Not unless the Taliban becomes involved."

Awalmir shrugged. "We are not friends of the Taliban."

Samroz leaned forward. "Is this disregard of our harvests permanent?"

"I don't know," Brannigan answered truthfully.

"What are you going to do about the ones who murdered the Swatis?" Awalmir asked.

"I'm waiting for orders," Brannigan said. "But I know for sure we will be told to hunt them down and capture them for punishment."

"What if they won't surrender?" the Yousafzai *khan* asked.

"We will kill them."

"Russians and Pashtuns too?"

"All of them," Brannigan stated.

"Even if some are Russian?"

"We will kill *all* of them," Brannigan repeated.

"In that case, you are the enemy of my enemy," Awalmir said. "I will help you in the coming battles."

SEALS
COMBAT ALLEY

JACK TERRAL

JOVE BOOKS, NEW YORK

THE BERKLEY PUBLISHING GROUP
Published by the Penguin Group
Penguin Group (USA) Inc.
375 Hudson Street, New York, New York 10014, USA
Penguin Group (Canada), 90 Eglinton Avenue East, Suite 700, Toronto, Ontario M4P 2Y3, Canada
(a division of Pearson Penguin Canada Inc.)
Penguin Books Ltd., 80 Strand, London WC2R 0RL, England
Penguin Group Ireland, 25 St. Stephen's Green, Dublin 2, Ireland (a division of Penguin Books Ltd.)
Penguin Group (Australia), 250 Camberwell Road, Camberwell, Victoria 3124, Australia
(a division of Pearson Australia Group Pty. Ltd.)
Penguin Books India Pvt. Ltd., 11 Community Centre, Panchsheel Park, New Delhi—110 017, India
Penguin Group (NZ), 67 Apollo Drive, Rosedale, North Shore 0632, New Zealand
(a division of Pearson New Zealand Ltd.)
Penguin Books (South Africa) (Pty.) Ltd., 24 Sturdee Avenue, Rosebank, Johannesburg 2196,
South Africa

Penguin Books Ltd., Registered Offices: 80 Strand, London WC2R 0RL, England

This is a work of fiction. Names, characters, places, and incidents either are the product of the author's imagination or are used fictitiously, and any resemblance to actual persons, living or dead, business establishments, events, or locales is entirely coincidental. The publisher does not have any control over and does not assume any responsibility for author or third-party websites or their content.

SEALS: COMBAT ALLEY

A Jove Book / published by arrangement with the author

PRINTING HISTORY
Jove mass-market edition / December 2007

Copyright © 2007 by The Berkley Publishing Group.
Cover illustration by Larry Rostant.
Cover design by George Long.

ISBN: 978-0-515-14383-6

JOVE®
Jove Books are published by The Berkley Publishing Group,
a division of Penguin Group (USA) Inc.,
375 Hudson Street, New York, New York 10014.
JOVE is a registered trademark of Penguin Group (USA) Inc.
The "J" design is a trademark belonging to Penguin Group (USA) Inc.

PRINTED IN THE UNITED STATES OF AMERICA

10 9 8 7 6 5 4 3 2 1

Dedicated to
Commander Larry Foss, USN

Special Acknowledgment to
Patrick E. Andrews

NOTE: Enlisted personnel in this book are identified by their ranks (petty officer third class, chief petty officer, master chief petty officer, etc.) rather than their ratings (boatswain's mate, yeoman, etc.) for clarification of status and position within the chain of command. However, when a man's rating is significant in the story, he is identified by that designation.

TABLE OF ORGANIZATION
BRANNIGAN'S BRIGANDS

HEADQUARTERS

Lieutenant William "Wild Bill" Brannigan
(Commanding Officer)

Senior Chief Petty Officer Buford Dawkins
(Detachment Chief)

PO2C Francisco "Frank" Gomez
(RTO)

PO3C James "Doc" Bradley
(Hospital Corpsman)

FIRST ASSAULT SECTION

Lieutenant Junior Grade James "Jim" Cruiser
(Section Commander)

PO3C Earl "Tex" Benson
(SAW Gunner)

ALPHA FIRE TEAM

Chief Petty Officer Matthew "Matt" Gunnarson
(Team Leader)

PO2C Dennis "Tiny" Burke
(Rifleman)

PO2C Peter "Pete" Dawson
(Rifleman)

PO2C Josef "Joe" Miskoski
(Grenadier)

BRAVO FIRE TEAM

PO1C Montgomery "Monty" Sturgis
(Team Leader)

PO2C Andrei "Andy" Malachenko
(Grenadier)

PO2C Edward "Matty" Matsuno
(Rifleman)

PO2C Garth Redhawk
(Rifleman)

SECOND ASSAULT SECTION

Ensign Orlando Taylor
(Section Commander)

PO3C Douglas "Doug" MacTavish
(SAW Gunner)

CHARLIE FIRE TEAM

PO1C Guttorm "Gutsy" Olson
(Team Leader)

PO2C David "Dave" Leibowitz
(Rifleman)

PO2C Reynauld "Pech" Pecheur
(Rifleman)

PO2C Bruno Puglisi
(Grenadier)

DELTA FIRE TEAM

PO1C Michael "Connie" Concord
(Team Leader)

PO3C Arnold "Arnie" Bernardi
(Grenadier)

PO3C Guy Devereaux
(Rifleman)

PO3C Chadwick "Chad" Murchison
(Rifleman)

Excerpt from Sun Tzu's *Art of War*, as paraphrased by Petty Officer 2nd Class Bruno Puglisi of Brannigan's Brigands:

If you know both yourself and the enemy real good, you don't have to sweat even a hunnerd battles. If you know yourself but you ain't real familiar with the bad guys, you'll end up batting about .500 in combat. But, man, if you don't know either yourself or them rat bastards, you're gonna get your ass kicked ever'time. Now think about that.

PROLOGUE

TWELVE-YEAR-OLD Reshteen stood on the rooftop with his wool serape-like *pukhoor* hanging loosely over his shoulders. It was still a couple of months before the onset of winter, yet a rare preliminary coolness was in the air. After the heat of summer, it was a refreshing change. The steppes were much warmer and fifteen hundred meters lower than the Kangal Mountains to the east across the Tajikistan border. Up in that frigid high country, hundreds of glaciers had been carving through the depthless rock beds for eons. These deep slabs of ice, some more than five kilometers wide, eased across the mountaintops in a steady progression that was so slow the human eye could not perceive the movement.

Reshteen, like all boys his age, took his turn on lookout duty, and that's what he was doing on top of old Mohambar's house, which was the tallest in the village. This was a vital necessity in the living routine of the Pashtuns who inhabited the Pranistay Steppes. Fierce bandits roved unchecked through the area, and raids happened once or twice a year. Mostly, however, the attacks by the murdering robbers occurred when people, alone or in small groups, were traveling across the steppes to other settlements.

The boy guards like Reshteen kept part of their attention focused on the distant horizons to the south and west. When they turned to the north and east, they took extra time to study the view. That was where the rugged, boulder-strewn foothills of the Kangals joined the flat country, and it was much more difficult to discern anyone approaching from that direction.

Reshteen took off his *puhtee* and scratched his head as he gazed out across the steppes in boredom. There was nothing out there but a dancing blur on the horizon that distorted the distant view. During the long hours of guard duty, when he tried very hard, his mind could conjure up phantom donkeys or goats in the haze. This time his eyes could make up nothing to amuse him, and he swung his attention over toward the mountains.

"Awrede!" he hollered out loud enough for the whole village to hear. "Two horsemen to the east!"

VALENTIN Surov and Yakob Putnovsky reined in as the village came into view. Both horsemen wore a mixture of native costume and Russian Army uniforms. Their boots were definitely military-issue and the open-collar camouflaged jackets were the type used by the KGB border guards of the Soviet Union. The rest of their clothing was the traditional type found in Afghanistan and Tajikistan. The cartridge pouches across their shoulders were the leather type available in the bazaars of the larger towns. These were handmade and exhibited the fine craftsmanship of the saddlers who designed, cut, and stitched them together.

Putnovsky took his binoculars and studied the small community. "Is this the place we're looking for?"

"Just a minute," Surov said. He reached into his jacket and pulled out a map, unfolding it carefully.

Putnovsky glared at him. "Fucking officer!"

Surov sneered. Both of them were veterans of the Russian Army and the practice of not instructing enlisted men in map reading had been a Soviet tradition that remained in effect with some units of the new Russian Army. The reason behind the practice was to keep any discontented soldier with itchy feet from finding a route to flee from the Peasants' and Workers' Paradise. Surov studied the terrain around them, then traced his finger along an elevation line. "*Da!* This is it. Come on!"

THE fact that Reshteen had sighted only two riders did not alarm the villagers, but they fetched their weapons just the same. The pair could be scouting for a larger bandit gang lurking somewhere else nearby. Most of the men stayed inside their huts, ready for trouble. The women and children went about their normal activities whether it was indoors or out, while a half dozen men with their AK-47s concealed under their *pukhoors* lounged on benches in the village square.

The two Russians rode slowly and warily into the village, their AKS-74 assault rifles slung across their backs to make it obvious they had no bad intentions. Each was aware the locals were armed to the teeth and that suspicious Pashtuns had a disagreeable habit of shooting first and asking questions later, provided there was a survivor or two to converse with. The Russians brought their horses to a halt at the well, nodding to one of the men standing there.

"*Staray me she!*" Surov said in his working knowledge of Pashto. "Are any of your *spinzhire* around?" He used the Pashtun word for "gray-beards," which was the way they referred to their elders.

The Pashtun man called out, and an old fellow named Mohambar appeared in the doorway of the nearest hut. He said nothing, but looked up at the Russian on the horse. These men had been appearing on the steppes from time to time over the past few years. It was said among the Pashtun tribes that they gave competition to the traditional native bandit groups.

"I have been sent by Luka Yarkov to give you a message," Surov said. "He has been informed that this village made much money selling opium poppies to a fellow called Awalmir Yousafzai."

Old Mohambar nodded.

"Awalmir did not give Yarkov's share to him," Surov said. "It is a *malya*—a tax. Since you were paid money by Awalmir, you must give a share to Luka Yarkov because he has enough fighting men to control everything that happens on the steppes. Do you understand?"

Mohambar stared at him without expression or emotion.

"If you do not pay Luka Yarkov what is due him, he will be angry."

There was still no reaction from the elderly Pashtun.

With anyone but Pashtuns, this would have been the beginning of some sort of negotiations, protests, or a discussion. But Surov did not expect any verbal response to his announcement. It was enough that he had made it and that these villagers would pass the word on to their brethren across the steppes.

The Russian turned his eyes from the old man and glanced around at the other villagers who also did no more than gaze at him. He nodded, saying, "*Khuday pea man*—good-bye."

The two foreigners rode slowly from the village, their weapons still slung across their backs. The Pashtuns looked at each other, knowing this was the start of big troubles on the Pranistay Steppes.

CHAPTER 1

BRANNIGAN'S Brigands had seen off one of their own the evening before. Mike Assad, the Arab-American member of the detachment, had received orders transferring him to Station Bravo in Bahrain for an undisclosed assignment. The farewell get-together held in the ready room on that last evening had been a sad occasion. It was a time of quiet conversation punctuated by forced laughter during recollections of episodes concerning Assad's time in the detachment. And of course there was also serious speculation about where the SEAL might be going and what he might be doing during this unexpected change in duty assignment.

Assad was one of the original members of the outfit, and the other Brigands truly felt as if they were losing a member of their family. His best buddy, Dave Leibowitz, had a hard time containing his disappointment and outright grief regarding the transfer. He and Assad had been known as the

"Odd Couple" because of Assad's Arabic ancestry and Leibowitz's Jewish origins. The two American SEALs had ignored their different ethnicities and developed a deep friendship over the many months of serving together. The pair's forte had been reconnaissance, and they shared the vanguard in dozens of incursions into harm's way, being the first to come under enemy fire on most occasions.

Mike Assad had been separated from the group one time before when he was plucked from their midst to be inserted as an operative for the CIA within the al-Mimkhalif terrorist group. This organization operated in Pakistan and Afghanistan, conducting a jihad that had very real possibilities of overtaking even Usama Bin Laden's al-Qaeda. Assad worked smart and had come out of the assignment with enough intelligence data to bring about the destruction of the bad guys. His reappearance in the detachment was one that none of the SEALs would ever forget. He unexpectedly bumped into them in the middle of the Indian Ocean while they were on an operation in an ACV, but that wasn't the kicker. Mike Assad was in a stolen whaler boat with a beautiful German courtesan who had been a member of a radical sheikh's harem of European women. That unscrupulous gentleman happened to be the leader of the al-Mimkhalif, the same terrorist group that Assad was spying on. From that time on, nothing Assad did surprised anybody in the detachment.

FLIGHT DECK
0815 HOURS

MIKE Assad, dressed in a BDU, stood holding on to a pair of seabags with the rest of the detachment gathered around him. He had turned in his field gear and weapons to Senior Chief Petty Officer Buford Dawkins the evening before and now had only his personal clothing and gear to take to his new assignment. It was an awkward time for everybody. This was the moment of good-bye, not like the night before when the actual parting was still hours away.

The SEALs as human males weren't good at showing their real emotions, and they shifted their feet and spoke self-consciously among themselves. They and their departing buddy were all glad when the approaching Seahawk helicopter coming to pick Assad up swung in off the ocean and begin sinking down to the deck. The roar of the engines and deep whipping of the rotors saved anyone from having to say anything.

Leibowitz stepped forward and tapped Assad on the shoulder. When he turned around the two shook hands and exchanged quick smiles. Now, one by one, the other SEALs presented themselves. It was mostly quick handshakes, but now and then a pat on the shoulder was thrown in for good measure. They were all relieved when the unceremonious ceremony of farewell was over, and Assad trotted over to board the Super Stallion CH-53 helicopter to fly off to his new life.

Lieutenant (JG) Jim Cruiser summed up everyone's feelings very well with a simple remark: "The detachment just isn't going to be the same anymore."

THE REPUBLIC OF TAJIKISTAN

TAJIKISTAN is a former member nation of the now-defunct USSR. It is a mountainous, landlocked country bordered by Kyrgyzstan to the north, Uzbekistan on the west, and China to the east, while Afghanistan is on the southern border.

Although Russians make up only 4 percent of the population, their influence and language are still strong even after almost fifteen years of independence. Back in those days of the former Communist glory, the area was a most unpleasant duty station and the Red Army posted many of its trouble-makers and undesirables in the local garrisons just to be rid of them. The worst of these sites was an unhappy place located in the Kangal Mountains where the undesirables were isolated and cut off from the rest of the world. This included a particularly notorious military prison where some of the worst offenders of the armed forces were housed. Many were awaiting executions that never happened due to the convicts having been written off and forgotten by Soviet officialdom. They languished within the confines of the place, underfed, ignored, and miserable.

The commandant of the prison was a luckless man stuck in a thankless job. He barely had enough funds to feed his charges and only a small guard staff to look after them. Consequently, the prisoners, though securely locked up, were free to do pretty much as they pleased within the walls and razor wire. As in any criminal group, the toughest of the tough floated to the top in this stew of violence and took over as the uncontested leaders. The top hoodlum ended up being an ex–warrant officer by the name of Luka Yarkov who had been convicted of beating a soldier to death during a drunken rage. He had been awaiting his execution for more than a decade. While this wouldn't be unusual in the United States, condemned prisoners always were shot within a few days of sentencing in Russia.

The commandant, while ignoring the activity within the prison, had managed to make outside contacts among the civilian population. This brought him into touch with local politicians and bureaucrats who had taken advantage of the distance between themselves and the Kremlin to get into extracurricular activities to make money in various dishonest endeavors. This included the black market, loan-sharking, selling of stolen government property, and other nefarious undertakings. Now and then one or more of these entrepreneurs had special needs for muscle. They would bribe the prison supervisor to release a few prisoners to be employed as goons and debt collectors when necessary. The commandant received bribes for providing these services, and he turned to the head prisoner, Yarkov, to furnish these temporary employees who performed the deeds for a pittance and a paid visit to a miserable brothel at the edge of the nearby town of Dolirod.

When the Soviet Union broke up, the Russians simply abandoned the place, leaving the condemned men free to do anything they wished as long as it didn't include returning to

Mother Russia. Yarkov was not unhappy about being unable to go back home, since his crime would undoubtedly result in the application of the heretofore forgotten death sentence. In fact, he saw remaining in Tajikistan as a great opportunity to establish a personal seat of power in a country rife with banditry and lawlessness. He quickly organized his prison gang into a small army and equipped them with uniforms, equipment, and weapons left behind by the former guard detachment.

Yarkov knew he couldn't carry on criminal activities from a prison that was so close to civilization, so he took his men up higher into the wild highlands of the Kangal Mountains to establish a base of operations. The Russians were surprised when they came into immediate conflict with the local bad guys who resented their intrusion. These were Tajik bandits who had been raiding in both Tajikistan and Afghanistan for generations. However, it didn't take the ex-convicts long to overcome their new neighbors, and after a couple of pitched battles that resulted in a decimation of the bandits amid an orgy of rape and destruction, the surviving victims threw themselves on the mercy of the conquerors.

At that point, the vanquished outlaws became assets and advisors to the Russian newcomers. They taught them the way of the mountains and the value of horses for fast travel in a near-roadless environment. After acquiring the skills necessary to become horsemen, this newly organized gang, guided by their new friends, made raids down on the Pranistay Steppes to the south. Surprisingly, the Pashtun people living in the area had more valuables and possessions worth stealing than Yarkov expected. They also had weaponry and ammunition left over from their fight against the Soviet Army back in the 1980s. And there were times when they had plenty of cash on hand made up of euros, French francs, German marks, and even American dollars. Yarkov couldn't figure out how they came into so much money.

It was easy to prey on them because they lived in a far-flung system of small villages and it was only a matter of picking them off one at a time. It was also a good place to get women. Most of these stolen females, after fighting fiercely to protect their honor, were beaten into submission and ravaged by the Russians. A few died from the mistreatment and a couple committed suicide, though this was rare. According to Pashtun beliefs, any person who killed himself would be damned for an eternity of committing and recommitting the act. However, a kidnapped Pashtun woman could not return to her people without having to suffer being murdered in the name of honor by the men of her family. Therefore, if she wanted to live, she would have to become an infidel's woman. Surprisingly, some lasting and tender relationships developed between these women and the rough ex-convicts. The children of these unions offered a future to this community of violence and banditry.

Yarkov and his men went down into the town of Dolirod to make purchases with the stolen cash or to sell or barter looted goods. And there was also that bordello available for those who had yet to get women. The ex-convicts were welcomed by the eager shop owners who had plenty of merchandise to sell them. There were weapons, military equipment, saddles, clothing, miscellaneous items, and presents to give the women waiting up in the mountains.

It was during one of the visits that Yarkov struck up a conversation with a money changer while trading in stolen currency for Tajik somonis. The subject of the conversation was the amount and variation of cash among the villagers down on the Pranistay Steppes.

It was at this time that Luka Yarkov learned about the opium poppy trade.

SHELOR FIELD, AFGHANISTAN
3 OCTOBER
0915 HOURS

BRANNIGAN'S Brigands walked down the ramp of the USAF Pave Low helicopter and filed into the hangar behind Senior Chief Petty Officer Buford Dawkins. This was the large, empty structure they always used as a combination barracks and headquarters during stays at the Air Force facility.

The detachment officers—Lieutenant Bill Brannigan, Lieutenant (JG) Jim Cruiser, and Ensign Orlando Taylor—were gathered off to one side with two staff officers well known by the Brigands. These were Commander Thomas Carey and Lieutenant Commander Ernest Berringer. There were four other men present: an officer in the uniform of the Pakistani Army, a dark youngster wearing native Pashtun garb, and a short, pudgy fellow with a tall, slim man standing beside him. This latter pair was dressed in khaki safari getups.

Senior Chief Dawkins raised his hand to bring the column to a halt. "Alright! Y'all got your favorite places to bed down, so turn to. Don't bother to unroll your mattresses. Just dump ever'thing on the deck and get right back here. Go to it!"

The SEALs went over to one side of the building where they normally slept during their frequent visits. They were surprised to see a familiar figure already there. This was Tiny Burke, a huge, muscular Tennessean who had been with the detachment during Operation Battleline a few weeks earlier. He grinned at them, speaking in his drawl. "It's right good to see y'all again."

Doug MacTavish, from North Carolina, was happy to see his fellow southerner. "How'd you manage to get back here, Tiny?"

"They was fixing to ship me to Iraq when a yeoman come up and said there was orders sending me straight back to Brannigan's Brigands," he explained. "They said I was taking somebody's place."

"That was Mike Assad," Doug said. "He was hauled away somewhere aboard a chopper."

"Well, here I am again then," Tiny said happily.

Everybody quickly grounded their gear, maintaining assault section and fire team integrity to keep the equipment arranged in an orderly manner. Then, with Tiny accompanying them, they walked back and formed up in front of the senior chief. Brannigan turned from the officers and strangers, nodding to the detachment.

"Okay, guys," he said, pointing to three rows of chairs toward the back of the hangar. "You know the drill."

The SEALs walked over to sit down in the rows of chairs with the officers and visitors following. It was Commander Carey who went to the front of the group and took the floor. "How many of you guys can ride horses?" Everyone stared at him in perplexed confusion, and he repeated the question with a degree of peevishness. "Damn it! I asked how many of you know how to ride a horse."

Monty Sturgis, Tex Benson, Garth Redhawk, and Chad Murchison raised their hands.

Brannigan chuckled. "Hell! I didn't think *any* of 'em knew how."

"This complicates matters," Berringer muttered. "There're only four."

"It can't be helped," Carey said.

Bruno Puglisi, wanting to be helpful, held up his hand. "I can handicap horses, sir. I used to go out to the racetrack with my uncle Vito all-a-time when I was a kid. I even hit a three-horse parlay when I was thirteen."

"Shut up, Puglisi," Brannigan said.

"Aye, sir!"

"Okay, men," Carey said. "If you haven't already guessed it, there is a mission in the offing. But before we get into that, let me introduce these gentlemen with me. The first is Lieutenant Barakaat Sidiqui. He is the captain of the Pakistani Army Polo Team."

Sidiqui, a slim, handsome man with lively eyes and a neatly trimmed black beard, stepped forward and gave a snappy British-style salute.

"This young fellow," Carey said, pointing to a boy in his late teens dressed in bakesey Pashtun clothing, "is Chinar Janoon. He will be your interpreter and guide."

Chinar gave them a wide, pleased grin. "How do you do, sirs? I am most pleased to be serving you."

Now the two men in the khaki garb stepped forward, and Carey indicated the short, plump one. "You may have seen this gentleman on television back in the States. His name is Dirk Wallenger and the guy with him is his cameraman,

Eddie Krafton. They are from Global News Broadcasting and will be imbedded with you on this operation."

"Wow!" Joe Miskoski exclaimed. "Are we gonna be on television?"

"Indeed you will," Wallenger said. "I have requested to be assigned to a unit going on a special sort of mission. Permission was at last granted, so here I am complete with a cameraman."

"Welcome," Brannigan said. "We hope for some even-handed treatment in your broadcasts, Wallenger."

"I promise I'll tell your story to the American public as truthfully as I possibly can," Wallenger replied. He glanced over at Carey. "By the way, I am considered a rather skillful horseman back home. And Eddie rides with me occasionally on weekends."

"You two are probably going to come in handy," Brannigan said good-naturedly. "There're twenty out of twenty-four of us who will need some pretty basic instruction. But I believe we all know what a horse is."

Wallenger showed a grin. "That's a good start, I would think."

"Okay," Carey said. "Tomorrow morning the whole bunch of us is going to fly over to Sharif Garrison in Pakistan where their army's polo team is stationed. That is where you'll begin your equestrian training."

Puglisi was confused again. "I thought we was gonna learn how to ride horses."

"Shut up, Puglisi!"

"Aye, sir!"

CHAPTER 2

THE military post, built by the British Army in the 1880s, was located five kilometers south of Karachi on the coast of the Arabian Sea. It was not an important facility now as it had been during the days of Queen Victoria's reign. In modern times it was being used for extracurricular activities such as a beach resort for officers and their families, hostelry for important military visitors, and—most important of all—the stables and headquarters of the Pakistani Army's polo team. This sport was the most popular in the northern areas of the nation and was a traditional pastime that many believed dated back to pre-Christian times.

Brannigan's Brigands, along with Wallenger, Krafton, and Chinar the interpreter, had been flown down from Shelor Field the previous evening, and after settling in, were fed a late dinner of fried paratha bread, marinated baked chicken, vegetables, and a traditional dessert of custard made of rice and milk. The meal was consumed in the officers' mess without regard to rank, so that the officers, petty officers, and the three civilians all dined together. This broke with normal tradition, but the unexpected training mission had caught the garrison staff shorthanded.

The next morning, after arising at 0630 hours, they were once again taken to the officers' dining facility to eat. This time they were served a Western-style breakfast of steak and eggs. This was followed by a tour of the garrison, conducted by Lieutenant Sidiqui, who pointed out several historical sites of the post. He also delivered a short lecture on the background of the area and its functions during the glory days of the British Empire. It had been an embarkation and debarkation site for troops going to and from colonial postings.

After a visit to the garrison's small but impressive museum, the SEALs and their companions were bussed out to the stables to begin their lessons in the fine art of equitation, which Puglisi now knew meant horseback riding.

The classroom was a modern chamber complete with tables and chairs, a combination DVD and VHS player, whiteboard, and small library with books, pamphlets, and magazines pertaining to horses and polo. Lieutenant Sidiqui waited while his students settled down at the tables. Each seating place had a notebook, a textbook regarding horses, and an array of ballpoint pens.

Chief Petty Officer Matt Gunnarson, sitting with his good friend Senior Chief Petty Officer Buford Dawkins, leaned toward his companion. "This Pakistani Army is gonna spoil us, Buford."

Dawkins, looking around at the near-antiseptic learning environment, nodded in agreement. "The ready room back on the *Daly* looks like a pigsty compared to this place."

Sidiqui went to the front of the room and stood by the combo DVD and tape player. "I welcome you to the training facilities of our army's champion polo team. We are most pleased to be able to help you prepare yourselves for your upcoming mission."

"Excuse me, sir," Monty Sturgis said, raising his hand. "Are we gonna be riding polo ponies in the field?"

"Oh, heavens, no!" Sidiqui exclaimed with a laugh. "We have other horses here at Sharif Garrison. There is a ceremonial cavalry troop stationed here that goes about the country giving riding demonstrations in the old traditions. They have an excellent stable of trained military mounts from which you will draw your animals."

Chad Murchison had a question. "Sir, I have ridden a great deal at several local stables back home and am familiar with show horses and polo ponies. What I would like to learn is the criteria for a cavalry mount. What does one look for in these famous and traditional warhorses?"

"That is an excellent question," the Pakistani officer replied. "And after I have explained it to you, you will appreciate more the horses you will take on your mission." He paused for a moment of thought, then said, "A cavalry horse must be sound and gentle under the saddle. He must possess a prompt action at the walk, trot, and gallop. And, of course, be free of vicious habits."

Tex Benson, who had done less-than-genteel horseback riding during his Texas youth, was also curious. "What are them calvary horse supposed to look like?"

"In the Pakistani Army we prefer geldings from fifteen to sixteen hands high," Sidiqui explained. "They should not weigh less than nine hundred and fifty pounds or more than fifteen hundred. An age between four and eight years old is also preferable. As far as appearance goes, he should have a broad forehead with large eyes, shoulders sloping well back, a full, broad chest with forelegs straight and standing well under." He paused, then asked, "Do you require more information?"

Benson shook his head. "No, thanks, I was just looking for a casual description."

"What's a 'hand' when you talk about how high they gotta be?" Gutsy Olson asked.

"A hand is four inches," Sidiqui replied. "And the measurement is from the withers to the ground."

Brannigan now spoke up. "You'll have to excuse us, Lieutenant. Most of us are in complete ignorance about horses. What are the 'withers'?"

"Oh, pardon me, please," the Pakistani said. "The withers of a horse is where the back meets the neck. Thus, the average horse for military service would be five feet high from that point down to the ground." He looked around. "If there are no more questions, we shall turn to the DVD player. You will see an introduction and description of the things you will learn during your training here. After this, we will have another question-and-answer period, then go to lunch. When you have eaten, you will be taken to the riding hall where you will be introduced to the horse that will be yours during your operation."

LOGOVISHCHYEH, TAJIKISTAN

LUKA Yarkov and his gang of ex-military prisoners called their small village in the Kangal Mountains "Logovishchyeh," which is Russian for "lair." Logovishchyeh seemed a good name for the community since the men living there considered themselves beasts of prey. Their membership in that particular group was made known by the tattoos of a snarling wolf's head on their right deltoid muscles. It was during the dark days of their incarceration when the images were crudely imbedded under the skin by thousands of pinpricks from sewing needles after being drawn on with India ink. A couple of excellent artists among the gang did the illustrations, while the subject's buddies helped with the painful process of puncturing it into the skin. Any prisoner not a member of the gang that was discovered with the image engraved in his epidermis paid with his life for the affront. The corpse, with the tattoos sliced off and shoved into the victim's rectum, would be found in the morning by the guards.

As trained soldiers, Yarkov and his men knew how to select a secure place to live that would be easy to defend from outside attacks. Logovishchyeh was within a rocky valley on the top of a peak. A narrow cut in the mountains served as an entrance and exit. Several vantage points offered excellent views down to the lower countryside.

The dwellings in the hamlet were skillfully built by men who were the scions of countless generations who had lived through the most brutal winters on the surface of the earth. Logs were carefully chinked and stacked to form eight-foot-tall walls with openings for windows and front doors. Then a similar structure was built inside the first with five decimeters space between the two. This was then filled with packed earth to provide enough insulation to keep out even the bitterest of cold. It also served to maintain the domicile at relatively cool temperatures during the short warmer seasons. The roofs were arched with several layers of logs and earth to protect the inhabitants from above. A short hallway of five meters was built out from the entrance so that two doors could be installed as a buffer to keep frigid winds from entering during the comings and goings from the domicile. The windows were commercially available double-paned models, which, like the doors, had been ripped from the prison that once held the small community's inhabitants.

A further enhancement of American Coleman generators provided electricity for the community. These were used mostly for refrigerators and freezers. Vehicles such as Toyota pickups, Volkswagen vans, and old military DAZ/GAZ utility cars were owned by the inhabitants. One five-ton ZIL-157 Soviet Army truck was communal property for heavy hauling. Most of this transportation had been liberated from the prison.

Now, after the passage of three years, the hodgepodge of log huts had evolved into a comfortable settlement. Several mountain springs furnished fresh water that flowed so rapidly it did not freeze even during the darkest times of the winter. Deer, wild goats and pigs, and other game were available for fresh meat. These sources of protein were supplemented with purchases of staples and vegetables in season in the shops of Dolirod.

Between Logovishchyeh, Dolirod, and raids down on the Pranistay Steppes, life was pretty good for Luka Ivanovich Yarkov and his men. They had everything they needed: vodka, food, and women, along with assorted cash money.

SHARIF GARRISON, PAKISTAN
RIDING HALL
1300 HOURS

AFTER the DVD presentation and lunch, the Brigands and their companions were taken to the riding hall to be introduced to their horses and the gear they would need to control and care for the animals. Each mount was in a separate stall and, under Lieutenant Sidiqui's direction, the Brigands were assigned to an individual animal. The horse equipment had been neatly stacked just outside each location.

Pete Dawson, checking on his horse, looked over in the next stall where Tiny Burke was carefully inspecting his own animal.

"Damn, Tiny!" Dawson exclaimed, noting Tiny's large size. "They should have given you one of them Budweiser Clydesdales."

Somebody down the line yelled out, "They're gonna have to put that poor horse on extry rations."

The senior chief, irritated by the gab, bellowed for the Brigands to shut up and give their full attention to their mounts.

A couple of minutes later, Lieutenant Sidiqui decided it was time to begin the afternoon's routine. "You will note a piece of paper on top of the equipment. Please to pick it up and read it."

The SEALs did as ordered, perusing a list of things they were unfamiliar with, for the most part.

Saddle, Phillips, Model 1936—1 Each	Feed Bag—1 Each
Saddle Blanket—1 Each	Horse Brush—1 Each
Bridle—1 Each	Currycomb—1 Each
Saddlecloth—1 Each	Lariat—1 Each
Saddlebags—1 Pair	Picket Pin—1 Each
Cooling Strap—1 Each	Rifle Scabbard—1 Each

As the Pakistani officer called out each item, the SEALs fumbled around to find it, then held it up for Sidiqui to see. The journalists Wallenger and Krafton had no trouble because of their previous riding experience, but the Brigands groped a couple of times when they were confused as to what some of the items were. The young interpreter Chinar Janoon knew how to ride, but he didn't know all the terminology for the items in English. But eventually it was determined that everyone was properly equipped.

"Excellent," Sidiqui said. "Now we will begin our instruction. The first thing you learn to do is place the bridle on your horse. I want to emphasize to you to move slowly and carefully. These horses are all well trained and broken in, but if they sense nervousness on your part, they may become skittish."

At that point a Pakistani soldier led a horse out to the officer, holding a bridle in his hand. The well-disciplined mount walked beside his human escort, completely at ease in the surroundings that were so familiar to him. "And now," Sidiqui said, "I shall walk the trooper through the proper procedure to apply the bridle to the horse." He paused to make sure everyone was watching, then turned to the trooper. *"Bridle!"* the officer ordered, then looked back at the SEALs. "The first thing is for the trooper to approach the mount from its left, and slip the reins over his head and let them rest on his neck."

The trooper deftly and expertly performed the task.

"And now," Sidiqui continued, "he takes the crownpiece in his right hand and the bit in the left and places the crownpiece in front of its proper position. Then he inserts his thumb in the side of the horse's mouth and presses the lower jaw to cause him to open his mouth."

The trooper deftly and expertly performed the task.

Sidiqui went on, saying, "Insert the bit by raising the crownpiece and with the left hand calmly draw the ears under the crownpiece and arrange the forelock. Then secure the throatlatch."

The trooper deftly and expertly performed the task.

"It is very simple," Sidiqui said. "You will be doing this

automatically and instinctively before very long. Now we shall remove the bridle." Once more he addressed the trooper with an order. *"Unbridle!"*

The reverse procedure was followed militarily and correctly. At that point, the lesson was switched to the bit and bridoon. "Are there any questions?" Sidiqui asked. "In that case, we will break down into groups under the instructions of those SEALs that are familiar with equitation. I believe there are four of you. That means that each will take five of your comrades in arms and run them through the bridling and unbridling procedure." He glanced at the pair of journalists and the interpreter. "I shall be happy to serve you three."

"Excuse me," Dirk Wallenger said. "Since my cameraman and I are both experienced horsemen, perhaps we could be of some assistance in the instruction."

"How very kind of you," Sidiqui said.

Chinar Janoon, the interpreter, spoke up. "I am not familiar with many things in English for riding a horse. I would like to be a student, please."

"I see," Sidiqui said. "In that case, we shall break down into—" He thought a moment. "—seven groups of three. You will practice on one horse at a time with the rider assigned to it doing the work. When he is able to perform the function correctly, move to the next horse."

Senior Chief Buford Dawkins, in his role as detachment chief, moved into action. "Alright! Fall in by threes."

"We officers will be together," Brannigan said.

"Aye, sir!" Dawkins acknowledged. "The rest of you form teams and do it quickly!" Within two minutes the first bridles were being slipped over horses' heads.

AFTER three hours of hard work, the SEALs had not only mastered bridling and unbridling but also learned to "stand to horse." In this bit of drill, the rider is at the horse's left, standing at attention, grasping the reins six inches from the bit. It was simple enough, but now and then a nervous mount would toss his head and the SEAL was forced to gain control of him.

After this, they learned to "lead out," which is the manner in which the riders—a courtesy title since none of them had yet ridden their mounts—actually walked the horse from one point to another under the command of Lieutenant Sidiqui.

This latter exercise was expanded to actually taking the animals from the riding hall through a door to a corral outside. Then they were ordered back inside, going to various places within the large building as well as returning to the corral several times. This was more than just the practice of leading out; it was an opportunity for human and equine to become better acquainted and begin to bond together.

1600 HOURS

THE SEALs had gathered in the shade next to the building in the corral. The officers and chief petty officers were inside with Lieutenant Sidiqui and the two newsmen to discuss the week's coming events. In the meantime, the lower rankers and their interpreter enjoyed a rest after the day's work.

"Y'know," Pete Dawson said, "I'm really developing an affection for that horse. It's like the dog I had when I was a kid."

"Yeah," Guy Devereaux said. "I'm thinking of naming mine."

"I already did," Joe Miskoski said. "I'm gonna call him 'Lightning.' "

"That's a good idea," Doug MacTavish said. "I think I'll call mine 'Traveler.' That was Robert E. Lee's horse during the Civil War."

"Listen to this," Pech Pecheur said, "I'm gonna dub my horse 'Silver' like the Lone Ranger."

"You can't call him that," Matty Matsuno said. "Your horse is brown. If you're gonna name him 'Silver,' he's gotta be white."

"I don't care what color he is," Pecheur said. "I like the name and I got dibs on it."

Miskoski looked at his buddy Puglisi. "Hey, Bruno, what're you gonna call your horse?"

"I already thought that up," Puglisi said. "I'm gonna name him 'Ralph.' "

There was a stunned silence, then Miskoski asked, "What kind of name is that for a goddamn horse?"

"It's a good name," Puglisi argued. "I'm naming him after my favorite uncle."

"Well," Arnie Bernardi said. "I guess that makes sense."

"Sure it does," Puglisi said. "I'm gonna send a picture of me and Ralph to my uncle as soon as he gets out of solitary."

"He's in prison?" Matty Matsuno asked. "What'd he do?"

"There was a misunderstanding," Puglisi said. "It was something about four bodies found buried in a junkyard over in Jersey."

Garth Redhawk asked, "So why did he get thrown in solitary confinement?"

"Another misunderstanding," Puglisi said. "There were some stab wounds in his cellmate. They couldn't prove nothing against Uncle Ralph, but when they learnt him and the guy had been crabbing at each other the day before, they used it as an excuse to put him in the hole. He's been in there for almost six months now."

Further conversation was interrupted by a shout from Senior Chief Dawkins at the door. "Inside! On the double! Fall in by teams and sections." The SEALs hurried back inside and formed up properly with the officers off to one side. Lieutenant Sidiqui took the formation.

"Good job today, men," he said. "We could do more, but it might make the horses nervous. Therefore, for the next half hour I want each of you to go into your mount's stall and spend some time with him. Stroke him a bit and talk in a nice, soothing tone of voice. That way you will develop a friendly rapport with him. You may report to your horses."

The Brigands turned to, going to their assigned animals. When Puglisi walked into the stall, he began to gently stroke the animal's cheek. "Hi, ya, Ralph," the SEAL said softly. "How's it going, big guy?"

CHAPTER 3

DIRK Wallenger stood with his microphone across the road from the post's riding hall, mentally readying himself for his presentation. This would be the first taping of this assignment to be sent back to the Global News Broadcasting's home office. He was dressed in his khaki safari suit, complete with epaulets. He also sported a Kevlar helmet and body armor as he waited for his cameraman, Eddie Krafton, to prepare the equipment for recording. To further enhance the impression he was on the field of battle, he stood at the edge of a grove of babul trees that blocked any views of buildings, streets, or other manmade objects. On TV screens all across America, the journalist would appear to be in the wilds of Southwest Asia.

Wallenger and Krafton had spent more than a week getting shots of the SEALs' riding activities, along with an interview with Lieutenant Bill Brannigan. Now Wallenger would make his first intro into which all the previous taping would be edited at the Global News Broadcasting's Washington studio. The presentation was for the series to be aired over the GNB to their subscribers of independent local stations. Wallenger had titled his programming "Somewhere in the War." The idea came from recent research he had done on war correspondents and their reports in past conflicts. Most of the newspaper and magazine accounts written during World War I began with the words "Somewhere in France." Wallenger thought the intros gave an aura of urgent secrecy in a dangerous environment, so he adapted it for his own presentations.

"Okay, Dirk," the cameraman, Eddie Krafton, said. "Whenever you're ready."

"Right," Wallenger said. He took a deep breath and cleared his throat. "Five . . . four . . . three . . . two . . . one— Greetings, everybody, this is Dirk Wallenger presenting the first broadcast in my series 'Somewhere in the War.' As you recall in my last program from our studio in Washington, I apologized for inadvertently releasing an inaccurate news item. This was the result of my being given incorrect information by a previously unimpeachable source. At that time I stated that I was no longer going to sit in a studio and report on the war in the Middle East from my anchor desk. Instead I would be going out where the action is and getting the truth firsthand. So here I am 'Somewhere in Pakistan,' imbedded with a United States Navy SEAL detachment. Their commanding officer is Lieutenant William Brannigan, to whom his men refer as 'Wild Bill.' And the unit itself is known as Brannigan's Brigands, which gives you a pretty good idea of what these intrepid men are like. They are the roughest, toughest fighters around, let me assure you of that, and they are the quintessential United States Navy sailors. However, rather than being at sea, these SEALs are far inland, spending a week learning to ride the horses they will take into a land combat operation. You heard correctly! It is like stepping back in time before motor or armored vehicles existed. They have been transported to the days of the cavalry, the lancers, the hussars, and other elite mounted regiments and legions. This gives you some idea of the primitive environs in which the SEALs will conduct their combat operations. Thus, they are acquiring the skills of equitation to prepare for a secret mission of which I know absolutely nothing at this moment. But I have been assured that I will be allowed to accompany them straight into the middle of the action, where I will have complete access to the deadly battles. I can guarantee you that when that fighting begins, each of my broadcasts will be made under fire while locked in close combat against fanatical mujahideen warriors somewhere in Southwest Asia. All the details and information I will give you will be experienced by me firsthand." He paused, saying, "Okay, Eddie, let's cut at this point."

"That went well, Dirk," Eddie said. "It leads into the scenes of the riding instructions and the interview with Bill Brannigan."

Wallenger grinned. "You mean 'Wild Bill' Brannigan. I think using his sobriquet will add to the excitement of our broadcasts."

"You bet," Eddie agreed. "And referring to his guys as 'Brannigan's Brigands' is the icing on that cake."

"Okay," Wallenger said. "Now after this intro we just made, they'll show the riding lessons and interview. Then I'll sign off. That's going to be standard stuff since there's not really any excitement going on at the moment." He grinned. "But I hope this setup with the helmet, body armor, and trees will provide an ambience of dangerous adventure."

"It sure as hell will," Krafton said. "Y'know, we can do the sign-off now, if you want," Eddie suggested.

"Sure," Wallenger agreed. "Okay." He went through the five-to-one count, then said, "Now you've met the SEALs known as Brannigan's Brigands. This has been your chance to witness their determination and professionalism. And you're going to see a lot more of them and me in future broadcasts. Let me remind you yet again that this will be the real war, ladies and gentlemen, not sound bites or rebroadcasts from other sources. So, until the next time, this is Dirk Wallenger, 'Somewhere in Pakistan,' wishing you peace in a world gone mad." He lowered the microphone. "Okay, Eddie."

"Right," Eddie said. "As they used to say in the old days, it's in the can." He took the camera off his shoulder. "That 'wishing you peace in a world gone mad' makes a great sign-off."

"You're right," Wallenger agreed. "Now ship what we've got back to Shelor Field. I've made arrangements with the public information guy there to see that it will be forwarded on to the Washington studios."

"Okay," Eddie said. "They've got some kind of pipeline set up for journalists that can get their stuff express shipped back to the States. I'll take care of it."

"Alright," Wallenger said. "I think I'll go over and see how the guys are doing."

He left Eddie, going across the road to the riding hall. He saw that the SEALs were mounted, seated well in the saddle, going around in a circle within the confines of the large building. Under Lieutenant Sidiqui's direction, they were riding at different speeds from walks to trots, then back to walks, and finally coming to a halt.

"Good job, men," Sidiqui said enthusiastically. "Remember to keep your center of gravity in the saddle between your knees and heels. Stay relaxed; keep your reins long so your horses can extend their necks and heads. Now let's go another time. Forward, *march*!"

As the Brigands moved out, Sidiqui nodded to Wallenger. "They are doing quite well, Mr. Wallenger."

"Yes," Wallenger said. "They seem to be catching on quick enough."

The journalist was beginning to feel a sense of belonging with the group of SEALs, or at least he was very much at ease among them because of their collective friendliness. These professional fighting men were not like the cadets during his boyhood days at military school. During those unhappy times the other boys bullied him because of their rank and greater physical strength, while the Brannigan's Brigands simply took him as he was, without censure or hostility. He had enjoyed helping to teach them to ride, and they listened to him with good humor and respect when he gave pointers or criticism.

At first Wallenger perceived Bruno Puglisi to be a boor-
ish idiot. But as he got to know him, he realized the SEAL
was actually very smart when it came to basic intelligence,
i.e., the ability to adapt. Puglisi was the kind of man who
could be cast up on a deserted island and within a short period of time figure out which plants were safe to eat, how to
trap the local animals and fish, build a comfortable shelter,
and survive quite well in the feral surroundings. Wallenger
knew of college professors who would die of starvation
and/or the elements within a month or so if faced with the
same situation.

The reporter recognized Chad Murchison as a social
compatriot. They were both from backgrounds of privi-
lege and wealth, had been educated at private schools, and
had several mutual acquaintances up and down the eastern
seaboard. Murchison seemed out of place in the macho
SEAL world, but he had obviously proven beyond a doubt
that he belonged there; yet Wallenger perceived him as being in a sort of limbo, as if he were searching for who he really was.

The journalist turned his attention back to the riding. After a few moments, he asked Sidiqui, "When do you bring
them to the gallop?"

"Tomorrow," the Pakistani officer answered. "I hope you
will be able to help."

"I'm looking forward to it," Wallenger replied, making
a mental note to be sure that Eddie taped the event.

LOGOVISHCHYEH, TAJIKISTAN

AS could be expected, the hut belonging to the headman,
Luka Yarkov, was the largest in the village. It was more than
his home; it was also a headquarters, meeting hall, and storage area for weaponry, ammunition, and the more important
and valuable items used in the raiding operations he directed. The place was guarded by a quartet of the biggest ex-
convicts on a twenty-four/seven basis.

Yarkov had two women, both stolen from villages on separate raids. The youngest was fifteen-year-old Gabina, who he had kidnapped on his second raid onto the Pranistay Steppes. A year later eighteen-year-old Zainba was brought in to join the household. The two girls were similar in appearance in that they were young, plump, and had green eyes. Yarkov preferred his women to be teenagers with blue or green eyes, and a bit on the fleshy side. This was a strong resemblance to his older cousin Sofia, with whom he had his first sexual experiences.

Zainba and Gabina were from different clans, but formed an instant rapport in spite of past intertribal conflicts. In reality, both were disgraces to their families since they had been raped by an infidel. However, because of their friendship, they made some mutually beneficial decisions about how to deal with their fate. The two girls were practical and intelligent though completely illiterate and uneducated. They logically saw no advantage to ever returning to their villages where the men in the family would take their lives in honor killings. They decided to make the best of the situation in Logovishchyeh and live out their lives as peacefully as possible. On the plus side, their master never beat them, he praised and appreciated their food preparation and housekeeping abilities, took the time to begin teaching them Russian so they could all talk together, and seemed considerate when he was having his way with them. They could only guess about the sex since both had been virgins when captured, but Zainba's sister had told her what it was like to have a husband and submit to his physical desires.

The two Pashtun girls usually wore their native garb. But at special times, their master insisted that they don tight dresses with short skirts that were readily available in the shops in Dolirod. Since the women were not allowed out of the village, their masters did all the shopping. These garments were worn with the top buttons undone to afford a generous view of their cleavage. Individual men also picked out special outfits such as sheer slips and nightgowns for their women to wear at certain times. After years of imprisonment in a male convict society, the Russians were now able to satisfy desires that could only be fantasized in the past.

1900 HOURS

LUKA Yarkov had called a meeting of his underbosses in his home. These were Valentin Surov, Aleksei Barkyev, and Fedor Grabvosky. All three had the talents that had made them not only members of the hierarchy in Logovishchyeh but also during the long years in the military prison when they advised and directed Yarkov on running the gang.

Valentin Surov was an ex-officer, well educated and addicted to a gambling habit that had ruined his military career. He brought some sophisticated intellect to the table. Aleksei Barkyev was one of those rare individuals who was physically imposing, possessing great strength, yet had a keen and lively logic that enabled him to make accurate assessments of both tangible and abstract situations. Unfortunately that was where his aptitude ended. He could never figure out the right actions to take after his deductions. Fedor Grabvosky, on the other hand, was a small, sickly weakling, but he had a cunning intellect that not only aided him in surviving the savage environment of prison but made him a great planner. He and Barkyev together made one very imposing team.

Yarkov's wives had gotten several bottles of vodka from the freezer, along with the tall, narrow glasses traditionally used to imbibe the liquor. They set the servings down on the table as the four guests ogled them for their plump prettiness. This still made Gabina feel a bit uneasy, but Zainba's feminine ego was pleased with the attention. Such conduct would never have been permitted by a Pashtun man and would have led to a deadly confrontation with any other male who would dare show such disrespect to the women of his household.

After the girls withdrew to the kitchen, the Russians charged the glasses for the customary toast. *"Bogatstvo ee mestnost!"* Yarkov announced, asking for riches and well-being. They all knocked back the slugs of vodka in one swallow.

"So," said Surov, refilling his glass. "Why have you called us together, Luka Ivanovich?" He used the patronymic as was custom among Russians.

"It is time to begin preparation for the next opium harvest," Yarkov replied.

"I visited that village as you ordered," Surov said. "I took Putnovsky with me and we informed the villagers that they owed you a tax." He shrugged. "I must tell you that I did not feel that would accomplish much."

"I had you do that because of being counseled to do so by little Fedor Zakharovich," Yarkov said. "I will let him explain it to you."

The diminutive Grabvosky, who had been a payroll clerk in the Army, could imbibe a lion's share of vodka in spite of his small size. "The main job given us by the big boss in Khorugh is to take over the entirety of the poppy crops being grown on the Pranistay Steppes. However, we must do so in well-planned steps. It will give us time to develop alliances among the Pashtuns."

"We cannot go to the Pashtuns we've stolen women from," Surov pointed out.

"That still leaves us plenty since we have not gone to all the villages," Grabvosky said. "Our principal enemy will be the warlord Awalmir Yousafzai."

"Can't we fight Yousafzai by ourselves?" Barkyev asked.

"We need the Pashtuns to harvest the poppies," Grabvosky said. "You must remember that down on the steppes there are long and bitter feuds between the tribes. I believe you are aware that the last names used by the Pashtuns are their main tribal names. That is an indication of how important their clans are to them. They will not bear insults or abuse to be directed toward their kinsmen. Fortunately for us, there have been many conflicts that have left smoldering resentment that bursts out in bloody vendettas from time to time. And as I stated before, we will approach those tribes who we have not attacked."

"Ah!" Barkyev exclaimed. "So we will work one tribe against the other, eh?"

"*Tochno*—exactly!" Grabvosky exclaimed. "But there is

an additional requirement in order for us to be able to gain control and exert influence on the people of the steppes. They are all afraid of Awalmir Yousafzai, who is in actuality the warlord of the largest tribe in the area."

"Is he capable of crushing the others?" Surov asked.

"Not all at once," Barkyev replied. "But he can handle them quite easily one at a time. Our goal is to unite the tribes to go to war against him."

"Can we do that?" Yarkov asked. "Those tribes are not exactly friendly toward us since they consider us infidels."

"Ah, yes!" Grabvosky said. "But if we made treaties with them, we could unite them under your leadership. The first step is to go to the Mahsud tribe where Surov and Putnovsky informed them they owed a tax to you. Now you must 'forgive' the tax and tell them you want to be friends with them because you found out that the Yousafzai tribe is their enemy. You inform them that the Yousafzais are your enemy too."

Barkyev laughed loudly. "Of course! There is the old Pashtun proverb that says the enemy of my enemy is my friend."

"We could do this with other special villages and tribes until we and they are strong enough to defeat the Yousafzais," Surov remarked enthusiastically. "With them out of the way, we can control all the other Pashtuns on the Pranistay Steppes."

"The opium poppy harvests and sales will be ours," Grabvosky added.

"How many tribes are out there on the steppes with whom we can establish a rapport?" Barkyev asked.

"Let me think," Yarkov mused. "There are the Mahsuds and Kharotis. That's two."

"Do not forget the Ghilzais," Surov said.

"The last one is the Bhittanis," Grabvosky said. "That makes four."

"That is very good," Barkyev said. "That means there will be four against the Yousafzais. Counting us Russians, that gives us odds of five to one. The scales balance in our favor."

"Five to *three*!" Grabvosky corrected. "Our enemies are

the Janoons and Swatis, but they may or may not join the Yousafzais.

"Even if they do, we will enjoy a near two-to-one advantage," Surov said.

"No matter," Yarkov said. "It will be an easy victory. By the time of the next poppy harvest, the whole of the Pranistay Steppes will be under our control."

"By Lenin's ghost, boys!" Barkyev exclaimed. "We are going to start a war."

Yarkov raised his glass of vodka. "*Ko voina!* To war!"

The other three at the table joined the toast.

CHAPTER 4

THE riding instruction for the SEALs came to a close. At the end of the final lesson, every man was able to handle his horse in an acceptable manner. They were not experts by a long shot, but Pete Dawson and Dave Leibowitz had a surprisingly natural aptitude for equitation. Those talented rookies ended up being close in ability to the more experienced Tex Benson, Monty Sturgis, Garth Redhawk, and Chad Murchison. Lieutenant Barakaat Sidiqui was confident enough in the detachment's horsemanship to believe that any shortcomings in riding among the rest of the SEALs could be quickly made up with practice in the field during the operation.

Before the Brigands packed up gear and mounts for the flight to Shelor Field, their Pakistani instructor had a final surprise for them. He took the group out to the Army's jumping course, where the military team trained for international competition. The squad was well known in the sport, having participated in several Olympics. Sidiqui explained that the practice of jumping horses over obstacles was started many decades before in British cavalry regiments where the activity was considered nothing less than a necessary training exercise.

When the SEALs reached the course, they gathered at a good viewing spot just outside the fence. Eddie Krafton was already there with his camera, ready to record everything on tape. Chad Murchison looked around. "Where's Dirk?" he asked.

"You'll see real quick," Eddie said, making sure the lens of his camera covered the entirety of the riding field.

"May I have everyone's attention?" Lieutenant Sidiqui said. "You are about to see a demonstration of excellent horsemanship." He let out a loud, sharp whistle.

A horse suddenly appeared from around the far stables, and the rider took it at a canter into the interior of the fenced area. It was Dirk Wallenger, and he guided the mount onto the course. He rode smoothly and easily at the first obstacle, which was a collapsible wooden wall. The horse cleared it gracefully, not breaking stride as it headed for the next jump.

"You will notice," Sidiqui said loudly, "that Mr. Wallenger is making sure he adjusts his position in the saddle to not upset his mount's balance during the jumping maneuver."

Wallenger and his equine companion next went over a triple bar, cantered on to a couple of more in a smooth, even ride-jump-ride-jump-ride sequence. The SEALs cheered and whistled in appreciation of the performance. Next was a water jump that Wallenger took the horse completely across, clearing the brush at the front, the small pond in the middle, and lastly the lathe on the far side. The demonstration elicited more loud approval from his audience. He then went over three vertical elements of various heights before slowing to a trot and riding over to where the Brigands shouted their approval at him.

"Hell of ride, guy!"

"Well done, dude!"

"You are one badass cowboy, man!"

Dirk Wallenger was extremely pleased with the reaction. He grinned, blushing at the praise. "Well," he said, "I've had a lot of practice."

"That was most inimitable, Dirk," Murchison said. "Have you been in competition?"

Wallenger shook his head. "I'd have to take off about twenty-five pounds. This poor animal has earned his oats hauling me around that course." He dismounted as a Pakistani trooper trotted up to take the reins and lead the horse back to the stable.

Puglisi was mystified by the riding exhibition. "Can you teach us to do that, Dirk?"

"I think so," Wallenger said. "But it would require that our present animals be trained for the sport. I'm afraid it would take a long time."

"Man!" Puglisi said. "I'd give just about anything to be able to do that. It looks like a real kick in the head."

Another soldier appeared on the scene, this one wearing the insignia of the signals branch on his beret. He saluted Sidiqui and handed him a message. The lieutenant read it, then looked up at the SEALs with a sad smile. "This is saying that three United States Air Force transport aircraft will be arriving at the Karachi airport at fourteen hundred hours. They will collect you and your horses to return to Afghanistan. I would assume you will be going soon on your mission."

"That's what it is," Brannigan said. "Thanks for the good training, Lieutenant. It was hard work but satisfying."

"I am glad you approve," Sidiqui said. "And I shall miss you all. And may I say in all sincerity that you are the best class I ever had."

Senior Chief Buford Dawkins didn't like drawn-out good-byes. "Fall in! We've got a lot to do to get ready for this afternoon's flight. You got to do more than just look out for yourselves; there's them horses and all their gear to take care of."

As the men formed up, Puglisi glanced at Miskoski. "Damn! I sure hope Ralph can adjust to life in Afghanistan."

"I'm not even going to reply to that," Miskoski said.

ALTHOUGH the upcoming operation for Brannigan's
Brigands was not classified, the journalist, Dirk Wallenger,
and his cameraman, Eddie Krafton, were not permitted to attend the mission briefing. Regulations forbade outsiders access to the procedures since there was always the possibility
that sensitive material might inadvertently be brought up.
This prevented their presence even though the two men
would eventually be in the middle of the field operations.
Wallenger and Krafton waited in the officers' billets while
the SEALs retired to their hangar to do what they had to do.

To everyone's surprise, however, the young interpreter
Chinar Janoon was present when Commander Tom Carey
and Lieutenant Commander Ernest Berringer opened the
briefing. The first item on the agenda to be announced was
that Chinar was more than an interpreter. He was, in fact, a
fully qualified asset to the point he would be indispensable
to the SEALs on the mission that had now been named Operation Combat Alley. The young Pashtun would also be giving part of the presentation.

Now that the entire detachment was seated in chairs at the
usual briefing spot in the hangar, Carey began his dissertation from the podium. "Before we get into the nitty-gritty,"
he said, "I want to mention you'll be in another opium poppy
growing area as you already have been a couple of other
times before. But on this occasion you'll not be taking action
against growers, smugglers, sellers, buyers, or anybody else
involved in the activity."

"That makes sense." Lieutenant (JG) Jim Cruiser said.
"The harvest is over with anyhow."

"That's not the only reason," Carey said. "The tribes benefit too much from growing the stuff, so it has been decided
that there are certain areas where the government is going to
look the other way. This will continue unless the farmers begin dealing with the Taliban, who will use the money to buy

arms, ammunition, and other war-making tools. As a matter of fact, part of your mission is to keep an eye out to see if the Taliban is creeping around out there."

"And if they are, sir?" Ensign Orlando Taylor asked.

"Then report it ASAP through the net," Carey replied.

"I thought the farmers were already being bribed not to grow the poppies," Taylor remarked.

"That funding has dried up until a new budget is worked out by the Afghanistan government," Carey said. "Anyway, let's get into the briefing." He opened the folder he had put on the podium. "Okay. The name of the mission is Operation Combat Alley, and here's the situation where you're going. The area is the Pranistay Steppes where several Pashtun tribes are scattered among thirteen villages. The population of the area is a total of a bit more than six hundred fighting men. We don't know how many women and kids and old folks are in the place, since the Pashtuns on the steppes only count those men and boys of war-making age."

"What's steppes?" Puglisi asked.

"Prairie or flatlands," Carey answered, slightly annoyed. "However, in this case, the description 'steppes' is not quite accurate. There are plenty of gullies and shallow valleys that give it a rugged quality. This makes motor transportation difficult, thus going by horse or donkey is the only way to get around reasonably well. The area is approximately eighteen hundred square miles, so there's plenty of space between the settlements. It's high desert country that is baking hot in the summer and freezing cold in the winter—pardon the clichés—with hard-packed sandy soil. However, there are certain areas where creeks and ponds abound that provide the fertile areas to raise food and those opium plants. At this point I'll let your asset, Chinar Janoon, give you some more info on the people that live on the Pranistay."

Now that the young Pashtun had been identified as an asset, the SEALs were a lot more impressed with him. This meant he had some sort of connection, either official or quasi-official, with the Afghanistan government and/or military. The fact that he was educated and could speak several languages was also an indication that here was somebody special even if he was only in his late teens or early twenties. And he had demonstrated that he was a damn good horseman as well.

"Good morning all," Chinar said cheerfully. He spoke in a sort of British accent. "I am going to discuss the demography of the Pranistay Steppes. There are a total of seven tribes of Pashtuns scattered about the area. The largest is the Yousafzai tribe, which has a hundred and twenty fighting men in three villages. They are well armed and relatively prosperous because of the poppies. Their leader is a warlord actually. His name is Awalmir. I give you only his first name because his last name, like all Pashtuns, is the tribal name. Since I am called Chinar Janoon, you may rightfully assume that I am from the Janoon tribe."

Ensign Orlando Taylor raised his hand. "Is your tribe a powerful one?"

"We rank fourth on the Pranistay with eighty-five fighting men dispersed between two villages," Chinar replied. "The weakest tribe would be the Ghilzai, who have fifty-five in their only village. The one thing we all have in common is that all our communities are ruled by the eldest men, to whom we refer as *spinzhire*. That means 'gray-beards' and is both a respectful and affectionate term. The name covers the several positions of local government. If a village has a headman, and many do not, he is referred to as the *malik*. There are also the scholars who are called *oleme*; the judges are referred to as *qaze*, and the *molla* are the Muslim clergy. Owners of large tracts of land or warlords are addressed as *khan*."

Puglisi had a question. "Do all you guys get along okay?"

Chinar shook his head. "I fear not. We have a long history of blood feuds and what would be termed clan wars. Alliances and dissolutions are erratic and varying, depending on the nature of the disagreements. A tribe may be involved in a bitter war with another, yet the next year they are united against a common enemy that has evolved during a more recent quarrel. And, of course, when bandits come into an area, the villages all unite against them, forgetting past grievances."

"Who are these bandits?" Chief Petty Officer Matt Gunnarson asked.

"They are outsiders who come out of the Kangal Mountains to the north," Chinar replied. "They are from Tajikistan and have been raiding down on the steppes for many generations. Mostly now, however, the cowardly wretches attack travelers and others who are too far from the villages to be helped by fellow tribesmen. I shouldn't think that you would have a bit of trouble with them. In fact, the local people will be only too glad to have you around to keep them away. Believe me, those criminals will fear you." He paused for a moment. "I have been told that you are acquainted with the proper way to conduct yourselves in the company of Pashtuns, so I needn't cover that. I have also arranged to have a donkey train available to carry heavy equipment and loads for you. My village will supply a half dozen along with drovers. And, now, if you have no questions, my presentation is finished. Thank you."

Commander Carey took over again. "So here is your mission statement: You are to deploy into the Pranistay Steppes of northeastern Afghanistan for the purpose of observing, aiding, and establishing friendly rapport with the indigenous people. That's it, plain and simple."

"I hope the execution portion is as assuageous," Chad Murchison remarked.

Carey, who didn't know what the word meant, ignored the remark and continued his dissertation. "You will be airlifted from Shelor Field via three C-130 transport aircraft just as when you returned here from Pakistan."

"Is it a long flight, sir?" Puglisi asked.

Carey shrugged. "I'm not sure. Why do you ask?"

"I was just worried about Ralph getting airsick again."

"Who's Ralph?" Carey asked.

"My horse," Puglisi replied.

"You named your horse Ralph?" Carey inquired with a very incredulous expression on his face.

Joe Miskoski interjected, "It's a long story, sir. You don't want to go there."

"I sure as hell don't!" Carey exclaimed. He gave Puglisi

another skeptical look before continuing. "Okay. You'll land at an area picked out by Chinar. It's marked on the maps you'll receive prior to leaving. He's assured us the terrain is firm and large enough to accommodate the aircraft. You will unload your gear, horses—including Ralph, of course—and get into your mission with Chinar as your guide and interpreter."

Now the Skipper had a question. "What about the reporters, Wallenger and Krafton?"

"They will go in imbedded with you as previously stated," Carey said. "But stay on your toes. If anything untoward that calls for 'special' action occurs, keep them away from it. As far as normal activities go, they are free to film, report, and interview anybody they want to. The official word is for you to cooperate with them."

"Aye, sir," Brannigan said. "And what about our resupply?"

"As soon as you pick out a place or places, you inform the SFOB aboard the USS *Combs*," Carey said. "They'll see that anything you need, including fodder for the horses, is delivered to you." He looked over at Doc Bradley. "You will be expected to aid the locals in case of sickness or injuries, so whatever medical supplies you need will be made available through resupply."

"Yes, sir," the hospital corpsman replied.

"I doubt if you guys will be needing more than a basic issue of ammo unless you end up doing a lot of hunting," Carey said. "Chinar tells me there are deer, wild pigs, and goats in the foothills of the Kangal Mountains."

"Christ!" Guy Devereaux exclaimed with a chuckle. "And they're calling this Operation Combat Alley? They should've named it Operation Candyass Lane."

"It won't be all that easy," Carey said. "You'll have calluses on your asses from all the riding you guys are going to do."

"What about commo?" Frank Gomez, the detachment RTO, asked.

"Follow the SOI," Carey said. "We won't be doing a briefback. This mission is simple and tame. Work out your own wants and desires when it comes to taking in supplies and goodies you want. And don't forget you'll have a donkey train to transport heavy or bulky equipment." He closed up his notes. "That's it! Turn to!" He glanced over at Puglisi. "Tell Ralph I hope he has a nice trip."

"I sure will, sir," Puglisi said.

CHAPTER 5

THE six Russians rode slowly for an essential reason: They did not want to alarm the Pashtuns in the village they were now approaching. Each also had his AKS assault rifle slung muzzle-down across his back to illustrate the peacefulness of their intentions. However, these were violent, suspicious men, and they had Tokarev 7.62-millimeter automatics out of sight but readily available in their waistbands.

Valentin Surov and Yakob Putnovsky, who had visited the little community almost three weeks previously to tell the Pashtuns they owed a tax, were two of the riders. The other four were Luka Yarkov, the headman; Aleksei Barkyev, an underboss; and two hard cases named Vilgelim Dalenko and Lev Shinskovsky.

The boy guard on duty had already alerted the villagers, and when the unexpected visitors entered the community proper, they saw the usual peaceful scene of oldsters sitting around the communal well, smoking their pipes with languid puffs as if they had no worries in the world. The Russians knew the placid impression was false, and that they were under the guns of hidden males in the surrounding houses.

Surov, with his rudimentary knowledge of Pashto, rode forward and came to a halt. *"Stari me shey!"* he greeted politely.

One of the old men nodded to him. *"Salamat osey!"*

"Do you remember me?" Surov asked.

"Ho," the oldster answered affirmatively. Then he pointed to Putnovsky. "And I remember him too."

"May we speak with your *malik?*" Surov requested. "Our *khan* is here with us and would like to make friends with him."

Mohambar the elder was summoned and he appeared ten minutes later from a doorway not more than five yards away from the well. He approached Surov and the others, looking up into the Russian's face. "We have no money to pay your tax."

"That is alright," Surov said, knowing there was plenty of cash among the hamlet's population. "Our *khan* is here. His name is Yarkov and he wishes to meet you."

Yarkov urged his horse over closer and nodded down to Mohambar. When he spoke, he did so slowly to allow Surov to translate. "When I asked you to pay me a tax, I thought you had cheated me. Now I find that the bad man Awalmir of the Yousafzai tribe was trying to make trouble so you and I would not be friends."

Mohambar stood silently, waiting for the man to continue with whatever it was he had to say.

"I am going to take care of selling your opium powder from now on," Yarkov said through Surov. "I will pay you a much better price than that scoundrel Awalmir. That is why he does not want us to be friends. He is selfish and evil, stealing money from you with his lies and cheating. He wants to get rich by taking advantage of you. What do you think of that?"

"If you pay us more, we will be your friends," Mohambar announced. The old men behind him nodded their approval.

"I want to show you I am a nice fellow," Yarkov continued. "You will see I am honest and deserve your trust." He reached in his haversack and pulled out a roll of bills. "This is a token of my respect and affection for the Mahsud people. It is five thousand afghanis. You see? I pay you in the money of this country not the somonis of Tajikistan. And this is a gift. Consider it an extra offering to mark this new arrangement between us. For your crop this year I will pay a total of ninety-five thousand afghanis to each family in both the Mahsud villages."

Old Mohambar generally kept his emotions hidden, but this offer of one and a half times the usual amount caused him to lose control before strangers. Pashtun style. He raised his eyebrows, and the old men by the well all murmured, "Mmm!"

Mohambar said, "We will accept your offer, Yarkov Khan." The addition of the honorific title to the Russian's name was a sign the elder had placed his people under Yarkov's command.

Now Surov spoke for himself. "My chief is very happy that you have accepted both his friendship and partnership for the next poppy harvest." He raised his hand in farewell. *"Khuday pea man!"*

"Khuday pea man!" the old men responded happily.

BETWEEN THE JANOON TRIBE'S VILLAGES
1400 HOURS

THE engines of the three C-130s were idling as the Brigands, along with the two journalists and Chinar Janoon, led their horses down the ramp and off the aircraft. Although the animals had been flown before their transfer to Shelor Field from Sharif Garrison, they were skittish from this most recent flight. The mounts tossed their heads and stomped their hooves as the riders took them fifty meters away from the aircraft to set up a picket line. As soon as they had some distance between themselves and the transports, the well-trained horses settled down and allowed themselves to be attached to the picket pins driven into the hard earth.

After the animals were situated, Senior Chief Buford Dawkins assigned one man each to watch over three horses as the first two aircraft revved their engines for takeoff. The disturbance might spook some of the more nervous horses—and Puglisi's Ralph was the worst—but the presence of the SEALs speaking to them in soothing voices would keep them calm.

The remaining dozen petty officers hurried over to the third aircraft to begin unloading the weapons, munitions, gear, horse furniture, bales of hay, and bags of oats. Rather than stand around watching the heavy work, the three officers and the senior chief pitched in to haul the stuff to a central location for stacking. Chinar had already left the scene to walk the kilometer of distance to the main village to bring back the donkeys and their herders. They would be hauling the heavy stuff to a spot just north of the smaller village that the asset had chosen for the SEALs' first bivouac.

1600 HOURS

WHEN Chinar returned from the village, not only did he have the donkey skinners with him but he was also accompanied by some three dozen laughing, shouting men and boys. They gave the SEALs friendly grins and boldly started poking around the gear that was stacked up near where the third aircraft had been before taking off for the return flight to Shelor Field. The Brigands, well used to Pashtuns, made them laugh with their funny accents when they said something in Pashto to them. Chinar quickly instructed the donkey skinners to bring the animals closer so that they could be loaded for the trip to the bivouac area.

Each skinner had his own unique manner of loading the two animals he had brought with him. A total of ten Pashtuns and twenty of the sturdy little donkeys had shown up for the hauling job. The skinners, while joking and conversing loudly with their tribal brothers, worked hard at arranging the bundles on the animals. They used sacks, ropes, leather straps, woven hemp, and other means to put such large loads on the beasts that it looked as if they would collapse under the weight. But the donkeys stood steady and calm, completely unaffected by the heavy burdens. Now and then one would bray and kick, more disturbed by the noisy people than the weight that he bore.

The senior chief was standing beside Chinar, watching the work. Dawkins asked, "Do y'all use donkeys for all your heavy hauling?"

"Yes, we do, Senior Chief," Chinar replied. He had heard the others address this oldest SEAL in that manner, and his training for the diplomatic service had taught him to follow examples of protocol. Besides, Dawkins looked as if he might be a *spinzhire* of the United States Navy.

"Then it really is impossible to use some sort of motor vehicle in this area, huh?"

Chinar nodded his head. "It is exactly as Commander Carey stated; the majority of the terrain on the steppes is rugged and uneven, with natural obstacles that only horses and donkeys can negotiate effectively."

"What about them little motor rickshaws you see so much in this part of the world," the SEAL asked. "Couldn't they be used?"

"Only in a very few areas, Senior Chief. That is why tribal villages are no more than a kilometer or so apart. If there is trouble, one group can quickly go to the aid of the other on horseback without having to worry about the lack of roads."

"Maybe it'd be better if you folks all lived together in one group," Dawkins suggested.

"Sometimes it is better for clan harmony if there is separation between certain family groups," Chinar explained.

"That's true in America too," Dawkins said with a grin and a wink. He glanced over at the picket lines where the SEALs were saddling the horses and arranging the gear in front of an appreciative audience of friendly Pashtuns. "I'd better go make sure the guys will be ready to move out when them donkeys are all loaded."

Dirk Wallenger and Eddie Krafton, with their own horses ready for the trek, were busy taping the Pashtuns, who were pleased to be pictured for television. The closest they had to the medium were DVD players used by government visitors who would come around to show programs on nutrition, safety, health issues, and other useful information needed by isolated communities far from civilization's amenities. Many times the visitors had camcorders and taped the residents then showed the results on the machines. It was always a moment of both awe and hilarity for the villagers when they saw the moving, talking images of themselves and their neighbors.

Finally all was in readiness and the senior chief had everyone stand to horse in section and team formations. As the officers rode off to one side, the old salt bellowed the orders he had learned from Lieutenant Sidiqui in the classes on military equitation and drill.

"Prepare to mount! *Mount!* Twos right! At a walk, *march!*"

The detachment, after going from the line into a column of twos formation, headed out of the area as the donkey skinners followed with their heavily burdened pack animals. Brannigan laughed aloud. "Why do I keep expecting John Wayne in a cavalry uniform to show up any minute?"

Jim Cruiser also chuckled. "And he would probably be chased by a crowd of howling Apache warriors, right?"

"No way," Brannigan said, leading Cruiser and Taylor toward the column. "It would be the other way around."

The Brigands rode slowly across the steppes. Now Operation Combat Alley—or Candyass Lane, as it was being referred to—was on the ground in what seemed to be a very passive mission.

LOGOVISHCHYEH, TAJIKISTAN
1900 HOURS

LUKA Yarkov relaxed on the floor in front of his hearth, resting on a feather-stuffed pallet. He was tired after a long day of visiting a total of four villages on horseback. But the day's traveling had been well worth it. His approach and the counterfeit afghanis he had passed out had bought him the loyalty and support of a total of 340 armed fighting men among four of the seven tribes living on the Pranistay Steppes. Combining those Pashtun bumpkins with his 110 Russians gave him a formidable force to take over the local poppy business, and crush Awalmir Yousafzai and his allies.

It was times like this that he wished he was completely independent. But he owed allegiance to the Russian crime syndicate headquartered in the city of Khorugh through their support and influence with the Tajik authorities. However, Yarkov considered this no more than a temporary inconvenience. With cunning and care he would eventually wrest control of the operation from the Big Boss. Then all the profits would be his and his alone.

Zainba brought him a cup of steaming tea heavy with cream and plenty of sugar. He took the brew and treated himself to a preliminary sip. As he watched the girl walk back to the clay oven to help Gabina with the preparation of the meal, he wondered if she were pregnant. He was always aware when one of the girl's menstrual cycles was in progress. It had been ingrained into them it was a time when they were unclean. They would not prepare food or have sexual intercourse or any other sort of intimate touching. After the period was over, they went through a purification process of careful bathing before things got back to normal. Yarkov thought it had been around two months since the eighteen-year-old girl had exhibited any evidence of menstrual bleeding.

If Zainba was pregnant, the Russian wasn't sure if he wanted to keep her or not. Better to give her away before she shit the little bastard out into the world. Yarkov was not very fond of children and having one underfoot would spoil the harmony of his house. On the other hand, Zainba was attractive and he hated to lose such a pretty sexual playmate. He knew he couldn't get her to give the baby away. Vilgelim Dalenko made one of his women do that and she tried to kill him for it. When that failed she went over to the edge of the encampment and threw herself over the side, her body bouncing off boulders all the way down to the slopes where the steppes began. Dalenko lost her anyway, so he should have traded her for another female or just given her and the kid to one of the other guys.

At any rate, there was more to occupy his mind at this particular time. He would have to strike the other tribes fast while he still had the loyalty of the four tribes he had bribed. The Yousafzai was the largest enemy clan, and Awalmir Yousafzai was their leader. It was true they had the usual council of elders, but Awalmir ran things his way without consulting them. The second strongest group were the Janoon. Perhaps it would be better to hit the weaker Swatis first. If he wiped them out, it would shake up the Janoons, and there was a good chance they might join him then. That would mean the Yousafzais would be all alone against the whole of the Pashtun families. At that point, their elders might force Awalmir to abdicate and join Yarkov's organization as poppy growers.

But no matter what tactics and strategy he adopted, Yarkov knew he would have to launch his campaign at the earliest possible moment. Even his planned rebellion against the syndicate would have to wait. His thoughts were interrupted when fifteen-year-old Gabina called to him in her halting Russian. *"Tih khochyetsa?"*

"Yes," he replied, getting up. "I am hungry." He walked over to the table where a large serving of chicken, rice, and flat bread awaited his pleasure.

SEALs BIVOUAC
PRANISTAY STEPPES
19 OCTOBER
0800 HOURS

THE night before had been cold. The SEALs had brought sleeping bags with them, but they were designed for temperate zones and would not be much use when the temperature really dropped on the steppes. But the Brigands had managed to stay reasonably comfortable by sleeping with poncho liners wrapped around them while snuggled deep into the bags. Chinar, with almost his entire life spent on the steppes, had his own Pashtun blankets and had been completely comfortable. Wallenger and Krafton had come with arctic sleeping gear and had been warm and cozy through the night.

Now, with the sun well up and quickly warming the chill out of the air, the men sat around in groups downing MREs heated in FRHs. The donkey skinners had returned to their village the previous day since there wouldn't be much for them to do for a while. The feed and gear they brought over on their animals had been dropped off and covered by tarpaulins. Although they were only part-time employees, funds to pay them for full time had been allotted to Brannigan. They appreciated the generosity and promised to be available whenever needed.

The two journalists ate with the officers, sharing the GI rations since they had been provided with the same government rations as the SEALs. Wallenger was looking forward to some excitement. He gave Brannigan a look of eagerness. "What's on the agenda for today, Bill?"

Brannigan took a bite of scrambled eggs from the packet, then answered, "The first thing we have to do is organize the camp. Then the officers and chiefs will go over to the village with Chinar to meet the headmen and establish a rapport of sorts."

"We should take Doc Bradley with us, sir," Jim Cruiser said. "There might be something for a corpsman to do over there. Remember how he helped that little boy down in South America?"

"Good idea," Brannigan said.

Wallenger and Krafton looked at each other with raised eyebrows. Could Brannigan's Brigands be the guys involved in the massacre of the villagers in Bolivia a while back? They both quickly recovered from the startling realization and turned their attention to the meal.

"When that's done I'll start sending out patrols of individual fire teams," Brannigan continued. "So this base camp will be home for a while."

"What are these patrols going to be doing?" Wallenger asked.

"They'll be checking out the area," Brannigan replied. "And maybe introduce themselves to anyone they meet." He took another spoonful of the food. "You can go along if you want. I've been told to let you have full access to our activities."

"I believe we'll do that," Wallenger said, thinking that there was going to be some great opportunities to pick up some very interesting information—either past or present.

CHAPTER 6

IT was obvious the people were anticipating the visit from the SEALs. Events such as a group of visitors suddenly showing up were rare. It was almost like a holiday, and it put the people in a mood to celebrate. Everyone was at the edge of the village, gathered behind the august figure of old Quajeer the headman. They grinned in happy anticipation as their guests rode up. Willing hands of young boys took the reins of the horses as the Americans dismounted and approached the elder. Chinar solemnly introduced the oldster to the strangers, referring to their ranks in Pashtun: *Turan* Bill Brannigan, *Dvahom Baridman* Jim Cruiser, *Dreyom Baridman* Orlando Taylor; *Krur* Buford Dawkins, *Loi Bresh* Matthew Gunnarson, and *Bresh* James Bradley. These were actually army ranks, since landlocked Afghanistan did not have a navy, but the villagers could relate to the titles. The interpreter used *zhornalisanet* for Dirk

Wallenger and Eddie Krafton to identify them by their profession.

Krafton immediately began taping as the SEALs took turns shaking hands with Quajeer. The village chief gave a short speech, punctuated with exaggerated gestures, in which he welcomed the Americans and thanked them for hiring the donkey skinners, which would bring an influx of cash into the community. He then asked if there was anything else the Janoons could do for them.

After the translation, Brannigan greeted the old man and his villagers through Chinar. "My men are grateful for your kind welcome to us. We are here through the courtesy of the Afghanistan government and are in their service. Your friendly offer of help to us is greatly appreciated. We also hope that if there is any service we might do for you, that you will feel welcome to make a request. The Taliban is gone from here and—" He was interrupted by catcalls and angry yells as the people expressed their dislike of the religious gang that had ruled over them for several years. Brannigan continued, "—we will be on the alert in case they try to return and make trouble. We are also on the lookout for bad people among you who want the Taliban back. If you are troubled by them, please let us know and we will see that they are taken away."

Quajeer seemed genuinely pleased by the last statement. "There were those of the Mahsud tribe who have been with the Taliban. They are bad people and hid guns to use to kill us if the Taliban came back. They also have money given them by the Taliban. We told some British soldiers of this, and they came and found the guns and took the bad ones away to be punished. But the money was hidden and could not be found."

"We will visit the tribe you told me about and make sure they behave," Brannigan promised.

This elicited more yelling among the people, and Chinar explained the outpouring to the SEAL officer. "The Mahsud are our enemies, Lieutenant Brannigan. Our very worst enemies. You must keep a close eye on them. We have a saying,

'Marane zda kawem darghal le Mahsud.' That means, 'Serpents learn treachery from the Mahsud.' "

Brannigan grinned. "Christ! That pretty well describes the bastards, doesn't it?" He turned and motioned Doc Bradley to come forward. The hospital corpsman presented himself, and the Skipper once again addressed Quajeer. "This man is like a doctor," he said. "He knows many things about medicine. If you ever have any sick or injured people, he can help them."

Upon being given the news the elderly Pashtun's eyes opened wide. "We have a man who had cut himself very deeply two days ago. Can you help him?"

"I can help him," Bradley said through Chinar. "Take me to him."

Excited murmuring broke out in the crowd and they made way as Chinar and Quajeer led Bradley toward the man's house. "His name is Sangin and he was hurt while butchering a goat."

They were taken some twenty meters deeper into the village to a house near some goat pens. When they went inside, a woman looked up startled, but Chinar calmed her by explaining that the American had come to help her injured husband. Krafton, who had been busy taping everything, had to stay outside.

Bradley found his patient resting on a pallet in a far corner. He knelt down and took the unresisting man's arm. He undid the bloody bandage covering the wound and found a deep gash across the forearm. "I can't see good enough in here," the SEAL said. "Tell him he must come outside."

Sangin allowed himself to be taken from the house out into the sun. He grinned at the people gathered around his pallet, proud to be the center of attention. Bradley looked at Chinar. "Tell everybody to stand back. I need room."

Chinar issued the order and the Pashtuns obeyed, anxious to watch the American black man work. Krafton and Wallenger moved closer, and since Bradley had no objections they continued taping. The first thing Bradley did was inject a local anesthetic of 200 milligrams of lidocaine. It took effect rather quickly and the growing comfort was obviously very soothing to Sangin. He began to wave the arm around until Bradley gave him a ferocious glare. When the patient settled down, the corpsman began cleaning the wound, remarking, "There's bits of meat in here."

"Probably goat," Chinar remarked.

"Damn!" Bradley said. "He'd've had gangrene in another week." He gave a second shot—this one a tetanus toxoid— then began a debridement procedure of gently cutting away infected tissue from the wound. None of it had become mushy, so the Pashtun was not yet in danger. The SEAL worked slowly and steadily, obviously sure of himself as he cleaned the wound and applied an antiseptic solution to ward off any further infection.

Sangin thoroughly enjoyed the procedure, watching with interest as what had been a dirty injury beginning to fester now appear clean and open. The suturing absolutely fascinated him. With all that finished, Bradley dabbed on a good coating of old-fashioned iodine, then applied a fresh, neat bandage.

"That's it," the corpsman announced, standing up.

Sangin got to his feet too, and began walking back and forth holding up the injured limb for all to see. "I'll come back in a few days to take out the stitches," Bradley said to Chinar. "Tell him to keep the bandage on, make sure it stays dry, and don't get any dirt on it." As Chinar delivered the instructions, Krafton zoomed in with his camera to get a good close up of the translator and the injured man.

The Americans were ready to leave and everybody again crowded around and followed them back to their horses. The SEALs mounted up, making good-byes to their new friends. Senior Chief Dawkins reached back into his saddlebags and pulled out some wrapped rock candy, and began tossing it out by the handful at the kids. Even the adults joined in the scuffle for the sweets as a minor riot broke out in the rush to get a share of the goodies.

Now forgotten in the melee, the SEALs wheeled their horses and began the ride back to the bivouac.

KHORUGH, TAJIKISTAN

THIS city of a bit more than 33,000 is located to the
northeast of the Kangal Mountains almost on the Afghanistan border. The nearest other municipalities of any size
were in Pakistan and Uzbekistan. While the official language of Tajikistan was Tajik, the large number of Russian
expatriates in Khorugh meant that their mother tongue was
also prominent in the area. There was also a strong criminal
connection between the underworld of that city and the
Russian Mafia in Moscow.

Aleksander Akloschenko was a former Soviet bureaucrat
who had been stationed in Khorugh during the glory days of
Communism. Like all prosperous Russians, or those in
cushy jobs, he had put on a lot of weight and his facial features had softened from his life of ease. Now in his late for-
ties, he had ended up a corpulent, short, balding man with an
extremely large stomach.

During his career in Tajikistan, Akloschenko was chief of
government property, buildings, and land, and the long distance between his office and that of his immediate supervisor back in the USSR meant he was a virtual potentate
without superintendence. His only obligations were a series
of monthly activity reports and inventories he dispatched
back to Russia. Once a year, when inspectors were sent out
for examination and audits, they were always so nervous and
physically shook up after the frightening Aeroflot flight on
ancient, creaking aircraft that all they wanted to do was con-
sume vodka to both soothe their nerves from the nerve-
wracking journey as well as fortify themselves for the
hazardous return. Their inspections of property books and
budget outlays were superficial at best, done with quick half-
drunken scans of the documents that Akloschenko trotted
out for them to peruse. Most embezzlers keep two sets of
books, but the inefficiency of the Soviet system did not make
that necessary in Akloschenko's case.

Consequently, with this blessed independence, the bureaucrat was able to gleefully sell government vehicles and

equipment on the black market that serviced not only Tajik-istan but Afghanistan, Pakistan, and Uzbekistan as well. Additionally he hired out convicts from the military prison as laborers to private construction contractors who were also using government-owned building materials purchased from Akloschenko. These arrangements included furnishing tough guys for anyone who needed some physical pressure applied to debtors and/or business rivals.

All this brought in beaucoup shekels for Akloschenko's private coffers. It was true he had to lay out bribes and kick-backs among several branches of Soviet agencies within the local government net, but the men running those organiza-tions had as much self-sufficiency as Akloschenko, thus these arrangements were mutually beneficial. When the USSR collapsed, he could have returned to the new Russia and that had been his preliminary intention. But when several col-leagues were assassinated by the emerging crime syndicates in the home country, he decided to stay put. And just to re-ally play it safe, he used ex-convicts who had recently been freed from the prison as bodyguards. He established him-self on the top floor of a poorly constructed downtown four-story building—Khorugh's equivalent of a skyscraper—and switched from being a crooked bureaucrat to being a crooked businessman. This latter endeavor eventually evolved into his being the head of his own crime syndicate that emerged out of the situation.

Akloschenko's latest and pet project was a scheme to take over the opium poppy harvest and smuggling on the Pranistay Steppes in Afghanistan with Luka Yarkov. He supplied the brains and money to get things rolling while Yarkov and his gang contributed the muscle. He had made secret arrange-ments for sales known only to him and his closest associate, Pavel Marvesky. Even Yarkov was unaware of the arrange-ment with the hush-hush customer.

The two advantages Akloschenko enjoyed in the scheme were that any resistance could easily be handled in that desolate area and that he had the luxury of time, since there was the entire winter to consolidate and organize the ef-forts.

AKLOSCHENKO'S OFFICE
1400 HOURS

PAVEL Marvesky stepped into the reception area, laying an appreciative gaze on the pretty blond who screened the visitors to her boss. He winked at her, saying, "Hello, Ekaterina."

She did not smile back. Her boyfriend, Maks, who was afraid of Marvesky, would beat the hell out of her if he heard about any flirtation with the gangster. And that would end with Marvesky either shooting Maks or beating him to death. Maks was a little fellow who was a clerk in public works and wouldn't stand a chance against the large, muscular Marvesky, who had been a champion weightlifter back in Russia. Maks was cute and she liked him, so the young woman decided any show of defiance toward Marvesky was up to her.

Her voice was coldly businesslike when she announced, "Mr. Akloschenko said you were to go straight in when you arrived."

"*Spasebo*," Marvesky said, winking again. He stepped through the door and closed it, giving a little wave to Akloschenko. "Hello, Chief."

"Hello, Pavel Dimitrovich," Akloschenko said. He shoved the papers he had been studying aside and gave his full attention to his caller. "Sit down."

"Thank you, Chief," Marvesky said. "It is starting to get cold outside. Winter is just around the corner."

"One season follows the other," Akloschenko remarked. "What is going on out there?"

"Things look good," Marvesky replied. "The Pashtuns are all set to plant in the early spring. I have made arrangements for transport to the new distribution spot in Dusanbe. An excellent warehouse has been obtained there, and we can keep the trucks in storage until needed."

"*Prevockodnie!*" Akloschenko said. "They will be protected from the weather."

"It is a sound structure," Marvesky assured him. "Parts of it can be heated so there is no danger of the oil or lubrication getting too thick and stiff."

"You have done well on your end," Akloschenko said. "Just remember to keep the identity of our customer to yourself."

"Of course, Chief."

"Now I am ready to expand your responsibilities," Akloschenko said. "This will include some very sensitive matters."

Marvesky, expecting this development, nodded. "I suppose that will concern Yarkov and his boys, hey?"

"Exactly. Tell me, Pavel, what do you think of that fellow Surov who is in Yarkov's gang?"

Marvesky thought for a moment. "An ex-officer, as I recall. He held the rank of captain, I believe, when he ended up in prison for embezzling regimental funds to pay off loan sharks and gambling debts in Saint Petersburg."

"Correct," Akloschenko said. "Now tell me what you think of Luka Yarkov?"

"He is a natural leader," Marvesky said carefully, "but not everywhere. In prison his toughness and ruthlessness worked well for him. The life inside was primitive and many times a matter of kill or be killed. He excelled in the dangerous existence. No doubt about that."

"You are making a good point," Akloschenko said. "But what about outside of prison? How do you think he has conducted himself thus far?"

"He is doing quite well up there in Logovishchyeh," Marvesky allowed. "His men are both respectful and loyal toward him. He is able to carry out assignments quite efficiently. He was a *praporschik*—a warrant officer—in the Army." He thought a moment. "He was under a death sentence for killing a soldier. He beat the life out of the guy. I do not recall the dead man's offense, except that it was considered rather trivial."

"It would seem that Yarkov's efficiency goes to hell when he loses his temper," Akloschenko remarked.

Marvesky knew exactly what his boss was thinking. "Perhaps he should be subordinated to Surov." He shook his head. "*Nyet!* That could not happen. Yarkov would have to be eliminated."

"It is early yet before the harvest and all the attending complications," Akloschenko said. "But perhaps if you visited Logovishchyeh, you could sort of sound Surov out. You know what I mean; be subtle and try to discover how deep his loyalties are to Yarkov."

Marvesky smiled. "I would think that since Surov was an officer he has resented having to serve a former subordinate. It makes sense that he would prefer to be the boss of that gang. But there is another problem you're not taking under consideration, Chief."

"What's that?

"Perhaps the other convicts would not accept Surov as their leader," Marvesky said. "If you had Yarkov removed and put Surov in his place, those guys might decide to kill him."

Akloschenko laughed. "Back in the old Soviet bureaucracy we would classify that as an adjustment of personnel status."

CHAPTER 7

DIRK Wallenger used the notes he had made during the taping at the Janoon village to write out his latest presentation for broadcast. Since he would be unable to make a voice-over on the scenes he would have to rely on the editing people back in the Washington studio to match up his spiel with the correct sound bites. This unconventional method would have been irritating enough to the micromanaging journalist, but he also had to rely on unscheduled resupply flights to get his tapes back to Shelor Field for mailing to the States. That was one problem he hadn't envisioned when he first decided to get imbedded with a combat unit.

Now, fifty meters away from camp, Wallenger waited as Eddie lifted his camera into position. "Okay, Dirk."

"Right. Five . . . four . . . three . . . two . . . one . . . Greetings from somewhere in Afghanistan," Wallenger began. "The SEAL detachment known as Brannigan's Brigands is now on the ground and running, or perhaps I should say 'galloping' straight into their mission that has been dubbed Operation Combat Alley. Yesterday we went to a Pashtun village to become acquainted with the local natives, and had the very real pleasure of making friends with a group of exotic people who have inhabited this part of the world for eons. The Pashtuns are fascinating, and just happen to be the largest tribal society in the world today. Their actual origins are obscure and they refer to legends to mark the beginning of their existence, mingling historical fact with myth. They are a passionate people who do not hesitate to turn to violence to deal with disagreements with not only outsiders but their own kind within their many clans. Here, in this part of Afghanistan, there are seven tribes who share a history of peace and war in which temporary alliances and hostilities have whirled and mingled throughout their existence." He stopped speaking to refer to his notes.

Eddie relaxed, taking the camera from his shoulder. "Man, oh man! I can't wait to see these tapes."

"They'll have been broadcast many weeks before we get to see the final results of our efforts," Wallenger said. "Okay. Let's roll again." He waited for the cameraman to get ready, then immediately took up where he left off. "The Pashtuns live by a series of codes that reflect a male-dominated society. This set of laws demands that they be hospitable to strangers as well as strictly observant to matters of honor. This latter edict is what seems to lead to most of the violence in their lives, and informed sources here have told me that, for the most part, this involves matters between the sexes. Any disrespect to a woman, which can include even a casual glance, demands that the males of the family retaliate immediately and fiercely to maintain their honor. Note that I said *their* honor, not *her* honor. If a woman of their family engages in sinful conduct, she will be murdered by male relatives in an act termed an 'honor killing.' Accordingly, a woman who is raped must produce witnesses to testify that she resisted the assault with all her strength, or she too will be slain or ordered executed by a Muslim judge. Strangely enough, killings because of male-female issues do not have to be revenged. And, speaking of revenge, when custom demands it, the Pashtuns respond accordingly, setting up vendettas that can go on for generations. On a somewhat more civilized side, if a Pashtun submits himself to the mercy of another, begs to be forgiven for some wrong while humbling himself completely, the subject of his pleas is not only required to grant the requests but is expected to be generous about it. Go figure."

Eddie stopped taping as Wallenger signaled him to stop. "I can make a few additional notes on this background shit to tape later. I must find the stuff I wrote about Doc treating that guy's cut arm." He fumbled through his papers. "Ah! Here it is. Ready to go?"

"You bet."

"The SEAL you see coming out of the hut with the injured man is Hospital Corpsman James Bradley, who is called 'Doc' by his comrades in arms. The village chief requested medical aid for this fellow being carried on the pallet, who had cut himself badly while butchering a goat. As you see, Corpsman Bradley has begun treating the man. This is a lifesaving situation, ladies and gentlemen, since the arm is infected and would eventually fester into full-blown gangrene. That, of course, means the patient would have died unless someone amputated the arm. That is hardly a surgical procedure that could be performed satisfactorily in this wilderness. What we are witnessing here is an unselfish act of kindness of one human being to another; in this case an American serviceman is ministering to a primitive Pashtun, literally saving his life before our eyes. Cut, Eddie."

"That was good, Dirk."

"Right," he said absentmindedly while he turned to his notes again. "I'll do the sign-off now, then tomorrow I want to embellish some of this. Okay, here we go."

"I'm ready," Eddie announced.

". . . Four . . . five . . . And so, ladies and gentlemen, you can see it's not all killing and maiming out here. Within the violence of war are small acts of kindness and charity that might be taken for granted back home, but are ever so meaningful out here on the war front. These incidents are like a few bright stars in a bleakly dark night. This is Dirk Wallenger, somewhere in Afghanistan, wishing you peace in a world gone mad. Cut!"

"This is getting better all the time," Eddie said. "I'd be willing to bet your 'Somewhere in the War' series is going to get you not only an Emmy but a Pulitzer too, Dirk, if you also write a book. Think about making guest appearances on talk shows."

Wallenger smiled with pleasure at the thought. "And I, of course, will remember my intrepid cameraman when I accept my accolades, kudos, and praises."

"Your gratitude warms the cockles of my heart," Eddie said with a chuckle, knowing that as soon as they returned stateside, he would fade into obscurity in the same proportion that Wallenger's fame would grow.

As they walked back to the bivouac, Wallenger glanced over to see a couple of the SEALs giving their horses some exercise out in the open. "Say, Eddie, do you suppose these guys were part of that massacre of those Brazilian villagers down in South America a year or so ago?"

"I don't know," Eddie said. "I remember your report, but I wasn't down there with you."

"Jim Cruiser did make that remark about Doc Bradley helping a sick child in South America," Wallenger reminded him.

"He sure did," Eddie replied.

"The thing kind of blew over, but it was obvious that someone massacred a village of men, women, and children in cold blood," Wallenger said. "While I was at the scene, I interviewed a guy who claimed to be a witness. He said his wife and kids were shot down by American Green Berets during a dawn raid. He claimed the perpetrators included African and blond men who spoke English."

"I saw the photographs you brought back," Eddie said. "Those were dead civilians, no doubt. And, like you said, included women and kids. I recall there was a lot of rioting down there in South America when the story came out."

"They found the guy I interviewed later in the uniform of a Fascist revolutionary army," Wallenger said. "He had been killed in a battle and was pretty torn up. But he seemed to be the same guy."

"Sometimes a corpse is hard to identify," Eddie pointed out. "Especially if a violent death is involved. So there's always the chance it was somebody else."

"Well, I'll tell you something," Wallenger said as they neared the bivouac. "I'm going to snoop around and make some innocent-sounding inquiries among these Brigands."

"It could amount to a significant scoop," Eddie opined.

THE SWATI VILLAGE
1530 HOURS

THE men of the hamlet had armed themselves to the extent that they wore extra bandoleers of magazines for their AK-47s crisscrossed over their torsos. Each weapon was fully locked and loaded with one round in the chamber. The women and children were inside the huts, lying on the floor, while a few of the bolder boys peered from the windows. The fighting men were unable to determine the exact number of weapon-toting unfriendlies approaching their community from off the steppes, but it was obvious the intruders badly outnumbered the locals.

The group of outsiders, made up of fifty Russians and seventy-five Pashtuns from the Mahsud tribe, came to within fifty meters of the village, forming a semicircle that covered it on three sides. Valentin Surov, accompanied by a Mahsud war leader named Dagar, rode forward to within twenty meters of the Swati community. The Russian called out, "*Salamat osey!* We would speak with your *malik*!"

"What do you want to talk about?" came a shout from the interior of the hamlet.

"It is too important to bellow back and forth about," Surov said. "My friend Dagar and I will come closer to you. You will see we mean no harm because if there is trouble we will be the first to die."

A few minutes passed, then two elderly men appeared from the mud buildings and advanced ten meters toward the visitors. Surov and Dagar rode forward, then halted and dismounted, holding the reins of their horses. Dagar knew both of the Swatis. He pointed to one, "That is Abasin, the *malik*," he said to Surov. Now he indicated the other. "And that is Tolwak, a *molla*."

Surov displayed a friendly smile. "We are here on behalf of Luka Yarkov, our chief. Yarkov has great affection for all Pashtun people, and that includes the Swatis. He is going to take over the selling of the entire opium poppy crop of the Pranistay Steppes. To show his respect for your tribe and all the tribes, he is going to pay you one and a half times the price that Awalmir of the Yousafzai paid you in the past. He is most generous, is he not?"

Abasin ignored the remarks. "You Russians stole five of our women and girls. You must pay us for them."

"I speak of a subject more important than females," Surov said. "This is a big thing that Yarkov does. Awalmir trembles in his hut, afraid of Yarkov. Already we have made alliances with the Mahsud, Kharoti, Bhittani, and Ghilzai tribes."

"We want to be paid for the five women," Abasin insisted. "You must pay us one thousand afghanis for each one."

Surov frowned in anger. "Do not be disrespectful. Yarkov has more than three hundred men. You don't seem to realize that he is a *khan*."

Tolwak, the clergyman, glared furiously at Dagar. "You have taken sides with an infidel against true believers of Islam."

Dagar grinned. "Are you deaf, old man? Did you not hear what Surov said? His words are not idle boasting. There are four tribes of the faithful already joined together to sell their harvests to Yarkov."

"We will not speak of anything until the Russians pay us five thousand afghanis," Abasin insisted. "You cannot take women and expect to get away with it."

"Yarkov will not give you a single afghani for all the Swati women in the world," Surov snarled. "And if you choose not to sell us your poppy harvest, we will take it from you."

"You will take nothing from us!" Abasin snapped. "If you

want crops from our tribal fields, you will have to fight for them!"

"Then we will kill you all," Surov threatened. "And leave your pretty women alive so that we can take our pleasure with them."

"Listen to him," Dagar said. "Surov speaks the truth. Already five of your women will burn in hell forever for fornicating with the infidels. Do you want more to spend eternity in the fires of hell?"

"You have much to lose," Surov said. "We will go now. You think over the offer and be grateful for Yarkov's generosity. We will return for your friendship or your lives and pretty women."

Abasin and Tolwak stood silently as the two swung themselves back up into their saddles, then wheeled around and galloped back to rejoin their friends.

LOGOVISHCHYEH, TAJIKISTAN
1800 HOURS

YARKOV and his underbosses had gathered once again in his large domicile for a strategy meeting. This time they had company: Pavel Marvesky from Khorugh was in attendance. They were well aware of the importance of the man closest to the Big Boss making a personal visit to their home base.

A fire, built by Gabina, crackled in the hearth while several bottles of vodka recently retrieved from the freezer were sitting in an ice bucket in the middle of the table. Gabina had spent the afternoon preparing *samosas* and *pakoras* for snacks. Yarkov was in a good mood. The girl worked alone serving him and his guests because Zainba had begun menstruating. The gang leader was glad she hadn't ended up pregnant.

Now the five Russians drank toasts to their motherland, each other, and the boss of all bosses, Aleksander Akloschenko. With the cold vodka in their bellies, they consumed a couple of the snacks each before settling down to business. Marvesky, as a courtesy, allowed Yarkov to open the informal proceedings.

"Alright, brothers," Yarkov said, wiping at the crumbs in his beard. "We are honored to have Pavel Dimitrovich Marvesky come to visit Logovishchyeh. And without further delay, I invite him to address us as to his purpose for the journey from modern Khorugh to our primitive little town."

"Thank you, Luka Ivanovich," Marvesky said. He chuckled. "Do not worry, brothers, I will not be here boring you for long." He waited for the polite laughter to die down. "I wish I had been with you during the visit to the villages. It would be most convenient for me to actually get a look at the Pranistay Steppes. But, at any rate, I am only here to get the latest news to take back to the Big Boss. And I am ready to hear how things are progressing in the plan to take over the harvest."

"Everything goes well," Yarkov informed him. "We now have the four strongest tribes on our side. I followed the Big Boss's instructions and promised them one and a half times the usual price. That was enough to make our offer more interesting to most, and they quickly abandoned Awalmir Yousafzai completely."

"Where were you earlier today when I arrived?" Marvesky asked.

"We paid a visit to the weakest tribe on the steppes," Yarkov answered. "But they refused our offer. Instead they want us to submit an honor payment of five thousand afghanis to them for some women we took last year."

"That seems strange to me," Marvesky remarked. "I admit I know little about these damned Pashtuns. Why would money compensate them for the loss of female relatives?"

Surov interjected, "According to their religion, the women are disgraced because of having been fucked by us. Thus, they want an honor payment to satisfy their dignity. On the other hand, if we returned to the women to the villages, the bastards would murder them as if they were sick lambs."

"That is true," little Fedor Grabvosky said. "They believe these women have sinned and will go to hell."

Marvesky was confused. "But they were kidnapped and

raped. It was not the women's fault." He suddenly laughed. "And I know they didn't fall in love with you ugly lugs, so they probably fought like hell when you laid hands on them."

"Oh, yes," Aleksei Barkyev, the largest of the under-bosses, said. "But once they're beaten up and given a damn good screwing, their fighting spirit evaporates like piss on a hot stove. In their minds, they have lost everything by then. They are doomed both on earth and in the hereafter."

"Well, I know the Big Boss is not going to want any 'honor payments' made to those bumpkins. It would be a sign of weakness. And he will not tolerate their refusal to join us either. I am sure you know what that means."

"Of course," Yarkov said. "We must make an example of them to convince the other tribes of the wisdom of join-ing us."

"How many tribes still remain obstinate?" Marvesky asked.

"Counting the Swatis, there are three," Surov answered. "The Janoons and the Yousafzais. The last two have the most people, and we are taking the poppy business away from the warlord of the Yousafzais."

"Then wipe out the Swatis," Marvesky said. "If they're a small group, their poppy fields can be divided up among our allied tribes." He poured more vodka into his glass. "Re-member we will eventually expand to other areas and other tribes, so don't leave a man, woman, or child alive. You must make a strong impression that will become well known throughout all Pashtun groups in Afghanistan." He noticed one of the snack dishes was empty. "Are there more?"

"Of course, Pavel Dimitrovich," Yarkov said. He turned his head toward the other room. "Gabina! More *samosas*!"

CHAPTER 8

IGOR Tchaikurov had been a member of the *Spetsnaz* Special Operations Detachment of the Soviet KGB Border Guards before running afoul of the law. The elite unit he belonged to performed some of the most daring and clandestine duties for the Communist regime in operations along the entirety of its immense border. Tchaikurov was among the best in the dark missions and was a career warrant officer until his sentence for murder that brought about his incarceration in the military prison in Tajikistan. Although condemned to be shot, he languished like all the others awaiting capital punishment, enduring more than a decade of brutal confinement.

Tchaikurov had killed a fellow soldier because of an infatuation with the man's wife. She was blond, pretty, and desirable, and Tchaikurov was having an affair with her. He reasoned that by ridding her of the husband, the woman would be his alone. It turned out he was only one of a trio of lovers whose attentions she enjoyed while her husband was away patrolling isolated areas of the international border. After learning of the competition, he killed her too. Unfortunately he had been spotted entering her apartment by neighbors in the crowded building.

At his sentencing the colonel who presided over the trial stated that he didn't blame Tchaikurov for slaying the woman, but killing a valued *Spetsnaz* soldier was unforgivable. Therefore, he recommended the prisoner be taken to the nearest military prison for execution. The other officers of the tribunal agreed and sent the disgraced border guard to Tajikistan to have the sentence carried out. Follow-up orders never arrived, and the double murderer languished in confinement as a bureaucratic unperson.

Now, in the predawn hours, Tchaikurov trod silently and swiftly across the hard-packed soil of the Pranistay Steppes. He approached the outlying huts of the village and paused to see if any dogs might have been aroused. The only sound was that of the wind, showing that the local canines were snug asleep in the huts of their masters. The Russian knew exactly where he was going. It was the building where the boy guards stood their watch. It was easy to find, since a ladder was propped up to allow the lads access to the flat roof. Tchaikurov ascended without a sound, pausing when he could peer over the top. He saw a small figure sleepily manning his post, gazing out into the darkness. Within quick seconds the ex-*Spetsnaz* man was over the top, moving to a position just behind the boy. The garrote went around the small neck and was violently jerked taut. The youngster lost consciousness much quicker than would a full-grown man. After lowering the limp body to the rooftop, Tchaikurov pulled the flashlight from his jacket. A red lens cover blinked scarlet as he signaled that all was clear.

Luka Yarkov was at the head of 150 men as he moved toward the village. Fifty of this force were Mahsud tribesmen with a history of conflict with the Swatis. They looked forward to this opportunity to settle a few old scores that popped up when their foes had refused to join in Yarkov's operations. When the group of attackers was within twenty-five meters of the nearest huts, half the tribesmen scurried around to cut off any escape routes on the far side while a couple of dozen Russians split into two groups to cover the sides of the hamlet. The remainder of the gang moved straight into the village.

The slaughter began when the first doors were kicked in and assault rifles fired into the interior of the mud homes. All hell broke loose and the sleepy dogs who had been dozing suddenly awoke to begin useless, loud barking that was cut short by combinations of 7.62- and 5.45-millimeter bullets. Yarkov, with his military training, had planned a *blitzkrieg*-type attack with initial rushes of heavy fire followed up by groups of riflemen who mopped up survivors. When the firing began, those on the flanks quickly joined the battle, charging into the melee.

It was butchery by bullet as the village men did their best to respond to the fiery assault. Most managed to get off no more than one short burst before being cut down in the houses as their women and children died around them. The few fighters who managed to get through a door and outside were blasted down in swarms of bullets coming at them from different directions.

The heavy initial killing took only ten minutes, but another half hour was necessary until every single inhabitant of the Swati village was either dead or wounded. The latter were quickly dispatched with pistol shots. No pity was shown to the vanquished. Old people, men, women, children, and infants lay scattered around, their clothing turned to bloody rags from the gaping wounds of dozens of bullet strikes. There would have been looting except so many household items, like the people, had been shot to pieces. A few of the lucky killers did manage to pull rings and bracelets off a few of the women while other took wristwatches from the male corpses.

Yarkov kept his men searching for possible survivors until dawn began to glow behind the Kangal Mountains. By then the area had been searched over, a few weapons picked up from the dead, and every victim the attackers examined had been determined to be a corpse. The Russian boss yelled orders to withdraw while Surov repeated the instructions in Pashtun.

They went back to the horses that were being held by a couple of dozen Mahsud boys in the area from where the assault had been launched. The grim job was over, and the attackers mounted the horses for the ride back to their quarters. The Russians headed toward Logovishchyeh while the Mahsud split off to return to their two villages.

SEALs BIVOUAC
23 OCTOBER
1015 HOURS

EVERYONE was surprised by the sight of the patrol made up of Lieutenant (JG) Jim Cruiser, Petty Officer Third Class Tex Benson, and Alpha Fire Team returning so early from what was supposed to have been a four-hour trek to the north.

Brannigan walked up to them with Senior Chief Buford Dawkins as they reined in their mounts. The Skipper noted the serious expression on Cruiser's face, but decided to be a bit flippant anyway. "Since you can't run out of gas, did you come back early because you ran out of oats?"

Cruiser ignored the lighthearted greeting. "Sir, we dropped in on the Janoon village and the people say that another village was wiped out. Everybody was killed."

"Jesus!" Brannigan said. He looked over at the headquarters spot. "Hey, Chinar! Come here!"

The young interpreter trotted up, quickly noting this was not a festive occasion. "Yes, Lieutenant?"

"Cruiser says your folks over at the village said a Pashtun group has been massacred," Brannigan reported. "Let's go check it out."

"Did they say who was killed?" Chinar asked.

"They told me the tribe's name, but it went right over my head," Cruiser said. "Evidently some of the locals had gone to deliver some donkeys that were sold to them, and they found everybody dead."

"Oh!" Chinar exclaimed. "It must have been the Swatis."

"Can you lead us to their village?" Brannigan asked.

"Yes, sir!"

Brannigan yelled out, "All hands! Now hear this! Grab your gear and saddle up!" He glanced at Dawkins. "Senior Chief, you and Gomez stay here and mind the fort."

Now Wallenger trotted up with Eddie at his heels. "What's going on, Bill?"

"It sounds newsworthy," Brannigan answered. "A local village has been wiped out by somebody. Since you're imbedded with us, I can see no reason you can't go along."

"Mmm," Wallenger said thoughtfully. "That's an interesting development. Who do you think the perpetrators are?"

Chinar answered, "I think it would be other Pashtuns. Perhaps a feud has broken out."

"It must have been pretty serious if it deteriorated to genocide," Brannigan remarked.

"Indeed, sir!" Chinar said. "It could be that a woman in somebody's family was treated with disrespect."

"And for that a whole village would be wiped out?" Brannigan asked.

"Indeed, sir!" China repeated.

In ten minutes the detachment was mounted, armed, and ready. Brannigan pulled a "John Wayne," personally leading his troops on a gallop across the steppes with the faithful Chinar at his side.

THE SWATI VILLAGE
1130 HOURS

THE Second Assault Section under Ensign Orlando Taylor had been detailed to clear the village. The rest of the detachment formed a loose defensive perimeter around the area while the hamlet was checked out.

Dirk Wallenger, with his powerful binoculars to his eyes,

surveyed what he could. "There are obviously a lot of bodies sprawled around," he remarked to Eddie Krafton, who had his camera on his shoulder. "But it's difficult to determine how many."

"We'll find out soon enough," Eddie said.

Taylor and Connie Concord appeared at the community's edge, trotting toward Brannigan and Cruiser. The ensign's face was twisted into a grimace. "Everybody is dead, sir," he reported. "There're even little dead babies in there."

"Alright, Orlando," Brannigan said. He turned to the rest of the detachment. "Okay! Let's move in by fire teams and check the place out. Be prepared! It's not a pretty sight."

Doc Bradley literally ran into the place ahead of the others to begin a desperate search for wounded that might need medical aid. The rest of the Brigands walked slower, going between the buildings where corpses were sprawled in the violence of their death. It was obvious that most had been riddled with bullets after falling to the ground, since no human could have taken so many hits before collapsing.

The interiors of the homes were like slaughter pens. This was where the majority of the dead children lay huddled in death as they cringed in the midst of the horror blasting down on them. Some cribs had been kicked over and there was evidence that a couple of the infants had been stomped to death.

Puglisi noticed a pile of cartridge cases, surmising that several of the shooters must have stood in a group firing at targets of opportunity who were no doubt running for their lives. He knelt down and picked up some of the brass. "Skipper!" he called out.

Brannigan walked over. "Find something interesting?"

"Maybe, sir," Puglisi said, standing up. "There's two kinds of cases here. Seven-point-six-two and five-point-four-five. The first group is prob'ly AK-47s. Them kind of weapons are pretty numerous around here since the Russkis invaded this place back in the eighties. That's where the locals got most of 'em from. But I'll bet a year's paydays that these smaller ones are from AK-74s. The Russkis started making 'em when they felt the larger calibers was turning obsolete. It was an answer to our five-point-fifty-six. I'll bet you anything these are AK-74-Ms, the latest models in that line. They got short-barrel versions too."

"It looks like the tribes are modernizing, Puglisi," Brannigan said, examining some of the evidence.

"I don't think so, sir," Puglisi said. "I bet there's some goddamn Russkis around here someplace."

The remark set Brannigan to thinking. Puglisi was verbose, unpredictable, and impetuous, but behind that bluster was an analytical mind. Stupid blowhards don't make it through BUD/S, and the Italian-American was a prime example of the best of the best. Puglisi had an innate talent to figure things out. When he was confused or wondering about something, all his impulsiveness melted away and he fell into methodical thinking. And Brannigan could not recall his ever being wrong.

"Lieutenant Cruiser!" Brannigan bellowed.

Cruiser appeared from between a couple of hutches and reported in. "Yes, sir?"

"Your Bravo Fire Team are the best recon guys, right?"

"Yes, sir," Cruiser replied. "That's Sturgis, Malachenko, Matsuno, and Redhawk."

"I have a mission for 'em," Brannigan said. "I want 'em to check out the area for any tracks left by the attackers. Then follow the bastards as far as possible. Right to their fucking hometown, if they have to."

"Aye, sir!" Cruiser said. He turned and hurried back to his section.

Doc Bradley walked up to the Skipper, sadly shaking his head. "No survivors, sir. And I counted twenty-one bodies with multiple wounds, including headshots at close range. To me that means they were among the wounded finished off while still alive."

"God!" Brannigan exclaimed. "This just keeps getting worse."

Dirk Wallenger and Eddie Krafton walked amidst the carnage, recording the scenes to be sent back to the States. Although they had seen violent deaths before as news reporters, what they witnessed at that moment shocked them into somber silence as they worked.

Suddenly Pete Dawson shouted from a rooftop. "Hey! There's a kid up here and he's alive!"

Doc Bradley rushed over to the mud house and made his way up to the ladder leading to the roof. When he arrived, he found Dawson kneeling beside a frightened boy, obviously in shock. There was a raw, bleeding wound that went around his neck and throat. He allowed himself to be helped to his feet and guided to the roof edge. Bradley got onto the ladder, and Dawson helped the boy over the side so the hospital corpsman could carry him down to the ground.

Several of the Brigands came over to help, and they laid the kid down on a blanket brought from a house. "What's the matter with him?" Tiny Burke asked.

Doc looked up, answering, "The little guy's been garroted. He's lucky to have survived."

Gutsy Olson looked up with a sad expression. "Wait'll he finds out what happened to his family."

DIRK Wallenger and Eddie Krafton had finished taping the scenes of carnage in the village after methodically covering the entire area. All that would be interspersed and spliced into Wallenger's narrative. Now it was time for the spiel, and Eddie had his camera rolling as the Skipper stood off to one side waiting to be interviewed.

"This is Dirk Wallenger somewhere in Afghanistan. The view behind me is a stark testimony to the inhumanity of mindless war. The bodies of dozens of men, women, children, and the elderly are sprawled in and around the simple mud dwellings that once housed the entire population of a Pashtun village. The United States Navy SEAL Detachment with which I am imbedded was informed of this atrocity earlier this morning by donkey herdsmen from another village. It was they who discovered their slaughtered clansmen in this scene of utter horror. The Americans responded quickly, rushing here in the hopes of saving lives, but there was only one survivor. This was a frightened young boy who had huddled in horror on the roof of his house while terrorists roamed through this once peaceful hamlet, systematically

killing everyone they saw. Lieutenant William Brannigan—
known as 'Wild Bill' to his men—is here with me."

Brannigan walked into view and stood with his arms
folded across his chest, his M16 slung over his right shoulder. He nodded to Wallenger. "Hello, Dirk."

"Hello, Lieutenant Brannigan," Dirk said. "Do you have
any idea who committed this unspeakable crime?"

"At this point we don't have a clue," Brannigan responded.
"The native peoples in this area are known for blood feuds,
but my local advisor and translator has now ruled this out.
He is a Pashtun and has made inquiries and was told that
this particular tribe had been getting along fine with the
others lately, and although they have a history of participat-
ing in intertribal conflicts, this doesn't seem to add up as
one."

"What about the Taliban?" Wallenger asked. "Could this
be the work of religious fanatics?"

"That is a very real possibility," Brannigan said. "They've
been kicking up their heels lately and have made trouble in
other parts of Afghanistan. It is possible that they passed
through here with the idea of setting an example."

"What actions will you take in regards to this incident,
Lieutenant?"

"I'll transmit a report to our operational base, of course,
and send out patrols to see if some meaningful information
might be dug up."

"You seem determined to take revenge against the murderers," Wallenger stated. "Is this assumption on my part valid?"

"Let me say this," Brannigan replied. "If I am ordered to
hunt down and attack the murderers, I will do so with a great
deal of enthusiasm. And that goes for my men too."

"Thank you for the input, Lieutenant Brannigan," Wallenger said. "We'll look forward to talking with you again."
He began walking away, leaving Brannigan out of camera
range as he spoke to his unseen audience. "You may de-
pend on being kept fully informed of this situation, ladies
and gentlemen. And may I say that at this particular moment I am of the opinion that it is an absolute necessity that
coalition troops maintain their presence here somewhere in

Afghanistan. This is Dirk Wallenger, wishing you peace in a world gone mad."

1645 HOURS

MONTY Sturgis rode at the head of Bravo Fire Team as they approached the Swati village after four and a half hours of following the trail of the murderers. They found Brannigan with Jim Cruiser, Orlando Taylor, and the other SEALs watching a group of Janoon Pashtuns hard at work burying the dead. Chinar had gone to his home village to bring back men to inter the corpses, since Islam decrees that the dead should be buried as soon as possible after death. Certain other preparations, such as washing the bodies with soap and water, then binding them in white cloths, were required. But under the present circumstances this was not possible. The best that could be done for them was to make sure the corpses faced Mecca. The men working with the shovels also called out the first part of the *shahuda*, "There is no God but God!" as they shoveled the dirt over the dead.

Sturgis and the rest of the Bravos led their horses to the officers. The team leader saluted. "Sir, we found some boot tracks a few meters out and they led to where some horses had been kept. That was where they the attack started from. The killers mounted up at that spot to return to wherever it was they came from. It was hard to tell the exact number of 'em but it was at least a hunnerd and prob'ly a lot more'n that. We followed the trail toward the Kangal Mountains and determined they split into two groups. One headed southwest and the other left the Pranistay Steppes to head up into the high country. They had to be going to Tajikistan. No doubt of that."

"Okay," Brannigan said. "It looks like we've done all we can here." He turned to the others. "Alright! Mount up! We'll head back to the bivouac and leave these Pashtuns to finish taking care of the dead."

The men, glad to get away from the butchery, headed toward the picket line where their horses were secured.

CHAPTER 9

THE population was quiet, going about their daily activities while speaking in muted voices. Even the women inside the huts did their best to keep from banging pots and pans as they prepared the day's meals. No one had decreed a period of silence, but stillness was being observed voluntarily because their chief Awalmir Khan was holding an important conference in a grove of *mana* trees a few meters from the village.

Awalmir had called a session of his principal war leaders, including the village *molla* Shamroz. He also invited Quajeer, *malik* of the Janoon tribe, to attend the get-together. Both groups had a shared history of cooperation in peace and war that nourished a genuine trust between them. Quajeer had sent word the evening before that he had important news to discuss, and Awalmir, aware of unrest on the steppes, had quickly arranged a meeting with the other leader. Now, as they squatted in the trees, Quajeer began speaking.

"Early yesterday morning, some of my kinsmen went to deliver donkeys that had been sold to the Swatis," he began. "When they arrived they found everybody dead."

Paywastun, Awalmir's chief lieutenant, looked over at Quajeer with his one good eye. A deep scar from a shrapnel wound ran down the left side of his face and the eye socket was no more than a small mound of disfigured flesh. "What do you mean by everybody, brother?"

"Exactly as I have said," Quajeer said. "Every man, woman, and child had been slain except for a young boy who had been missed by the murderers. The elderly and infants are among those martyred. I sent word about the massacre to the Americans who are encamped on our lands."

Awalmir was a green-eyed muscular man with a square jaw. He did not like foreigners. "And what was the reaction of the infidels?"

"They went to investigate," Quajeer replied. "They have a medical man with them. He treated the boy's wound where he had been choked with a rope or something."

"Is he the one who bandaged Sangin's gash?" Awalmir asked. Nothing that happened on the steppes got past him.

"Yes. He is a black man and very skillful in the art of healing. Sangin is doing very well."

"Let us return to the subject of the attack," Awalmir said. "Is there anything else you can tell me about it?"

"There were two kinds of cartridge cases lying around the village," Quajeer said. "One type was very small. I had never seen any like that. My kinsman Chinar, who is a guide for the Americans, brought me one." He reached inside his *pukhoor* and pulled out the brass tube. "Here it is."

Awalmir examined the case. "This is from those accursed Russians! I know all about those sons of Satan. Perhaps they are seeking vengeance because we defeated their invasion of our homeland. Or perhaps a few are with the Tajik bandits."

"Mmm," Paywastun agreed. "Perhaps they are not bandits. They could be soldiers using the bandits."

"It is all very confusing," Awalmir complained.

"One more thing," Quajeer said. "Chinar looked around at the footprints. Among the marks of boots were many *tsaplan*. That means there were Pashtuns among the *wazhunkan*."

"The Mahsuds!" Awalmir said. "Who else?" The volatile man seethed for a moment, having trouble speaking in his rage, but after a few deep breaths he had his temper under control. "We will take no action now. However, I will see to it that men will patrol and stand guard between our three villages."

"We do that now with our own hamlets," Quajeer said. "And the Americans are near us too."

"Perhaps the Americans will deal with the murderers," Paywastun suggested.

"Who knows?" Awalmir commented. "One way or the other we must observe *badal* in the name of our Swati brethren."

A gleam came into Paywastun's eye. "Then we will have a war, will we not?"

"If Allah so wills it," Shamroz, the *molla*, interjected.

SEALs BIVOUAC

THE Brigands learned that the surviving boy's name was Emal and that he was twelve years old. Doc Bradley had cleaned and dressed his wound once more after they arrived in the bivouac from the Swati village. He had evidently turned slightly during the garroting, and that's what saved his life. Chinar had wanted to take him to the Janoons to live with a family there, but the youngster refused the offer. In his fear and grief he had seen Pashtuns as well as whom he perceived as Tajik bandits murder his people, and he was more at ease with the Americans. Doc was kind and gentle with his injury, and the others showed genuine friendliness and sympathy toward him. The Americans gave him a feeling of security as well as evidence that not everyone in the world was cruel and merciless.

1300 HOURS

THE entire detachment had finished tending to their mounts, breaking up hay bales, and putting on feed bags after taking the horses over to a nearby creek to be watered. The animals were now connected to the picket line as their riders gathered around the headquarters area to answer a pithy summons from the Skipper.

"Now hear this," Brannigan said to the men who were grouped informally to his direct front. Some were sitting, others kneeling as they awaited the word from the Old Man. "I've contacted the SFOB on the *Combs*—that means Carey and Berringer—and they've given us instructions to stay close to the bivouac here but maintain vigorous patrolling within the immediate area to maintain security."

"Sir," Chad Murchison said, raising his hand. "Do they have any cognition as to the identity of the depredators of the village?"

"Uh . . . well . . . no," Brannigan said. He had to listen carefully to Murchison's novel way of speaking as did the rest of the Brigands. "But they think there's a good chance it was the Taliban. Or perhaps Tajik bandits. Does that answer your question?"

"Yes, sir," Murchison said. "Thank you, sir."

"While we keep patrols out and about," Brannigan continued, "we are to contact the two largest tribes on the steppes here. That would be the Yousafzai and the Mahsud. The idea is to establish friendly ties with them and get all the information we can as to what's going on around here."

Puglisi, who was chewing a hunk of MRE chocolate, asked, "Can we be sure they'll be friendly toward us?"

Brannigan glanced over at Chinar. "What do you think?"

"They will be most suspicious," Chinar replied. "However, I do not believe you will find them outright hostile. But the Yousafzai and Mahsud are bitter rivals and will hesitate to form any friendship with you when they discover you will be talking to both of them."

"Who do you suggest we contact first?" Brannigan asked.

"The Yousafzai," Chinar answered. "They and my tribe are very friendly."

"At any rate we'll have to be diplomatic," Brannigan said. "Carey gave me explicit orders that we are to assure all the Pashtuns here that we have no interest in their opium poppy crops. This is a blessing for the local farmers since they make a hell of a lot more money selling the powder from the plants than wheat or barley."

"Sir," Ensign Orlando Taylor said. "I have researched that subject, and it is indicated that the highest bidders for the narcotic are the Taliban. Surely we must make them understand we cannot tolerate that."

"We'll try not to be so direct, Ensign," Brannigan said. "We'll emphasize that the Taliban are bad people and shouldn't be dealt with. The Pashtuns around here aren't that fond of those religious nuts anyway."

"Money talks, sir," Taylor reminded him.

"You're right," Brannigan agreed. "But we must emphasize the protection afforded the locals by the Coalition Forces in Afghanistan. And we've got good ol' Doc Bradley. He's our best ambassador of goodwill with his medical skills."

"There's another angle, sir," Arnie Bernardi reminded him. "What about hidden weapons and ammo?"

"We'll let that slide by," Brannigan said. "Carey emphasized that we are not to interrogate or search the Pashtuns for arms, ammo, or other contraband. We are, in fact, gentleman, the good guys." He gave a concentrated glance at the tough, armed SEALs he was addressing. "Well, fairly nice guys anyhow."

LOGOVISHCHYEH, TAJIKISTAN
2330 HOURS

PAVEL Marvesky, with Andrei Rogorov, his combination bodyguard and chauffeur assigned to him by Aleksander Akloschenko, used the illumination from the settlement's windows to light his way to his destination. When they reached the hut, Marvesky pounded on the door. "Valentin Danielovich!"

The door opened and Surov, clad in a thick robe, stood in the entrance with a glass of vodka in his hand. Music from the building's interior could be heard. "Ah! It is you, Pavel Dimitrovich. Come in."

The bodyguard, a beefy man who barely acknowledged pain and completely disregarded any sort of physical discomfort, stayed outside in the night chill as Marvesky went into the domicile. Surov's woman, a sixteen-year-old named Aghala, was off to one side mixing dough for the next day's baking as the two Russians settled down. Surov's record player was an ancient hand-cranked model manufactured during the old Soviet days, and it played only 78-rpm recordings. He turned the machine off, then handed a glass and a bottle of vodka to his unexpected guest.

"Was that Tamara Sinyavskaya on that last record?" Marvesky asked.

"Yes," Surov answered. "She was singing 'Katyusha.' One of my favorites."

"Ah, *da*, I know it well," Marvesky commented. "But give me Alexei Martynov's rendition of 'Kalinka.' What memories are brought back by those old songs."

"I feel closer to Russia when I listen to the Motherland's music. It soothes my troubled soul."

Marvesky took a deep swallow of vodka. "Do you miss Russia much, Valentin Danielovich?"

Surov nodded. "There are times when I must confess to a feeling of deep sadness in my aching heart. Ah! How I miss the vibrancy of winter nights in Moscow. The Novaya Opera, Bolshoi Ballet, and concerts at the Tchaikovsky Hall." He sighed. "I suppose I shall never enjoy those cultural venues again."

"What would you think about the opportunity to return to your beloved Moscow?"

Surov sensed a profound meaning behind the question, but he made an effort not to indicate any outright reaction to it. "What a beautiful thought."

"And what if you could return without having to worry about the authorities?" Marvesky continued.

"A wild dream," Surov said. "I still have several years left on my sentence." Now he knew that Marvesky's visit was much more than a casual call at his home.

"Your criminal records could be expunged under the right circumstances," Marvesky said. "It would be—ahem—a matter of where your basic loyalties lay."

Surov poured himself another glass of vodka, then recharged his guest's drink. He slowly and thoughtfully set the bottle down on the table. "My gratitude would be limitless," he said. "In fact, I would kill for such a blessing in my wasted life. Sometimes my descent into this hell seems more a nightmare than reality."

Marvesky's voice was lowered as he said, "I will discuss this subject with you later." He took a deep swallow of vodka, then leaned back in his chair, speaking in a normal tone. "Let's hear another song, Valentin Danielovich."

"Certainly! How about *Podmoskovnite Vechera*?" Surov said. "I have Vladimir Troshin's interpretation."

"*Udivitelnbiyeh*—wonderful!" Marvesky exclaimed.

Surov put the record on, and both Russians sipped dreamily from their glasses as the sounds of the old melody filled the hut. Outside, the bodyguard Rogorov stood stoically in the cold, noting the sparse snowflakes that had begun to descend lightly over the Kangal Mountains.

YOUSAFZAI MAIN VILLAGE
25 OCTOBER
0930 HOURS

THE session was in the usual place preferred by the Awalmir Khan. He and his *molla*, Shamroz, sat on one side in the small clearing among the *mana* trees, facing their visitors. Chinar, the Janoon interpreter; Lieutenant Bill Brannigan, Lieutenant (JG) Jim Cruiser, and the hospital corpsman, Doc Bradley, sat opposite the Yousafzais. The mood of the session, while not obviously unfriendly, was formal and serious. Awalmir seemed suspicious of the Americans, and Shamroz was reserved and solemn.

Brannigan spoke through Chinar, saying, "We bring you greetings as representatives of the American government here on the Pranistay Steppes. I also speak for the Coalition Forces who are dedicated to protecting you. This man on my right is my second in command. His name is Cruiser. This other man is our medical specialist, whose name is Doc."

Shamroz, also speaking through the interpreter, asked, "Are you the one who treated the bad cut suffered by the Janoon brother?"

Doc answered with an affirmative nod.

Brannigan continued, "We are concerned about the horrible massacre in the Swati village. I took my men there and we saw the dead people. Do you have any idea who might have done this thing?"

"I know exactly who committed the atrocity," Awalmir replied in a cold voice. "It was those demons from the Mahsud tribe. Also I would think the Kharotis, Bhittanis, and Ghilzais were there too. They did it with the Tajik bandits. And we think Russians also."

Brannigan's eyebrows raised. Could it be that Puglisi was right in his assumption that the former Soviet Union was involved? "Who are these Russians?"

"Well," Awalmir said hesitantly, "perhaps they were all Tajik bandits or even soldiers from their army. At any rate, whoever they are, we cannot know for sure. It is very difficult for us to get across the international border without having trouble with the authorities."

"What do you know about the bandits in this area who may be Russians?" Brannigan asked.

"Nothing for certain, just suspicions," Awalmir replied. "If there are any, someday we will catch them, but I fear it will be only a few at a time." He abruptly changed the subject. "Are you going to destroy the next poppy crops?"

Brannigan shook his head. "No. My orders are to leave the harvest alone." Then he added, "Unless the Taliban becomes involved."

Awalmir shrugged. "We are not friends of the Taliban."

Shamroz leaned forward. "Is this disregard of our harvests permanent?"

"I don't know," Brannigan answered truthfully.

"What are you going to do about the ones who murdered the Swatis?" Awalmir asked.

"I am waiting for orders from my superiors," Brannigan said. "But I know for sure we will be told to hunt them down and capture them for punishment."

"What will you do with those that do not surrender?" the Yousafzai *khan* asked.

"We will kill them."

"Russians and Pashtuns too?"

"All of them," Brannigan stated.

"Even if some are Russians?"

"We will kill all of them," Brannigan repeated.

"In that case, you are an enemy of my enemy," Awalmir said. "I will help you in these coming battles." He looked at Chinar. "I think the Janoons will help too."

"Quajeer has already said he will join the fight," Chinar said.

Awalmir turned his attention back to Brannigan. "When you have your orders you tell Quajeer and me. Then we will meet and decide what must be done." He stood up to signal he had no more to say.

At that point the meeting broke up and Chinar handled the protocol of parting, then the Americans went to their horses. Brannigan swung up into the saddle, glancing at Cruiser. "The first thing I'm gonna do is contact the SFOB and tell Carey about those goddamn Russians."

"As that old American saying goes,' Cruiser said with a wry grin, " 'the shit is about to hit the fan.' "

CHAPTER 10

BRIGADIER General Gregory Leroux, United States Army, was the angriest man in all of America's armed forces. He was a highly decorated Special Forces-, ranger-, parachutist-qualified graduate of the United States Military Academy at West Point, New York; holder of the combat infantryman's badge; an experienced combat leader of units from platoons to entire combined-arms brigades; and had been stuck aboard a United States Navy guided-missile destroyer where he was forced to direct special operations while confined within steel bulkheads in a clandestine headquarters belowdecks. The general swore if he ever found out who came up with the idea of establishing an undercover SFOB aboard a ship, he would wring the son of a bitch's neck.

It didn't matter to the general that this small headquarters was unique since, unlike other such directional centers, his responsibilities of command and control were for very high-level, special operations far out of the norm. These missions called for an intense focus of effort and concentration with little outside interference. And that was the main reason for the isolation of a floating, movable operational base aboard a warship far from other administrative and logistical sites.

But what really bugged the old soldier was his constant exposure to naval terminology such as somebody replying "aye, sir" to his orders, having to call a floor a deck, a wall a bulkhead, a latrine a head, refer to left as port, right as starboard, front as fore, back as aft, and dozens of other terms. After being in the assignment for a month, he had posted a sign on the door leading to the compartments he used as offices:

WARNING!
DO NOT USE SAILOR TALK
PAST THIS POINT

The crew aboard the *Combs* returned the general's irritation in spades.

1515 HOURS

COMMANDER Tom Carey and Lieutenant Commander Ernest Berringer, naval operations and intelligence officers respectively, sat in chairs across the desk from General Leroux. Over to the side, occupying another piece of metal furniture, was a man who had just been introduced to them by Leroux. The stranger wore a battle dress uniform that bore no insignia of rank or military unit. This individual also sported a 9-millimeter Beretta automatic in a shoulder holster.

This was Spencer Caldwell, a CIA case worker stationed in Khorugh, Tajikistan, in a deep undercover assignment. He was about as happy as Leroux in regards to his present location. The unexpected summons that had brought him to his present physical locality was more than inconvenient; it was downright dangerous. He was one of those unknown entities in a shadow world of intrigue, adventure, danger, and dirty tricks that left the inept and/or unlucky extremely dead when misadventures occurred.

Now he and the two navy officers sat silently while Leroux perused a file of radio messages and INTSUMs from higher headquarters. Finally, the general took his glasses off and laid them down on his desk. He turned his eyes on Caldwell. "What we need to know from you is if there are any fucking Russians up in those Kangal Mountains?"

"Yes," Caldwell replied. "They are former convicts of a Soviet Army prison that had been established in that country during the Reds' glory days." He was a man obviously in excellent physical condition, mentally alert and harboring a streak of meanness just under the surface. "Most of them were either lifers or condemned to executions that were never carried out."

"Why the hell not?" Leroux asked. "Were the sentences commuted?"

"It was a typical glitch of the gigantic Communist bureaucracy," Caldwell explained. "The paperwork to send them to the place was never followed up with orders to shoot the rotten bastards. So when the Soviet Union came apart at the seams, nobody knew what to do with them. Requests to transport them back to Russia by the new Tajik government fell through the cracks or went unanswered."

Leroux displayed his lopsided grin. "So what happened? One day somebody forgot to lock the front gate and the sons of bitches just walked out?"

"Something like that," Caldwell said. "The prison population was run as a gang during their incarceration and continued in that manner after their release. They couldn't return to Russia without proper passports or ID, so they formed into a gangster band and raided across the border into Afghanistan. As ex-soldiers they're pretty formidable, and now have a town all their own up in the Kangal Mountains."

Carey nodded. "That was what Brannigan needed to know. A Pashtun village was wiped out a while back, and there was some confusion as to whether some of the raiders were Russians or Tajiks."

"Actually," Caldwell said, "the ex-convicts subdued the local bandits. Now they claim the Kangal Mountains and Pranistay Steppes as their turf."

Berringer, ever the intelligence officer, asked, "Are the Russians independent?"

Caldwell shook his head. "They have contacts with the local crime syndicate in the city of Khorugh. I'm pretty sure they receive instructions from the big boss whose name is Akloschenko. I've yet to determine if that's a permanent arrangement or just temporary for special jobs."

"Do you have a mole somewhere in that mess?" Berringer asked.

"No," Caldwell replied. "I've been working hard on that for the past two years. So far all I've been able to develop is underworld informers. And they're not always reliable."

"Tell me something," Leroux said. "Have you been turning in INTREPs on this situation to your bosses in the CIA?"

"Of course I have," Caldwell said, irritated by the insinuation that he had been sloppy in his work.

"Then why the fuck wasn't it shared?" Leroux snapped.

"How the *fuck* should I know why the *fuck* it wasn't shared?" Caldwell shot back. "Goddamn it! I'm over there in that fucking place with no backup, trying to organize a net, and get pulled out to come over to this shit-eating ship to answer a bunch of stupid questions while I got more important things to do."

Leroux, who was never upset by a busy man having good reason to lose his temper, calmly asked, "If we saw that you got a Russian speaker, could you get him inserted into that bandit gang?"

"He'd have to be a native," Caldwell answered. "And be able to fit in perfectly. One little slip and he'd be dead meat."

"Shit!" Leroux cursed.

"Wait a minute!" Carey exclaimed, suddenly having an idea. "I know the perfect guy."

THE LSPO used the standard arm-and-hand signals as he brought the Super Stallion chopper in for a landing on the *Combs'* helicopter pad. The aircraft settled down only long enough for a lone figure to leap off to the deck before the pilot revved back up into the sky.

Petty Officer Second Class Andy Malachenko of Brannigan's Brigands, wearing a rucksack on his back, an M16 rifle over his shoulder, and carrying a seabag, walked over to the superstructure where Commander Tom Carey and Lieutenant Commander Ernest Berringer waited for him. The two officers greeted the SEAL, then led him into the interior of the ship for a quick trip belowdecks where they went directly to General Leroux's bailiwick.

When they reached the general's office, Malachenko left his gear outside the door but kept his weapon over his shoulder as he followed his escorts into the interior. Besides Leroux, the CIA operative Spencer Caldwell was seated at one side of the compartment. The general waved away the navy personnel's salutes. "No time for bullshit protocol. Who's this guy?"

"The one I told you about, sir," Carey said. "He's the man we need for that special assignment."

"He looks alright," Leroux said. He spoke directly to Malachenko. "This guy beside me has some questions for you."

"Yes, sir," Malachenko replied suspiciously.

Caldwell asked, *"Vi gavarit pa'Ruski?"*

Malachenko replied in Russian, saying, "Yes. I speak Russian."

"You are obviously quite fluent in the language," Caldwell remarked. "No trace of an American accent."

"I was born in Russia, sir," Malachenko said, sticking to the language. "I grew up speaking Russian before I learned English in the States."

"What brought you to America, Malachenko?" Caldwell inquired.

"My parents immigrated in 1994 when I was ten," he answered. "We lived in Brighton Beach, New York. That's where I learned English."

"Did you continue to speak Russian in your home?"

"Yes, sir. As a matter of fact the whole neighborhood spoke it. Most of the stores had Russian language signs. But us kids picked up English real quick in school, and since we learned early in life, none of us have Russian accents. It's easy when you're young."

Caldwell glanced at Leroux, going back to English. "He'll have to be brought up to date on the latest slang. And, of course, he'll need a cover story."

Malachenko was slightly alarmed. "What the hell is going on?"

Leroux leaned back in his chair. "Tell me something, Malachenko. We need a Russian-speaking volunteer to go on a dangerous mission that may last a few months. You will also be exposed to the constant danger of being compromised. If that happened, you would be shot immediately if not sooner—if you're lucky. In the event your luck had run out, they would make the execution a three- or four-day celebration. What do you say?"

"Sure, sir. What do you want me to do?"

"We need you to infiltrate a Russian criminal gang up there in the Kangal Mountains that border the current OA where your detachment is stationed."

Malachenko chuckled. "How about that!"

Leroux gave the SEAL a close study. "I believe you're one of Brannigan's bunch. Is that so?"

"I sure am, sir."

The general laughed aloud. "Well, there's no doubt you're a damn good man. I'll let Caldwell explain the mission to you."

"It isn't real complicated," Caldwell said. "And I'll be your asset since I'm assigned to the area. You will enter Tajikistan in the guise of a guy on the run from the Russian law. Documents will be made available to back up your operational role. Your first port of call will be the city of Khorugh. That's where you'll be able to 'run into' some of the local Mafia types. You give them your cover story and they'll see that you link up with the gangsters living in the mountains. From that point on, you get all the intel possible on the group to include their purposes, intentions for the immediate future, and methods of operation. Then exfiltrate back to your guys on the Pranistay Steppes. Depending on what you're able to learn, action will be taken to eliminate that threat."

"We think they were the ones who massacred a whole village of people, sir," Malachenko said. "It was enough to make you sick."

"Then you realize fully who you're dealing with," Caldwell said.

"There was some Pashtuns with them," Malachenko added. "You can't trust nobody out there."

"Well, that goes to show how hairy your mission is gonna be," Leroux remarked dryly.

Malachenko showed a grin of resignation. "Hell! If I ever have an easy mission, I'll prob'ly drop dead from shock and surprise."

PRANISTAY STEPPES
1045 HOURS

ENSIGN Orlando Taylor and his entire Second Assault Section held their horses to a walk across the open country in a column formation. Chinár, the young interpreter, rode beside him, while Doug MacTavish, the SAW gunner, was close behind. Dave Leibowitz was up forward on point, and his teammate Bruno Puglisi was the Tail-End-Charlie, charged with security at the rear. Delta Fire Team furnished two flankers—Guy Devereaux on the left and Chad Murchison on the right—as the section continued on their patrol mission of observance and exploration in that area of the OA.

The terrain over which they traveled was mostly flat, but the evenness was broken here and there with slight dips and small streams that had to be crossed. The weather was chilly and everyone noticed that the snow on the highest peaks of the Kangal Mountains had increased over the previous few days. The SEALs wore field jackets, but had not buttoned the hoods on just yet, nor were any gloves in evidence among the riders. Chad Murchison, born and raised in Massachusetts, found the lower temperature invigorating. He was hoping that if it snowed on the steppes perhaps they could get some cross-country skiing in. As he continued the slow ride on the flank, Chad kept his eyes on the horizon from the right front all the way around to the right rear. So far there was nothing but an empty horizon beneath a bleak prewinter sky.

Then he sighted a line of horsemen.

"Brigand Two," he said, raising Taylor on the LASH. "There's a half dozen riders at four o'clock." He put his binoculars to his eyes and studied the strangers for a moment. "They're Pashtuns."

"Roger," Taylor said, acknowledging the information. "All hands! Right flank, march!"

The section wheeled their horses directly to the right, forming into a skirmish line. Chad was now in the direct front, nearest the strangers. He was quickly joined by Chinar, and they led the way toward the unknown riders.

The Pashtuns now sighted them, and all removed their AK-47 rifles from their shoulders. Chinar glanced at Chad. "We must hold up our empty hands and show that we have no unfriendly intentions." Taylor ordered everyone to halt, while the duo continued drawing closer.

"*Munzh yu melgerane*—we are friends!" Chinar shouted.

Suddenly a pair of shots came from the Pashtuns, splitting the air above Chad and Chinar's heads. Chad immediately pulled his M16 from the saddle scabbard and shot back. Taylor ordered the rest of the section into a gallop, yelling over the LASH. "Return fire!"

It was impossible to aim properly at a full gallop, and all the rounds flew harmlessly through the air. The Pashtuns responded by turning away, pounding across the steppes with the SEALs in pursuit. The chase went on for almost a quarter of an hour before the natives charged into a gully. At that point they halted, dismounted, and took up positions with their assault rifle muzzles pointed at the Americans.

"Cease fire!" Taylor said after noticing the Pashtuns were not shooting at them. "Halt!"

After stopping, the SEALs swung from their saddles, turning the reins over to a previously appointed horse handler team made up of Pech Pecheur, Doug MacTavish, and Arnie Bernardi. The remainder of the SEALs moved forward in a skirmish line, ready to respond to any hostile action taken by the Pashtuns. After a couple of moments a shout could be heard, and Chinar spoke into his LASH to Taylor. "They are calling for us to identify ourselves."

"Tell 'em who we are," Taylor instructed.

"Munzh yu Amrikayi payra!" Chinar yelled, identifying the SEALs as an American patrol. This was followed by a couple of exchanges between the Pashtuns and the interpreter. Chinar informed Taylor they would be coming out and not to shoot.

Within ten minutes both groups were together, and the meeting resulted in Chinar explaining that the Pashtuns thought the SEALs were Tajik bandits or Taliban. This was followed by apologies all around, and the ensign gave the natives permission to continue across the steppes after they explained they were a hunting party.

When the Pashtuns rode off, Taylor expressed relief that none had been killed. "This would have been catastrophic and set our efforts here back," he said.

"I don't know," Chinar said. "Those men are from the Bhittani tribe and they are bitter enemies of my clan. I think they became friendly when they saw we outnumbered them. If not, we would have ended up like the Swatis who were massacred."

Taylor frowned. "Do you think those guys had anything to do with that?"

"If not, they certainly knew about it before it happened," Chinar said.

The two fire team leaders, Gutsy Olson and Connie Concord, looked at each other. Gutsy slung his M16 over his shoulder, saying, "I got a feeling that the situation out here is gonna start deteriorating *real* fast *real* soon."

Connie shrugged. "Tell me something I don't already know."

CHAPTER 11

SPENCER Caldwell, the CIA operative working a highly dangerous solo assignment in Tajikistan, had become something of an expert on the Russian Mafia and its fellow travelers. The first thing he learned was that they were not an independent crime organization that worked alone, but were made up of numerous "syndicates" with their own agendas and goals. When he was given the task of preparing SEAL petty officer Andrei Malachenko to infiltrate the gangs in Tajikistan, he began the orientation by explaining they were multilayered loose groups. The one the SEAL would concentrate on was run by a conniving ex-Soviet bureaucrat named Aleksander Akloschenko who was more or less sponsoring a group of ex-military convicts in a project to wrest control of the opium poppy harvest from Awalmir Khan, the principal warlord on the Pranistay Steppes. And since it was the convicts Brannigan's Brigands had to deal with, the best way for Andy to reach them would be through an initial contact with Akloschenko's organization.

The exchange of ideas and suggestions between Andy and Caldwell was a valuable learning experience for both men. They agreed that Andy should avoid making any contact with Caldwell, who would be returning to Khorugh before Andy was inserted into the mission. The CIA operative, who had built up his own cover as a freelance archaeologist, had worked himself into a position where he was able to wander around the area without arousing suspicion. Caldwell coldly explained that if Andy suddenly showed up unexpectedly on his doorstep, the operative would send him away—or worse.

0100 HOURS

PETTY Officer Second Class Andy Malachenko wore a jump helmet as well as a parka and coveralls over civilian clothing of a heavy shirt, wool trousers, and hiking boots. Additionally he packed a Tokarev automatic pistol with shoulder holster for both protection and appearance. Now, in the dim overhead lights of the SEALs' hangar, he struggled into the RAPS for the HALO insertion he was to make into Tajikistan in a few short hours.

A Russian fur cap was stuffed into the jacket pocket for use after his parachute entry into the mission. And, rather than a rucksack, he was jumping with a relatively small sport backpack in which he carried extra clothing, magazines and ammunition for the pistol, and 300,000 rubles in cash that amounted to about $10,000 American. An entrenching tool to bury the helmet, coveralls, and RAPS was to be attached to the backpack, then discarded by tossing it somewhere into the brush after use.

The last item of his mission inventory was a forged passport made out in the name of Jan Kowalski as a preliminary cover. This was an obvious forgery meant to be discovered, at which time he would produce another ID document that indicated he had been born Mikhail Molotosky in Moscow, where he was involved in various criminal activities.

The DZ he would be using was several kilometers outside Khorugh. After landing and disposing of his equipment, he was to walk to the city and make his way into a Russian neighborhood called Krasgorod by the locals. Once there, he would find a bar called the Domashni Tavern that was a hangout for the local Russian Mafia, where he was to make inquiries about a fellow named Ivan Karlovich Gelshenov. Spencer Caldwell was aware that Gelshenov was found murdered in that same neighborhood six months earlier, so Andy's claim of knowing him could not be disproved.

Andy had been given the two cover stories by Caldwell to present when he first made contact with the Russian gangsters. The first was purposefully designed to be extremely weak and easy to see through. The SEAL was to say that he had come to Tajikistan in order to find work as an automobile mechanic. That would make little sense to anyone familiar with the high unemployment rate in the country. The criminals would be immediately suspicious and certain to suspect him of some underhanded dealing. However, Andy was to stick to the story stubbornly, while insisting on seeing Gelshenov.

At that point he would be taken to see his "friend." However, there was no doubt that the gangsters would actually escort him to a special place for a more thorough examination. This, of course, would include a vigorous punching around. The SEAL was to take all he could stand, being careful not to sustain any serious injuries, then admit that he was fleeing from the Moscow police who wanted to question him regarding extortion and protection shakedowns of local kiosks. He was to also reveal that he had spent three years in the Army, serving in a motorized infantry regiment stationed near Saint Petersburg.

SOUTHWEST TAJIKISTAN
0445 HOURS

THE hum of the aircraft's engine had faded away in the dark sky as Andy's feet hit the ground with a slight crackling sound. The mountain meadow chosen as his DZ was covered with a thin sheet of ice, and the SEAL appreciated the warmth provided by the thick down parka and the heavy sweater beneath it. He dumped the harness after loosening the chest strap and the waistband, standing still for a moment in the surreal windless environment. This area was desolation pure and simple, making Andy suddenly feel isolated and lonely. Being on his own is tough for a man who normally depends on teamwork with trusted buddies to get assigned missions done. It was obvious to the SEAL that he would have to adapt to a new mind-set if he was going to succeed on this latest operation.

Andy shook himself out of the mental doldrums and immediately gathered up the folds and straps of the RAPS, carrying the whole thing over to a thicket of brush some twenty-five meters away. He was glad there was no permafrost as he began to strike the ground with the entrenching tool, digging up chunks of dirt that would have been frozen solid within a couple of months. The top layer was a bit difficult, but by the time he was about six inches down the task became easy. He kept going until he had cleared out a one cubic yard mini-excavation. He felt a tug of sadness when he shoved the parachute into the hole. It had saved his life, bellowing open to stop his earthward plummet, then obeyed the tugs he made on the toggles with the accuracy of a faithful guide dog. Now it was doomed to rot in a hole out in the middle of nowhere in Southwest Asia.

With the concealment done, Andy swung the backpack over his shoulders and set off walking eastward in the direction the ground sloped. It took him a half hour of rapid travel before he reached the road. He turned south and went a hundred meters to find a badly faded and bent sign that informed him that Khorugh was twenty kilometers away. Andy quickly converted the kilometers to miles in his head by multiplying the number by .6, coming up with twelve miles. Not too bad a walk for a guy in excellent physical condition. The cold weather helped kick up his energy level as he briskly stepped out toward his destination.

0715 HOURS

THE whine of a truck engine in lower gear as it went downhill could be heard in the distance behind Andy. He turned and saw a Mitsubishi five-ton hauler coming toward him at about twenty miles per hour. He waved at the driver, and the guy put on the squeakiest brakes the SEAL had ever heard, bringing the vehicle to a shuddering halt. The trucker, showing a wide Slovak face, grinned at him. "Where are you going, brother?" he asked in Russian.

"To Khorugh," Andy said, opening the door and hopping into the cab. "I have been walking all night."

The driver pressed on the accelerator, setting the truck back into motion. "You will find some vodka in the glove compartment. Take a couple of swigs, brother. It is cold outside."

"*Spasebo*," Andy said, thanking him. He opened the compartment and pulled out a half-liter bottle of cheap vodka with the brand name Zavalinka. After a couple of gulps, he replaced it. "Whew! That was refreshing."

The man grinned. "I thought you needed a good old-fashioned jolt of vodka after such a long walk through the frigid darkness." He eased back on the speed as the road steepened downward. "My name is Yuri Petrovich."

Being a spy was not second nature to Andy, and he almost blurted out his real name, but he recovered quickly. "I am Jan Kowalski."

"So what brings a young Russian lad like you to Tajikistan?" Yuri asked. "I can tell by your speech you are from far up north, but your name is Polish."

"My grandfather served in the Great Patriotic War after joining the Red Army when they liberated Poland," Andy said. "I am in Tajikistan because a friend has gotten me a job as an auto mechanic."

"You are indeed lucky, brother," Yuri said. "There is not much work in these parts. I used to drive this same truck when I worked for the local commissar of property in the old days. Without that experience, I would have had to return to Russia."

"Well, there is no work up there either," Andy remarked.

"You see?" Yuri said. "I am a lucky fellow, hey? But I will be glad to leave this cursed place someday. Will you work in Khorugh?"

"Yes. I must find my friend in a part of the city that is called Krasgorod."

"Of course," Yuri said. "That is where most of the Russian population lives. I will be going quite near the locality. You will not have far to walk when I let you out."

"Then I am a lucky fellow too," Andy said.

Both fell into silence as Yuri negotiated the curving mountain road. Andy's loneliness came on him again as he stared out at the bleakness of the Tajik mountains. This was a shitty assignment. He should have told that goddamn Army general back on the *Combs* to piss up a rope.

They hit the flats, and Yuri began running through the gears as he picked up speed.

KHORUGH, TAJIKISTAN
0810 HOURS

YURI came to a stop at a red light. "Here is where you get off," he said, pointing to the right. "Stay on that street and it will take you straight into Krasgorod where Russians live and work. Good luck."

"Thank you," Andy said.

He stepped down to the street and trotted over to the curb, then settled into a slow walk in the indicated direction. The area was drab and shabby with down-at-the-heels shops and apartment buildings built right up to the sidewalks. A few kiosks were scattered along the street offering a variety of simple fare: canned goods, vodka, magazines, newspapers, cheap notions, and other similar merchandise. All the signs on the establishments were in the Cyrillic alphabet, and the young Russian-American could pronounce the words but couldn't understand them. He realized then that the Tajik language used the same letters as Russian. He saw a kiosk obviously dealing in tea and coffee. The sign said чои ва

КАВА, but in Russian it would have had the words ЧАИ и КОФЕ. After examining a number of others, he found a few words he could figure out. Now he realized that if his mission went completely to hell and he was on his own, he would be traveling through a country where it would be impossible to speak or understand the people. And he couldn't go looking up Spencer Caldwell either. The best thing he could do would be to make a rapid exfiltration due west.

However, after he had gone three blocks, a few signs in Russian appeared, then increased in number as he continued walking deeper into the neighborhood. Eventually all the signs were in the language brought into that part of the world by the Soviet Union.

A man wearing a worn quilted jacket and an old cap with loose earflaps sat on a stool in front of an apartment house. Andy went over to him to ask for directions to the bar where he was supposed to mingle with the locals. *"Dobroye utra,"* he greeted him. *"G'dyeh Domashni taverna, pazhzhaista?"*

The man, with a deeply lined face, looked up at him with pale blue eyes. "Who has the money to go to the Domashni Tavern?"

"I do not know," Andy replied. "I want to know how to get there."

"Can you read?"

"Of course I can read," Andy snapped. He knew how to deal with such impudence in a Russian and put a threatening tone in his voice. "Where is that restaurant?"

"Stay on this street and look at the signs," the fellow grumbled, uncomfortable under the younger man's glare. "And since you can read, you will see the name you are looking for."

Andy continued on his way, looking for both the sign and a building that appeared as if it were a combination restaurant and bar. After going two more blocks, he saw what he was looking for. The SEAL hurried across the street and went inside. A quick glance showed the place was not unlike a traditional combination café and saloon in Russia. A couple like it had been established in Brighton Beach by immigrants from the Motherland. A bar that ran the entire length of the establishment was on one side, while a row of a half dozen tables was on the other. Some booths that went the rest of the way down the narrow room completed the picture.

Andy took a stool at the counter. When the barman came up, he ordered a coffee and omelet. The guy shouted the order down to a cook stationed in the center of the bar, then turned back to the new customer. "Do you need an eye-opener?"

"Vodka," Andy said. When the guy returned, he had a tumbler instead of a shot glass filled with the liquor. This made Andy grin inwardly. He was really back into the Russian culture where the national drink was consumed lustily and often. He took a sip, then asked, "Do you know where I might find a fellow by the name of Ivan Karlovich Gelshenov?"

The bartender's eyes opened wide at the mention of the name. "Is he a friend of yours?"

"Yes. He is an old friend, as a matter of fact."

"I can make a call and get a message to him," the bartender said. "But you might have to wait for a while."

"I have nothing else to do," Andy said.

The man turned and went down to the cash register where a phone sat. He picked it up and dialed.

DOMASHNI TAVERN
1830 HOURS

ANDY Malachenko alias Jan Kowalski alias Mikhail Molotosky nursed his fourth cup of coffee as he sat at the bar. He had turned down more offers of vodka, feeling that this was a situation that could very well require quick reactions of sobriety rather than the stumbling slowness of drunkenness. And once more he wished like hell he was back with the Brigands. An unexpected tap on his shoulder caused him to snap his head around.

A large man stood there, looking at him with open curiosity. "Are you the fellow who looks for Ivan Gelshenov?"

"Yes."

"What is your relationship with Ivan Karlovich Gelshenov?"

"He is a friend of my uncle," Andy replied.

"What is it you wish? To say hello? Deliver a message?"

Andy looked into the man's eyes, sizing him up as a real bad character. "That's my business."

"There is nothing in Khorugh that is *your* business," the stranger pronounced softly but with a threatening tone. "I ask you again. What is it you wish with Ivan Karlovich?"

"He sent word to me that he could get me a job as a motor mechanic."

"Alright," the man said. "Come with me."

AKLOSCHENKO'S OFFICE
1115 HOURS

THE only light coming into the room was dimmed by the dirty windows. There was a single lamp for illumination, but it was not turned on. Andy Malachenko sat in a chair, his jaw aching from the numerous punches he had taken. Three men had situated themselves at each side and to his rear while a very fat individual sat at the desk to his direct front. When he first walked into the office, he had been jumped and wrestled to the chair and forced to sit down. A rough search of his person produced his weapon, the passport, and his money. This was the prelude to some very impolite questioning, and each answer that displeased the interrogators earned Andy a hard smack in the face. At this point he knew it would only take another series of blows before he would have a loose tooth.

It was obviously the right time to "give in."

"Alright," he said, rubbing his sore chin. "I do not know Gelshenov. I heard of him through a cousin of his in Moscow. He is a close acquaintance who lived in a flat on the same floor as mine. I'm in some trouble with the police in Moscow. My pals and I have been selling 'protection' to kiosks in a couple of neighborhoods. One of the bastards blabbed and they had begun arresting the guys I work with. It was time for me to make a run for it. I got into the gang's stash of cash and hid out while Gelshenov's cousin made arrangements to get me a passport. That's not my real name."

"So you're not Jan Kowalski, eh?"

"No."

The man who had met him in the restaurant laughed. "That is a Polish name. Do you realize that?"

Andy grinned slightly. "It was the best that could be done in such a short period of time. At any rate, I was hoping that Gelshenov could get me a new start down here."

The man at the desk finally spoke. "Ivan Gelshenov is dead. But since you do not really know him, you will not mourn, hey?"

"No."

"So what is your real name?" the man at the desk asked.

"Mikhail Andreovich Molotosky," Andy replied.

"I am Aleksander Akloschenko," the man at the desk said. He dismissed the other two thugs, leaving the guy who had met Andy in the tavern. "This fellow is Pavel Marvesky." He gave Andy a friendly look. "Well, Mikhail Andreovich, if you are looking for a job, I believe we can be of a great deal of help to you."

CHAPTER 12

THE Russian gangster Andrei Rogorov was concentrating on being more chauffeur than bodyguard for his boss Pavel Marvesky. It was in this role that he drove his boss and the new gang member Mikhail Molotosky up into the Kangal Mountains. The destination of that midmorning ride was the gangster village of Logovishchyeh.

Andy Malachenko, in his cover as Molotosky, sat in the backseat with Marvesky exchanging occasional comments during the monotony of the journey. The big boss Akloschenko had returned Andy's pistol, money, and passport to him, and all was safely nestled in the backpack he had placed between his feet. The vehicle they rode in was a badly used 2000 Mercedes-Benz Kompressor Sedan with a battered, dented body that was rusted along the bottom of the chassis. The car's paint was so faded it was difficult to tell if the original color had been robin's-egg blue or azure. The appalling condition of the expensive automobile was as much the result of the freezing corrosion of the Tajik winters as Rogorov's careless driving. Fender benders were so frequent among the local motorists that if no one was injured and both cars could still be driven, the incidents were forgotten.

Marvesky, who had been gazing absentmindedly out the window, turned toward Andy. "We realize you are used to a big city, Mikhail Andreovich, but the only work we have for you is in the country."

"That is better than nothing," Andy remarked.

"We forgot to ask if you had any military service."

"I was in the Army for three years as a conscript," Andy replied, wondering if that part of his cover story was important. "I served as a rifleman in a motorized infantry regiment."

"That is excellent," Marvesky said. "You will be in the company of ex-soldiers, and a knowledge of military tactics and weapons will come in handy."

"What sort of work will I be doing?" he asked.

"It is very interesting," Marvesky said. "You will actually be going into Afghanistan a lot."

"Whew!" Andy said. "My military service occurred long after that unhappy time because of my age. But I do not feel good about going there even if the war is over. I have spoken with a lot of veterans who say that was a bad time for them."

"This is an entirely different situation," Marvesky informed him. "We are in complete charge of the countryside where we operate, and even have some of the Afghans as our friends. They are part of our group."

"That's much better than it was in the 1980s."

"Of course. However, it is very important that you learn how to ride a horse," Marvesky informed him.

"I already know how to ride a horse," Andy said, instantly regretting blurting the information out. He really needed more practice when it came to being an undercover operative.

Marvesky gave him a hard look. "Where in the hell did you learn how to ride a horse in Moscow?"

Andy thought very quickly, then spoke in a matter-of-fact tone. "I used to work at a riding stable in the suburbs." He forced a laugh. "Mostly I shoveled shit in the stables, but one day I asked my boss if I could learn to ride. He thought it would be a good idea since I could help out with the kids' classes."

"That is very fortunate," Marvesky said. "Who were the people using the stables?"

"The *nobodniks*," Andy answered.

Marvesky frowned. "I do not believe I am familiar with the term."

"Those are the newly rich of the Russian Federation," Andy explained. "Most of them were former bureaucrats under Communism who signed government property over to themselves. They usually sold it for inflated prices, or used the land to start businesses. But now there are other emerging entrepreneurs who are making the big rubles. And dollars, and deutschmarks and francs too. They all thought owning horses and going riding like the nobility in the Czar's days was the 'in' thing to do. They have many trendy attitudes."

"I have been here in Tajikistan since I was a boy," Marvesky said. "My father was a bureaucrat." He frowned. "But he was too much of a damned drunk to do himself or us any good after the Soviet system fell."

"Bad luck," Andy said.

"I must warn you about something, Mikhail Andreovich," Marvesky said. "When you arrive in our organization, you will be tested. By that, the other men will want to see what you're made of. Do you understand?"

Andy nodded. "Certainly. It is like hazing in the Army when the older soldiers bully the new recruits."

"It will be worse," Marvesky warned him. "All these men were confined in a military prison. And most had been there for many long years."

"Alright," Andy said. "Thanks for the warning, Pavel Dimitrovich."

DOLIROD
1300 HOURS

THEY reached the small town of Dolirod after turning off the main highway. Marvesky pointed out the window. "You will find this a handy place to visit," he explained to Andy. "It is a market center with a few shops to purchase necessities and there are a couple of blacksmiths and artisans who manufacture iron and leather goods. Most of the fellows at Logovishchyeh purchased leather bandoleers here to hold the magazines for their assault rifles."

Andy glanced around as they rolled through the little hamlet. "I see there are some trucks parked by that gasoline station."

"Yes," Marvesky said. "The drivers can also get simple meals to fill their bellies at the restaurant inside." He chuckled. "There is also a bordello. If you do not end up with a woman, you will no doubt visit the place with the boys from time to time."

"What are the women in there like?"

Marvesky now emitted a loud burst of laughter. "Look at the place. What do you think?"

Andy grinned. "Better than nothing, hey?"

LOGOVISHCHYEH
1330 HOURS

ANDREI Rogorov went up the narrow rutted road like it was a modern highway in Europe. The Mercedes's shocks contracted and expanded violently as the tires went in and out of the deep furrows worn in the dirt. Andy Malachenko was tempted to bellow at the driver to slow down, but decided silence was best since Pavel Marvesky didn't seem to notice anything untoward about his chauffeur's driving.

They were in a narrow valley with high sides, and Andy's finely honed military instincts gave him the distinct impression that they were being watched from the heights. No doubt the automobile was recognized by those standing watch among the boulders above, thus its arrival on the scene was not challenged. After ten minutes of the rough ride, they emerged into an open area where a small log settlement was located. The journey smoothed out at that point and they slowed down to a crawl.

Andy took in the view around him, and it reminded him of illustrations and photos he had seen in old Russian books his parents had. The place looked like a farming village from bygone days, with the sturdy structures that obviously served as homes and storage buildings. There were also children of mixed blood playing soccer in an open area.

Several men, clad in a combination of civilian attire and bits and parts of Army uniforms, nodded politely at the car as it crawled by. Andy saw evidence of many *gymnastiorki*— the pullover shirt-tunics that were traditional military attire based on old peasant shirts. These garments had high military collars, cuffs, and loops on the shoulders on which to fasten epaulets indicating insignia of rank. Andy had one at home that had belonged to his great-grandfather, who had served in the Czar's Army during World War I. It was a simple olive-green item of clothing with epaulets of the same color that bore the two stripes of a *mladshi unteroficier* that was the equivalent in rank to a modern corporal.

Then he spotted a couple of women. They carried jugs on their heads, walking with slight sways under the load. When he saw some water slosh out of one of the containers, it was obvious there was a complete lack of plumbing in the community. No doubt the females just visited a communal well. Andy was surprised that they were Pashtuns, and he wondered what they might be doing in this place with nothing but European men. Surely their male relatives would have objected to their presence in the place, but the females seemed unfazed by their surroundings.

The car came to a halt in front of a building that was larger than the rest. Marvesky used a nod of his head to indicate that Andy was supposed to unass the automobile. He grabbed his backpack and got out to be led to the door. They stepped inside a narrow hall or foyer—Andy wasn't sure which it was—and Marvesky knocked on the door.

A young and plump Pashtun girl responded to the summons. She seemed to recognize Marvesky and stated, "V'stupate," inviting them to enter.

Andy, well briefed in Pashtun etiquette, gave her only the quickest of glances, noting that she did not show the usual shyness displayed by the females of her culture while in the presence of unknown males. A Russian man who was smoking a pipe sat in a chair next to the hearth. He stood up and embraced Pavel Marvesky respectfully, then turned his attention to Andy.

"Who is this fellow?"

"His name is Mikhail Andreovich Molotosky," Marveksy replied. "He has come to join your band. He showed up in Khorugh looking for Gelshenov."

"That bastard!" the man said. "He owed me some money." He glared at Andy. "Are you related to him?"

"I do not know him," Andy replied. "A cousin of his sent me down here to see him about work."

Marvesky looked at Andy. "This man is Luka Ivanovich Yarkov. He is the chief of this group."

Andy shook hands with the other man.

"Mikhail Andreovich is in big trouble with the Moscow police," Marvesky said. "He served three years in the motorized infantry and can ride a horse. Akloschenko wants you to take him on."

"We can use the help," Yarkov said, taking what the underboss said as Gospel. "Tell me, Molotosky, why are the Moscow police looking for you?"

Andy fell into his cover story, telling about shaking down kiosk owners and other petty crimes, then, when the police were closing in, grabbing the money from his gang's hideout. After that he hurried to Gelshenov's cousin to arrange for transport and a passport.

Marvesky laughed. "They gave him one with a Polish name."

Yarkov chuckled. "When one must move fast, one must sometimes take what is offered without argument or protest." He looked over at the Pashtun girl. "Go fetch Surov and tell him to come here."

The girl left and now another one appeared. This one carried a tray of vodka and *samosas*. She set it down as Yarkov invited his guests to take seats. The new girl served the men, then withdrew. Marvesky took a deep drink, then spoke to Yarkov. "I need to have a talk with you, Luka Ivanovich. But it can wait until Molotosky is situated."

Yarkov took a bite of a *samosa*. "I have to find someone who can teach these women to cook in the Russian way." He rolled his eyes upward. "Ah! I would die for the taste of some pancakes stuffed with sour cream. And sturgeon, herring and onions, eggplant, caviar, and—" He stopped speaking, looking a bit sad. "Never mind. I torture myself."

"At least you eat better than the fellows in the barracks," Marvesky reminded him. "They have to fix their own meals or have it done by that little Pashtun queer."

"They should get women," Yarkov said. "I tell you the truth, Pavel Dimitrovich, I think some of them prefer the company of men."

"Too many years in prison," Marvesky said. He grinned at Andy. "Do you see what you have to look forward to in the barracks?"

"It is better than the Moscow jail," Andy said. "At any rate, perhaps I can get a woman of my own. How does one arrange for a mistress?"

The other two burst out laughing. Yarkov wiped the tears from his eyes when he settled down, saying, "You steal her during a raid, young fellow. Or maybe buy one from another man."

A knock on the door heralded the arrival of Valentin Surov. He was introduced to Andy, then told to take him to the barracks and get him settled in. Surov gazed at the newcomer, thinking, *This is a tough guy who can take care of himself*. After a nod to Yarkov and Marvesky, he gestured for Andy to follow him out of the house. Once more Andy grabbed the precious backpack.

The two walked from Yarkov's house, dodging running children a couple of times as they made their way through the hodgepodge of other buildings to a long structure. Surov came to a halt, pointing to it. "That is the *kazarma*—the barracks—where the fellows without women live. It is a bit crowded but none have the desire to build a place of their own. I suppose after years of prison they prefer company."

"Marvesky told me they're a pretty rough bunch," Andy remarked.

Surov nodded his head. "You must keep in mind that many of them are murderers and under normal circumstances would have been shot long ago. The *kapo* is the toughest."

"That is not surprising," Andy said. "The barracks chiefs in the Army always were."

"Be especially careful here," Surov warned him. "Our *kapo* is a former *Spetsnaz* soldier. He murdered the husband of the woman he desired, then ended up murdering her too when he found out she had other lovers besides him."

"A trigger-happy fellow, no doubt," Andy remarked casually.

"He used a knife in both instances," Surov said. He took Andy into the building, moving toward the center where the stove was located. This was a typical arrangement; the toughest of tough had their beds near the source of heat in the winter, and far away from it during the warmest parts of the year. Igor Tchaikurov was in a partitioned-off area where he caught the full benefits of the stove. He stood up respectfully as Surov walked up to him with Andy in tow.

Tchaikurov greeted Surov politely as he gave Andy a baleful gaze. "Hello, Valentin Danielovich. Who is this?"

"A new man," Surov replied. "His name is Mikhail Andreiovich Molotosky. He is from Moscow. Find him a place and let him settle in." With the simple formalities taken care of, he turned and made an abrupt exit. In truth, Surov did not like visiting the barracks.

Tchaikurov grinned at Andy, then motioned to him to tag along as he walked down toward the end of the building. The SEAL was beginning to weary of being led from pillar to post, but he followed after the *kapo* as they threaded their way through the bunks. The men lounging around the barracks gave the newcomer their full attention. Andy noticed there was a semblance of neatness in the way the men had arranged their bunks, storage containers, and other belongings.

Clothing was hung up neatly on pegs driven in the wall and a few had made simple wardrobes to hold their attire. These were signs of military experience.

Tchaikurov stopped and pointed to a couple of empty bunks with locker boxes. "Take your choice."

"Thank you," Andy said.

"Or, if you see another you prefer, feel free to take it from the present owner," Tchaikurov invited.

"I am not the type of fellow who looks for trouble," Andy said.

Tchaikurov grinned humorlessly at him. "We shall see to getting you some bedding later. And a weapon and ammunition too."

"I shall look forward to it," Andy said. He watched the man head back to his cubicle, then set his backpack on the bunk and sat down beside it. He knew what was coming and he was ready.

He didn't have long to wait.

A man a couple of beds down got up and stared at him. The guy was big with a lanky muscularity. He wore an undershirt, revealing a myriad of tattoos on his arms and shoulders. He walked down to Andy, then bent over and picked up his backpack.

"Put that down," Andy said.

The man ignored the command and began undoing the straps. Andy stood up slowly, then exploded into a single straight punch as he drove the heel of his hand in an upward motion to the guy's chin. The tormentor's head snapped back and he collapsed to the floor, hitting heavily, completely unconscious and unmoving. Andy retrieved his backpack, then dragged the guy down to his bed and left him.

Suddenly another barracks dweller jumped up and charged straight at Andy, leaping over a couple of bunks. It appeared the SEAL was going to meet the charge, but he suddenly stepped to one side at the last moment, reached out, and grabbed his assailant's right wrist while spinning around. Now the guy was moving in the opposite direction, and a kick in the ass propelled him into a sliding fall across the floor. Andy rushed up and placed his foot on the back of his neck, pressing down hard.

"Mmm," the SEAL mused. "Do I step down quickly and kill you straight off or just keep applying pressure until a loud crack announces your broken neck?"

The others were now grinning at their buddy on the floor, who mumbled, "You are not very sociable. Do you not prefer to get along with your new friends?"

Andy knew he had passed the test, and he lifted his foot. "Sure. I think you all are a bunch of very nice fellows. But I do not appreciate it when my belongings or I am personally trifled with." He glanced around. "None of you had better do that again."

Now Tchaikurov was back, chuckling. "Tell everybody your name."

"I am Mikhail Andreovich Molotosky," Andy announced.

"Very well, Mikhail Andreovich," Tchaikurov said. "Come with me and let us see to your blankets and weapons. We can do that now since you are still alive. You may leave your backpack on the bunk." Then he added in a threatening tone as he looked at the others. "Nobody will touch your possessions."

At that point Andy was no longer worried

AS the day passed, Andy alias Molotosky settled in and began to make friends with the others. He learned that for a payment of seventy somonis a month he could have meals prepared for him by a young Pashtun man who lived in one corner of the barracks. The others informed him that the guy was a homosexual who had been found wandering alone and shunned on the Pranistay Steppes. His people could have killed him for his sexual orientation, but the tribe had not expected him to live long out in the wilderness anyway. His name was Gulyar and he had several boyfriends among the ex-convicts. Normally this would have been violently condemned, but after so many years of incarceration, the veteran prisoners tolerated the relationships.

As Andy settled in, he acquired a few bottles of vodka from a crippled peddler who was called Torgovyets—the Russian word for "merchant"—by the others. Torgovyets lived in a small hutch near the entrance to the settlement and hitched rides into Khorugh, where he bought items he could resell for a profit to the other inhabitants. His lameness was the result of slashing his Achilles tendons to get out of hard labor during his prison days. He made himself useful to Yarkov's organization by standing double stretches of guard duty at night.

2030 HOURS

RUSSIANS like vodka. Andy Malachenko alias Mikhail Molotosky was no exception. His father kept his vodka on the windowsill of their Brighton Beach apartment during the frigid months of winter. In the summertime it went into the freezer of their refrigerator. Vodka had been a very important part of the Malachenko family's social life with their expatriate neighbors.

Now Andy was in the company a group of ex-convicts knocking back deep gulps from tumblers as they sat around inside the barracks. Andy's treatment of his tormentors had been a cause for celebration as he was accepted as a full member of their group. Even the two men he had humiliated—Yakob Putnovsky and Timofei Dagorov—joined in the celebration with no hard feelings. Although pretty drunk, Andy was still under control and gave everyone his cover story *in toto*, telling of the extortion of kiosk owners, service in the Army, working at the stables for the *nobodniks*, and buying a passport in order to flee south to get away from the Moscow police. Everyone thought it was great, and they peppered him with questions about the modern Russia that they had never seen. He knew enough to be up-to-date from what his parents had told him of their former lives, along with information gleaned from letters sent by relatives. But instead of hearing about their motherland making the men homesick, it convinced them they could never go back to such an unorganized, wheeling-and-dealing society. And, of course, those under a death sentence would face extremely fatal consequences if they wandered back across the border.

As the drinking increased and the conversation became more animated and interesting, someone suggested they load into a couple of the cars and go down to the whorehouse in Dolirod.

The group, leaving behind a trio of hardcore drinkers who preferred inebriation to sex, staggered out of the barracks into the cold. A driver and a couple of the quicker men got into the cab of an ancient Soviet GAZ transport truck while Andy and the others clambered into the back. It took a bit of doing to turn the motor over, but within ten minutes the vehicle and its shit-faced passengers were bouncing down the mountain road toward the town. The wind in the back was frigid enough that everyone ducked down to avoid the blast. Andy stood up for an instant to look ahead, noting that only one headlight seemed to be working. He sat back down, hoping like hell they would make it safely to the lowlands without skidding off the road to plunge into a deep mountain ravine.

The arrival in the town came to a halt in front of the bordello. Only it, the bar, and the restaurant displayed any evidence of electric lighting. The other buildings showed flickering lanterns in the windows. Andy followed the others as they left the truck and lurched toward the whorehouse.

His last intimacy with a female had been aboard the USS *Dan Daly* when he had a brief affair with a young lady petty officer who worked in the ship's navigation team as a quartermaster's mate, so he was primed for a sexual encounter. The bordello was not as large a building as Andy expected, since the women entertained their clients in rooms where they lived. The available prostitutes waited in a communal parlor for customers since there was no madam or pimps.

Andy staggered and lurched into the place among the others and wasn't sure how he ended up with the woman who led him back to her quarters. She was a slim Tajik-Russian who looked attractive to him in the vodka haze that danced through his brain. Being a young man he was able to satisfactorily conclude the transaction in spite of being shit-faced. Afterward he offered her a drink from the bottle of liquor he had with him. She refused, speaking in broken Russian. "I not drink. It a sin."

"Does that make much of a difference now?" Andy asked.

"Yes. Allah knows my life is hard. It is written in the Qu'ran that he is benevolent and munificent. So he understands and forgives for what I must do to feed myself and my children."

Andy considered what she said. She was using religious rationalization to convince herself that everything would be fine in the by-and-by. The SEAL looked up into her face, searching for some sign of emotion in the unfortunate woman. She smiled sadly at him, then stood up and took his hand to return to the waiting room.

LOGOVISHCHYEH

WHEN the partying group got back to the barracks, they stormed inside. Igor Tchaikurov, the *kapo*, stepped from his cubicle and called out to Andy. "Hey, Mikhail Andreovich. First thing tomorrow go to the stables. We will fit you up with a horse."

"Sure," Andy said. "What is the rush?"

"You are going with a group to do a reconnaissance patrol down on the Pranistay Steppes," Tchaikurov answered. "It will be a good experience for you."

CHAPTER 13

AFTER the excellent training in military equitation under the Pakistani Lieutenant Barakaat Sidiqui, Andy Malachenko found his new Russian companions a bit on the sloppy side when it came to riding horses. Although they were all ex-soldiers, they had never served in a cavalry unit and knew nothing about mounted formations or maneuvering on horseback. The leader of the group was Valentine Surov, who had surprised Andy with his fluency in Pashto. No doubt the ex-officer was one of those rare individuals who had a flair for the acquisition of foreign tongues.

Now, in the early afternoon chill, Andy was among a disorganized crowd of a half dozen Russians cantering across the steppes toward the Bhittani's main village for a confab. When he learned of the destination, the SEAL felt it would be a good idea to wear shades just in case some Pashtun might recognize him.

Andy felt a slight hangover from the unaccustomed amount of vodka consumed the evening before, although his cohorts didn't seem the worse for wear. The SEAL had gotten a bit out of shape in handling the aftereffects of the strong liquor since he hadn't been home for a while.

When they reached the outskirts of the village, the group slowed down to a walk, wending their way through the huts to the square. The *malik*, Ghatool, had already been apprised of their approach by lookouts and was waiting with a couple of the *spinzhires* and a tribal warrior at his side. After the Russians dismounted, some boys rushed forward to take the reins of their horses and lead the animals out of the way. The *malik* and Surov greeted each other, then sat down. The other visitors remained standing in a semicircle around the ex-officer and the Pashtun elders. Surov and Ghatool immediately fell into an intense conversation, with the warrior joining in from time to time to add his own comments. After twenty minutes, Surov stood up and addressed the Russians.

"Ghatool has just told me there was an encounter with American soldiers," Surov explained. "This man was present at the scene." He pointed to the warrior. "His name is Mirzal, and he says there was an exchange of gunfire."

Andy's jaw tightened imperceptibly, knowing that the American "soldiers" would be nobody else but Brannigan's Brigands. "Were there any casualties?" he asked, putting his mouth into gear before his brain. It was a stupid thing to do, but his lack of experience as a spy had betrayed him once again.

Surov was confused as to why Andy would care, but he replied, "Nobody on either side was shot."

"How many Americans were they?" Igor Tchaikurov inquired.

"Mirzal says there were ten and that a Pashtun by the name of Chinar was also with the group. He is from the Janoon tribe and is acting as the Americans' translator."

Another Russian, Yakob Putnovsky spat. "Shit! This means big problems for the opium harvest. That is one sure thing the *amerikanski* are more concerned about than anything else. Those bastards will be out chopping down the first plants that appear in the spring."

Andy knew that wasn't the case; at least not at the present.

"This is going to make things a hell of a lot more difficult," Tchaikurov said.

"It is bad news alright," Surov agreed. "I am going to cut this patrol mission short and get back to Logovishchyeh as quickly as possible. Yarkov must learn about this new development immediately. Some serious preparations are going to have to be made if we are to deal with it effectively."

He gave a loud whistle, and the Pashtun boys brought the horses back for the visitors. In less than a half minute they were mounted up and galloping across the steppes in the direction they came from.

SEALs BIVOUAC
1520 HOURS

DIRK Wallenger watched with extreme satisfaction as the USAF Pave Low chopper lowered toward the landing spot designated by Frank Gomez, who was the detachment's acting LSPO. This was a resupply flight that meant that Wallenger could also send out his tape cassettes for shipment back to the Global News Broadcasting studios in Washington. He and Eddie Krafton had done some interviewing with Janoon tribesmen while using Chinar as an interpreter, and the effort resulted in some excellent human interest features. The journalist was sure the tape would give the GNB ratings an extremely big boost. He could already see the Emmy within his grasp. If not that, the Stensland Communications Award was a sure thing.

As soon as the helicopter touched down, Senior Chief Buford Dawkins had the working party hurry aboard to wrestle the incoming cargo out of the fuselage. The shipment included hay and oats, MREs, the long-awaited arctic sleeping bags, beer, snacks, small gifts to be given to the Pashtuns, reading material, and—most important—the mail. After more than a year overseas, mail call was an all-important event in the lives of Brannigan's Brigands. Another of Gomez's "acting" jobs was that of postal clerk. He even had a small briefcase in which he kept stamps and various forms to transfer mail deliveries and send in changes of address for detachment members who had been shipped out or sent TDy to other duty stations. While the unloading was going on, he went inside the aircraft for the mailbag, taking it over to his hootch to sort it out for distribution to the detachment.

There were several letters for everyone and some packages that meant extra goodies that would be shared among the Brigands. This was always a morale builder. Homemade pastries and candies were welcome additions to the bland diet of MREs. When Gomez was ready, he went around to the other hootches, dropping off the mail for the inhabitants to pick up when the supply work was finished. The officers were standing together observing the unloading of the chopper, giving Gomez the opportunity to save some steps by handing the envelopes to them personally rather than go to each of their hootches.

Ensign Orlando Taylor had a letter from his father, Lieutenant (JG) Jim Cruiser had three from his wife, Veronica, and the Skipper had one from his spouse, Lisa. It had been a while since Lisa had written, and Brannigan was anxious to read his mail. He quickly left the area, going over to his living quarters. The letter was dated a week previously and had been mailed from NAS North Island in Coronado. He opened the envelope and pulled out the single sheet of paper that bore Lisa's small, neat handwriting.

Dearest Bill:

I know you must be on a combat operation someplace, and I feel like hell writing this to you. I wanted to see you in person, but there is no telling when we could be together again, and this is something that must be dealt with now.

I am asking you for a divorce. I won't go into a lot of detail about how our marriage has been so difficult due to long separations, though I am sure that has

*something to do with it. I have found someone else.
He is a Naval Reserve aviator who lives in San Diego.
I met him during some fleet training exercises and I
guess we just saw too much of each other. He is a
freelance writer of aviation articles for magazines
and newspapers. I'll be staying in the Navy, and
Craig is already back in civilian life. He is able to re-
locate easily when I am given transfers. He works out
of a home office and can reside anywhere and still
meet his contractual writing obligations.*

*I guess I am a weakling, Bill, and I know you have
such contempt for that, but I cannot help myself under the circumstances. I hope you don't hate me.
There will always be a place for you in my heart.*

Lisa

Bill Brannigan set the letter down, turning his head to
gaze out the hootch. He did nothing for a few moments except watch the work of unloading the helicopter. Then he
busied himself heating up some water for a cup of MRE coffee. When the brew was ready, he sipped it slowly and con-
templatively, leaning back to rest against his rucksack.

He was sad, not angry, because he really couldn't blame
her. The marriage that started out happy and bright had deteriorated into a sham several years before. He never did fit in
well with her flying friends, and she was right about those
long separations. Bill Brannigan and Lisa had enjoyed an
exciting courtship after their first meeting at the North Island Officers' Club. He had gone there to try to score with
one of the many civilian women who hung around the place
looking for romance with a handsome naval officer. But instead of one of them catching his eye, it was a beautiful lady
aviator in a khaki uniform by the name of Lieutenant (JG)
Lisa Gordon. The mutual attraction was so strong that the romance started about two quick minutes after he invited her
to join him in a drink.

Their love for each other was initially deep, but after a

couple of years a few rough patches in the relationship emerged. They went through several crises common among couples who both serve in the military, but things always eventually smoothed out. The real tension come from the fact he couldn't stand her aviator friends. His attitude as a SEAL did not meld into that culture, and eventually none of her fellow fliers cared very much for him either. There were a few incidents and confrontations at affairs where the drinking had been particularly heavy, and Lisa was embarrassed by the events. All the unpleasantness kept adding up, until they both instinctively tiptoed around each other, putting a lot of effort in not offending or angering one another. This was not the basis for a real successful marriage under any circumstances.

So another guy came along and that was that. She could continue the naval career she loved so much, and her new husband could stay at her side. Of course they would be apart during those six-month outings with the fleet, but he would be home waiting when her tours ended, whether it be in North Island, Pensacola, Whidbey Island, or whatever NAS was her duty station.

Brannigan looked around at his surroundings. He sat under a tarpaulin, wearing a dirty BDU with an M16 rifle, ammo bandoleers, web gear, and other war-making accoutrements around him. His branch of the service was nothing like Lisa's. This was what and who he was; a warrior who met the enemy face-to-face. His type of military service was termed "soldiering." He participated in most active ops exhausted, hungry, and thirsty, with the proverbial wind blowing either hot or cold in his face for weeks at a time. He was no different than men who had served in the Roman legions, Napoleon's Imperial Guard, or the Poor Bloody Infantry of Britain's Thin Red Lines. He attacked, defended, and endured long moments of lonely waiting in an atmosphere where men were killed and maimed in primitive conditions within grenade-throwing range of each other.

Brannigan finished the coffee, then got to his feet to go out and see how the cargo job was coming along.

TAJIKISTAN

THE mountain bandits of the country had a long tradition of murder, rapine, and plundering. Generations back they had preyed on travelers negotiating the great passes of the high country, raided small villages from time to time, and even made warring expeditions onto the Pranistay Steppes to invade the fierce Pashtun tribes that dwelt there. This latter activity called for much guile and surprise to succeed. Their ancestors learned the hard way not to attack established villages. The warrior people living in them were always alert and ready for an enemy to appear. Generally this ended up with the bandits becoming the victims before they even reached their objective, and it would be they who fled for safety rather than the Pashtuns. It was best for the Tajik outlaws to go after small groups or isolated camps of herders and hunters if they wanted to prey on the inhabitants of the Pranistay Steppes.

As things continued to evolve through the decades, the bandits committed most of their crimes in the lowlands of Tajikistan. In more modern times they hijacked trucks on isolated stretches of highways, robbed buses, or caught occupants of occasional automobiles that happened to travel through their raiding grounds. Now and then the police would come looking for them, but the lawmen were easy to evade.

Then the Russians showed up in the Kangal Mountains.

The bandits didn't know where they had come from, they just suddenly appeared. When raided, these newcomers defended themselves ferociously, then counterattacked. And, unlike the police, they didn't mind getting off the roads and up into the high hill country to search out the Tajiks. The bandits learned these murderous men were former convicts who had been locked up many years for the worst of crimes. Eventually, the ex-prisoners subdued all the bandits' camps, and a truce was agreed to in which the robbers would conduct their activities in way that did not upset the cruel Russians.

LUKA Yarkov sat in his chair looking down at the two
Tajik bandits who knelt on the floor to his direct front. The
one was Akali, a chief, and the other his subchief, a wily looking fellow by the name of Buxari. The little gay Pashtun cook
named Gulyar was also present. He spoke Tajik and would act
as a translator for everybody. He had once lived in Khorugh
with a Soviet bureaucrat who had returned voluntarily to
Moscow after the fall of the Soviet Union. The man wanted
to get back to the gay bars of the big city to find real romance. He had been exiled to Southwest Asia because of his
sexual orientation, but with the establishment of the Russian
Federation, that had come to an end.

The pair of Tajiks had been summoned to the Russian's
presence the day before and had reluctantly presented themselves to the headman of the ex-convicts. Generally this
meant a dirty or dangerous job that paid little. Unfortunately
for the bandits, any refusal or hesitation on their part could
result in a raid on their camp.

After seeing they were served coffee, Yarkov announced,
"I have a task for you."

"How much will it pay?" Akali asked through Gulyar.

"Fifteen hundred somonis," Yarkov replied.

The two Tajiks looked at each other. They would keep
half and split it, then take the other half and divide it up
among their subordinate bandits.

"There are some Americans down on the Pranistay Steppes
in Afghanistan," Yarkov said. "We want you to search them
out and attack them. Kill them all."

Akali swallowed nervously. "Those Americans are nasty
fellows."

"There are only ten of them," Yarkov assured him. "I
know this for a fact because my good friend Ghatool of the
Bhittani tribe has seen them and talked to them."

Buxari still didn't like the idea. "But how can we find

them? We could search the steppes for weeks and never see any Americans. It would be like trying to find a mouse in a mountain range."

"Ghatool says you can probably make contact with them in the Derdala area," Yarkov replied.

The Tajiks liked that. It was a good place for an ambush with all the gullies and dips in the ground. But Akali did not show any enthusiasm. "Fighting Americans is very dangerous, even if there are only ten. Fifteen hundred somonis is not enough."

"You know I do not like to bargain over fees," Yarkov said with a frown. "However, I will give you one thousand rounds for your AK-47s. You will not need to shoot that much to kill less than a dozen men."

Ammunition was precious to the isolated bandits, and lately the shortages had reached critical levels. Akali quickly ran the matter through his mind, thinking that if a proper ambush were staged, ten Americans could all be killed with less than a hundred rounds. That would leave at least nine hundred left over.

"We accept the job," he announced.

"Excellent," Yarkov said. "I will have the bullets brought over for you. Would you like another cup of coffee?"

"Do not forget the money," Akali said.

MAHSUD MAIN VILLAGE
PRANISTAY STEPPES
6 NOVEMBER
1000 HOURS

MOHAMBAR, the *malik*, Dagar, his young war leader, and three other *spinzhiri* were seated on the benches in front of the well. Two chairs and a rickety stool had been set out for their visitors. These august persons were Lieutenant Bill Brannigan, Lieutenant (JG) Jim Cruiser, and Hospital Corpsman Doc Bradley. Standing beside them, in his usual role as interpreter, was Chinar of the Janoon tribe. Farther to the rear, Alpha and Bravo Fire Teams, along with Tex Benson, the SAW gunner, were kneeling or standing as they saw fit. At the edge of the crowd, not exactly menacing, but looking businesslike, were a couple of dozen fully armed fighting men of the Mahsud tribe.

After an exchange of polite greetings, Brannigan took the floor. Chinar was ready to translate as the Skipper spoke. "We Americans are here to offer you our friendship. The President of the United States is very fond of his Pashtun friends and has sent us here to help you in any way that we can. The President has instructed me to tell you that in no way will we interfere with the harvest of next spring's opium poppy crop."

Mohambar nodded as a sign of approval. "We are happy to hear you say that. The poppies are very important to us. And if we do not have to worry about anybody chopping them down, we will be able to plant a larger crop and make more money. Our people can purchase many things that they need and life will be good for them."

"We also have another way to show our desire to help you," Brannigan said. He nodded to Bradley, who stood up. "This man is like a doctor. Although not a surgeon, he is able to cure many ills. Have you heard what he did when we visited the Janoon tribe?"

Mohambar again nodded. "It is said that he made a man who had infection in a bad cut be cured and keep his arm."

"That is what he did," Brannigan said. "Do you have any ill people here?"

Now Dagar spoke up, his voice somewhat enthusiastic. "Many of our children have tapeworms. We fed them charcoal, but the tapeworms did not go away. Can this man who is like a doctor help them?"

"I can help them," Doc said. He was familiar with desperate primitive people feeding charcoal to tapeworm sufferers in the hope that the parasites would die of starvation. Unfortunately, the nourishment of the victims also deteriorated. The SEAL corpsman looked around, spotting a large, spreading *chicku* tree. "I will take my medicine over there. Bring me your sick children."

Even as he picked up his medical kit and began walking

over to the spot, several of the Mahsuds rushed away toward their homes to bring back their ill kids. By the time Doc got the kit open and organized his medicine, there were thirty youngsters lined up. It took him a half hour to determine that the children truly displayed the symptoms of the infections. This malady is worldwide and not necessarily confined to backward places.

Now the entire population, including the leaders, also gathered around. "This is going to take five or six days," Doc announced.

Mohambar asked, "What is your treatment?"

"Every morning before they eat they must take two of these pills," Doc explained, holding up a bottle of niclosamide. "You must not fail. This will kill the tapeworms. I will come back in the afternoon of the fifth day and continue. At that time I will go to the home of each child and administer an enema."

Chinar explained what an enema was and what would result. There was a bit of hesitation, but the young interpreter reminded them of Doc's skill in helping a man who would surely have died of gangrene or gotten his arm cut off without the American's ministrations. And the amputation would have been enough to kill him if it was not done by a proper surgeon.

"None of the children must eat the next morning," Doc continued. "I will give them an antiemetic. That medicine will keep them from vomiting up the dead tapeworms. Two hours later I will give them another enema. This way the dead tapeworms will come out their little bottoms. Understood?"

Dagar was skeptical. "And that will rid them of the illness?"

"I promise you it will rid them of the illness," Doc said confidently.

1130 HOURS

THE Americans had gone and the *malik* Mohambar and Dagar stood alone at the edge of the village watching the departing visitors fade into the haze of the distant horizon. Mohambar turned to the young man. "What do you think of the Americans?"

"I do not trust them," Dagar said. "They will wait until they find out where all our poppies are planted, then call in the Afghanistan Army to cut them down. And do not forget that the Russian promised to pay us a bonus for the crop."

"But the black American gave us the opportunity of having the sick children cured," Mohambar argued.

"We will let the black man apply his skill to them," Dagar said. "But before this winter grows deeper and colder, we will have to kill him and the rest of the Americans."

"As Allah wills," Mohambar said solemnly. "I will send a message to Yarkov that they have come to visit with us."

CHAPTER 14

BUXARI, the Tajik bandit subchief, rode slowly up the slight rise of the ground with the other two members of the scouting party flanking him. This was an area with a terrain layout that rolled and dipped in the midst of a series of gullies. The ravines that cut through the firm terrain were anywhere from a single meter to three deep, with very few sinking as much as five meters into the earth. Several series of these ground features ran into each other and branched out like the flow of creeks and rivers coming together to form deltas. Others continued their course to dead ends, their lengths ending abruptly as if the ancient glaciers that gouged the earth had been suddenly halted by some celestial command.

These scouts, like the dozen other men in the main body with their chief, Akali, were armed with AK-47s and carried extra bandoleers of ammunition provided by the Russian

Luka Yarkov. For rations they had canned meat and *chapatti*, carrying water in secondhand military canteens. There was no liquor in the group. These were all Muslims and followed the dictates of Islam by avoiding alcohol. Each bandit also had been paid fifty somonis—almost $18 American—while Akali and Buxari had taken half the payment handed over by Yarkov and split it evenly between themselves. They each had the equivalent of $135 American. When Akali handed out the bandits' shares, he did it individually, whispering to each recipient, "Don't tell the others what I paid you. You're more valuable to me than any of them, so you have some extra." The bandits smiled smugly to themselves, each thinking they had been paid more than their companions.

"Diqqat!" one man suddenly exclaimed, pointing off to the west.

Buxari looked in the indicated direction and spotted a double column of horsemen traveling at an angle toward them. He quickly led his party down into a gully, then dismounted and crawled up to where he could see the strangers. He counted five men and noted the direction in which they were traveling. It was due north toward the place where Akali waited with the rest of the bandits. Buxari pulled an ancient British telescope from his haversack. It had been in his family for four generations after a female ancestor had taken the spyglass from the body of a British major. She had finished mutilating the corpse after a long-ago clash between the natives and elements of Queen Victoria's army. Buxari slid the focusing tube back and forth until he was able to get a clear view. These were all foreigners of some kind, and they wore camouflage uniforms. The Americans!

It took the scouting party twenty minutes of hard riding through the confines of the natural trenches before emerging to gallop to the spot where the main body waited for them.

When Buxari reached his clansmen, he dismounted and knelt down beside Akali, who sat on the ground smoking a cigarette. "We have spotted five Americans over to the west. They are traveling northeast on the long level strip of land where the gullies lead up to the foothills of the Kangal Mountains."

Akali leaped to his feet. "Allah has answered our prayers. The infidels are riding straight into the best ambush spot."

0900 HOURS

IT wasn't too far to the place where the Tajiks knew the American would have to cross. The bandits were illiterate and untaught, but they were geniuses in their knowledge and instincts of warfare in the land where their people had fought and killed for uncounted generations. They surmised the infidels were going to take a circuitous course through the Derdalas, then go along the foothills before making another turn that would put them on a direct route back in the opposite direction. Akali could even make an accurate estimate as to the exact location where the infidels would make the maneuver. The bandit chief led his men to a spot where two gullies came close to converging. The Americans would ride straight into that area, then go through the narrow gap of flat terrain with the idea of emerging at the foothills. That was where the ambush would be set up.

DELTA Fire Team, under the command and control of Petty Officer First Class Connie Concord, rode lethargically along, taking care to avoid riding down into the deep gashes in the terrain that could lead to only God knew where. They stayed topside and alert, reinforced by Doug MacTavish and his SAW. Chad Murchison was on point, but no flankers were out because the nature of the terrain made that impossible. A deep chill hung still and penetrating in the air, and the recently arrived arctic sleeping bags had been well appreciated by the SEALs the night before.

By now Brannigan had reached a conclusion that the slaughter at the Swati village had been a local feud. Things had been quiet for the past seventeen days, and all the patrolling activities had ground down to be no more than uncomfortable rides in the cold weather with nothing to show for the discomfort and frustration. However, the mission orders plainly stated they were to keep a watch on the area and, without helicopters, the only way to do their duty was horse patrols.

The sudden blast of gunfire broke the silence like a clap of thunder. Chad Murchison looked as if he had leaped backward from his saddle before falling heavily to the ground.

THE BATTLE

THE SEALs immediately returned fire as Connie Concord jumped from his horse and ran over to Chad while spurts of dirt flew up around his feet from incoming fire. "Give me cover!" Connie ordered through the LASH as he quickly checked out the wounded SEAL. Chad was conscious, but bleeding heavily from his right side. He rolled over to his hands and knees.

"Oh, drat!" he said. "Help me back on my horse, Connie."

"Right, but hurry up. We're under fire."

"I have determined those circumstances," Chad remarked with a grimace of discomfort.

As the two struggled at the task, Doug MacTavish sent out heavy bursts from the SAW, sweeping down the gully where he perceived the location of the unfriendlies. A minute later, with Chad leaning forward in the saddle, he and Connie cantered rapidly back toward the others. Connie quickly sized up the nearest place of safety. It was the ravine on the west side of the battle zone. He ordered the team down into it, glad to see it was deep enough to give some cover.

AKALI was furious. "You idiots!" he screamed at his men. "All that firing and all you have done is shot one infidel."

"We do not get enough target practice, Chief!" one of the nearby bandits protested.

Buxari, however, was in a good mood. "The Americans went into the gully to the north! It is a dead end. Let us mount up and ride after them."

Within seconds all seventeen were in the saddle and

heading to a spot where they could quickly emerge from the
gulch and ride up to higher ground. They rode down the side
of the gully where the SEALs were, traveling parallel to the
infidels' route. After a mere five minutes the bandits had
drawn up even with their quarry, and Akali ordered his men
to hold fire until the Americans had to stop at the dead end.

GUY Devereaux was on the point, holding his horse to a
fast walk because of Chad. Connie had come over the LASH
and told him to take it easy because of the wounded SEAL's
heavy bleeding. What the fire team needed was a good gallop to put plenty of distance between themselves and whoever the rotten bastards were that opened up on them. They
had been caught in the open with their heads up their asses.
The quiet monotony of the previous weeks had lulled them
into utter stupidity.

Suddenly Guy reined in. "Dead end!" he yelled over the
LASH. "This fucking ravine has come to a stop!"

Less than a minute later the others caught up to him. The
horses crowded together at the narrow terminus, pushing
and bumping against each other. Connie Concord quickly
noted there was no way out; not to the front, the sides, and
certainly not the rear. That was where the bad guys would
be. Chad suddenly slumped over to one side, then fell heavily to the ground. Arnie Bernardi leaped down and opened
up the BDU jacket. Connie hadn't had time to tend to Chad's
wound at the ambush point, but now Arnie ripped open his
first-aid packet and pulled out a battle dressing. He applied it
directly over the gunshot injury, then wound the bandage
around Chad's waist, tying it off tight.

"Man!" Chad said, his eyes opening. "I could feel myself
falling, but I could do absolutely nothing about it. What an
abashment!"

"Yeah," Arnie said. "I really hate it when I get, er, abashed."

"It means embarrassed," Chad explained as he winced
from the tightness of the dressing.

Connie issued terse orders. "Devereaux! MacTavish! Take
the west side. Work your way up to the top of this fucking

ditch and keep an eye out. Bernardi! You and I will take the east."

Chad struggled to a sitting position. He was still numb and at that time felt no severe pain though he was experiencing waves of dizziness. "Somebody give me my M16! I can cover the coulee."

Within moments the defensives were formed. Connie pulled out his map, then turned to the LASH again, hoping the AN/PRC-126 radio's range would be extended over the flat terrain. "Boss, this is Delta. Over."

No answer.

MacTavish yelled, "I hear horses coming this way!"

"Goddamn it!" Connie cursed. "Boss, this is Delta. Over." Pause. "Boss, this is Delta. Over."

The crackling sound of Frank Gomez's voice faintly sounded over the earphones. "Delta, this is Boss. You're coming in low and garbled. Over."

"We are under attack," Connie said, looking at the map. He had not brought his GPS since it didn't seem necessary for the simple patrol mission. The team leader had to use another tried-and-true method of noting his physical location. "Map coordinates three-seven-two-five-seven-zero-three-three. I say again. Map coordinates three-seven-two-five-seven-zero-three-three. We are trapped and under attack by unknown enemy. Over, goddamn it!"

Gomez spoke again. "This is Boss. Map coordinates three-seven-two-five-seven-zero-three-three. Roger. Out."

SEALs BIVOUAC
0920 HOURS

LIEUTENANT Bill Brannigan quickly mustered the three officers, two chiefs, and thirteen petty officers of the detachment. This latter bunch was immediately sent to the horse pickets to saddle and bridle every mount. Meanwhile, the Skipper quickly briefed his section commanders and team leaders, who had been ordered to bring their maps with them.

"Get the charts and check out the location of coordinates three-seven-two-five-seven-zero-three-three," the Skipper ordered. "Everybody find it? Alright! I've already worked the distance to be twenty kilometers. As you can see by the contour lines, there are fingers of gullies and ditches and whatever running all over the fucking place. Delta Fire Team is in a defensive hold at those coordinates I just gave you. No doubt they're holding out in one of those deep depressions."

Ensign Orlando Taylor, commander of the Second Assault Section to which the Delta Fire Team belonged, spoke up. "Sir, they have MacTavish and his SAW with 'em."

"There's one plus at least," Brannigan said. "As soon as the horses are ready I want you to have every man cram all the ammo he can into his combat vest and grab his weapon. I'll see that Doc Bradley brings his medical kit. We have about an hour of hard riding to get there. Move out!" He turned to Senior Chief Buford Dawkins and Frank Gomez, the RTO. "Senior Chief, you stay back to take care of the home front. Have Gomez by the Shadowfire to relay any commo we might have for Shelor Field or General Leroux."

Dirk Wallenger, trailed by his faithful cameraman, Eddie Krafton, had heard the commotion and came running from where the newsmen had been taping some ongoing commentary for sound bites. "Bill!" he hollered out. "What's going on? Is it alright if Eddie and I come along?"

"Sorry, no," Brannigan said, checking his combat vest. "You'll have to stay here. No time to talk about it."

Wallenger knew better than to argue or try any cute tricks, and he remained quiet as he watched the organized commotion rattling on around them. In spite of the mixing of sections and fire teams, the detachment managed to maintain unit integrity as they rushed through the preparatory activities prior to the rescue attempt.

BATTLESITE

AKALI and his men were forced to stay on the east side of the gully into which the SEALs had ridden. In order to deploy any men on the other side, the bandit chief would have had to delay his pursuit while they rode a couple of kilometers back to where it was possible to cross over to the west.

The Tajiks had no idea where the Americans might be in the ravine, and the only way to find out was to send a couple of men to draw fire. Akali was not about to risk any of his better men for the dangerous task, so he called out for two guys named Jugil and Imoxra. Jugil was a fully qualified village idiot while Imoxra's IQ would be sorely pressed to measure up to the mental capacity of a sand flea. The two came forward, halting next to their chief.

"Gardonho!" he said, getting their attention. "We must find out where the Americans have stopped. Ride the length of the gully until you see them. Then come back and tell me where they are."

"What if they see us first?" Jugil asked in a rare moment of perception. "They might shoot at us."

"If they do, just duck your heads," Akali advised. "Then ride back here and tell us where they are."

Jugil glanced over at his pal Imoxra. "Do you understand? If the Americans shoot at us, we must duck our heads."

"That is a good idea," Imoxra replied agreeably. Then a thought occurred to him. "But what if their bullets strike us?"

"Do not worry about that," Akali said. "If the Americans shoot you, we will hear them and know where they are. We will go there and kill them."

"Yes, Chief," Jugil said. "That is a fine plan." He gestured to Imoxra. "Let us go quickly."

Akali shook his head in dismay as the two dimwits headed down the gully, breaking into a gallop.

CONNIE Concord and Arnie Bernardi had found an excellent firing position along the top of the ravine. They had good footholds on a small ledge and were both able to see clearly in the direction the attackers would be coming from.

The two SEALs discerned the sound of galloping hooves

before a pair of riders came into view. The enemy rode directly toward them, about ten meters out from the gully. "I'll take the one on the left," Connie spoke in a whisper. He and Arnie aimed carefully, and it was Arnie who fired the first round while Connie acted a split second later. The first man jerked backward in his saddle, caught his balance for a couple of seconds, then fell from his saddle. The second took a solid strike in the chest that hit so hard his hands flew up in the air as he tumbled backward over his horse's rump.

"Those were recon!" Connie said in the LASH. "The others will be here real quick. Ever'body get ready!"

AKALI, with Buxari staying beside him, responded to the sound of shooting by signaling the ten surviving bandits forward. They charged blindly toward the Americans, not knowing if they were in the gully or out in the open. Sudden fusillades of three-round semiautomatic fire plowed into the group, knocking three down. The others spun around and headed back where they had come from. But before they could get out of range, two more were hit, unhorsed by strikes of the bullets.

GUY Devereaux and Doug MacTavish could see plainly that there was no attack on the west side of the defensive position where they were located. They quickly scampered across to join Connie and Arnie.

"How many of them do you think there are?" Connie asked.

"I couldn't tell," Arnie replied. "Our view is too constrained from here. We'd have to climb out of here to see more. But there didn't seem to be a lot of 'em."

"Maybe there's a bigger bunch coming up," Doug suggested, arranging his magazines around him within easy reach.

THE blasts of firing had ended abruptly, but Lieutenant Bill Brannigan was going to assume the worst-case scenario as he led the column of twos toward the fight. Because of the map coordinates Connie had transmitted, the Skipper knew the exact location where Delta Fire Team was holed up. He spoke into the LASH as they drew closer to the objective. "Follow my orders. We're going to make an old-fashioned cavalry charge. I didn't hear any heavy machine guns or mortars, so I'm going to assume this is a small-arms battle. We'll go in with pistols, but be ready to dismount and go to rifle fire if we have to."

The SEALs loosened their M16s in the saddle scabbards, then pulled the Beretta automatics from their holsters, locked and loaded with one round in the chambers.

"Column left, *march*!" Brannigan said.

The formation made a left turn, following the leaders around in that direction. They were now parallel to the battle.

"By the right flank, *march*!"

Everyone swung directly to the right, forming into a single line of mounted skirmishers facing straight at the battlesite.

"At a gallop, *charge*!" Brannigan said, grinning slightly to himself as he thought that John Wayne would be proud of him. The SEALs instinctively cheered amid the thunder of hooves across the rigid ground.

The only thing lacking was a bugle call.

AKALI, with his best friend, Buxari, at his side, had turned the five surviving bandits around and ordered them forward into the attack once again. The chief and subchief were at the rear of the formation, as the charge gained speed. After going fifteen meters, Akali and Buxari made an abrupt turn to the rear to gallop for their lives, leaving their men to fend for themselves.

THE Skipper was the first to fire into the five horsemen coming toward them. In an instant the other eighteen SEALs joined in, the sounds of the pistols barely audible in the noise of the galloping horses. It was impossible to aim effectively while bouncing in the saddle, but the volume of bullets was concentrated at a small compact group of the enemy. Two fell to the side as they twisted from their saddles, a single man pitched over his horse's head. In only a moment last two took hits and hit the ground bouncing and rolling.

Off in the distance, too far away to catch now, two other riders could be seen making a successful escape. Brannigan ordered a halt, bringing the charge to a close next to where Delta Fire Team had crawled up out of the ravine. Connie Concord yelled, "We've got a wounded man. Chad is down there in the bottom of the gully!"

Doc Bradley leaped from the saddle, grabbing his medical kit as he ran over to the edge of the high ground. He slid down to Chad, who was now moaning softly with pain. The hospital corpsman went to work, taking off the field dressing to inspect the wound. The Skipper scrambled down the earthen wall and joined him. "How's it look, Doc?"

"Soft tissue wound, sir," Doc answered as he prepared a shot of morphine. "Not too serious except it appears to involve leakage from intestines into the stomach cavity. That could cause toxic shock. We need a medevac, and we need it *right* here *right* now! We can't chance taking him back. He'd have to be moved too slowly. By the time we reached the bivouac, he'd be dead."

"Damn!" the Skipper said. He spoke into his LASH. "Gomez, this is the Skipper! Get on the Shadowfire radio and call in a chopper to pick up Murchison immediately if not sooner. You know the coordinates. Out!"

A few minutes later Connie Concord's face appeared over the top of the gully. "The aircraft is on the way, sir."

CHAPTER 15

LOGOVISHCHYEH

ANDY Malachenko had been worried about not knowing the latest and trendiest slang expressions and colloquialisms of modern Russia. This seemingly minor detail could easily blow his cover, resulting in some very uncomfortable and fatal consequences. However, after the days he spent with his Russian companions, the SEAL discovered he was more up-to-date than they. Their long years of incarceration in Tajikistan had cut them off from the Motherland, and Andy had been more or less kept up-to-date from letters sent to his parents by relatives still living in Russia. His cover story was reinforced every time one of them asked what he meant by a remark or word he had employed in conversation. He was even able to tell some trendy jokes he had picked up in the correspondence from the old country.

However, Andy was becoming more and more impatient and frustrated with the passing of the days since he really didn't know what he was supposed to be looking for. In truth, his orders for the mission were ambiguous, leaving him to nose around until he found something relevant. The only information he had gleaned so far was that all these guys were former military convicts—which was pretty well known already—and they were in cahoots with a crime syndicate operation out of Khorugh. This was also information in the current files. The big boss's name was Aleksander Akloschenko, whose main man was Pavel Marvesky. Maybe the headquarters weenies didn't know about them, but their names didn't seem important to Andy. The Russians wanted to take over the opium harvests in Afghanistan, but who really cared? The word was to leave the farmers alone and let them grow their crops in peace. What difference could it possibly make if the poppy gum was smuggled out by Russian gangsters, the Sicilian Mafia, or any other crime cartel?

Andy figured the best thing he could do was to continue to play it by ear until he came across something that would seem important to SPECWARCOM or some other staff entity in the perplexing and convoluted world of command headquarters.

THE KANGAL MOUNTAINS
9 NOVEMBER
0915 HOURS

THE sun was up just above the eastern mountain peaks, but was too weak to radiate any warmth into the chilly air. Andy Malachenko, mounted on one of the horses from the communal stables, huddled in his parka as the animal's hooves clacked over the icy glaze of the rocky path he was following.

If he wasn't gathering much intelligence, the SEAL figured the next best thing would be to plan ahead in case he would have to make a sudden exit from the present scene. Whether it be to get back with some timely information or to haul ass to safety, it would be a good idea to pick out the best route before it was really needed.

The main road out of Logovishchyeh led down to the town of Dolirod, and from there out to the highway. Obviously if he had a hundred or so pissed-off Russian gangsters after him that would not be a prudent route to follow. His self-appointed mission that day was to find a quick way out of the Kangal Mountains, down to the Pranistay Steppes while avoiding built-up areas. He rode slowly along, scanning the ground and the surrounding hillsides to see if there was a hidden pass or ravine that would allow access to the lowlands.

The chill seeped through his clothing and he had to wiggle his toes in the stirrups to keep them from growing numb during the ride. A couple of times, when his feet had begun to feel like dead lumps, he had gotten off and walked to get the circulation in his lower extremities back to normal. He knew he was descended from ancestors who had endured eons of murderous cold, but sometimes it got the best of him. The one thing he liked about Southern California was that he didn't have to wear a lot of clothing. Even in the winter months of January and February, a light sweater would suffice to keep a guy comfortable, and there never was any use for gloves.

The trail he spotted was not exactly that. Instead of being a path, it was no more than an elongated rock formation that led downward from a stand of boulders. Andy urged the horse over to the spot, then pulled the reins to get the animal moving downward with the natural slope of the terrain. As he progressed toward the lower altitudes, the SEAL grew more confident even though the trail narrowed into a ledge in a couple of places that was barely wide enough for the horse. Finally he reined in when he reached a spot where he could gaze out at the steppes through a cut in the mountains. From that point on, the slope gentled out enough that he could gallop all the way down at top speed if he had to.

Satisfied that he had discovered an excellent escape route, Andy turned the horse and headed back up the mountain.

STATION BRAVO, BAHRAIN
STATION HOSPITAL
1415 HOURS

CHAD Murchison's eyes fluttered open, then closed, and he sank back to sleep as he had done a half dozen times in the previous few hours. His slumber was shallower this time, and within another twenty minutes he had come awake enough to stay that way. As his consciousness cleared, he looked around as best he could by turning his head on the pillow. He was in a bed in a long line of other beds in which men displaying various types of bandages were resting, reading, or listening to music through earphones. Chad looked the other way and noticed a couple of intravenous drips leading from bottles down to his arms. The needles were covered by gauze and tape.

"How are you?"

The feminine voice startled him and Chad turned his face back the other way to see a pleasant young woman in nurse's garb standing by the bed. He nodded to her, and had to take a breath before he could speak. "I am fine. Thank you."

"You woke up at an opportune time," the nurse said. "The doctor is making his afternoon rounds and is about three beds away." She straightened the sheets over the patient. "Is there anything I can get you?"

"No, thank you," Chad replied. Now he wondered where the hell he was. "What is this place?"

"You're in the hospital at Station Bravo," the nurse said. "You came in here last night and went straight to the operating room."

"Well—" He started to speak, then fell back into silence as he began to remember the ambush and the battle that followed. "I was wounded, was I not?"

"Oh, yes, indeed," the nurse replied. "You were most certainly wounded."

Now an army officer with a stethoscope around his neck stepped into view. "Hello, Petty Officer Murchison. How're you doing?"

"To tell you the truth I am in somewhat of an addled state," Chad replied. "I cannot tell you if my physical condition is good or bad."

The doctor smiled. "You'll have to rely on me for that. I operated on you last evening. While I was patching you up, I did some exploring around and noticed that your bladder and a kidney had been nicked by either a bullet or shrapnel."

"It had to be a bullet," Chad said. "There were no heavy weapons involved in the battle."

"Well, whatever it was, those injuries call for a urologist," the doctor said. "We're going to ship you to Germany for the proper treatment. After that you'll be headed stateside. Your other wounds are going to heal fine and I'm certain there'll be no serious problems with your urinary parts. Sending you to Germany is a purely routine matter. No need for alarm." He patted the SEAL on the shoulder. "You just relax and concentrate on getting better. I'll take one more look at you before they bundle you off tomorrow morning for the flight to Europe."

"Thank you, sir," Chad said.

The doctor started to walk over to the next bed, but he turned back. "By the way, I took out your appendix while I was in there. It was real handy, so I snipped it."

Chad grinned. "Thanks. I really do not require the organ, do I?"

"Not if what they told me in medical school is true," the doctor replied with a grin.

"I'll be back to see you later," the nurse said.

Chad suddenly felt very tired.

1615 HOURS

A female medical yeoman walked up to Chad's bed. She was a plump redhead with a lot of paperwork under her arm, and she gave the SEAL a wide smile. "Hello. I came by to talk about where you want to go from Germany. I take it you've been informed about that."

"Yes," Chad said. "The doctor apprised me of the situation."

She set her folders down and fished his file out of the pile. "Let's see. Your hometown is Boston, so I take it you'll want to go to a medical facility in that area."

"No," Chad said. "I would rather go to Balboa Naval Hospital in San Diego."

"Really?" she remarked. "Most guys want to go to their hometowns to be close to their families and friends."

"Not me. San Diego will be just fine."

"Listen, sailor," she said, "are you sure you aren't groggy from your operation? Once I do the paperwork it can't be changed."

"United States Naval Hospital, San Diego, California, if you please," Chad said.

She shrugged. "Okay, sailor."

LOGOVISHCHYEH
YARKOV'S HOUSE
10 NOVEMBER
0845 HOURS

THE two Tajik bandits were plainly upset, and their usual fear of the Russian gangster chief had been smothered by their bad mood. Akali and Buxari refused an offer to sit down, though they did each take a mug of hot, strong coffee that Gabina had brewed. The little gay interpreter Gulyar was nervous, since he was well aware that the Russian was not the type to take a lot of disrespectful complaining and finger-pointing, particularly from a couple of hill bandits.

"You told us there were only five Americans!" Akali said through Gulyar's translation. "So I took no more than twelve of my best and bravest fighters with me."

Buxari interjected, "That would have been more than enough to fight a successful battle against only five."

"But there were ten times that!" Akali exclaimed. "Fifty Americans charged us on horseback. We would have fled, but honor bade us stand and do our best to defend ourselves against such overwhelming odds. We fought a long battle before all my men lay dead and riddled by bullets at our feet."

Yarkov nodded as he listened to Gulyar change the Tajik to Russian. He knew the two bandits had never been in any fight in which they didn't have the advantage in numbers and position, and they would not have attacked so large a force of heavily armed Americans. He figured that they blundered into a small group that was quickly reinforced by a larger. And he also would bet there were no more than ten to twenty Americans involved.

Now Buxari joined in again. "We shot up all our ammunition."

"Yes!" Akali exclaimed. "I demand a payment for the loss of my men and ten thousand bullets."

"Mmm," Yarkov mused. "I am curious as to how you two got away."

"How?" Akali said. "I will tell you how. Buxari and I fought like tigers and they finally fled from us, leaving us in the carnage of that awful battlefield."

"Allah had mercy on us," Buxari added. "And there were helicopters too."

"Yes!" Akali cried. "What were we to do? We have no Stingers like the Pashtuns had when they fought you Russians and your Hinds. Rockets and bombs exploded all around us."

"Were there tanks?" Yarkov asked, trying hard not to burst out laughing.

"I believe I saw one, maybe two," Buxari said, as the story grew wilder.

"I think there were three," Akali said. "The situation was impossible. We are lucky to be here."

Yarkov was tempted to run the two liars off, but he needed the bandits from time to time during his operations. If he got rough with them, they would gather up their women and children and flee to the highest ranges of the Kangal Mountains. It would take an army to dig them out, and they would stay there until they all either starved or eventually wandered off to more hospitable climes where there were good hunting and robbing opportunities.

"I will give you another thousand somonis," Yarkov said. "And five hundred bullets."

Akali spoke angrily. "That is not enough!"

Yarkov knew the two would keep all that for themselves without giving a thing to the families of the dead men. "I have just told you what I am going to pay in compensation for your troubles. So take it and go." He snapped his finger at Gabina. "Fetch Surov!"

THE BARRACKS
1030 HOURS

ANDY Malachenko was lying on his bunk reading a year-old Russian weightlifting magazine when a slight disturbance at the other end of the barracks interrupted him. He sat up and noticed that Igor Tchaikurov was talking loudly. Since everyone seemed interested, Andy dropped the magazine and went down to see what was going on.

The former *Spetsnaz* man was laughing. ". . . And those two idiots Akali and Buxari spun this tale of almost single-handedly fighting off hundreds of American soldiers. Luka Ivanovich told me they said there were even helicopters and tanks, and all their men were killed until only those two were left standing. But finally they scared off the Yanks by their ferocious two-man counterattack and they managed to escape before enemy reinforcements arrived."

As Tchaikurov continued his own version of the wild story the two Tajik bandits had told Yarkov, it became obvious that a few Americans had won a decisive victory over the bandits. Andy wondered if those attackers had been Brannigan's Brigands.

"Luka Ivanovich gave them some more money and ammunition to placate the lying bastards," Tchaikurov said. "But he is worried that the Americans have come into the area to make sure there are no poppy harvests next spring and summer."

One of the gangsters complained, "That would be a disaster for us. It is the only thing that is going to allow us to continue our lives here."

"Do not fret," Tchaikurov said. "The boss is going to contact Akloschenko in Khorugh. He can make arrangements to get us reinforced with some tough guys from Moscow." He looked over at Andy. "Hey, Mikhail Andreovich. There might be some of your old pals in that bunch, huh?"

"I would not doubt it," Andy replied.

"And do not forget the Tajik Army," another Russian added. "There are some big shots in the government that want their piece of that opium pie, hey? They will send at least a couple of rifle companies to reinforce us."

"Of course," Tchaikurov said. "And that might include real tanks and helicopters instead of those dreamed up by bandits."

Now Andy had some intelligence to pass on. If a formidable force roared out of the Kangal Mountains down onto the Pranistay Steppes, the detachment would be cut off, then slaughtered. The only way that could be prevented was to make sure reinforcements were brought in from Coalition troops before the attack.

Andy would give himself a few more days of observation, then make his break and return to the SEALs.

SEALs BIVOUAC
1400 HOURS

WHEN Frank Gomez got on the Shadowfire radio to call in the medevac for Chad Murchison, Dirk Wallenger asked him to raise Lieutenant Bill Brannigan on the LASH and see if it was alright if he and Eddie Krafton returned to the battlesite with him. With everything down to a dull roar, Brannigan gave his acquiescence, and the two journalists saddled their horses and rode back with the RTO. When they arrived, the duo did a thoroughly comprehensive taping of the scene.

Now, back in the bivouac, they were ready for Wallenger

to do his voice-overs for the tapes that Eddie had recorded. Wallenger did his countdown, then launched into his spiel. "Good evening, ladies and gentlemen, this is Dirk Wallenger continuing my series 'Somewhere in Afghanistan.' A little more than twenty-four hours ago, a patrol from the SEAL detachment known as Brannigan's Brigands was ambushed by insurgents in the outlying areas of the Pranistay Steppes in northeastern Afghanistan. Although outnumbered, the patrol leader managed to pull his men back to a defensive area and put up a fierce resistance after calling for reinforcements. Lieutenant Wild Bill Brannigan immediately mustered his hardy SEALs and literally galloped to the rescue." Wallenger paused. "Okay, Eddie, cut. This will do for the lead in."

"Right," Eddie said. "How about the scene of the battle with the dead lying all over the place?"

"Okay," Wallenger said. He referred to his notes, then continued. "Five . . . four . . . three . . . two . . . You see here the scattered bodies of twelve dead insurgents who had attacked the SEAL patrol. An inspection of the corpses revealed these were not Taliban mujahideen, but Tajik bandits who have a history that includes decades of raiding into Afghanistan, murdering and pillaging the small outlying villages. When they decided to take on a patrol of tough U.S. Navy SEALs, they made a bad mistake. Two of the number managed to escape, fleeing before the battle was terminated. There was only one casualty on the American side, and that was a wounded man who was flown out for medical treatment. I am most happy to report that he is expected to make a full recovery from his combat injury. We are not allowed to reveal his name pending notification of next of kin. I can tell you, however, that he was one of the original members of this detachment that was activated as a platoon. Of the sixteen men who made up the new unit, I am sorry to have to tell you that three have been killed in action. There have been other losses, but those numbers have not been made available to me. This is a brief report because the battle fought here was also brief in spite of a dozen deaths and a wounded man. Many of the clashes all over Afghanistan are quick, bloody affairs that do little to advance the overall strategic design of the military commanders. It is these unexpected happenstances that make it so dangerous for our armed forces in this portion of the war on terrorism. This is Dirk Wallenger, somewhere in Afghanistan, wishing you peace in a world gone mad." He dropped his microphone to his side. "Cut, Eddie."

Eddie lowered the camera.

CHAPTER 16

THE invitation to eat out with Pavel Marvesky and Valentin Surov down in the town of Dolirod had surprised Andy Malachenko. He knew the reason for it must be more than simply to make him feel welcome as the new guy on the block. Since Marvesky was the number one rep of the Big Boss Akloschenko, and Surov was part of the leadership under Yarkov, the SEAL figured something big was going on. He joined them in the Mercedes for the trip to town. As usual, the taciturn Andrei Rogorov was the driver. After the others entered the eating establishment, he remained outside, standing watch by the entrance, seemingly immune to the bitter cold.

They found a table right away, settling down to drink from the bottle of vodka that had been served them even before the waiter took their orders. The restaurant was a log building with rough-hewn furniture and a dirt floor covered by sawdust. The other customers were truck drivers and a small assortment of travelers with a couple of locals wrapping up a long day of work with a late meal.

After being served dinners of goat and potato soup along with a large loaf of coarse bread, the trio dug in. Surov was silent, obviously waiting for Marvesky to open the evening's agenda, so Andy waited patiently as he ate. He ripped off a hunk of bread and dipped it into the soup. A couple of minutes of silent munching passed, then Marvesky looked up from his meal, turning his eyes directly on Andy's. "Aleksander Ivanovich Akloschenko has grown disenchanted with Yarkov's brand of leadership."

"Mmm," was all that Andy said, now knowing that a new chief was in store for the Russian gangsters. He was extremely curious about why they were making him privy to the plot.

"The Big Boss wants to put Surov in charge, understand?" Marvesky continued.

"Sure," Andy responded. "But why are you telling me about it?"

"Because you have no allies among the others," Marvesky explained. "Without any close pals, we know you will be a trustworthy comrade in this change of command."

"What difference does that make?" Andy asked.

"Because you are going to kill not only Yarkov, but his loyal follower Igor Tchaikurov," Marvesky announced calmly. "It might be difficult to get one of the old sweats to do the job. Hardcore loyalties were made in prison while that bunch rotted there." He chuckled slightly. "And some of those fellows are more than a little crazy anyway."

Andy said nothing, but his mind was racing. He fully realized that if he refused to commit the assassinations, he would never return to Logovishchyeh alive. He was trapped in the plot whether he liked it or not.

Now Surov joined the conversation, asking Andy, "Any problems with the arrangement, Mikhail Andreovich?"

Andy shook his head, deciding to fall into a criminal mind-set. "What's in it for me?"

"A bonus payment," Marvesky said. "You can have fourteen thousand Tajik somonis or twenty-two thousand Afghanistan afghanis. Both come to approximately a hundred and forty-five thousand rubles."

Andy did some quick math in his head, noting the amount added up to nearly five thousand American dollars. He frowned and grumbled, "I would think the job would be worth twice that, if not three times."

Marvesky's eyes went cold. "Aleksander Akloschenko does not bargain over payments. That is what he is offering. Period."

"You will also get some miscellaneous bonuses," Surov pointed out. "I will be moving into Yarkov's house and you can have mine." He winked. "You could get a woman of your own when you leave the barracks."

"Or *women*," Marvesky added, now in better humor.

"Count me in," Andy said with a slight grin. "How are things going to be set up?"

"I am going to tell Yarkov that there is a special situation involving the final arrangements for the coming spring's poppy harvest," Marvesky said. "He is to take you and Tchaikurov to a spot on Highway Panj at kilometer twenty-five between Dolirod and Khorugh."

Surov explained, "Tchaikurov is fanatically loyal to Yarkov. With him there, Yarkov will not be suspicious."

"Won't he be mistrustful about me coming along?" Andy asked.

Marvesky shook his head. "I will inform him that we are going to include some of your Moscow contacts. It will involve large profits that we do not wish to share with the rest of the gang. In order to keep things low-keyed you three will come on horseback rather than driving down to the rendezvous. I will tell Yarkov we wish for things to appear as if you are going out for a recreational ride."

"That makes sense," Andy said.

"When you reach the meeting place, shoot both immediately," Marvesky continued. "Then wait for the Big Boss to show up with me in the Mercedes. When it arrives, get in and you will be driven back up to Logovishchyeh, and Akloschenko will announce the change in command."

"Agreed," Andy stated.

"Let's drink to it," Surov suggested.

The three stopped eating long enough to raise their glasses in a toast. Andy wasn't as casual about it as he appeared. The SEAL foresaw the possibility of several dangerous eventualities. Not only from Yarkov and Tchaikurov, but from the two men he dined with. They might soothe any hard feelings among the ex-convicts by announcing he had shot Yarkov and Tchaikurov during an argument. The conspirators would then claim they killed him in revenge. Everybody satisfied. Case closed.

SEALs BIVOUAC
13 NOVEMBER
0745 HOURS

LIEUTENANT Bill Brannigan, Lieutenant (JG) Jim Cruiser, and Senior Chief Petty Officer Buford Dawkins sat on the ground outside the Skipper's hootch, drawing up a resupply request for the next delivery. It was a routine but vital task and a couple of points of priorities had to be gone over. These involved some comfort items, additional blankets, and some extra medications and drugs for Hospital Corpsman Doc Bradley's medicine chest. But finally, with all the ducks put into a proper row, the senior chief was able to take the completed list over to Frank Gomez for transmission back to Shelor Field.

"Got a minute?" Brannigan asked Cruiser, who started to get to his feet and leave. "At least a little time for a cup of coffee?"

"Sure, Skipper," Cruiser said. "This damn cold is seeping down to my bones."

The two officers crawled into the hootch, with Cruiser somewhat curious about the invitation to a coffee klatch. Brannigan retrieved his field stove from its niche, and set a pot of water on to boil. After the passage of some ten minutes, both settled back against the earthen walls with steaming cups of MRE coffee. Brannigan reached inside his field jacket and pulled out an envelope, handing it to Cruiser.

"What's this?"

"It's a letter from Lisa," Brannigan replied.

"You want me to read it?"

"Sure."

Cruiser set his cup in the dirt and pulled the missive from the envelope. He read the short but significant letter, then looked up at his commander and friend. "I'm sorry, Bill."

"Yeah," Brannigan said. "I guess it was bound to happen sooner or later. Inevitable, know what I mean?"

"Veronica saw Lisa a few months back at University Towne Centre," Cruiser said. "They had a short conversation, but she said nothing about a boyfriend or anything." He paused to pick up his coffee for another sip. "How're you doing, buddy?"

"Kind of sad," Brannigan admitted. "Mostly because what we once had is gone. Shit! It happens a million times a day between couples, huh? Especially those who live apart most of the time."

"Yeah," Cruiser said. "Veronica and I are getting along pretty good. We're both growing weary of this long separation, but no problems are growing out of it."

"You two are a strong item," Brannigan said.

"Listen, Bill," Cruiser said, "when we get back to California, Veronica and I will want you to spend some time with us."

"Thanks," Brannigan said. He grinned slightly. "Don't worry. I won't make a nuisance of myself."

Cruiser smiled back, then finished his coffee. "I've got to get over to the section. I called a team leaders' meeting for zero-eight-thirty. See you later, Bill."

"Okay," Brannigan said. He waited for Cruiser to crawl out of the hootch, then reached over to his admin bag to pull out the ammo inventory report that would be due in three days.

LOGOVISHCHYEH
YARKOV'S HOUSE
1400 HOURS

LUKA Yarkov and Igor Tchaikurov sat sullenly at the kitchen table, a half-empty vodka bottle between them. Yarkov poured some into a tumbler and downed it all. "This is the last for me. I want to be cold sober and alert this evening."

"Good idea, Luka Ivanovich," Tchaikurov said. "And I will have no more either." He drained his own glass with a couple of swallows.

Zainba and Gabina were leery and worried. The two men were not acting normally, and things were obviously going terribly wrong for some unknown reason. The two Pashtun girls silently withdrew to the back of the house and sat down together to wait and see what was going to happen.

Out in the kitchen, Yarkov sat with both elbows on the table. "They are out to get us, Igor Igorovich. We have our backs to the wall."

"That bastard Mikhail Molotosky was sent down here from Moscow to kill us," Tchaikurov said.

"With Akloschenko behind this, there is no escape for us," Yarkov opined.

Tchaikurov took a deep breath, then let out a sigh. "He and Marvesky will pay off the rest of the fellows to back him up. Those ungrateful bastards do not care. Our years in prison together mean nothing to them."

"It was strange the way Molotosky suddenly showed up, was it not?" Yarkov remarked. "One fine day that son of a bitch Marvesky arrives here in the Mercedes and drops him in our laps."

"I never liked the fellow from the first time I laid eyes on him," Tchaikurov growled. "And now we are told to ride down to the highway for a supersecret meeting because his Moscow pals are going to join in the opium poppy syndicate, hey?"

"They must think we are stupid!" Yarkov exclaimed in fearful anger. "That fat bastard is forgetting that prison made us cunning. One develops a strong instinct for survival behind bars."

"But what are we to do, Luka Ivanovich?" Tchaikurov asked.

"What else can we do?" Yarkov replied. "We will go to the meeting as ordered. But as soon as that Mercedes shows up, we go into action. You shoot Molotosky and I will turn my AKS-74 on the automobile." He was thoughtful for a moment. "I must be careful not to damage the engine. We can use it to get as far from here as possible."

"But where will we go, Luka Ivanovich?"

"What difference does it make as long as we put a great deal of distance between ourselves and this place," Yarkov said. "We have no choice in this matter other than to stay alive and flee the area. Maybe we could reach one of the Tajik bandit gangs."

"They would kill us, Luka Ivanovich," Tchaikurov said.

"You are right," Yarkov said. "They hate our guts."

"I know something better that we might do," Tchaikurov said. "We could get up to one of the former Soviet Republics that is in revolt against the Russian government. If we join a winning side, we will be safe."

"And if we do not, we will be killed," Yarkov pointed out.

"What does that matter?" Tchaikurov asked. "If we return to Russia they will carry out our executions anyway. That is our only chance."

Yarkov grimaced. "We are truly desperate men, Igor Igorovich."

SEALs BIVOUAC
1900 HOURS

IT had been a long day for Lieutenant William Brannigan, USN. No matter how busy he was, feelings about his failed marriage taunted him until he was almost driven to distraction. Now he stood at the edge of the bivouac, staring out over the Pranistay Steppes, his mind filled with thoughts of his soon-to-be-ex-wife Lisa. The real hurt of the breakup

had finally settled in hard, bringing along a heavy load of regret.

For a brief instant that afternoon he had seriously considered writing her a letter asking for a chance to try to mend
their failed relationship. Fantasies of reconciliation floated
through his consciousness, but were suddenly dashed by reality. That simply would not happen. She had another man
she loved, went to bed with, and she was now looking forward to a new romantic beginning in her life.

"Bill."

Brannigan turned to see Dirk Wallenger standing behind
him. "What can I do for you?"

"I was wondering if there would be any more excitement
forthcoming," the journalist said. "I hate to bother you, but
I'm here to get stories. But I understand it's the tactical situation that drives things here in the combat area."

"Yeah," Brannigan said, glad to turn his mind from his
failed marriage. "We either wait for orders or for a situation to
develop that we must react to. Things have been quiet lately."

"Sure," Wallenger said. He sank into silence, recalling
that on the first morning in Afghanistan, Cruiser had made a
remark about Doc Bradley helping a boy down in South
America. The journalist cleared his throat. "Ahem. There's
something I've been meaning to ask you about. I bumped
into a story during an assignment while I was in South
America several months back. A group of Brazilian settlers
was wiped out down in Bolivia. Much like what happened to
the poor people in the Swati village. In fact, it was that incident that reminded me of the earlier one."

"Yeah?"

"Yeah. American Green Berets were accused of the
crime, but nothing came of it," Wallenger said. "Do you happen to know anything about it? I thought you might, since
you're in the 'business,' if you know what I mean."

"I'm afraid I don't."

"I interviewed a survivor," Wallenger continued. "At least
he said he was a survivor. He claimed he was a Brazilian and
spoke Portuguese. He had photos of the crime scene he said
had been taken by an itinerant priest."

"It sounds like an unusual situation," Brannigan commented dryly.

"It was," Wallenger agreed. "The guy was found dead later after a battle with unknown forces in that same area. He was wearing the uniform of a Fascist revolutionary army. Further investigation showed he was from Portugal and had deserted from the Spanish Foreign Legion."

The memory banks of Brannigan's mind kicked up remembrances of the Gran Chaco area of Bolivia and a mission the Brigands had gone on there. It was their second sortie into combat as a group. The enemy in that instance had been Falangist Fascists who were making a mad bid to begin a revolution that would encompass all of South America. And the Brigands had been horrified by the slaughter of the illegal immigrant Brazilian farmers. It all came to an end in a final showdown at the site of the Fascist base camp. Two of the key men, both renegade Chilean paratroopers, were captured, but they later escaped in what was considered an inside job. Now both were thought to be somewhere in Europe, being hidden by neo-Nazis while waiting to try again.

Brannigan looked at Wallenger. "I don't know a thing about it. Have a nice evening." He turned and walked back to his hootch.

LOGOVISHCHYEH
14 NOVEMBER
0200 HOURS

THE night was cold and raw as Andy Malachenko, Luka Yarkov, and Igor Tchaikurov rode from the stables out to the road that led down to Dolirod and Highway Panj. All three were fully armed with concealed pistols and AKS-74 assault rifles in their saddle scabbards.

The three men huddled down into their heavy coats, the earflaps of their fur caps pulled down and tied under their chins. Heavy mufflers covered their faces against the buffeting of the freezing wind. Andy was in the lead with his companions behind him as they left the Russian settlement and reached the bucolic route leading to their destination.

"*Z'dyehs*—stop," Andy said, raising his hand after they had gone a hundred or so meters.

Yarkov was ready to reach for his Tokarev pistol. "What's the matter?"

"You are heading for a trap," Andy said. "Marvesky and Surov want you both killed."

Tchaikurov looked first at Yarkov, then back to Andy. He didn't know whether to trust the Muscovite or not. The ex-*Spetsnaz* decided to sound him out. "And how do you know of that?" He was also ready to shoot the SEAL out of the saddle.

"They want to get rid of you two so Surov can take over the gang," Andy explained. "I am supposed to shoot you before we reach the highway, then join them in the car to drive up here. That was when they were going to announce Surov as the new leader."

Now Yarkov and Tchaikurov were looking at each other. Yarkov rode up close to Andy. "And what has made you change your mind and decide not to kill us?"

"I want to get you both out of here and down into Afghanistan," Andy explained. "I will take you to the Coalition Forces where you can give them information on the gang and the crime syndicate in Tajikistan."

"Maybe we should shoot you," Tchaikurov growled. "Then knock off the two bastards in the car, and take it for ourselves."

Andy shook his head. "Why do that? You'll end up with no place to escape to. If you go with me you will be rewarded." He now noted both had pistols in their hands, and he grew nervous. "Listen! You will have a chance to go to America."

"Ha!" Yarkov laughed. "How are you going to get us to America, Mikhail Andreovich?"

"I am an American," Andy announced.

"I speak English," Tchaikurov announced. "I studied the language for three years in KGB school." He switched to the language, saying, "Tell me about yourself."

"I know a safe way out of the Kangal Mountains down to the Pranistay Steppes," Andy explained in English. "From there I will take you to the Coalition Forces. I was born in Russia but grew up in Brighton Beach, New York." He paused. "Hell! If I wanted to shoot you two guys, I could have done it before now."

Tchaikurov stared at him openmouthed, then turned to Yarkov. "He is telling the truth. The fellow is an American alright!"

Yarkov stuck his pistol back in its holster. "So just what the hell are you doing out here? You must be CIA!"

"We do not have time for a lot of chitchat right now," Andy said. "I will explain all later. Right now, we should make a run for it."

Yarkov chuckled. "In that case, lead on, *Amerikanets*."

Andy pulled on the reins of his horse, heading for the route he had discovered during his covert reconnaissance some weeks earlier.

CHAPTER 17

THE wind was freezing and vicious as it buffeted the trio of riders going down the icy slope toward the lowlands. Andy Malachenko was in the lead with Luka Yarkov and Igor Tchaikurov following. The group allowed their horses to pick the best route across the rocks. As they neared the steppes, particles of stinging dust were picked up by the swirling airstream to add to the discomfort.

Yarkov kicked his horse in the flanks and trotted up beside the SEAL. "How far do we have to go?"

"I do not know," Andy replied. "Do either one of you have a map?"

Yarkov shook his head. "They would do us no good. Map reading is not part of Russian military training unless one is a commissioned officer."

"In that case, we shall continue riding due east," Andy said. "Eventually I will spot a landmark I recognize. But we have to avoid the Pashtun villages. I do not know which tribes to trust, so it is best to stay away from all of them."

"I agree," Yarkov said. "At any rate, here are a few who would love my and Tchaikurov's heads."

Eventually the three instinctively formed into a wedge formation with Andy in the advanced center position. As the ride continued, the trio settled into the discomfort with soldierly stoicism, doing their best to ignore the stinging cold dealt them by the elements.

0800 HOURS

YARKOV left his spot and once again joined Andy. The Russian leaned close so he wouldn't have to shout over the loud whistling of the wind. "We must rest our mounts. There is no forage for them, so we cannot ride them too hard."

"Good idea," Andy said, not having enough experience with horses to consider their welfare.

They rode into a dip in the ground that offered some protection from the wind, and dismounted. The saddles were taken off the horses, and after securing the animals the humans turned to their own comforts. Andy reached into his saddlebags and pulled out some packages. "I knew we would be going for a long ride, so I brought along some extra rations. I have chocolate, instant coffee, some cheese and sardines."

The Russians laughed hard, and Yarkov said, "We bought food too. As we told you earlier, we knew there was something suspicious about going down to the highway, so we were prepared to knock you off along with whoever was in the car. Then we were going for a long drive."

"We have extra money too," Tchaikurov added.

Andy grinned. "Well, let's eat then. Did you bring any bread?"

"Yes," Yarkov said. "And strawberry jam."

"We will have a *pir*," Tchaikurov said. "A feast, eh?"

They broke out their goodies and made some comparisons about who had what and how much, then divvied everything up. Within a few minutes, the one camp stove that Andy had bought was lit up to boil water in the pot that Tchaikurov contributed. Yarkov took a bite of a Nestlé chocolate bar and glanced over at the SEAL. "Where are we headed, Mikhail Andreovich? And what is going to happen to us there?"

"I should tell you something now," Andy said. "I serve in the American Navy SEALs. My real name is Andrei Malachenko. You will first visit my commanding officer at our bivouac for a brief introduction. From there you will be flown from Afghanistan to an American base. That is where you will be given a thorough debriefing."

"What about that reward you talked about?" Tchaikurov asked.

Andy wasn't certain about any rewards or special treatment, but he knew enough to put a positive spin on his remarks. "That will be taken care of when you get to America. That's far above my station. You will eventually meet the people who will bring you through that phase. The U.S. government has a special protection program that provides new identities, jobs, and money."

The two Russians grinned at each other and turned their attention to the snacks. Andy settled back, satisfied that he was bringing two valuable assets into the system.

1000 HOURS

THE three evaders were back into the humdrum riding through the cold that dominated the monotonous terrain of the steppes. Andy Malachenko referred to his compass now and then to make sure they stayed on an easterly course. The sun, high and distant, did little to raise the temperature; even its illumination was weak and wintry.

The crack of a bullet broke the air around them and was quickly followed by the sound of a gunshot. The riders twisted in their saddles and looked to the rear. A dozen or so riders galloped toward them, firing erratically and inaccurately in their direction. A quick look around showed the only cover available was some distant boulders near the northern foothills. No orders were necessary as they galloped toward the protection with Tchaikurov in the lead.

After going a hundred meters, Yarkov's horse went down and the Russian hit the dirt hard, rolling violently over the unyielding terrain. The ever loyal Tchaikurov wheeled around and galloped back to his chief. Andy reined in and pulled his AKS-74 from the scabbard, providing covering fire while Yarkov jumped up behind Tchaikurov. Then they renewed their race for the rocky area.

It took ten minutes to reach the site, and all three jumped from their horses and took up firing positions. Yarkov had only his pistol since his rifle was back with his horse, and he held his fire to wait for their pursuers to draw closer before taking any shots at them. Andy and Tchaikurov squeezed off a couple of rounds each to discourage the attackers, but they continued closing the distance.

Then the bad guys quickly dismounted too, turning their mounts over to a couple of horse handlers. With that done, they scampered from boulder to boulder to close in. A few more shots were exchanged with no casualties on either side. Within a couple of minutes they were within the range of Yarkov's pistol. He took careful aim, then stopped as he suddenly yelled out, "Hey! *Mo budem Rusho!*"

The firing ceased as Tchaikurov took a close look. "Those bastards are Tajiks."

"Correct," Yarkov said. "And one of them is that idiot Akali." He yelled out again, this time in Russian. "Akali! I am Luka Yarkov!"

Now all the Tajik bandits stood up and looked at each other in confusion. Akali, with no knowledge of the language, recognized the Russian. He waved and began walking toward the three men in the cover of the larger boulders. Andy relaxed now as the bandits approached. He counted ten of them, with the two in the distance holding the horses. Both Russians stood up and the bandits grinned at them as they drew closer.

"Now!" Yarkov said in a low whisper.

He and Tchaikurov opened fire on the Tajiks, the latter's

selector on full automatic. The victims had only a couple of brief seconds of surprise before the bullets ripped into their bodies. One man, lagging behind the others, tried to run, but he too was toppled by quick bursts of 5.45-millimeter slugs.

Yarkov turned to Andy as the echoes of the volleys died off into the distance. "If they discovered we were fugitives and alone, they would have shot us down like mad dogs. But we fired first."

"Right," Tchaikurov said. "The Tajiks are very brave when they outnumber you."

Andy frowned. "It would seem you are very unpopular with the natives."

Yarkov chuckled. "We have treated them badly in the past. They undoubtedly feel they had some old scores to settle with us."

Andy looked off in the distance. "Those guys minding the horses have ridden off. It looks like they've turned the animals loose."

Tchaikurov pulled himself back into the saddle. "I will go get you one, Luka Ivanovich. Then we can ride back to your horse and get your rifle and gear."

Andy decided to wait with Yarkov.

**LOGOVISHCHYEH
16 NOVEMBER
0815 HOURS**

CLOSE to a hundred of the Russian ex-military convicts had gathered in a group, pressed close together because of the cold. To their direct front stood three men: Aleksander Akloschenko, Pavel Marvesky, and Valentin Surov, who leaned against the Mercedes. Andrei Rogorov, bodyguard and chauffeur, stood off to the side. He was ready for a confrontation. His eyes scanned the crowd, looking for signs of trouble.

Marvesky and Surov helped Akloschenko up on the bumper, then gave him a boost as he stepped onto the hood of the car. The corpulent man looked down over the sullen faces gazing at him with suspicion in their demeanors. The crime boss crossed his hands across his chest and stood defiantly with his feet apart. "Alright, brothers! I have some startling news for you. Through my system of informers, I recently discovered that the man Molotosky who came here was not who he said he was. In fact, Molotosky was a gunman for the Moscow Mafia who want to move in here and take over the opium harvest for themselves, see? I am sure you all remember he showed up with a lot of cash. Well, he had even more than any of us thought, and he had bought off both Luka Yarkov and Igor Tchaikurov to join his gang in their scheme. They were going to knock off me and all my boys over in Khorugh."

The little underboss Fedor Grabvosky was in the front. He looked up into Akloschenko's face. "How could three men arrange a takeover of so many others?"

Akloschenko had expected challenging questions, and gave an immediate, confident answer. "The Moscow syndicate was going to send down enough men to handle the operation here after most of us had been eliminated." He paused to check the men's reactions to the news. He liked what he saw. "After I learned about the plot, I decided to trap those three bastards, but they somehow got wind of it and escaped. I do not know where they went, except that Yarkov and Tchaikurov could not go back to Russia. But Molotosky would have no trouble, and I am sure he is hiding from his pals who will want to settle with him about fucking up their plans."

"What are we going to do now?" a voice asked from the crowd.

"I have placed Surov in charge," Akloschenko announced. "You will obey every command he gives, because he now represents me. In other words, he has taken Yarkov's place."

The diminutive Grabvosky spoke again. "But is not the Moscow Mafia powerful and well financed? Surely they can send enough men down here to get what they want."

"I have taken that into consideration," Akloschenko said,

elaborating on his falsehoods, "and turned to my contacts in the Tajik government. These politicians and bureaucrats are going to use official funds to invest in the opium harvest. And they will add some two hundred soldiers to the mix. That is more than enough to handle a few city boys from Moscow. I will tell you something surprising that has been kept a secret until this very minute. We will all become rich, because the entire harvest will be sold to the Taliban. They will take care of all smuggling, transport, and distribution. All we must do is let them know where and when to pick up the powder and gum."

Aleksei Barkyev, another of the underbosses under Yarkov, stepped forward. "I thought the Taliban were on their last legs."

"They have grown stronger, brother," Akloschenko said. "They have financing from Saudi Arabian oil princes. They will use the money they earn from the sales of the opium to finance arms dealing, training camps, and provide aid to several of the former Muslim countries of the old USSR. Such as Chechnya."

One of the ex-soldiers was confused. "Excuse me. But are not those Muslims fighting against our own people?"

"Brother," said Akloschenko, "we no longer have our 'own people.' Every person you owe allegiance and loyalty to is gathered here and now."

The truth of the statement was instantly recognized by the former convicts, who expressed their acceptance of the changes with silent looks of acquiescence.

YARKOV'S FORMER HOUSE
17 NOVEMBER
1000 HOURS

THE rusted-out Toyota pickup without doors rolled up to the front of what had once been the home of Luka Yarkov. The rear was filled with the household belongings of Valentin Surov and his sixteen-year-old Pashtun woman,

Aghala. They hadn't needed to bring a lot since Yarkov's property was still in place and that included his two women, Zainba and Gabina. The pair had stayed with the house because no one had told them what to do after their master's disappearance, and they had no other place to go anyway.

Surov and Aghala got out of the truck cab and walked to the front door. Surov led the way into the house with the girl following him. Zainba and Gabina stood nervously in the kitchen waiting for them. At this point Aghala stepped around the Russian and walked up to the other two Pashtun girls. She gave them a look of haughty contempt, showing what was more of a sneer than a smile on her young face.

"You are to stay here," she announced to them in Pashto. "You now belong to Surov and that makes me the *wrumbanay shedza*—the first wife."

Zainba spoke up angrily and loudly. "I am older than you. That makes me the first wife."

Aghala showed a furious scowl. "Surov has already told me I am the chief woman! And if you do not obey me, I will have you taken down to the barracks and thrown in for the men's enjoyment. You would not survive past the third night of their rough treatment."

Zainba and Gabina looked at each other, realizing that they were completely at the other Pashtun girl's mercy. They both bowed their heads to indicate they accepted the conditions imposed on them.

"That is much better!" Aghala said. "Now there are some things in the back of the truck outside. Fetch them in here and I will show you where to put them. I will also organize the sleeping arrangements. *Tadi kawa*—hurry up!"

A moment after the two girls scurried through the front door, Akloschenko and Marvesky entered with Surov. The three men went to the kitchen and settled down at the table. With the others fetching and toting, Aghala took care of serving the men vodka, then quickly withdrew to further instill her authority over the house.

Akloschenko took a full swallow of the liquor, looking at

Surov. "Everything went fine with the men. They will obey you with the same willingness they did Yarkov."

"Yes," Surov agreed. "As long as they are able to earn money and live safely and comfortably here, everything will be satisfactory."

Marvesky finished off his vodka and refilled the glass. "Now that we have solved the problem of acceptance, we can begin laying down our plans for the winter."

"Exactly," Akloschenko agreed. "Before the harvest this spring, we must consolidate the Pashtun tribes on the steppes. They must all swear allegiance to us. Those who refuse will be forced to participate."

"The problem is the two holdout tribes," Surov said. "Both the Yousafzais and the Janoons are strong clans. It will be difficult to defeat them."

Akloschenko smiled. "We will be able to use the Taliban to put more pressure on them. They will be the only customers for the harvest, thus those two tribes will be at our mercy."

"For any reluctant tribesman, it will be a case of join or die," Marvesky said.

"That is an enticement that never fails," Akloschenko said in agreement. He looked at the liquor bottle on the table. "I hope you have better taste than Yarkov, Surov. This is a very bad quality of vodka."

"I will rectify that situation as soon as possible, Aleksander Ivanovich."

THE PRANISTAY STEPPES   .
19 NOVEMBER
1300 HOURS

CHARLIE Fire Team rode slowly along in a diamond formation. Dave Leibowitz was to the front, Pech Pecheur on the left flank, and Bruno Puglisi covered the right, while team leader Gutsy Olson performed as Tail-End-Charlie. They were on a perimeter patrol moving in a circle while maintaining distance of a couple of kilometers away from the bivouac. This was strictly a security job since the Brigands were more or less stood down until some assignment or reassignment popped up with something to keep them busy.

The wind was strong enough that it howled across the countryside, creating a windchill factor that made the temperature feel fifteen degrees colder. The SEALs wore mittens with trigger fingers along with ski masks and heavy parkas. They dismounted and walked as much as they rode in order to keep the circulation moving through their lower extremities. They had gotten back into the saddle a few minutes before and settled down to cover their fields of fire when Puglisi suddenly spoke.

"Hold it!" he said in the LASH. "I just sighted something at three o'clock." He pulled his binoculars from their case and scanned the distant horizon. "Three riders . . . mmm, not Pashtuns . . . Europeans . . . Christ! It's Andy Malachenko and two other guys."

"Right flank," Gutsy ordered.

They broke into a trot, going straight toward the trio of riders. When they rode up, the SEALs greeted Andy, who was obviously very pleased to see them. Charlie Team gave his Russian companions stares of unabashed curiosity. "Who are them two guys?" Puglisi asked.

"I'll explain later," Andy said. "I got to get back to the Skipper immediately if not sooner."

"What the fuck's going on, Andy?" Gutsy asked.

"A whole lot o' shakin', as the old song goes," Andy replied.

Gutsy spoke into the LASH, "Brigand, this is Charlie. We've made contact with our wandering boy. He's brought two friends for dinner. We'll be there pronto. Out."

The column of horsemen turned west.

SEALs BIVOUAC
1325 HOURS

LUKA Yarkov and Igor Tchaikurov had been relieved of their weaponry as soon as they rode into the camp. For a brief moment it appeared as if they were going to resist, but the sight of a couple of dozen tough Navy SEALs convinced them there wasn't much they could do. Now they sat scarfing up MREs while Tiny Burke and Joe Miskoski watched over them. Frank Gomez had been ordered to send a message to the USS *Combs* to inform General Leroux of Malachenko's return with two defectors.

Due to the sensitivity of the situation, Dirk Wallenger and Eddie Krafton had been sent over to their own quarters and told to stay there until further notice. The two journalists' instincts told them a big story was going down, so they did their best to pick up information by listening to conversing SEALs as they walked past.

Andy Malachenko had been called over to the Skipper's hootch for a confab with Brannigan, Jim Cruiser, and Orlando Taylor. Brannigan only asked one question but it was a meaningful one that set Andy off with a rambling oral report on his mission.

"So, Malachenko," Brannigan said. "What's been going on?"

"Well, sir," Andy began, "them two Russians I brung with me were being set up to get bumped off so that another guy could take over their gang. There's a crime syndicate in the city of Khorugh, Tajikistan, run by a guy named Aleksander Akloschenko, who is planning on muscling in on next season's poppy harvests. I think he's got some loose connections with the Mafia in Moscow. Anyhow, he's got these ex-convicts from a Russian prison working for him. They've been raiding down in Afghanistan stealing women and stuff. They're in a settlement up in the Kangal Mountains and go down to a town at the nearest highway called Dolirod for R and R. I also heard enough about the massacre at the Swati village to think they might have something to do with it."

Jim Cruiser grinned. "Listen up, Malachenko. Get some paper from the detachment chief and write out a report. He's got a manual that will show you the format to follow. I know there's a lot more for you to tell us."

"Aye, sir," Andy said.

"Meanwhile, you can act as an interpreter," Brannigan

said. He signaled over to Tiny Burke and Joe Miskoski, indicating they were to bring the Russians over. They immediately complied, escorting Yarkov and Tchaikurov into the Skipper's presence. The two fugitives sat down, and the Skipper began grilling them through Andy, although Tchaikurov had a good working knowledge of English.

Yarkov immediately spoke up. "We demand political asylum in the United States of America. If we are returned to Russia, we will be executed."

"I can't arrange that," Brannigan said, "but you can certainly apply for the protection when the right moment arrives." He wanted to get information, not discuss the two men's welfare. "What do you know about the killing of the population of a small Pashtun village?"

"We know nothing," Yarkov said. "We fight only Tajik bandits."

"What is your connection to the opium poppy harvest?" Ensign Orlando Taylor inquired.

Tchaikurov fielded that one, saying, "The crime boss in Khorugh wanted to hire us to make arrangements for purchases from the farmers on the Pranistay Steppes."

Cruiser started to speak, but was interrupted by the arrival of the RTO, Frank Gomez. He handed a message to the Skipper. "This just in, sir."

Brannigan quickly read the neatly handwritten missive. "Okay. It says here we are to do no debriefing of the Russians. They will be airlifted out of here to parts unknown for examination." He looked up at Miskoski and Burke. "Take 'em back where you had 'em." Then Brannigan turned to Cruiser and Taylor. "There're also orders here to bring the steppes completely under our control. We are to take our Pashtun allies and go after our Pashtun enemies. We're to give them a chance to change their minds."

Cruiser let out a low whistle. "There're three hundred bad guys while between us, the Yousafzai Tribe, and the Janoon Tribe, we only have about two hundred total."

Brannigan shrugged. "That's three-to-two odds against us. Not too bad, really."

"What about reinforcements?" Taylor asked.

Brannigan shook his head. "The last sentence in this message reads 'No troops available to aid you.' That pretty much sums that up."

"Did you expect anything else, sir?" Cruiser asked.

"One can always hope," Brannigan remarked.

CHAPTER 18

CHAD Murchison, thanks to determination and excellent physical conditioning, made a nice recovery from his two operations. He healed fast with plenty of pep and a good appetite, and was now officially classified as ambulatory on the ward. This meant he didn't have to use a bedpan anymore, though he had cheated on those instructions by waiting until night to sneak from his bed and hobble down to the end of the ward where the head was located. That morning they also gave him the good news that he would be allowed to leave for overnight liberty from the facility any time he wished.

Now, sitting in the small ward lounge, he had settled down to read a novel he had gotten off the library cart that was wheeled into the ward each day. The deliveries were made by a nice lady volunteer who worked in the hospital with a group of similar women dedicated to making the patients' stays as pleasant as possible. The book Chad had chosen was titled *The Brothers Karamazov*, by the Russian writer Fyodor Dostoyevsky. Chad had always liked Russian novels because of the spiritualism and complexities woven through the characters and the storyline.

His reading was interrupted when a hospital corpsman came down from the ward office and tapped him on the shoulder. "Hey, Murchison, they just called to say you got a visitor waiting for you in the reception area."

Chad frowned, wondering who would be calling on him. It couldn't be any of his relatives since they were so dedicated to proper protocol and etiquette they would never arrive unannounced. Not even a long flight from the East Coast would be an excuse to drop in for an unexpected visit. He took the book back to his bed stand, then walked from the ward out to the hallway.

The reception area was on the other side of the building. It was a meeting place with vending machines and comfortable furniture that was designed as a pleasant locale to get away from the antiseptic qualities of hospital life. When Chad stepped through the door, he stopped short, his eyes wide open with surprise.

Penny Brubaker got to her feet and rushed to the SEAL, embracing him and kissing him hard on the lips. "Oh, Chaddie!" the beautiful honey-blond cried, stepping back and looking at him. "I was so worried when I heard you had been wounded!"

He stared at her in dumbfounded silence. When he requested hospitalization in San Diego, he had done so to be as far as possible from his hometown of Boston where former friends and acquaintances would come to visit him. The SEAL wanted no contact with his past. But, between the trauma of getting shot and the sedatives during medical treatment, he had completely forgotten that Penny had taken a home in Coronado just across the bay from San Diego. And she had her married cousins Harrington and Stephanie Gilwright living with her.

"Are you alright?" Penny asked. "Were you hurt bad, Chaddie?"

Chad recovered enough to speak. "I'm, uh getting along, y'know, fine."

Penny was more than just a little put off by his lack of enthusiasm at seeing her. She took his arm and led him over to a sofa by the window, helping him sit down. Then she positioned herself close to him, an arm around his shoulders. "How long will you be in the hospital, darling?"

"I don't know when I'll be released back to duty."

"Why didn't you write me?" she asked with an accusatory tone in her voice. Then she answered her own question, saying, "You weren't up to it, were you? Poor Chaddie!"

"Mmm," he mumbled under his breath.

"Can you get permission to leave for overnight visits?" she asked. "We have plenty of room over at the beach house. We have a lovely view of the bay and a nice patio where you could sit and relax." She pecked him on the cheek. "And of course I would be there to wait on you hand and foot."

"I'll have to ask," Chad said. This was the very last thing he wanted. Most of the turmoil and unhappiness in his life, outside of Hell Week during BUD/S, had come from his relationship with Penelope Brubaker. They had been childhood sweethearts all through high school, but during his freshman year at Yale, she had thrown him over for a jock. He had been hurt badly by the rejection, and that was the principal reason for his joining the Navy. The fantastic accomplishment of earning the trident badge of the SEALs had wiped away the old hurt, and it was a brand-new, rebuilt, energized, dedicated, and badass Chad Murchison who had emerged from the challenges and ordeals of qualifying for one of the toughest branches of the armed forces.

"Chad," Penny asked, "are you on sedatives?"

"Not right now."

"Then what's the matter? Are you going through a flashback or something? I've heard of that. I even had some bad episodes after I returned from my UN job in Afghanistan. Wasn't it a hoot for us to run into each other over there? I bet you were really surprised when I told you I had broken up with Cliff, huh?"

"Yeah," Chad replied. He also recalled how much he

resented the fact the egotistical young woman had assumed he wanted to renew their romance.

"Harrington and Stephie are looking forward to seeing you again," she said. "Well, Steph is. Harrington is usually so shit-faced he doesn't really know what's going on. We've had a whole string of Mexican maids working for us. Harrington always manages to insult them or make them feel uneasy with his drinking and leering. What a lech! I think we're on our eighth or ninth by now. I lost count."

"Mmm."

"Chaddie, I'd like you to have dinner with us tomorrow night. Can you do that?"

He started to turn her down, but knew he was only putting off the inevitable. "Yeah. I can get out, I guess. I'll ask."

"Can you spend the night?"

"I'm not well enough," Chad lied.

By all rights he was a young man, and sleeping with Penny would be pleasurable, but having sex with the girl would only put him deeper into a situation he wanted to get out of.

"Well, you'll get a nice meal and we can spend some quality time together," she said, cuddling against him.

Chad stared out the window at the traffic on Pershing Drive.

FOULED ANCHOR TAVERN
CORONADO, CALIFORNIA
1930 HOURS

WHEN Brannigan's Brigands were at their home station at the Naval Amphibious Base in Coronado, they spent most of their liberties at their favorite watering hole, the Fouled Anchor Tavern. This establishment of revelry was owned by Salty Donovan, a leathery SEAL veteran who ran the place with his wife, Dixie. Salty served in the Navy from 1967 to 1997, going to such lovely places as Vietnam, Somalia, and the Gulf War. He came out of his career with a locker box full of decorations that included the Navy Cross. The stories of his exploits were still part of SEAL legend.

It was arguable whether Salty or Dixie was in charge of the tavern. They were both in their fifties and as an evening of boozing progressed, Dixie let Salty come out from behind the bar and sit with his old retired buddies and the young guys on active duty, to knock back endless rounds of brew. Though he drank his share of the pitchers and then some, Salty was most certainly not a tub of beer guts. Even after a long session of drinking, he would still be out early the next morning double-timing down Silver Strand Boulevard— AKA State Highway 75—for a distance of ten miles. After the vigorous jog, Salty would arrive back home invigorated and ready to take on the world for the rest of the day.

Dixie, though not much for exercise, didn't smoke or drink except for an occasional glass of wine. She and Salty didn't have any kids, but they lavished whatever parental instincts they had on the youngsters who patronized the tavern. Sometimes, when a couple of young SEALs had a disagreement, Dixie would break up the fight all by herself with a motherly smile and a hard grip on the collars of the combatants until they calmed down. Since the lady did not allow grudges, the pair of scrappers was always made to shake hands and let bygones be bygones.

On that particular night, Chad had gone to the Fouled Anchor for the express purpose of seeing Salty and Dixie while maybe getting together with some acquaintances from other SEAL outfits. He walked into the tavern, going directly to the bar where Dixie was working with the barmaids serving out pitchers of beer to the customers. When she saw Chad walk in, she almost dropped the pitcher she had just filled. "Chad Murchison!" she yelled out.

Chad, delighted to see her, smiled widely. "Hello, Dixie. I came by to see if you had run Salty off. If so, I'm ready to beginning courting you as only a lady should be."

Dixie laughed loudly. "No, I ain't run him off."

"I should be so lucky," came a gruff voice behind him.

Chad turned around to see the rugged features of Salty Donovan twisted into a tight grin. The young and old SEALs shook hands, and Salty gave Chad a quizzical look. "You been wounded, boy?"

"Yeah. How'd you know?"

"You got the look, son," Salty said. "You're not quite yourself yet."

"It wasn't a grave injury," Chad said. "I'll be returned to full duty very soon."

"That's good," Salty said, but he thought the younger man looked a bit wan. "Let's get you to a booth with a pitcher of beer."

"Right," Dixie said, drawing the brew. "This first one is on the house."

"Yeah," Salty said with a wink, grabbing the pitcher and a couple of glasses. "Then we'll charge you double after that."

Chad grinned as Salty led the way to a back booth in a corner. They slid into the seats across from each other. Salty did the honors, passing a full glass to his companion. "So how's it been going with the Brigands? We heard about the KIAs."

"Yeah," Chad said. "Of the original platoon we've lost Milly Mills, Kevin Albee, and Adam Clifford. Then some other newer guys later on."

"It's a shame," Salty said. "O'course, it's us that put ourselves in harm's way, and that's something outsiders can't understand." He shrugged at the ignorance of candyasses. "So what's been your latest type of missions?"

"We've been operating off that new amphibious assault ship, the *Dan Daly*," Chad said. "They've set no limits on our time over there, so we've been hitting it full tilt. Mostly in Afghanistan. A lot of sneaking and peeking."

"Yeah," Salty said. "The same old game, huh?"

They downed a few beers as Chad hit the high points of previous missions while leaving out classified facts such as illegal excursions across international borders. Dixie showed up with another pitcher, setting it down on the table. She scowled at Salty, saying, "Get your ass up and lend a hand back of the bar. I'm short two of the girls tonight and I'm waiting tables myself now."

Salty winked at Chad. "Duty calls!"

Chad watched him and Dixie disappear into the crowd, then poured another beer, gazing out over the groups of

SEALs, feeling very lonely for the Brigands. He could have gone out and found some acquaintances to share the evening with, but he was a little tired after the cab ride over from San Diego. It showed he still wasn't quite a hundred percent.

When that second pitcher was done in, Chad signaled to one of the barmaids for another. After being served, he settled back to enjoy some more solitary drinking and contemplation. His mind turned to his time in BUD/S, that school that turns ordinary guys into SEALs. Chad grinned as he suddenly remembered the time when some Twinkies were discovered in a student's room. The instructors made the poor guy spend all the breaks the following day double-timing around the training site singing out, "I love Twinkies! I love Twinkies! I love Twinkies!" Each time he made a complete circuit of the class area he had to drop down for a dozen eight-count push-ups before leaping up to continue the routine.

And there was the unforgettable and very scary "drown proofing" in the CTT. Chad had been brought up around boats, both sail and power, and had spent a lot of time out on the water. Like most rich kids, he had learned to swim early in life in case of falling overboard as well as for sport. But having his hands and feet tied before jumping into the tank unnerved him. The idea was to sink to the bottom, then come up for a breath of air before submerging again. The first couple of times convinced him they would be fishing him out for resuscitation, but he quickly caught on and it became routine, although he hoped he would never have to do it for real.

The low point of BUD/S for Chad had been when he was assigned to the Goon Squad. They were the hapless students who performed the worst in training. The goons were the slowest of the slow, the most awkward of the awkward, and the least likely to succeed. This lack of aptitude resulted in their being assigned to the lowly team with the insulting name. The instructors figured none of them would make the grade, and wanted to save the Navy the time and expense of carrying their useless asses through too much more of the training. They were the ones who were made to come out of the frigid surf and roll on the beach to get "wet and sandy."

They also had to do bear crawls, buddy carries, and other chickenshit stuff to drive them to quit. But Chad, chafing from being dumped by Penny Brubaker, was determined to make good and he refused to give up. He took an amazing amount of punishment, actually gaining strength and courage as the mistreatment continued with increasing pressure. He realized later that this was why he was eventually given extra encouragement, because the instructors came to admire the fighting spirit in his skinny body.

Mind games were also a big part of the curriculum. Most of the time, the team that finished last in a training exercise received extra PT as a punishment. But Chad remembered once when he was in the *fastest* group to complete a run, and the instructors chose to punish them instead. And, of course, there were those 120 hours of Hell Week with five days of tougher discipline, frigid cold, constant wetness, wrestling inflatable boats and logs; all on a grand total of four hours of sleep.

Now, sitting half drunk in the Fouled Anchor Tavern as a decorated combat veteran of numerous SEAL missions, Petty Officer Second Class Chadwick Murchison grinned to himself. Would he go through it again?

Damn straight, pal!

PENNY'S BEACH HOUSE
21 NOVEMBER
1845 HOURS

PENNY pulled off the street and into the driveway, taking the BMW down to the garage. Chad glanced over at the patio when they came to a stop. He saw Harrington and Stephanie Gilwright sitting at a table. The married couple was next to a portable heater that was going full blast to give some comfort from the cold air coming off San Diego Bay. Stephie got to her feet and walked toward the car as Penny and Chad got out.

"My God, Chad!" Stephie exclaimed giving him a hug. "You look like a rugged movie star!"

Chad hugged her back. "How are you, Stephie?"

Penny led the way to the patio as the other two followed. Harrington remained seated, and Chad could see he was drunk. The SEAL nodded to him. "Hello, Harrington."

"Nice to see you, Chad," he said. "Care for a drink, old boy?"

"I could use a beer."

"Coming up," Harrington said. He reached over and picked up a small bell, tinkling it. A young Hispanic woman appeared and was given a curt order to bring a beer for the visitor. She disappeared back into the house as Chad and the two girls sat down. Harrington took a sip of his martini, studying Chad. "You've changed quite a lot, old boy."

"Yeah. I have."

"So you're what is known universally as a SEAL, what?" Harrington inquired.

"Yeah."

"I've seen those chaps running around the beach, carrying boats and rolling around and doing an obscene amount of exercise," Harrington said. "What's that all about?"

"That's the training course," Chad said. "When they finish it, they will be SEALs."

"And you did that?"

"Yeah."

"Damned senseless, if you ask me," Harrington said.

Stephanie actually sneered at her husband. "Well, nobody's asking you."

"Well, it's a bother, whether anybody asks me or not," Harrington shot back.

The maid reappeared with a bottle of Corona beer and a glass. She carefully poured the brew, bringing up the right size of head. Chad nodded his thanks to her with a smile and took a sip.

"How are you doing, Chad?" Stephanie asked. "We were very concerned when we heard you had been wounded."

"Ah, yes," Harrington said. "Interesting, I'll say. What happened, old boy?"

"I was shot," Chad explained. To save other questions, he added, "It was in Afghanistan in a firefight with Islamic insurgents. I came out of it fine."

· "Thank God," Penny said. "That's something we're going to have to talk about, Chaddie."

"My wound?"

"No. About when you're getting out of the Navy."

Harrington interjected, "You look like a tough fellow, Chad. When you get back to Boston, are you going to look up Cliff Armbrewster and give him a jolly good thrashing for taking Penny away from you?"

"Shut up, Harrington," Stephanie said. "Penny didn't stay with Cliff very long."

"Oh, come now, Steph," Harrington said as he mixed another martini in the shaker. "You've always had a big crush on our Chad here. I knew that even before we got married. As I recall you were quite happy when Penny took up with that oaf Armbrewster. Thought you were going to have Chad for yourself, hey?"

"I think that's enough," Penny said. "Just get as quietly drunk as you wish, Harrington, and never mind the commentary."

"I'll tell you one thing," Harrington said. "I wouldn't be a SEAL." He poured the freshly prepared martini into the glass. "Damned if I'm stupid enough to go through that ridiculous initiation or whatever it is they call it." He laughed. "Nobody needs them anyway. If the President wants to get rid of terrorism in the Middle East, he should just drop a nuclear bomb on the place. Boom! Problem solved, hey? Turn that whole bloody part of the world into a parking lot that glows in the dark, what?"

Chad grinned, trying to picture what Harrington would be like in BUD/S. "Maybe you're right, Harrington."

"Perhaps I am," he said.

Further conversation was interrupted when the maid came out again to announce that dinner was ready. The four followed her inside, going to the dining area. Chad saw that the meal was catered. A couple of servers dressed in white waiter jackets stood behind a buffet that offered soup, salad, New York strip steaks, lobster, potatoes au gratin, and mixed vegetables. For dessert there was chocolate mousse and coffee. Three different wines were available on the table for the quartet of diners. Chad felt guilty as he picked up a plate and began walking down the line to be served. He knew that Brannigan's Brigands' evening meal would have been MREs eaten outside by the hootches as a freezing wind blew in over the Pranistay Steppes.

2230 HOURS

THE caterers had taken away all their things, the maid had cleaned the kitchen and dining room, Harrington Gilwright was passed out up in his bedroom, and Stephanie had withdrawn to the living room to wind down with a glass of sauvignon blanc. Penny took advantage of the quiet time to take Chad out to the patio to gaze out over San Diego Bay.

The heater made it comfortable, and Chad turned to look at Penny in the dim light coming from the kitchen window. Her features were particularly lovely in the soft illumination, and he spoke to her in a low voice, saying, "I don't think we should see each other anymore."

The slight smile of contentment she had lasted only another millisecond before her expression turned into one of angry surprise. "What? I can't believe you just said that to me. To *me*!"

"I apologize for my obtundness, Penny," Chad said. "But it is an unpleasantness we must face up to."

"I can't see where you're coming from!" she snapped. "What brought this nonsense on?"

"People change."

At first she just stared at him as if he had uttered the vilest declaration of which a human being was capable. She recovered a moment later, crying out, "Don't you love me, Chad?"

"No."

"You *must* want me!" Penny cried. "I could have my choice of men!" She calmed down a little. "I don't believe you mean it. You've always loved me. Admit it!" She felt a flash of embarrassment and anger as her feminine ego reeled like a rose in a stiff wind. "Fate meant us to be together always, Chad! It was fate that brought us together over in Afghanistan.

Twice! That meant we were supposed to be a couple forever!"
When he made no reply, she continued, "It's your terrible experiences in the war that have affected you. And your wound
has unsettled you too. You simply must get out of that stupid
Navy!"

Chad turned away and stared out over the dark waters.
"You are from a part of my life that I have abandoned, Penny.
It was a time when I was not at my best. I was a skinny, awkward kid, unsure of myself and also untested." He looked at
her. "I want to get away from that and not go back to anything or anyone that has anything to do with those years that
I consider no less than awful. It was a time of frustration and
strong feelings of inadequacy. And you were the cause of
much of that."

Penny looked at him in silence, barely able to compre-
hend words she thought would never be directed at her.

Chad decided to keep it cruel and short. "I do not love
you, Penny. I do not want you."

"The why did you choose to go to the hospital in San
Diego rather than one in Boston?" she asked.

"I forgot you were here."

The words hit her hard as she realized he meant exactly
what he had just said. Penny abruptly left the patio, going
into the house. Chad waited a few moments, then followed
after her. He went through the kitchen and dining room into
the living room where Stephanie sat, looking in puzzlement
at the stairs that the weeping Penny had rapidly ascended.
She turned her eyes on Chad. "What happened?"

"I need to call a cab," he said, ignoring the question.

"The phone is over by the door," Stephanie said. "There's
a phone book too."

Chad went over and turned to the Yellow Pages. After
punching in the number of a taxi company and summoning a
ride, he hung up and went out the door to wait at the curb for
the ride back to the hospital.

CHAPTER 19

STATION BRAVO, BAHRAIN
BARRI PRISON

THE two Russian fugitives, Luka Yarkov and Igor Tchaikurov, had been flown directly from the SEALs' bivouac to Station Bravo for confinement and questioning. Petty Officer Andy Malachenko had been extremely surprised when he was ordered to accompany them on the trip. Neither he nor Lieutenant Bill Brannigan could figure out why such instructions had been passed down unless it was because of his fluency in the Russian language. The whole thing pissed off Brannigan since he had thought Andy was back for duty. With Chad Murchison gone, that meant a continuance of being shorthanded, this time in both the Bravo and Delta Fire teams.

Yarkov and Tchaikurov were classified as "sensitive personnel" by the Special Warfare intelligence staff in the operational area, and Brigadier General Greg Leroux had sent an urgent notification to Fred Leighton, the senior interrogator at Barri Prison, that they were to get a particularly thorough examination. However, he was to leave out any undue physical or psychological pressure unless absolutely necessary.

LEIGHTON'S OFFICE
22 NOVEMBER
0815 HOURS

THE mysterious Fred Leighton's home address, i.e., the organization he reported to, was not generally known among the prison staff, and that included the commandant. Leighton wore a BDU, but the uniform bore no insignia of rank or military organization. However, his authority was absolute and he seemed to operate with a fund so large that it was rumored there was no limit to the amount of money for his mysterious activities.

Andy Malachenko sat across from Leighton's desk, completely uneasy about this clandestine nonregulation environment he had been cast into. For some reason it seemed even more ominous than his infiltration into the Russian gang. After meeting Leighton and being invited to sit down, the interrogator said to Andy, "We're going to get you a navy officer's uniform, Malachenko. You're going to be a lieutenant (JG) during your visit to our happy abode."

"What's that shit all about?" Andy asked, not happy about the idea.

"It is a very important part of our program with your Russian pals," Leighton said. "And I want you to know that I'm very happy to have you here. Perhaps I should say that I'm glad to 'have you aboard,' as it is expressed in the Navy."

"Whatever," Andy remarked sourly, wanting to get back to the Brigands.

"So what I'll do is prepare you to interrogate those two," Leighton said. "The questioning will go in planned and scheduled steps, but it must appear to be spontaneous to them. We want them to think that we have lot of information they don't know about, but we don't want them to get the idea we're being tricky. Understand?"

"Yeah."

"I've already had a quick go at 'em," Leighton continued. "I got pretty much the same basic story out of both, but I picked up some hesitancy on their part when it came to revealing a lot about the activities of that Russian gang. The Taliban was a subject they found sensitive as well. They readily admitted to being in a military prison, but they claimed it was for mistreatment of recruits. A quick check with some of my contacts in the FSB revealed both men were murderers under sentences of death that were obviously not carried out."

"Yeah, that's true," Andy said. "I got to know all those guys and they were a tough bunch. It seems they got lost in that Soviet bureaucracy and became unknown entities that had dropped through the slats. They would have rotted in jail if the Communists hadn't gone out of business."

"What about that Pashtun village that was wiped out?" Leighton asked.

"We have some strong suspicions that the Russians were involved," Andy said. "I made some inquiries while I was staying in their settlement, but nobody would talk about it. I guess I was too new to be fully trusted."

"Okay. The first thing is to get to the truth of that particular matter. If the Russians are responsible it will make it easier to make deals with them. We can threaten them with crimes against humanity charges. Even deportation back to their home country for surefire executions."

"I got to tell you something, Leighton," Andy said. "I'm no expert interrogator. The only training I have is when you're in the field and need some important information real quick. I'm talking about taking the prisoner flying in a helicopter and threatening to throw him out if he doesn't cooperate. If you've got several EPWs, you can always go ahead and toss one out to scare hell out of the others."

Leighton chuckled. "We can operate with a lot more finesse here at Barri, so forget battlefield interrogation. You're valuable to us because you speak Russian. Even though Tchaikurov speaks passable English, he'll respond better to you in his native tongue. And I'll be coaching you through the process."

"So why do I have to be an officer?"

"Because both those guys are long-term professional soldiers," Leighton explained. "They were *not* career criminals. At one time they willingly subjected themselves to military discipline, and obviously did fine since both attained warrant officer rank. Ergo, they'll respond better if they're dealing with a man who is superior to them in rank."

"Fuck it," Andy said. "Hook the bastards' balls up to a field telephone and turn the crank. They'll talk quick enough."

Leighton shook his head. "That won't work, my friend. Physical torture will only make the subject say things to make you quit hurting him. Then you end up with a lot of information that could be more made-up than fact. You get absolutely nothing but a mixture of truth, lies, and errors."

"Okay then," Andy said. "I'm ready to have a go at 'em."

INTERROGATION ROOM
1315 HOURS

PETTY Officer Andy Malachenko wore the service dress blue uniform of a U.S. Navy lieutenant (JG) with a quarter-inch gold stripe over a half-inch gold stripe on each lower sleeve. He carried a briefcase as he stepped into the room where Luka Yarkov sat at the table. Andy walked up, removed the white service cap, and set it on the table. He gave Yarkov a stony glare.

"I believe it is proper for a warrant officer to stand at attention when a commissioned officer enters the room."

Yarkov immediately got to his feet with his heels locked.

"Sit down," Andy said, as he took a seat. He fished some papers out of the briefcase and scanned the top one for a moment. Then he glanced at the Russian. "I am very disappointed in you."

"Why is that, sir?" Yarkov asked.

"According to these papers, you were in prison for beating a recruit to death in a drunken rage," Andy said. "We may have to turn you over to the Russian government for the final disposition of your case."

"I was framed!"

"Well," Andy said, "let's discuss other matters now. What about that horrible massacre of an entire Pashtun village? Men, women, and children were slaughtered like cattle."

"I know nothing about it."

"We understand there was another Pashtun tribe involved, but there were foreigners also."

"That could be true," Yarkov said. "But if there were foreigners, they would be Tajik bandits. Those rotten bastards have been raiding into Afghanistan for generations. Why would we Russians wish to kill a crowd of Pashtuns?"

"Who do you sell opium poppies to?"

"We have done nothing with opium poppies," Yarkov said. "But we were planning on taking over next season's crops. The crime syndicate in Khorugh was going to run the show, see? You know Aleksander Akloschenko quite well. He was the fellow in charge of the operation."

"Then who would Akloschenko sell the crops to?"

Yarkov shrugged. "The Moscow Mafia, I suppose."

"What about the Taliban?"

"I was working for Akloschenko," Yarkov said. "You'll have to ask him about that."

Andy wrote down a few notes, then put the papers back in his briefcase. When he stood up, Yarkov immediately assumed the position of attention. Andy picked up his cap. "This will do for now, Yarkov. But I will be back as we uncover more information."

Yarkov relaxed when Andy went through the door, then sank back down into his chair with a deep feeling of apprehension.

1530 HOURS

IGOR Tchaikurov did not have to be told to show the proper respect for an officer. The instant that Andy entered the room in his uniform, the former warrant officer was on his feet. Once again the SEAL turned to his act of angry disappointment.

"You lied to me, Tchaikurov!" he snapped. "You said you were jailed for mistreating soldiers, but we have learned that you killed another soldier and his wife in a love triangle."

"I swear I am innocent!" Tchaikurov insisted. "The woman was having affairs with me and some other fellows. After they murdered the couple, they made it look like I had done it."

"The United States government may decide to return you to the Russian authorities over this," Andy said. "You had better keep that in mind."

"Yes, sir!"

"Sit down."

"Yes, sir!"

"Let's turn to that Pashtun village that was wiped out," Andy said. "How were you involved?"

"I was not involved at all," Tchaikurov protested. "Some of the other fellows went along on the raid for a lark. The Pashtuns did all of the killing. They were angry with the other tribe for betraying them to the Taliban."

"Did this involve deals for selling opium poppies?"

"I know nothing of opium poppies except that we were going to be involved in next year's crops," Tchaikurov said. "We were contracted to do the work for Aleksander Akloschenko. You know all about him."

"Was he going to sell the crops to the Taliban?"

"I do not think so," Tchaikurov said, very much aware of the Americans' hostile attitude toward the Islamic terrorist organization. "We Russians do not like the Taliban any better than you do."

Just as he had done with Luka Yarkov, Andy ended the interrogation in a manner that made it obvious this would not be the last session.

CHAD Murchison sat in the outer office on a bench
along the wall. He was next to a desk manned by a yeoman
who was busy updating personnel records on his word pro-
cessor. The guy reminded Chad of Randy Tooley back at Shelor Field. Both Randy and the yeoman were among the
faceless crowd in the armed forces that kept administrative
and logistical operations moving along smoothly while un-
derranked and underpaid in the jobs. Their successes were
credited to officers who benefited with great notations in
their OERs. These commanders, however, were appreciative
and smart enough to see to it that these efficient subordi-
nates were kept as happy as possible. These talented individuals were given privileges far beyond those received by less
valuable personnel.

The intercom on the desk buzzed and the man answered
it. He switched it off, then nodded to Chad. "Commander
Wilson will see you now."

"Thank you," Chad said. He went to the office door,
knocked twice, and stepped inside, delivering a salute.
"Petty Officer Murchison reporting, sir."

Commander Wilson returned the gesture, obviously in a
hurry. "What can I do for you?"

"Sir, I've just been returned to duty status from the hospital," Chad said. "I received orders to report to a SEAL team
aboard the base, but I would like to return to my outfit in Afghanistan instead."

"Well, Petty Officer, that's too damn bad," the commander said. "This is the Navy and right now we're involved
in a hell of a war. Individual wants and desires must be put
aside at times like this. We all must do what the Navy wants
us to do."

"Sir, I am not seeking a cushy berth," Chad said. "I want
to return to combat."

"You can go back to the battle zone when your new unit is

ordered overseas," Commander Wilson said. "You are dismissed, Petty Officer!"

"Aye, sir," Chad said, saluting again.

He left the office, walking across the base deep in thought. He had promised himself when he first enlisted in the Navy that he would never take advantage of his status or the valuable connections within his family. But now he had no choice but to do exactly that. He found an open area and pulled out his cell phone. After punching in the numbers for a direct-dial long-distance call to Washington, D.C., he waited for an answer.

"Office of the Chief of Naval Personnel."

"Hello," Chad said. "I would like to speak to Admiral Murchison, please."

There was a pause, then a new voice came on the phone. "This is Admiral Murchison speaking."

"Hello, Uncle Ed," Chad said. "This is Chad. I was wondering if I could ask a favor of you."

STATION BRAVO, BAHRAIN
BARRI PRISON
LEIGHTON'S OFFICE
24 NOVEMBER
0800 HOURS

FRED Leighton had his feet up on his desk, gazing out the window at the desert sky. Andy Malachenko had taken off the service blue coat and hung it on the rack by the door. He had a notebook in his lap, doodling idly as Leighton thought aloud.

"Now let's see," the interrogator mused, "both those Russian reprobates claimed they were framed for the crimes they were convicted of . . . Yarkov says the foreigners at the massacre in the Pashtun village were Tajik bandits . . . but, on the other hand, Tchaikurov admits some of the Russians were present during the atrocity."

"Right," Andy interjected. "He flubbed it a bit when he told me the killings happened because the Pashtuns were angry at the other tribe because they had betrayed them to the

Taliban. Which makes me want to ask him, 'Then why were the Russians there if they don't like the Taliban?' "

"Right," Leighton said. "Yarkov says the opium harvest is going to be sold to the crime syndicate in Khorugh . . . then it will go to the Russian Mafia in Moscow . . . but Tchaikurov claims he has no idea who will buy it."

"And Yarkov said he knows nothing about the Taliban," Andy pointed out. "He says if we want to know about them, we must ask Akloschenko."

"Those inconsistencies are a sure sign there is lying being done by both men," Leighton said. "But we have some great leverage to bring them down since if we send them back to Russia they'll be shot for those long-ago crimes. The only problem is that we're in a bit of a rush now, so it will take too much time to concentrate on both men. We'll have to choose one to lean on."

"Well," Andy said, "keep in mind that Yarkov was the head man while Tchaikurov was only a barracks boss and an enforcer."

"Right," Leighton agreed. He sat in silent thought for the next few minutes as he turned the situation over in his mind. When he reached a conclusion, he put his feet down on the floor and turned in the chair to face Andy. "Okay! You'll concentrate on Yarkov. Here's what you're going to do."

Andy leaned forward as Leighton began giving his instructions.

INTERROGATION ROOM
0900 HOURS

YARKOV sat in the chair, sweat glistening on his forehead, as he faced Andy Malachenko. Andy had his cap pushed back on his head, and he had turned the chair around. He sat in it, leaning against the back as he pointed a finger straight at the prisoner.

"You're a convicted murderer, Yarkov! If the United States returns you to Russia, some of your comrades are going to drag you to the nearest wall and shoot you! We also know you have committed crimes against the Pashtun people by raiding their territory and even stealing their women. Hell! You know damn well that I have seen them in your town. And many have been made pregnant by you guys. The Afghans may request that we turn you over to them instead of the Russians. What would happen to an infidel in an Islamic court, Yarkov? What kind of mercy would you get from them if convicted of kidnapping and raping Muslim women?"

Yarkov's face went pale.

"And we know you are up to your eyeballs in dealing opium poppies to the Taliban," Andy continued. "All the facts add up to that. One of the biggest and best financed buyers of the crops is the Taliban, who are financed by al-Qaeda and probably Syria and Iran too. Thus it is obvious they are the customers of the crime syndicate because they will pay the most money."

"Wait a minute!" Yarkov cried. "I have no say in who buys the opium."

"We have been informed by certain Pashtun tribal leaders that you yourself offered one and a half times the usual price for the crop. I would say that shows you are well financed and directed by the Khorugh crime syndicate. You are one of their lapdogs, Yarkov, and you knew you would be dealing with the Taliban."

"I know nothing of any deals with the Taliban!" Yarkov protested. "The crop was to be sold by Akloschenko. We were never sure who he would sell to. He kept that information to himself. Maybe Marvesky knew about it."

"I do not believe you," Andy insisted. "It does not add up if you were offering the Pashtuns money for next season's poppies."

"It was not *my* money!"

"You are lying!"

Andy paused a bit to let all the accusations sink into Yarkov's mind. Leighton had explained that the Russian's emotions were going to be swirling at this point, and he would want to reveal the truth. But he needed a good rationalization to do it. Even if he was scared shitless, he was soldier enough not to want to show fear until he absolutely had to. Now was the time for Andy to give the former warrant officer the proper motive to give up all he knew.

Andy got to his feet and leaned across the table. "You are under the command and control of the United States Armed Forces, Yarkov! You are subject to that military discipline! And I am an officer in the United States Navy who outranks you! I *order* you to tell me the truth, the whole truth, and nothing but the truth! As a soldier you have no choice but to obey me!"

Yarkov's military side came out and he leaped to his feet and saluted. "Yes, sir! I will tell you anything you need to know!"

"Good," Andy said calmly. He walked to the door and opened it, gesturing to the guard who stood out in the hallway. "Bring Mr. Leighton and a stenographer in here."

CHAPTER 20

THE tension in the steel compartment was so thick it could have been cut with the proverbial knife. This was the first time that the men sitting on the theater-like seats had ever been in this inner sanctum of Brigadier General Gregory Leroux. The fact they were there foretold matters of the utmost importance in the offing. The other times they had audiences with the general, it had been in front of his desk in his small office. There he had expressed curiosity, praise, criticism, and commentary replete with expletives in a roaring voice. Those sessions were experiences not to be forgotten.

Commander Thomas Carey, Lieutenant Commander Ernest Berringer, Lieutenant William Brannigan, Lieutenant (JG) Jim Cruiser, and Ensign Orlando Taylor maintained a nervous silence among themselves as they sat waiting for the Great Man to appear. The quintet of navy officers glanced at the large map of the OA to their direct front, noting that it was bare of markings and designations usually found on tactical charts. Whatever was coming up was brand-new and completely unexpected.

The door to the compartment opened and the familiar bellowing of Leroux's voice blasted into the interior like the detonation of an 81-millimeter mortar round. *"Keep your seats!"* He walked directly up to the front of the audience, grabbing a podium near the bulkhead. He dragged it to a convenient position that allowed him to face the five officers.

"Happy Thanksgiving," he said. "Nice to see you again." He opened a portfolio he had brought with him, perusing a document inside while continuing to speak. "By the way, that was a hell of a fine job by that guy Malachenko. The information he brought back from the little sojourn as well as his participation in the interrogation of those Russians started the boys in G-2 to filling in a hell of a lot of holes in their own files. I take it he has returned to you."

"Yes, sir," Brannigan said. "He returned late last night by the same chopper that hauled us over here. He came in with one of our wounded men who was returned to duty. So we are back to full strength."

"Good," Leroux said. Now he looked at them with a satisfied, almost smug expression. "Big stuff going down, yessiree-bob! We now know the truth about what was behind the rather puzzling order to not interfere with the Pashtuns' poppy harvest next year. It was not—I say again—*was not* because of a lack of funding for the Afghanistan police to control the activity. As a matter of fact, the enforcement detail had plenty of money. But a certain individual issued specific instructions to allow the crop to be grown and gathered without interference. That man was a government official by the name of Zaid Aburrani."

"Wait a minute!" Brannigan exclaimed. "That name is familiar."

"As well it should be," Leroux said. "You know him from your outfit's very first operation in Afghanistan. You were supposed to pick up a defector, as I recall."

"Yes, sir," Brannigan replied. "But the situation deteriorated rapidly once we were on the ground. This was mainly caused by the fact that the defector had been compromised and eliminated."

"A bad case of SNAFU," the general commented. "At any rate, this Aburrani was the special envoy who joined you after the defeat of the two warlords. He was supposed to be acting as a go-between for the Coalition Forces and the native peoples of the area. It is now known he was profiting a great deal from the opium trade. This fact popped up unexpectedly when the information provided by the two Russian defectors was combined with known intelligence by our intrepid intra-service staff. Those clever boys put two and two together and came with a solid irrefutable conclusion, i.e., Aburrani is in cahoots not only with that Russian crime syndicate in Tajikistan but also with the Taliban. The profits from the coming harvest were to go to only one source: the terrorists."

"What about Aburrani?" Berringer asked. "What's his status now?"

"Even as we speak, our friend Aburrani is in the hot seat," Leroux replied. "He had been named in a warrant issued by our government to the Afghanistan authorities. However, because of certain hypersensitive aspects of the case, the Afghans don't want to participate in the apprehension of the gentleman in question. However, they will make no overt response to his arrest by any Coalition Forces." He grinned. "That's somewhat of an understatement, as I'm sure you realize."

"Is that the only action going to be taken in regard to this incident?" Brannigan asked.

"No way," Leroux said with firm assurance. "I have been put in command of a two-pronged effort. The first thing we must do is pacify the hostile Pashtun tribesmen on the Pranistay Steppes."

Young Ensign Orlando Taylor sat up straighter with excitement. "What's the other prong, sir?"

"Oh, something right up the Brigands' alley," Leroux said. "How does an illegal attack to wipe out the Russian town in the Kangal Mountains of Tajikistan sound to you?"

"Most interesting," Orlando said.

"I'm sure it will be," Leroux said. He looked at Brannigan. "Give me a quick oral SITREP, Lieutenant."

"I have twenty-three SEALs under my command," Brannigan reported. "We are at full strength, including horses, well supplied with all requisitions filled at the moment. Our present resupply situation is good enough that we can bring in any additional necessities quickly. I also can muster a hundred and thirty fighting men of the Yousafzai Tribe and eighty-five from the Janoon Tribe. That gives me a total of—"

"Two hundred and thirty men," young Taylor interjected quickly. "The bad guys on the steppes have a total of three hundred and forty men belonging to four tribes."

Leroux actually gave the ensign a fond smile. "Ah, yes! There is nothing better than the keen participation of an eager young subaltern."

"Thank you, sir," Taylor said, pleased.

"Alright!" Leroux said. "Brannigan, I want you to organize your entire force of natives and SEALs, then produce an OPLAN to be submitted to me through Commander Carey. Your mission will be as I already stated, i.e., pacify the bad Pashtuns out on the steppes. I might add that you are authorized to use extreme prejudice in accomplishing that goal."

"What about that Russian town, sir?" Cruiser asked.

"That is a separate action and will not be undertaken until the Pranistay Steppes are a hundred percent contained," Leroux replied, pawing through his papers until he found the notes on Logovishchyeh. "Okay. The place you're talking about is called—" He studied the word in the document. "—shit! It's a long fucking name. There must be a Russki law that none of the words in their language are allowed to be under fourteen syllables. Anyhow! The place is occupied by approximately a hundred former Russian military convicts. When you're finished with the steppes, draw up an OPLAN to remove that thorn in our sides."

"I'll have a fine asset in Petty Officer Malachenko, sir," Brannigan said. "He knows the area well."

"Right," Leroux said. "You are now aware of what the preliminaries are, so don't waste time." He slammed the portfolio shut, saying, "I am inviting you to join me in a Thanksgiving feast aboard the *Combs* in a couple of hours."

Messieurs Brannigan, Cruiser, and Taylor declined with thanks.

Leroux understood where they were coming from. "It would be a hard thing to do knowing your men were sitting out there in the cold chomping on MREs while you're chowing down on a traditional meal, huh? Well, I have good news for you officers *and* your guys. A mess crew with thermal cans of turkey, dressing, mashed potatoes, gravy, and the whole nine yards will accompany you on the chopper back to your OA. Happy Thanksgiving!"

"We thank the general," Brannigan said gratefully.

"As well you should," Leroux said. "The chopper and chow are waiting for you on that flat area on the back of the ship."

"That's the aft end of the main deck, sir," Ensign Orlando Taylor informed him. "It's called the fantail."

"I almost give a shit," Leroux growled.

SEALs BIVOUAC
1700 HOURS

THE thermal mess cans were empty. The Brigands, along with three chopper crewmen and the mess cooks, had just consumed the last of the pumpkin pie, completely depleting the entire amount of chow brought in for the holiday. The cooks were packing up with the help from a quartet of SEALs, as the festivities ground down to a satisfactory conclusion.

"The only thing missing was a football game to watch before and after chow," Bruno Puglisi remarked.

Brannigan was standing off to the side with Dirk Wallenger and his cameraman, Eddie Krafton, watching the men pack up. The Skipper turned his attention to the newsmen. "By the way, before it slips my mind, I wanted to tell you that I stumbled across an interesting human interest story over at Shelor Field while I was gone. I even got a clearance for you to talk to the individual concerned."

"A human interest story, huh?" Wallenger remarked. "We could use something, Bill. Frankly, there hasn't been a hell of a lot of interesting things going on around here."

"And there won't be," Brannigan said. "We're due for a long quiet time here in the OA."

Eddie was interested in the story. "What did you dig up for us?"

"There's the weird kid over there by the name of Randy Tooley," Brannigan said. "He's the one who is the mover and shaker for the site's activities."

"I remember him," Wallenger said, grinning. "He doesn't like to wear a uniform, and he drives around in a dune buggy, right?"

"Right," Brannigan said. "Colonel Watkins, his CO, said he would be willing to be interviewed too. The kid is an eccentric thrown straight into in the middle of military operations and he's reputed to be the most efficient American serviceman in the Middle East. And he's funny as hell too. He has a lot of amusing anecdotes as well as some strange and colorful opinions he's not shy about expressing."

Eddie was enthusiastic. "That would make a great story, Dirk!"

"Hey, it sure would," Wallenger agreed

"You can hitch a ride on this chopper," Brannigan said. "They can drop you off, then you can come back with the next resupply when you've got your feature."

"Jesus!" Wallenger said. "We better pack our stuff. That chopper looks like it'll be ready to go pretty soon."

"I'll make sure they wait for you," Brannigan said.

Within fifteen minutes, the two journalists were back with bag and baggage, climbing onto the chopper that already had its rotors turning. The pilot increased the rpm until the aircraft rose slowly, turning south toward Shelor Field. Brannigan, with his hands in his pockets, calmly watched the Super Stallion disappear in the distance. When it was no more than a black dot in the sky, he turned toward the headquarters hootch.

"Senior Chief! Fall the detachment in! I have an announcement to make."

THE SKIPPER'S HOOTCH
2100 HOURS

THE sides of the shelter were rolled up to allow the smoke from the small fire in the interior to find its way out. Unfortunately it meandered around a bit before exiting, getting into everyone's faces and eyes.

Lieutenant Bill Brannigan supervised the get-together that consisted of Jim Cruiser, Orlando Taylor, and Chinar, the interpreter. The latter had returned earlier after delivering Emal, the Swati boy who had survived the massacre of his village, to a Janoon family who wanted to adopt him. They had lost a son his age to sickness the previous year. Emal, who needed the affection and care the SEALs could not provide for him, had been happy to return to a normal Pashtun family life.

"Now," Brannigan said. "The mission is to pacify the hostiles among the Pashtuns here on the steppes. The main thing I want everyone to keep in mind is that we must avoid civilian casualties if at all possible."

Cruiser was not optimistic. "Attacking villages will make that goal unattainable, sir. You have to keep in mind that there are seven of them."

"I'm afraid you're right," Brannigan said. He spoke to Chinar. "Do you have any suggestions regarding the problem?"

"Yes, sir," the young Pashtun said. "I think if we started with the Mahsuds and concentrated all efforts on them we could keep down the deaths of many women and children while we bring them under our control."

"Good suggestion," Brannigan said. "We could do such things as stop their hunting parties and search them. That will cause some unease in their lives. And then turn our attention on their smallest village."

"Yes, sir!" Chinar said. "That hamlet has only fifty fighting men."

"Alright then," Brannigan said. "We'll go there and search for weapons and contraband. We can tear things up and throw stuff around like a bunch of cops going through a crack house."

"I also suggest that you bring along some Yousafzais and Janoons and let them rough up the men," Chinar said. "It will cause the Mahsud males great embarrassment and humiliation."

"Yes, sir," Orlando Taylor said. "And take prisoners for questioning. Hold them until the rest of the Mahsuds come roaring out looking for a fight. They'll be in the open away from the women and kids."

Brannigan nodded his head. "Let's see. That will give us a good advantage since we will outnumber the tribe. But we have to give them a good ass-kicking before the other clans rally to their side. When the Mahsuds ask for *nonwatai*, the others will think twice before resisting us."

Chinar cautioned him saying, "It will not be that easy, sir. There will be a battle or two—maybe three or four—before the others give up."

"Yeah," Brannigan remarked. "And we've also got Murphy's Law to contend with."

LOGOVISHCHYEH SUROV'S HOUSE

THE relationship between the Pashtun girls in Valentin Danielovich Surov's household had been one of pure hell for Gabina and Zainba, who had lived there with Yarkov. Surov's woman Aghala bullied the two unmercifully. She did not work herself, bossing them through all the chores, even creating make-work tasks to add to their misery.

Gabina and Zainba dared not protest to Surov for fear he would become annoyed with them for disrespecting Aghala. If that happened, there existed a very real chance that he might throw them out of the house, leaving them homeless. That would put them in a precarious position. They could not return to their villages since they would suffer honor killings at the hands of their male relatives for fornicating with infidels. In order to save their lives they would have to offer sexual favors to the Russians in exchange for some crusts of bread and shelter. If they were very lucky, one of the men might decide to take one or both of them as his women. But the chance of that happening was very small.

Then an unexpected development occurred. Zainba was eighteen years old and growing more attractive as she matured. When Surov moved into the house he slept with both her and Gabina between times with Aghala. This, of course, had fueled Aghala's fury, and she was twice as mean to them after each episode. Then Surov began ignoring the fifteen-year-old Gabina, and within a few days also quit sleeping with Aghala. From then on he doted on Zainba with a special fondness. At that point, Zainba realized he had become infatuated with her, and her female instincts kicked in. Although not trained in seduction or the use of feminine wiles, the intelligent girl instinctively began using her beauty to advantage, going out of her way to pleasure him during sex.

Eventually, Aghala began to sense a marked weakening in her position in the household. She made some clumsy attempts to win back Surov's affections, but the fifteen-year-old didn't have the looks or experience to get the job done. She reacted to this embarrassing situation by turning her anger completely on Zainba while pretty much ignoring Gabina. One day, while Surov was gone, she flew into a jealous rage and punched Zainba in the face several times. Zainba did not resist, allowing the younger girl to leave some marks on her features.

When Surov returned home that evening, Zainba feigned great pain and injury. When Surov demanded to know what had happened, it was Gabina who told on Aghala. Surov responded by giving Aghala a good beating while bellowing at her for being mean to Zainba. Then he made the girl take all her belongings out of his bedroom, and he moved Zainba in.

The female hierarchy was turned upside down.

Now it was Aghala's turn to get the worst of the deal. Zainba was loyal to Gabina, considering her no less than a sister. From that point on the two ruled the roost. It was they who sat around while Aghala fetched and carried, doing all the work under the threat that if she complained, Zainba would ask Surov to throw her out of the house.

While all this turmoil was going on in his home, Surov was busy consolidating his hold over the other Russians. He also worked with Aleksander Akloschenko and Pavel Marvesky in planning an attack on the uncooperative Pashtuns down on the Pranistay Steppes. Akloschenko had emphasized that they must be able to get the entire poppy harvest grown in the flatlands in order to deal with the Taliban. Any rebellious tribe might easily plead *nonwatai* to the terrorist group and strike their own deal.

CHAPTER 21

NADER Abiska, using the code name Ilyas, was a supervisor-at-large for the CIA in Afghanistan. He operated out of a gunsmithy in the small town of Baghlan, conducting most of his business from his small office as contacts stopped by to pass on information, receive instructions, or enjoy a safe place to rest and recuperate after a harrowing mission. Abiska's slight pudginess belied his excellent physical fitness. He happened to be one of those individuals with a genetic propensity toward body fat. But beneath that soft layer of flesh was a finely tuned muscularity that provided strength, suppleness, and quickness to his physical actions.

The bearded man with dark skin had emigrated from Afghanistan to America with his parents at the age of thirteen. Brilliant in mind and restless in spirit, he was an excellent scholar, earning an MBA at the Harvard School of Business at the age of twenty. But instead of accepting a position with the several prestigious firms who wished to employ him, Abiska's yen for adventure brought him into the service of the Central Intelligence Agency. His ethnic background and language skills got him assigned to the Afghanistan desk in Washington. After a bit more than a year he grew bored with the paperwork aspects of the job and requested a transfer to clandestine operations in the field.

One of Abiska's best operatives was an athletic, dignified individual by the name of Ahmed Bariyan. He was the scion of a wealthy Pakistani family, educated in public schools in Great Britain in the classics, rugby football, and pub crawling. This latter activity was in direct disobedience to his Islamic upbringing, and his efforts to end the habit after graduation were for naught. Bariyan really liked to party hearty. Rather than return to Pakistan, the young man went to the United States, where he found employment on the faculty of Georgetown University as a professor of literature. After three years of teaching, Bariyan had developed a genuine love for the USA, eventually becoming a citizen. He continued imbibing the forbidden fruits of alcohol, pursued young women successfully and often, yet managed to remain a bachelor. He also played on a local rugby team as a star winger, a position similar to a running back in American football. An American teammate who had adapted well to the game recognized something special in the Pakistani, sensing some great potential in him that would serve well in the black game of espionage and spying. This employee of the CIA subtly and skillfully recruited this superb athlete into the intelligence organization.

It was Ahmed Bariyan who, under the code name Ishaq, acted as the asset for Brannigan's Brigands on their first mission as a unit. Bariyan, out in the cold in the Afghan hinterlands, had recruited a defector who could provide the West with a great deal of useful information in the War on Terror, and he needed help getting the guy out. Brannigan and his Brigands were chosen to go into the OA and extract the man, but he had been compromised and tortured to death by the local warlord before the SEALs even left the States. This led to Wild Bill Brannigan et al. having to fight their way through hostile territory almost immediately after the insertion.

0200 HOURS

NADER Abiska and Ahmed Bariyan, with the former in the driver's seat, sat in a Honda Accord in a grove of almond trees. They were close enough to the road to have a good view of the immediate area, but far enough back to remain out of sight. The half dozen spike strips they had put out on the dirt highway were concealed by a covering of earth. The vicious sharp points were exposed, silent and waiting like the two men who had positioned the devices where they would do the most good.

"Well, here we are then," Bariyan said in the upper-class British accent he had never lost.

"Yep," Abiska agreed. "And there won't be anyone else coming down this lonely road except our quarry."

Bariyan chuckled. "There'll not be a shred of rubber left on the wheels after the car rolls over those spikes. We shall bring our quarry to a complete stop within a quarter of a mile."

"This night's operation is not too surprising, is it?" Abiska stated as a rhetorical question. His manner of speech was pure American New England, molded by his exposure to the elite of that part of the country.

"Bound to happen," Bariyan said. "I just wonder what took them so long to act. Good God! We exposed the rotter almost two years ago."

"That's easily explained by an old cliché," Abiska remarked. "They wanted to give him enough rope to hang himself."

"I don't know about that," Bariyan said. "I'm of the opinion that something special has come up rather unexpectedly, what? And our target for this lovely evening will serve well in this particular instance."

"Could be," Abiska replied with a shrug. He checked his watch. "Ah, he's due any time now."

"And he's a punctual chap."

"Sure," Abiska answered. "He keeps regular habits and hours. The guy is one government official that doesn't have to worry about terrorists."

"Bloody right," Bariyan said. "That's the advantage of being in bed with the bastards, hey?"

"Too bad about his driver though," Abiska remarked. "I guess we'll have to chalk him up as collateral damage. He's not going to get much protection in that car. You had the correct information on the vehicle, right?"

"Believe it or not, it's one he's been using for the past eighteen months," Bariyan remarked. "It's not armored. Not even bulletproof glass."

"I would wager that you even know the license number."

"Sure. Would you care for me to recite it?"

Abiska laughed, then they fell into silence, relaxed but alert. Abiska had his favorite Beretta 9-millimeter automatic with him, while Bariyan was more formidably armed. His weapon for the evening's activities was a Steyr AUG assault rifle configured as a carbine. The magazine was filled with forty-two 5.56-millimeter armor-piercing rounds.

A couple of minutes eased by, then the sound of an approaching vehicle could be discerned, rapidly growing louder. This pleased the two CIA men. The faster it passed over the spikes, the quicker it would come to a nearly uncontrollable stop.

A series of pops, muffled by the sound of the car's engine, was followed by the flapping of shredded rubber. The auto swerved wildly past, and Abiska gunned the engine to rush out of the grove onto the road. He headed straight for the target that was now moving at somewhere around forty-five kilometers an hour. He easily caught up with it, moving to the left and pulling up even. The two men inside had expressions of helpless fright on their faces that showed in the dial lights of the vehicle.

Bariyan pointed the assault rifle at the driver's window and pulled the trigger. The weapon's selector was on full automatic and half the magazine's capacity was emptied, the rounds crashing through the glass to pulverize the man's body. The car swung to one side, then stopped as the engine quit.

Now Abiska hit the brakes, and Bariyan was out on the road, rushing to the car. *"Debandi!"* he yelled in Pashto. The man inside made no moves, so Bariyan reached through the shattered window and hit the button to pop the locks. He pulled the rear door opened, once more commanding, *"Debandi!"*

The man inside slowly and fearfully emerged, his hands in the air. Now Bariyan grabbed him, frog marching the guy to the other vehicle. The prisoner protested, "You must have the wrong man! I have friends in the Taliban!" Bariyan made no reply as they both got in the back. Then Abiska once more hit the accelerator, driving away from the scene of the kidnapping.

Zaid Aburrani was in custody.

SEALs BIVOUAC
0900 HOURS

THE C-130 was expected due to a radio alert transmitted to the Brigands from Shelor Field Operations. There had been no request for resupply, but it wasn't unusual for unexpected materiel or personnel to be dispatched into a situation that had strong probabilities of combat operations. It could be extra ammunition, chow, reinforcements, or even Commanders Tom Carey and Ernest Berringer coming in with some additional information or perhaps a briefing for a new operation.

When the distant drone of the four T56 turboprop engines could be picked up by the Brigands' dirty ears, all activity came to a halt. The arrival of a plane always meant there would be some tasks to attend to, and was a welcome break in the routine of the camp. Even the horses on the picket lines turned their heads toward the sound. The animals were well tuned in on the happenings and habits of their human companions, and knew the arrival of one of the noisy flying machines caused great excitement. Puglisi's Ralph snorted and stomped his hooves a bit, nervous about the airplane. He was not fond of flying.

The approaching aircraft was a black dot in the sky, closing in fast as the apparition morphed into that of a proper aircraft with wings. Lieutenant Bill Brannigan and Senior Chief Buford Dawkins had walked from the hootches out to the edge of the LZ to wait for the landing. It was cold and both men huddled into their parkas as they silently observed the visitor drawing closer.

"What the hell?" Brannigan exclaimed. He reached for the leather case on his pistol belt and withdrew the binoculars. He focused in on the aircraft, saying, "That's not military."

Dawkins snorted a chuckle. "What is it? United Airlines?"

"Take a look, Senior Chief," the Skipper said, handing over the field glasses.

Dawkins studied the sight, then said. "The damn thing is white. I think . . . yeah! I can see the letters now. It's a UN aircraft."

"Oh, brother!" Brannigan said. "What in the hell do they want?"

"I can't figure that out, sir," Dawkins said. "If they're thinking on working with the Pashtuns, they're gonna be shit out of luck. I'll bet they ain't got permission to come here." He was thoughtful for a moment. "Wait a minute! Gomez said they had clearance from Shelor Field Operations. How can that be?"

"I'll tell you how," Brannigan said. "This operation is classified. There's no way they can be kept out without tipping our hands."

Now the aforementioned Petty Officer Frank Gomez trotted up with a page ripped from his message pad. He handed it to Brannigan. "I just got this, sir. The commo center at Shelor ain't prioritizing their transmissions right today."

Brannigan quickly scanned the missive. "It's a good thing we got this, even if it was out of sequence. It tells me a UN mission is coming in and we are to keep them close to us and not allow contact with the Pashtuns. We're to tell them there's a blood feud going on and it's too dangerous right now. They are definitely not to go roaming around the Pranistay Steppes." He turned to the RTO. "Gomez, you go to each section commander and team leader. Give them that cover story and have 'em pass the word to their men ASAP. You tell Doc Bradley yourself."

"Aye, sir!"

At the moment Gomez ran off, the big UN plane touched down, its engine reversed as the pilot stood on the brakes to bring it to a halt. Rather than shut down one engine for unloading like most military planes, both power plants were cut, creating a dead silence over the area that had been engulfed by the roars of the turboprop quartet. The rear ramp immediately whined and began to lower. When it hit the ground, a familiar figure appeared. Dr. Pierre Couchier, the Belgian chief surgeon and head of the mission, looked out, then spotted Brannigan and Dawkins. He actually smiled, leaping off the ramp and walking rapidly over to the two SEALs with his hand outstretched.

Brannigan shook with him. "I'm glad to see you're not still angry with me, Dr. Couchier."

"Ah!" Couchier exclaimed. "*Mon cher lieutenant vaisseau,* I realize how unfair I was to hold you in total blame for the complete and utter destruction of my camp near the Iranian border. It was an honest mistake on your part."

Brannigan growled in his throat. "If you recall, Doctor, it turned out that the number of enemy were three times what you told me they were. That caused me to make a tactical error in my defenses."

"We are even, *Monsieur le Lieutenant* Brannigan," Couchier insisted. "I made a mistake in counting and you made one in your tactics, no?"

"No! Goddamn it! No!"

"Mmf!" Couchier said with a frown. "Well, *laisse tomber!*" He looked around. "Where is the best place for me to go to set up my operations, eh?"

"Your best place is right here," Brannigan said sternly. "It is very dangerous out on the Pranistay Steppes."

"Mmf!" the Belgian said again. "I am not afraid of things

dangereux! Nor are any of my people. We have a job to do and we will do it, *comprendez*?"

"There is a clan feud going on out there," Brannigan said. "I am working hard to bring peace to the area. Until I do, you will have to set up your operations right here."

"I insist in going wherever I might better serve the people who dwell on the steppes."

Brannigan gave the doctor a no-nonsense glare that spoke like thunder in the sky in spite of the silence.

Couchier shrugged. "Ah! *Très bien, monsieur le lieutenant*." He pointed over to an open, flat area. "*Là*—there?"

"That would be fine, Doctor," Brannigan said.

At that same instant, three females came out of the plane. The SEALs knew them from previous visits to the mission. They waved and hollered at the attractive young women. Irena Poczinska, a Polish X-ray technician; Josefina Vargas, an RN from Spain; and the German dietician, Ericka München, smiled back at the enthusiastic greetings. There was sensual quality about the women despite the rather baggy white coveralls they wore, and now their smiles turned to delighted laughter as they began to remember and recognize familiar faces among the Brigands.

The trio of females, like Dr. Couchier and the rest of the mission, were members of the United Nations Relief and Education Organization, or UNREO. They were part of a group of people that lived the real meaning of the United Nations. Dr. Couchier and his crew were not to be numbered among the embezzling, dishonest executives, the hypocritical senior ambassadors from nations led by despots, nor the American-baiting Third World cretins of the general assembly of that organization.

The UNREO mission, so splintered off from the main organization that no one was sure who they really belonged to, were the frontline soldiers of true humanity. They served in hellholes full of danger, deprivation, sickness, poverty, and hopelessness. Those people, like the three young women exchanging greetings with the SEALs, truly wanted to help humankind, and did so with shortages of funds while enduring harassment from criminal elements that were most times under the sponsorship of the national governments where the work was being done.

Couchier, knowing he would get nowhere arguing with the local military authority, left Brannigan to get his people to work unloading the plane. A good number of enthusiastic off-duty Brigands joined them in the job.

CHAPTER 22

THE conscious mind of Zaid Aburrani reeled in terror, the awful fear making his body shake as much as did the coldness of his steel surroundings. The utterly frightened man was clothed only in his undershirt, boxer shorts, and socks as he sat in darkness so complete the only thing he could see were floaters dancing around in front of his eyes. The man pressed up against a wall in an instinctive protective posture to draw away from the source of whatever danger he faced. The prisoner wasn't sure where he was, not even the location of the entrance to the mysterious chamber he had been cast into. If he had to guess, Aburrani would say it was a metal box. He was too frightened to move enough to pace the interior to determine the length and width, or reach upward in an attempt to find the height.

His mind had been clouded for an undeterminable amount of time, but seemed to be recovering from the confusion. His thoughts abruptly turned away from his present predicament to the incident that had led to his incarceration. It was a sudden remembrance that erupted through his mental turmoil, bringing back the sharp sounds and images of the strange car pulling alongside his own fishtailing vehicle, then the eruption of shooting, the cracking and breaking of the glass, and the driver's head exploding as he was flung across the front seat. Only the safety belt saved the poor man from being slammed against the opposite door.

Aburrani's mental state began to settle a bit now, and it was strange that he would impulsively recall the chauffeur that night was not his regular man. This was the brother of Kaid, who usually drove him; the brother had taken his place because Kaid wished to attend a program at his youngest son's school. The boy was going to play a piece on the piano. It suddenly occurred to Aburrani that Kaid's conscience would nag at him for the rest of his life because his brother had died in his place.

What tragic irony.

But irony is not supposed to be tragic, Aburrani thought. *Irony can be amusing, frustrating, or even contemptible if it smacks of stupidity or ignorance. But it should never be tragic.* The word "unfortunate" would normally fit in those circumstances, but this had been an undeniable tragedy.

A close association with violence was not a part of Aburrani's existence. He had read about it and heard about it, but he had never actually witnessed violence in his life. He had seen the result of it, of course; what person in Afghanistan had not? Dead and mangled corpses or maimed living people were common sights following bombing incidents, but he always felt distanced from such misfortunes as if he weren't at all concerned. No matter the bloodshed or suffering of the victims, he moved on through his life disconnected and remote from brutal behavior.

But now he had an intimate relationship with carnage after the ambush of his automobile. In a few stunning seconds he had been hurled into that abyss of violence that he had managed to avoid for so many years. As his mind continued clearing, he became aware of a slight discomfort in his right deltoid muscle. It was a sensation not unlike that experienced after getting a vaccination. He rubbed a hand over the sore spot on his shoulder. It was a sure sign he had been drugged sometime in the mishmash of confusion.

A door to his direct front suddenly opened, letting in a flash of brilliant light. Aburrani blinked against the brilliance as the figure of a man entered the chamber. The stranger knelt down and spoke in a concerned tone. "My dear Mr. Aburrani! I am so distressed to find you in this condition. I had no idea of your predicament until a short time ago."

Now another man came in, and Aburrani could make out he wore a camouflage-pattern uniform. He had a bundle of clothes of some sort that he thrust at the prisoner. Aburrani took them and held them close.

"Please get dressed," the first stranger said. "I must apologize that I cannot find your clothing, but I am sure it will be located eventually." He reached down and helped Aburrani to his feet.

Aburrani discovered he had been handed a pair of coveralls and some sort of slippers. As he dressed, he realized the stranger had been speaking to him in American English. It gave him a sense of well-being, as did the apologies he had just received. There is the explanation of this strangeness. A mistake! A colossal stupid mistake! They had obviously gotten the wrong man.

The clothing was much too large for him and it was difficult to walk in the slippers as he was gently led by the arm out into a corridor. The hallway was constructed of steel similar to the room he was taken from. He now fully realized it was a cell, and he was in a prison of some sort.

"Where am I?" Aburrani asked.

"I am afraid I am not at liberty to reveal that to you at this time," the stranger said as they walked down the corridor to a far door.

The man who had brought the clothing hurried ahead and opened the steel portal to allow them to enter a small room with a staircase. He stayed behind as Aburrani and his escort ascended the steps to the floor above. It was similar to the lower portion of the building, with a series of cell doors along the length of the hallway. They went halfway down to a door and the stranger opened it. When Aburrani obediently stepped inside, he saw that it was a paneled room with a couple of padded leather chairs that appeared to be most comfortable. A small table holding a coffee machine, cups, and a bowl of pastries was off in one corner. All these amounted to very good signs indeed.

Another feature of the place of which he was totally unaware was a hidden microphone that led to a recorder in another room.

"Sit down, Mr. Aburrani," the stranger said. "My name is Mr. Leighton."

"How do you do," Aburrani said, settling onto a chair.

"Can I get you a cup of coffee?" Leighton asked. "And perhaps a roll."

"Just a cup of coffee, thank you."

Leighton served them both, and then also sat down. After taking a sip of from his cup, he remarked, "You are a surprise visitor here."

"That unpleasant condition is mutual, Mr., er, Mr. Leighton," Aburrani said. "And I would like to be returned to where I belong. That, sir, is my office in Kabul."

"I hope that can eventually be done for you," Leighton said. "However, I do have some rather specific instructions regarding your stay here."

"Again, I ask you, where am I?" Aburrani said, becoming angry. Leighton's remarks made it appear as if his capture was planned after all. "I *demand* to know not only where I am, but the meaning behind the attack on me and the murder of my driver. What idiotic fool machinated that outrage?"

"You will learn all in due time, sir," Leighton said. "One of the subjects I have been charged with discussing with you is your ties to the Taliban."

"What an outright absurdity, sir!" Aburrani exclaimed. "And I resent it. I am in the employ of the government of Afghanistan."

"Mmm," Leighton mused. "You are not making a very good start, Mr. Aburrani. You see, we are well aware of your relationship with that particular terrorist organization, as well as your association with the smuggling of opium poppy gum out of Afghanistan to international criminals. May I suggest that you drop all pretenses and falsehoods and get down to the facts of the matter? It will save us both a lot of bother and unpleasantness that I am sure you wish to avoid as much as I."

"I deny your preposterous allegations!" Aburrani snapped.

"I shall ignore that last statement and go to work," Leighton said. In truth, just about everything about Aburrani's past was already known and documented. The purpose of this interrogation was to confirm the intelligence known, as well as get some of the finer details of the Afghan's dealings. "We will forget the Taliban for the time being. What I would like to discuss with you, for the moment, is your relationship with certain criminal elements in Tajikistan. Names, please."

Aburrani clammed up.

"You are not going to get anywhere with this bad attitude, Mr. Aburrani," Leighton said. "When I said I was distressed at finding you in your underwear in that cold cell, I was telling the truth. I thought it totally inappropriate for a man of your intellect and education. That is something that is reserved for those rough fellows that are dragged in from the battle areas. You are not a soldier, Mr. Aburrani. From your dossier, I would assume you do not even like soldiers very much."

Aburrani continued his silence.

Leighton got to his feet and went to the coffeepot. He poured himself another cup, then brought the container over and warmed up Aburrani's drink. After returning to his seat, he gave the prisoner a studied gaze. He took a long, slow breath, then said, "I can guarantee you a good amount of creature comforts, sir. Decent food, acceptable accommodations, and courteous treatment from the prison staff. Are you aware of the alternatives?"

Still Aburrani chose not to reply.

Leighton leaned back in his chair and began speaking slowly and methodically. "Well, let us see . . . you will be stripped completely naked . . . a cold cell with a brilliant light permanently illuminating your miserable abode . . . surly and brutal guards . . . awful food served irregularly and carelessly . . . a single bucket for urination and defecation that will be taken away and replaced only occasionally . . . not allowed to sleep . . . remain standing at all times . . . vicious and long periods of questioning . . . encouragement to respond truthfully with beatings . . . electric cattle prods inserted into your rectum . . . the unpleasant prospects of—"

"Which do you wish me to speak of first?"

"A brief history of your opium poppy deals would make an excellent start, Mr. Aburrani."

"I began with a warlord by the name of Ayyub Durtami," Aburrani said in a low voice. "I had accepted some bribes from foreign interests to make it easy for him to grow and harvest the opium plants. The arrangement was quite profitable."

"You say you 'began' with this fellow," Leighton said. "Was that relationship broken off?"

"Yes. Durtami was defeated during some activity in which some American Navy SEALs were supposed to bring out a defector from his compound. The man had been tortured to death before the Americans arrived and Durtami was foolish enough to try to keep them from leaving his domain."

"I take it the SEALs got away."

"More than that," Aburrani said. "They wiped him out and sent him and his surviving people fleeing. I know this for a fact because I was present in the area at the time as a representative of the Afghan government." He wiped away the perspiration that had begun to form on his face. "It is the truth. The name of the SEAL commander was Lieutenant Brannigan. William Brannigan."

"Alright," Leighton said. "Then what did you do?"

"Well, Durtami fled to the fiefdom of his brother-in-law, Hassan Khamami, who was an even stronger warlord,"

Aburrani continued. "Khamami made an attempt to wipe out the SEALs, and almost did it." His face assumed an expression of remorse and regret. "But he failed. However, I used my influence to keep Khamami from being completely destroyed and was able to protect his harvest after the Americans left. However, production was down."

"So your profits fell, hey?" Leighton remarked. "What actions did you take?"

"I was able to make arrangements through the Iranian Embassy to send the gum and powder through their country to Turkey," Aburrani said. "I had certain contacts in the Afghan Army to provide transportation. But—" He paused and sighed. "Once again that officer Brannigan showed up and not only brought my operations to a halt, but evidently foiled Iranian strategic goals for creating a large mujahideen force. They were using their share of the money to that end."

"Is that when you turned to the Taliban?"

"Yes," Aburrani admitted. "They had been getting money from Saudi Arabia to rebuild after their setbacks. My problem was that the most efficient and productive opium harvesting was being done on the Pranistay Steppes by the warlord of the Yousafzai Tribe. He was a fellow named Awalmir. But he refused to deal with me because of the Taliban. He hates them for the mistreatment they inflicted on his people after the Soviets had been driven out of Afghanistan."

"I see," Leighton said. "And who did you turn to at that point?"

"The Russian crime syndicate in Tajikistan," Aburrani said. "They are headquartered in the city of Khorugh near the Kangal Mountains."

"And the headman's name?"

"Aleksander Akloschenko," Aburrani answered.

"What did you want him to do for you?"

"To supervise the opium production on the Pranistay Steppes," Aburrani explained. "He was to gain control over the tribes and buy the crops for sale. I was, in fact, acting as an agent for both him and the Taliban."

"I see," Leighton said. "And what was this Akloschenko's attitude toward the Taliban?"

"He had no objection that they were involved," he replied with a shrug. "He would get his full cut."

"As I understand it, the Russian crime boss was going to make deals with the Pashtuns without you being outwardly involved."

"That is correct," Aburrani said.

"What methods was he going to use to form agreements with the tribes?"

Aburrani smiled slightly. "Capitalism, sir. Pure and simple. He was going to offer them a price one and a half times greater than what Awalmir of the Yousafzai had been paying."

"Did they go for it?"

"Unfortunately, not all," Aburrani said. "We did not take into consideration the plethora of blood feuds among the tribes. He was only able to get agreements from four of the seven clans."

"That's a majority, isn't it?"

"That was not good enough," Aburrani said. "The Taliban insisted that all the Pashtun people be involved in the deal. It would increase their prestige and influence among the native peoples."

"Where did that leave you?"

"I had to insist that Akloschenko use force against those who were less cooperative," Aburrani said.

"Did he have enough men to do that?"

"There were some renegade ex-convicts from the Soviet Army living in the Kangal Mountains that looked down on the Pranistay Steppes," Aburrani said. "They were led by a fellow named Yarkov, but Akloschenko did not care for him. He ran Yarkov off and replaced him with a former officer named Valentin Surov."

"All very interesting, Mr. Aburrani," Leighton said. He almost chuckled as he wondered if Aburrani was aware that Lieutenant Wild Bill Brannigan and his Brigands were also out there on the Pranistay Steppes. He cleared his throat to maintain his composure. "Ahem! What is the present situation regarding the Russians, the Pashtuns, and the poppy harvest?"

"The Russians are going to gather the Pashtuns who are

on their side," Aburrani said. "Then, as a group, they will attack the tribes who are holding out."

Leighton showed no emotion other than clenching his teeth. "Really? And when is this supposed to happen?"

"Any day now," Aburrani answered. He held out his cup. "May I have some more coffee, please?"

CHAPTER 23

THE Russian people have been known for centuries as being the quintessential stoics of the human race. They have endured the relentless, killing cold of their winters since time immemorial, tolerated the cruelties of despotic governments for countless generations, borne unspeakable periods of famine, bent under the rapine and ravages of foreign invaders, gone through the privations of smothering poverty, and suffered through imprisonment in dreadful Siberian labor camps. All this without outward complaints or protests, yet every once in a while, this dispassion erupts into the violence of striking out blindly and furiously in brief spasms of senseless fury in direct contrast to their compliant nature. This can be either to strike back at oppressors, or to inflict bloody misery on some other poor schmucks.

Such was the latter case on this frigid early morning in the flatlands of northeast Afghanistan. Eighty of Logovishchyeh's population of ex-convict soldiers rode through the whipping winds under the leadership of Valentin Surov as they headed for a rendezvous with a half hundred mujahideen of the Pashtun Mahsud tribe.

The journey had begun five hours previously with a ride down to the town of Dolirod, then a quick turn up Highway Panj to a spot where the foothills of the Kangal Mountains offered access to the Pranistay Steppes. The Russians went by this longer route because they were unaware of the more convenient way discovered by the SEAL Andy Malachenko when he was in their midst as an undercover agent.

Now, with the rising of the sun hours away, Surov's map reading skills had brought the group to the spot where the fifty Mahsuds waited for them. The Pashtuns, with near the physical and spiritual endurance of the Russians, paid scant attention to the cold temperatures as they stood with their horses in the confines of a large stand of boulders not far from the edge of the foothills. The war leader Dagar was squatting beside his mount, holding the reins lightly in his calloused fingers as the Russians approached. He watched them, seemingly with disinterest, as they drew closer. Even when they reined in their horses, the Pashtun made no overt gesture of greeting. Surov swung out of his saddle and walked up to the man. Only then did Dagar stand up. He sniffed a bit and rubbed his nose, then said, *"Pe khayr raghle."*

"Khayr ose," Surov replied. "Are you and your men ready?"

"Ho," Dagar replied. "I sent scouts out earlier, and they have returned. All is quiet at the village."

"Does it appear there are visitors there?" Surov asked.

Dagar shook his head. "There are no extra people. The only Yousafzai are those that dwell at the location."

"This should be done as rapidly as possible," Surov said in his crude but effective Pashto. "Because of the isolation we do not have to worry about noise. When we are a hundred meters away, we will all charge straight through the village and go out the other side for the first part of the attack."

"We do not know what a hundred meters looks like," Dagar said.

"Then tell your mujahideen to watch us," Surov suggested. "Do what we do when we do it. After the first charge, we will make another. Then I will direct the fight as the situation dictates. *Pohezhe?*"

Dagar nodded. *"Pohezham."*

With the basic plan taken care of, both turned to get their men onto horseback. With that done, the Russians went off at a trot with the Pashtuns following, spreading out along both sides at the rear of the formation.

THE village was the smallest of the Yousafzai tribe. As such it could muster no more than a couple of dozen fighting men, but it was part of a perceptive clan organization. It was more than lusty married couples that made their tribal family groups the most numerous of all the Pashtuns on the Pranistay Steppes. In the many battles in which they had participated over their eons of existence, their cunning instincts had kept their casualty rates down in campaigns that were nearly all victorious. It was because of those strong instincts for survival that they had adjusted their security routines to meet what seemed to be a changing situation in the locality.

These Yousafzais still used preteen boys for lookouts on the top of houses, but because of the unsettled conditions of late, tribal riflemen with AK-47s and bandoleers of ammunition had stationed themselves in depressions, behind rocky outcrops, and took advantage of other available cover around the hamlet on a twenty-four/seven basis. Their warlord, Awalmir, had paid a personal visit to the location a couple of weeks previously to satisfy himself that his kinsmen were taking the extra precautions that he had insisted on.

One of the adult guards on duty that night was an old fighter by the name of Reshteen. He had just turned thirty when the Russians invaded Afghanistan, and he had been among the first to offer resistance. He hated Russians more than he loved his own children, and the thought of any showing up to do harm to his home village was enough to put fire in the blood of the man who was now well into his fifties. His *pukhoor* was drawn tight around his body as he lay behind a rock a meter wide and half again as tall. He had the right side of the serape-like garment loose enough that he could easily bring his assault rifle to bear on any potential target. He had pulled the *puhtee* down to cover one ear for warmth. He alternated the arrangement from left to right every twenty or thirty minutes, so that his hearing would not be impeded.

Reshteen heard the clack that he instantly recognized as the strike of a horse's hoof against a rock. It was followed by a sudden influx of the noise, and he emitted a whistle to alert the others around the village. He grinned when he realized his warning had been sounded simultaneously by the others. That meant everyone on guard duty had heard the disturbance. Now he raised the sides of the *puhtee* so that both ears were unimpeded. Within a few moments, he could determine that the raiders were to his direct front. He would be the first they would come into contact with.

One of the best advantages a fighter can have during combat at night is to be low to the ground and looking upward into the lighter area of the sky. Reshteen enjoyed this benefit as the first row of horsemen came into view. He knew better than to try to use the sights in the darkness, so he raised his head to peer directly over the barrel of the rifle at the enemy. Two quick squeezes on the trigger sent nearly a dozen of the 7.62-millimeter slugs flying in a close-packed swarm at the attackers. One man was knocked off his horse and another hung on tightly in spite of being hit.

VALENTIN Surov saw the man crash to the ground at the same moment the incoming salvo exploded brightly ahead. Another man was obviously struck by at least one bullet and would be out of the fight. Surov's own AKS-74 barked a three-round automatic burst as he continued to ride forward, quickly going from a trot to a full gallop.

HORSES pounded past on both sides of Reshteen, and the next group that appeared after the first drove him to insane fury. Even in the dark he could tell they were Pashtuns, and he knew the sons of Satan had to be the cursed Mahsuds. He fired again, unsure if he had hit anything. He swung the muzzle of his weapon more to the left, but four simultaneous hits slammed into his shoulders, penetrating deep down into his torso, tearing up vital organs and arteries. The old fighter did his best to fire again, but the darkness of the night turned into the darkness of death, and he gave up the ghost as the Mahsuds galloped past him.

ZGARD, the guard at the rear of the village, leaped to his feet and ran to the right where his best friend Wakman was located in a depression that had once been a well. They were both in their late teens and anxious to make reputations as fierce warriors within the group of older men. When he reached the edge of the nearest house, he took cover and glanced out toward Wakman's position. He could see his friend already firing at the horsemen closing in on him. Wakman shot one off his horse, then was overwhelmed and gunned down, collapsing back out of sight into his fighting position.

At that moment the enemy attackers in the center of their formation had reached the interior of the village, galloping between the houses and firing into the windows and doors. By the time Zgard turned around, they had gone completely through the hamlet and were going out the rear. Zgard could easily make out the Pashtun riders in the group, and he began to methodically employ squeezes on the trigger, sending bursts of automatic fire into their midst. He shot down four before turning and running for cover between the mud domiciles.

SUROV led the men to a spot fifty meters past the village limits, then shouted orders in both Russian and Pashto. *"Brashaite! Aweshzi!"*

The attacking horsemen all wheeled around, the maneuver causing both ethnic groups to break up and mingle together.

Another bilingual shout from Surov ordered them to charge back through the village. They galloped into better illumination as the people opened windows where lantern light and flames in hearths exposed the crude streets to easy viewing. The raiders fired indiscriminately into the dwellings as they galloped by, inflicting casualties among women, children, and the elderly as well as the fighters who had come wide awake to repel the attack.

THE surviving man who had been on guard duty on the left side of the village had come in to join the fight in the interior. He teamed up with Zgard and two more men who had positioned themselves across a row of several houses to offer resistance. By the time the attackers had galloped through for the second time, all four of the Yousafzais were dead. The incoming fire from the overwhelming force of enemy was too heavy to stand up to.

THIS time when the attacking force turned around, Surov ordered the Russians to dismount while he sent the Pashtuns charging back through the village with instructions to wait on the far side. As the Mahsuds returned to the fray, horse handlers among the ex-convicts took the reins to hold the animals while the rest of the group moved on foot toward the houses. Each man had a traditional Russian army grenade sack across his shoulder holding three RGD-5 fragmentation hand grenades. These had been looted from the old prison's armory after the place was abandoned and stored in what had once been the back part of Luka Yarkov's house.

The Slavic fighting force formed into five skirmish lines of fourteen to sixteen men. This was part of ex-Captain Valentin Surov's tactics. The first two ranks, firing short full-auto bursts from the AKS-74s, moved rapidly through the objective, directing the salvos at targets of opportunities such as windows, doorways, and unwise villagers who exposed themselves. Their main job was to quickly knock down any outright or potential resistance. Behind them came the slow movers, doing mopping up chores with better aimed shooting and the tossing of grenades. When they had worked themselves through the houses and reached the out-skirts where the Mahsud mujahideen waited, all resistance within the village had ended.

"Pistolieti! Temanchan!" Surov ordered in both languages.

Now the Pashtuns dismounted and, like their Russian comrades in arms, those who had pistols pulled them from holsters. Thus began a systematic house-to-house search for survivors and wounded. All were given a final dispatch from this earthly life with shots to the head.

Step one of Aleksander Akloschenko's invasion was completed.

SEALs BIVOUAC
0930 HOURS

PETTY Officer Frank Gomez, sitting with the laptop computer across his legs, typed occasionally when the discussion going on around him required it. He was situated in the midst of the detachment's brains: Lieutenant Bill Branni-gan, Lieutenant (JG) Jim Cruiser, Ensign Orlando Taylor, and Senior Chief Petty Officer Buford Dawkins. Those learned gentlemen of mayhem were busy composing an OPLAN to be submitted to Brigadier General Greg Leroux through Commander Tom Carey. This involved the operation to bring the Pashtun tribes of the Pranistay Steppes under control. It was the preliminary step in Leroux's orders issued aboard the USS *Combs* on Thanksgiving Day.

An extensive program of recon and map sketching had been undertaken before they reached the point of actually putting the operational plans down on paper or, as in this case, into Gomez's computer. Unfortunately, the bivouac headquarters had no printer on which to produce a hard copy of the effort, so the OPLAN would be submitted on a disk to be printed out in Carey's office. It was tedious, but they ei-ther used that method or removed the Brigands' officers from the OA to do the work on the ship. That was not an acceptable alternative, given the potential of unexpected violence on the steppes.

The senior chief was in the middle of his dissertation on additional supplies needed for the coming activities when the sound of galloping hooves disturbed the calm. Everyone leaped to their feet, grabbing weapons as they readied themselves for a worst-case scenario. The entire detachment, including the men off watch, also responded with M16s locked and loaded.

The horses approaching were led by their asset Chinar, with several members of both the Janoon and Yousafzai tribes following him. Brannigan was surprised to see no less than the warlord Awalmir among them. The group came to a dusty, noisy halt at the headquarters hootch with Chinar and Awalmir leaping from their saddles. Chinar's eyes were open wide with excitement. "Skipper! A Yousafzai village has been destroyed earlier this morning. Everyone is dead!"

"Alright," Brannigan said in a calm tone. "Take a deep breath, then give me the details."

"Aye, aye, aye, sir," Chinar said. He had picked up this affirmation of orders from the SEALs but his excitement had caused him to add extra "ayes" to the mix. He inhaled, held it, then exhaled and immediately began talking. "Awalmir Kahn received word that the smallest village of his tribe was attacked and everybody there was killed, and it seems to be the same thing that happened to the Swatis. His warriors tell him many, many horsemen were there and they attacked and also they fought on foot. Awalmir Kahn is very angry. He has already sent his number one fighting man, Paywastun, to gather the tribe for war. We Janoons have sworn *badal* with our brothers the Yousafzai."

Brannigan looked over at Awalmir, who stood beside Chinar, nodding to him in acknowledgment of what had happened at the village. The Skipper turned back to the young interpreter. "Tell Awalmir I am very angry, as will be the American commanders when I tell them of the crime. Ask him to wait while I make contact and get their reactions. Make him understand they will not stand for this outrage."

"Should I tell him that they will swear *badal* with his people too?" Chinar asked.

"Yes!" Brannigan replied.

Chinar spoke rapidly to Awalmir. The warlord spoke a few terse words that Chinar translated. "He will stay here only until his clan is gathered to make war."

Brannigan quickly spoke up. "It would be better if we Americans, Yousafzai, and Janoons all fought together. I humbly beg Awalmir Khan to trust me enough to agree to that arrangement."

Chinar translated the request, and exchanged a few more words with the Pashtun war leader. Then he turned back to Brannigan. "Awalmir Khan agrees to what you suggest."

Brannigan went over to where Gomez stood with the laptop. He reached into the RTO's breast pocket and pulled out a message pad. After scribbling out a brief but fully descriptive SITREP, he handed it back. "Transmit this to Carey ASAP."

"Aye, sir!"

Brannigan whipped around to face Dawkins. "Muster the troops, Senior Chief!"

CHAPTER 24

SPENCER Caldwell had not been happy with his CIA assignment to Tajikistan. For more than a decade he had spent all his time in the former Islamic Soviet Socialist States of the USSR, and he found that setting up a net of operatives was all but impossible in those remote locations. Those nations where nothing much was going on offered little opportunity or reason to make any intelligence inroads. On the other hand, the ones filled with turmoil and strife attracted so much attention from the Russian Federation and its FBS that they were literally crawling with a plethora of spies, military infiltrators, informers, and turncoats. This mixing of causes made it impossible to determine any one person's reliability. Changing sides in issues seemed to be national pastimes in that part of the world.

Caldwell had at least developed an excellent cover that allowed him extraordinary access to the far reaches of the entire area. He posed as a freelance archaeologist and drove about in a battered Land Rover in the hinterlands checking out historical sites for relics and evidence of ancient peoples. It was ironic that he made several meaningful discoveries where ancient towns and settlements had once been located. In spite of his amateurish poking around, the locations revealed valuable antiquities. Caldwell obeyed the local laws by reporting his finds, and that resulted in the countries' own archaeologists, along with university students, joining him for further exploration. This increased his credibility and afforded him easier access to other parts of the desolate areas of Asia. Within a couple of years he was a well-known explorer, after being featured in newspapers and on television where he discussed his "career." No matter where he went, the local police always saluted politely as they waved him through their roadblocks without searches or inquiries. Additionally, he wrote articles about his discoveries that were published in several archeological magazines in Europe.

The CIA agent was also able to enjoy freedom of movement in cities by renting office space where he purportedly did all his paperwork. This was what led to his establishment in Khorugh. The shabby intelligentsia of the city were flattered that he had settled among them, and he was soon included in their social activities. These were no more than evening-long discussion periods in cheap apartments where the dialogue, though quite intellectual, was fueled by cheap vodka. It was typical Tajik custom that this was strictly a male activity, and the only women present were the hosts' wives, who served the second-rate snacks and liquor to the guests.

Not all the attendees at these affairs were academics. Educated people from other fields would show up, seeking the company of the scholarly elite to feed the cerebral hunger of their own excellent minds. Among these was a Tajik army officer by the name of Major Firdaus Khumar. He was a tall, slim man with graying black hair and a sophisticated demeanor. His beard was cut short, as was traditional among Islamic military men.

When Caldwell first met Khumar he immediately figured him as the somewhat ne'er-do-well son of a wealthy or important family. This would be typical in that part of the world when a prestigious clan would take the son who couldn't or wouldn't fit into the family's business and get him a commission in the army. It would be sort of a gentleman's existence for the reprobate that would keep him out of the way without becoming a total disgrace. However, after a half dozen or so conversations with Khumar, Caldwell found him to be extremely intelligent, well educated, and probably in possession of a genius IQ. This was a capable fellow who could do just about anything he desired. Besides his native tongue of Tajik, Khumar was fluent in English, Russian, French, and Arabic. And, most important of all, he held a responsible position in the Tajik Army's Intelligence Branch.

Needless to say, during those apartment get-togethers, Caldwell began keeping a close eye on Khumar. The man was an excellent candidate for any spy's stable of informants and confidents. He found out the officer was a married man with a couple of teenagers, and his wife was a schoolteacher. And, as soon as the major discovered Caldwell was an American, he warmed to him quickly. This put the experienced operative on his guard. Since Khumar was military intelligence, and Caldwell was an American, there existed the possibility of a deep probe despite the archaeological cover. In fact, it would be surprising if Khumar did not have some professional curiosity about him.

Thus began some subtle questioning and inquiries between them. After a while it was difficult to tell who was developing whom. But after a few months passed, Caldwell felt secure enough to invite Khumar to visit a site he was exploring in the nearby Kangal Mountains.

They took the Land Rover for a two-hour trip up into the trackless, barren hills until reaching a meadow between a couple of prominent mountains. The ersatz archaeologist explained this would have been an excellent spot for ancient peoples to have established a town or settlement, and he thought it worth the effort to do some exploratory digging. Khumar was enthusiastic about the prospects and volunteered to help with the shovel work. That one afternoon turned into several more trips and finally to an entire two-week campout as the searching continued.

A sincere friendship developed into evenings out enjoying the sins and delights of Khorugh. This involved drinking and whoring in places much like the apartments of the intellectuals. Khumar's conduct was most indicative of his lack of religious fervor, thus giving Caldwell some optimism in dealing with him.

The bars they patronized served cheap liquor in shabby surroundings, and the whores were young but not particularly attractive women who could be picked up and taken to cheap hotel rooms for quick unimaginative couplings. This desire for slatterns was not unusual for highly intelligent men, who found satisfaction and change in the grubby sexual experiences with females from the lower strata of society. It was after such activity on an early summer morning when Caldwell and Khumar were sitting at a kiosk drinking coffee. In spite of their hangovers, an understanding was reached.

Khumar wanted to defect with his family.

A few probing questions by Caldwell convinced him the man was sincere. Khumar wanted out of Tajikistan and had enough interesting intelligence regarding Russian activities in the area to make him valuable to the West. Caldwell promised to make "inquiries" and would get back to him. The result of a little giving-and-taking was that Khumar would go on a payroll, remain in his job, and pass on items of interest to Caldwell. When the time was right, arrangements would be made to have the major exfiltrated to America with his wife and two children to begin a new life free from the constrictions of Islam.

KHORUGH APARTMENT BUILDING
3 DECEMBER

THE men gathered for the evening's intellectual exercise were able to doff their heavy coats and throw them in the bedroom. The apartment was small enough and they were numerous enough that their natural body heat warmed things up enough that sweaters sufficed to keep the comfort at a bearable level. The bottles of vodka, as was customary in that part of the world, were kept out on the windowsill in the freezing temperatures to get cold enough for proper drinking. The host was a bachelor professor of history and he had purchased some bread, sausage, and cheese at a small shop on the corner for the enjoyment of his guests.

As usual there was no agenda for the evening's program, but the various discussions eventually narrowed down to one particular subject as they always did. The big topic was to express opinions on the question of whether the tenets of Islam could actually allow secular nations in the Middle East that could govern as true democracies. This set up some lively exchanges as the more devout insisted that it was a case of such governments adapting to religion, not the other way around, that would be the most beneficial to the people. Those less inclined toward worship argued that until the domination of Islam lessened considerably, there would never be any sort of true freedom or exchange of ideas.

Caldwell and Khumar sat off to the side, listening for the most part while making a contribution now and then. Generally, when the pair was not out at the digging site, they avoided any exchange of information or intelligence for security reasons. But this time Caldwell was forced to break that rule. As the evening's activities drew on he found it difficult to control his impatience. Khumar, who had gotten to know his friend quite well during the long hours of their friendship, sensed something was going on.

0230 HOURS

CALDWELL and Khumar made sure they were not the first to leave the apartment. It was best if they drifted away with several of the others to lessen the appearance of a close rapport. When they left, they accompanied four others out into the hall and down the stairs to the foyer. After brief good-byes, everyone walked out into the cold, with Caldwell and Khumar going down the street to where the Land Rover was parked.

Caldwell kicked the engine over, slipped it into gear, and pulled away from the curb. He drove slowly along the street with the wipers whacking at the snow falling against the windshield. "I have some information for you."

Khumar chuckled. "That will be a change. It is usually I with intelligence to impart to you."

"This will give your commanding officer the excuse to do what he's been longing for."

Khumar glanced over at his friend. "This should be interesting."

"The Russians have made a deal to sell the entire opium poppy harvest of the Pranistay Steppes to the Taliban."

Khumar nodded. "Am I correct in assuming you are discussing Aleksander Akloschenko and his syndicate?"

"You are," Caldwell said. "And the convicts hanging out in the Kangal Mountains are up to their ears in the plot."

Khumar turned his eyes back to the front, smiling slightly. Caldwell reached over and turned the heater on as they continued down the street.

THE PRANISTAY STEPPES
4 DECEMBER

IT hadn't taken Lieutenant Bill Brannigan long to organize his small "army" into a cavalry strike force. He pulled off a remarkable mobilization of his Pashtun allies through the efforts of Chinar making a demanding gallop to the friendlies' four villages. Within two hours of the young interpreter's Paul Revere imitation, every fighting man was at the SEAL bivouac, fully armed, equipped, and mounted for battle.

The Skipper's American command consisted of a total of four fire teams with two section commanders and a pair of SAW gunners. He would leave his headquarters intact to act as a mobile command post but break down the fire teams in separate echelons. His native contingent consisted of one hundred ten Yousafzai and eighty-five Janoon warriors.

Lieutenant Jim Cruiser and his gunner, Tex Benson, would

go with the Bravo Fire Team. They would take fifty-five fighting men of the Yousafzai tribe with them. Alpha Fire Team under CPO Matt Gunnarson would be an independent group with forty-three Janoons. Ensign Orlando Taylor and his SAW man, Doug MacTavish, had Delta Fire Team, along with fifty-five Yousafzai tribesmen. Charlie Fire Team, under the capable leadership of PO1C Gutsy Olson, reinforced with forty-two Janoons, made up the final combat element.

Brannigan knew the group who had slaughtered the Yousafzai villagers could be anywhere on the Pranistay Steppes. They fact they hit the smallest hamlet among the Pashtuns who refused to cooperate with them was a sure sign it had been done to set an example. After a consultation with Awalmir and old Quajeer, the *malik* of the Janoons, he determined the next assault would more than likely be the smallest Janoon community, which boasted some fifty fighting men. Since all the warriors of both tribes were now away from home and joined up with the SEALs, every bucolic little town on the steppes was in dire danger. The Skipper knew he had a bit of time on his side since the Russians would want to gather the entirety of their Pashtuns before striking out against the Yousafzai, Janoons, and SEALs. At this time it was an accepted fact that the ex-Soviet convicts were aware that Americans were in the area, though they probably had no idea of the exact number. However, with somewhere around 340 armed horsemen, they would be in a very confident mood even if they might have taken some casualties during the massacre.

0630 HOURS

LIEUTENANT Bill Brannigan had hoped to begin his operation two hours earlier, but the undisciplined Pashtuns had an annoying habit of wandering off to chat with friends and relations from other villages, going somewhere to tend to nature's calls, or brewing a pot of tea to share with their comrades. The Yousafzai, thanks to Awalmir and his chief lieutenant, the one-eyed Paywastun, were the first to gather their fighters into a group to be divvied up per the SEAL commanding officer's instructions. Not until Brannigan appointed a Janoon commander and subcommander did that tribe's men assemble properly. Those two leaders were Ghairat, a veteran of the war against the Soviets, and his brother-in-law Pamir who, though in his early thirties, had also fought the invaders.

When the Brigands first arrived on the steppes, Brannigan had ordered that all important locations, terrain features, and villages be noted using the GPS devices. All this data had been entered on everyone's tactical maps. The Skipper used his chart to figure out the combination hunt-and-destroy missions for that day. Brannigan ordered Chief Matt Gunnarson to take his fire team and the forty-three Janoons assigned to him to the smallest Janoon village. A little figuring had indicated they would be following an azimuth of seventy-two degrees.

The rest of the detachment would fan out on evenly spaced vectors toward the east in the search for the enemy force. Brannigan and his three SEALs in headquarters would go due east on ninety degrees. Their LASH systems gave them a marked advantage over the bad guys. An important piece of intelligence brought back by Andy Malachenko from his undercover work was that the Russians had no effective communications capabilities. That not only meant they would have trouble staying in touch, but could not split up too far from each other or they would lose all unit integrity.

When the preliminaries were taken care of, the teams of Americans and Pashtuns married up. All had bandoleers stuffed with ammunition, weapons locked and loaded, horses properly prepared, and every swinging dick was in the saddle and ready to rock and roll.

Awalmir was with Cruiser while his able assistant Paywastun rode with Orlando Taylor. Ghairat of the Janoons had been assigned to Chief Matt Gunnarson while his fellow tribesman Pamir would be the senior native under Gutsy Olson.

Now Brannigan sat his horse in front of the assembled force. A quick survey from left to right gave him ample evidence that they would never be better prepared than at that moment. "Go!" he yelled, then added in Pashto, *"Lar sha!"* The War of the Pranistay Steppes had begun.

CHAPTER 25

CHIEF Matt Gunnarson pulled his compass from his parka pocket and looked down at it in his gloved hand. During the more than three hours of travel across the steppes, one staggering disadvantage of the operation had immediately become apparent. The lack of language skills among both the American SEALs and the Pashtun fighters was causing confusion and a certain amount of pessimism.

Fire Team Alpha, made up of the chief petty officer, Tiny Burke, Pete Dawson, and Joe Miskoski, maintained a diamond formation for all-around security. However, the forty-three Janoons with them had proven completely unmanageable. Matt's attempts at conversing with Ghairat to get him to maintain closer management of his men proved futile. Neither man knew enough of the other's language to establish clear, unmistaken communication. The results were that the Pashtuns pretty much ambled along as they pleased, some keeping a watch on the horizon while others chatted among themselves as if the ride was no more than a recreational exercise.

Tiny Burke, who had been on the left flank, moved in closer to Matt. "Chief," he said. "Them guys are going along with their heads up their asses."

"Hey, no shit," Matt grumbled. "I don't know how to get 'em to close up. I been whistling and signaling but all the dumb bastards do is wave back at me. I tried talking to that guy Ghairat, but he just looks at me and gives me a shit-eating grin." He sighed. "I think they'll be more receptive once we're in a combat situation. Right now, they're not too concerned. I guess they just live in the moment."

"If we're gonna keep coming on operations out here, we're gonna have to learn their lingo," Tiny said. "Or at least some basic words to make 'em understand what they got to do."

"I believe they are aware their home village is in danger," Matt mused. "They just ain't the type to fret much until the shit actually hits the fan."

"Well, I understand that *we're* in danger," Tiny remarked. "I'm moving back to the flank." He pulled on the reins of his horse to return to his original position.

RUSSIAN/PASHTUN FORCE

VALENTIN Surov hadn't had much rest in the past forty-eight hours. The roundabout visits to the seven Pashtun villages had been frustrating and time-consuming. Gathering up the remaining seventy Mahsuds had gone relatively well during the visits to their two communities. The fact that five of their fifty brethren had been killed during the raid on the Yousafzais motivated them to *badal*. But getting them to turn out armed, equipped, and mounted had taken several hours.

Things turned even more inconvenient at the Kharoti, Bhittani, and Ghilzai hamlets, where a total of 215 fighting men were available to join the invasion force. Although it was obvious that there would be dead and wounded among their number, they treated the whole thing like a lark. Surov spoke to them as diplomatically as possible, but his efforts did little in getting them to do something as simple as moving faster in the preparations. Since there was no present danger, they scampered around, going into each other's houses and stopping in groups for excited conversations. At one point somebody threw a soccer ball at a small crowd of men saddling their horses. This erupted into an impromptu melee of kicking the orb around that went on for several long minutes.

But now, in a column of bunches, the small force of 79 Russians and 335 Pashtuns moved across the flat country toward the location of the smallest Janoon village. At this point Surov grinned to himself; the odds of the coming battle were approximately twelve to one. It shouldn't take as long as wiping out the Yousafzai hamlet. A couple of swift runs through the place should wrap up the job in under an hour.

At that point, his plans were to mop up the remainder of the Janoon tribe before turning his deadly intents back against the Yousafzai. Surov had been told the Janoons could muster 85 fighters at the most while the Yousafzai had 105. Even if some Americans were among them, there wouldn't be enough to make much of a difference.

The Russian commander stood in his stirrups to check on the positions of his point men. He had instructed Aleksei Barkyev and Yakob Putnovsky to ride in the direction of three prominent peaks in the Kangal Mountains to the north. They were to head directly toward the middle one to stay on the proper azimuth to the Janoon village.

1000 HOURS

LIEUTENANT Bill Brannigan and Chinar rode side by side as the headquarters group continued due east. Senior Chief Buford Dawkins and Frank Gomez were out on point, keeping them on course, while Hospital Corpsman Doc Bradley brought up the rear of the small group.

The going had been rough for a while after they ran into some terrain that included several deep gulley systems similar to the area where Chad Murchison was wounded. One area was so cut up that the group had to make a detour, going back in the direction they came from to swing out wider to the south. Following that disruption, they enjoyed five kilometers of easy riding across some flatlands before reaching an area filled with natural potholes. At that point the quintet had to slow down to avoid injuring the horses, who had to carefully pick their way through the pitted terrain.

As the ride progressed, Brannigan began to worry about the different teams spreading out too far. He checked his position on the GPS, then raised the section commanders to tell them to keep their people along the same longitudes as much as possible. If contact was made with the enemy, the response would have to be closely coordinated and timely.

1030 HOURS

CHIEF Matt Gunnarson was startled when the Pashtuns to his direct front suddenly broke into a mad gallop, heading straight ahead at breakneck speed. Within seconds the rest of the tribesmen joined them. Expecting the worst, the chief spoke into his LASH to the rest of the team.

"I don't know what goosed 'em," he said. "But expect the worst. Could be they spotted the enemy. Draw your M16s and form as skirmishers. Dawson and Burke, stay where you're at. Miskoski, pull up between me and Dawson." He waited until they were properly formed up. "At a trot, march!"

The SEALs sped up, riding across the open ground at a steady pace, each man holding his M16 ready. After a few moments passed they saw what had caught the Pashtuns' collective attention. The Janoon village was a couple of kilometers ahead. By the time the Brigands arrived on site, the Pashtuns were dismounted and mingling with the villagers, laughing and talking as they greeted each other.

At that point Chief Petty Officer Matthew Gunnarson lost it.

"Goddamn it!" he yelled in a fury. "What the fuck's the matter with you shitheads? Get some security out! The fucking enemy could be just over the horizon!"

The people, some grinning while others frowned in puzzlement, looked at the foreigner who was bellowing gibberish at them. The natives could see no point in being worried and upset. Everything was fine. At that point the SEALs made a simultaneous decision to set an example. Tiny Burke went to the front of the village and took up what was obviously a guard position. Joe Miskoski and Pete Dawson did the same thing to the right and left sides. Pashtuns may be excitable and impetuous, but they're not stupid. In less than a half minute they realized what the Americans were doing. The warriors immediately got their AK-47s and split themselves up to join the SEALs. Some others went to the far side of the village to stand watch there. Now the chief petty officer relaxed. Things were beginning to look better.

Then a salvo of shots came in from the left front, followed by some from the right front. A couple of beats later, incoming fire was directed at them from the direct front. Matt went to his LASH again. "Brigand Boss, this is Alpha at our objective. We are under attack. I say again. We are under attack. Out."

Now it was Brannigan's voice over the net. "Sections and teams report!"

"First Section, over!" replied Cruiser.

"Second Section, over!" answered Taylor.

Next came Fire Teams Bravo, Charlie, and Delta.

"All sections and teams, head for the Alphas at the Janoon village. Out!"

As the rest of the detachment along with their native allies swung toward the target area, Chief Matt Gunnarson joined the fighting lines. There wasn't enough time for any organization or direction. The enemy was already headed toward them at a gallop. To the defenders it appeared as if an entire cavalry corps was charging down their throats.

THE BATTLE

THE 79 Russians had broken down into previously organized echelons with Valentin Surov leading the most forward group of 28. Directly to his left rear came 25 more under the command of Aleksei Barkyev, while to his right rear, and spread out a bit more, came 26 led by Timofei Dagorov. All around them, riding insanely without form or discipline, were 335 close-packed Pashtun fighters, bumping against each other and breaking up the Russian lines as they intruded into their space.

THE SEALs and Pashtuns in the village began firing into the mass of horsemen pounding straight at them. Aiming wasn't necessary. They simply pointed the bores of their weapons at the horde and made rhythmic pulls on the triggers. Some of the ammo was tracer, and the fiery streaks behind the slugs lit the trajectories of the rounds. All went directly into the attacking formation.

SUROV had to swerve wildly around two men and their horses, who crumpled to the ground to his direct front. Humans and animals tumbled in a dust-raising mass of yelling and neighing.

At that point the Russian losses were light, but the crazy-ass Pashtuns were getting blown out of their saddles at a heavy but acceptable rate. The former army officer had plenty of natives to spare, and was not particularly concerned about the losses.

The attacking force went straight through the village, arriving on the other side in a disorganized jumble of Europeans and Pashtuns with their horses crowding and pushing together in a nervous mass. Surov shouted orders in two languages to restore some discipline to the formation, and the two groups began pulling apart to team up with their own ethnic brothers.

CHIEF Petty Officer Matt Gunnarson was an experienced combat leader with the ability to maintain a steady hand over the situation while keeping his mind working a few steps ahead of what was going on at any given moment. It took him only an instant to realize the attackers had been forced to pause to reform their ranks, and he immediately jumped into action to take advantage of the brief lull.

The first thing the chief did was go back to his bellowing and gesturing. The three other SEALs of Alpha Fire Team knew exactly what he had in mind, but their Pashto comrades in arms could only guess at what was wanted of them. Matt's primary concern at that point was to get all the women, children, and old people into a safer area. He decided to abandon the central and western parts of the village, and hole up in the eastern area. That way the civilians could crowd into the buildings and hunker down while the fighters positioned themselves for more assaults.

The SEAL team leader was relieved there were no heavy weapons, such as mortars and machine guns, to deal with, nor did any of the enemy seem to possess grenades. This was going to be a gunfight, pure and simple, and he had figured out a couple of ways to turn things to his favor. At least he hoped he could last until the rest of the Brigands arrived.

Within a minute, all the natives caught on to what was wanted of them, and the population began running toward the indicated area as their tormentors still milled around on the west end. They crowded into the homes and workplaces, getting within the walls that offered protection from the small arms fire. The valuable horses were also led into the structures without any protests from the people.

The chief spotted a pile of sandbags on top of the building that was used as a lookout post. He yelled over at Pete Dawson. "Get your butt up in that fighting position and cover us while we get organized down here."

Dawson obeyed wordlessly, scrambling up a ladder. A half dozen Pashtuns, seeing what was going on, reacted in their usual excitable way by following after him. Within seconds, the SEAL was nestled behind the barricade with three fighters on each side. He stood up long enough to glance out past the houses on the west side.

"Hey, Chief!" he yelled down. "It looks like they're gonna take another run at us!"

When the Pashtuns below saw the chief, Miskoski, and Tiny Burke run to places that offered excellent fields of fire, they followed suit. The group was no sooner situated than the pounding of hooves and yells of attackers could be heard thundering straight at their defensive positions.

The attacking mass was broken up by the scattered housing of the village, and this channeled their assault into a half dozen paths. The defenders concentrated their fire in those areas, but they were too few to make much of a dent in the 400 horsemen they faced.

GUTSY Olson and his Charlie Fire Team, along with forty-two Janoon fighters, galloped swiftly across the open country northward toward the village. The Janoons, in an area they knew well, were aware their destination was the smallest village of their clan. Although their knowledge of English was practically nonexistent, they instinctively sensed the very real danger for a group of their people. Illiterate people have a special instinct of comprehension that has not been dulled by memorizing symbols representing sounds that are then put together to form words. Their eyes perceive intent, purpose, and objectives in group activities such as hunting and war. This is done through instinctive interpretation of the physical action of people, animals, and, under certain circumstances, even climatic conditions. Sociologists, psychologists, and anthropologists refer to this collective sixth sense as the EAS, i.e., the Environmental Awareness Syndrome. Some consider the phenomenon spiritual or even supernatural, likening it to the primal but successful herbal and healing processes used by primitives all over the world.

SUROV ordered a halt on the eastern side of the village, but instantly changed his mind and led his force that now numbered a bit under 400 farther away to get out of range of the defenders' fusillades. Aleksei Barkyev rode up to the Russian leader. "Valentin Danielovich," he said. "We must keep up the pressure. Every time we hesitate, we lose more men when we charge again."

Surov laughed. "You mean to say, Aleksei Ivanovich, that we lose more miserable Pashtuns. No more than five of our comrades have given up the ghost in all this fighting."

Now Timofei Dagorov left his unit to join them. "How long is this going to take?"

"What's the rush?" Surov asked. "Do you have a crowded social calendar today?"

Dagorov grinned. "I am simply hungry and wish to eat. It has been a while since breakfast."

"Then I shall hurry things along," Surov quipped. "When I order the next charge, I want you two to have your men hold back long enough to let the Pashtuns get ahead of us. Then we shall follow them to the objective, using them as cover."

The pair swung their horses around to ride back to their units. Surov stood in his saddle with his AKS-74 above his head. *"Hamla kawi!"*

The Pashtun horsemen struck their animals with quirts, then stuck the whips in their teeth as they charged back toward the village. They immediately came under heavy fire from the close-packed defenders who once more delivered volleys from the cover of the buildings they occupied.

PETE Dawson, still on the roof, now had sixteen fighters who had joined him. Together the group poured sprays of 5.56- and 7.62-millimeter steel-jacketed slugs into the mass of men who galloped directly into their line of fire. Numerous figures were knocked spinning out of their saddles to bounce and roll across the walkways between the village buildings.

The return fire from the charging tribesmen of the Mahsud, Kharoti, Bhittani, and Ghilzai clans was not well aimed, but there was plenty of it. The uncoordinated but heavy swarms of bullets slammed into the defensive positions, gouging hunks of mud from the buildings and splattering into living flesh.

The Russians came in close behind them, protected by human shields as they swept through the village to the far side.

BILL Brannigan had maintained a canter to allow Charlie Fire Team to catch up with the five-man headquarters group. As soon as Gutsy Olson and his trio of SEALs joined them, the nine men broke into a gallop northward toward the scene of fighting.

Ensign Orlando Taylor, his SAW gunner Doug Mac-Tavish, and Delta Fire Team were only a scant five kilometers behind them, while up to the north Alpha Team was even closer to the besieged Janoon village. And close on their trail, Jim Cruiser led Tex Benson and Bravo Fire Team toward the same objective.

These SEALs brought a total of 152 Pashtuns to join the 4 Brigands and 35 Janoons fighting at the village.

BRANNIGAN and his bunch were the first to arrive at the battlesite. They came in from the north, the Americans spread out in a galloping line as skirmishers with the Pashtuns bunched up in their usual disorganized way. When they first spotted the enemy, the bad guys were on the far eastern side of the village, preparing to make another run at the defenders. The Russians and their pals were mingling as they formed up, making easy targets for the new guys in town.

When the mass of flying bullets crashed into the attackers, they instinctively pulled away from the source of incoming rounds. At the same time, Matt Gunnarson spotted the reinforcements, and ordered mass firing to increase the advantage. The result was a crossfire that emptied more enemy saddles. This time the Russians were dropping as thickly as their native buddies.

Surov did not have to give any orders to pull back, and it wouldn't have done him any good if he attempted to maintain control. The minute they tried to withdraw from the unexpected attack, another group hit them from the south. This was Ensign Orlando Taylor, his SAW gunner, and the Delta Fire Team. Five M16 rifles and the one M249 squad automatic weapon joined the salvos directed at the attackers. The Russians and Pashtuns were so close-packed that many of the falling corpses and wounded men collapsed on top of each other as they fell to the ground.

Now Lieutenant (JG) Jim Cruiser, Tex Benson, and the Bravo Fire Team joined in the melee. What had been a battle of resistance with little hope for the defenders had turned into a meat grinder for the attackers. Saddles emptied perceptibly as the Russian-Pashtun force made an impromptu and sloppy run for safety in an eastern direction. The SEAL relief force turned to follow as Matt Gunnarson's guys, along with their Janoon buddies, fetched their horses from the buildings to mount up to join in the chase.

By the time the run was at top speed only Valentin Surov and a half dozen Russians were still noncasualties. Of the original number of Pashtuns who rode with them, no more than 15 percent were still alive. After a kilometer of flight, the two groups instinctively split up, with the Russians galloping toward the nearby Kangal Mountains and the Pashtuns heading for their home villages.

The pursuers also parted company according to ethnicity. The SEALs pressed on after the Russians while the Yousafzais and Janoons, all swearing *badal*, furiously pursued their tribal enemies.

1645 HOURS

THE entire SEAL detachment was in the foothills of the Kangal Mountains, dismounted with a defensive perimeter formed around their impromptu bivouac. Brannigan ordered a halt to make a transmission to Brigadier General Greg Leroux aboard the USS *Combs*. Frank Gomez had brought the Shadowfire radio with him, and he raised the floating SFOB to send a SITREP to the cantankerous general.

The news of the victory on the Pranistay Steppes put Leroux in a near euphoric state of mind. All the problems with the poppy harvest and the Taliban had been wrapped up and tied with a bright red ribbon as far as he was concerned. The only thing to do now was to stand fast and let the brass upstairs make some very important strategic and tactical decisions on further steps that had to be made. The Brigands were to stand fast where they were and wait for the general, who would arrive ASAP with the latest poop.

THE Pashtuns back on the steppes were in a state of wait-and-see. The fighting men of the four tribes who had sided with the Russians had been decimated. They and their families were praying and preparing for what could very well be the end of their existence on earth. It appeared as if Allah's paradise would gain an influx of new arrivals in the next couple of hours.

The victorious Yousafzai and Janoon tribes now surrounded the main villages of the Mahsuds and Kharotis. The lesser Bhittanis and Ghilzais were being ignored at the moment. They would get theirs just as soon as the Yousafzai Awalmir Khan and Ghairat, the Janoon war leader, decided the fates of their vanquished enemies.

Fate had decreed one more paroxysm of bloodshed and violence over the expanse of the Pranistay Steppes.

CHAPTER 26

THE sudden windchill factor brought the temperature down a good twenty degrees as the rotors' blast of the Navy Super Stallion chopper whipped up a storm of stinging sand particles. Bill Brannigan, Jim Cruiser, and Orlando Taylor bore up under the discomfort as they watched the big machine land. Chinar, the interpreter, would normally have been there, but he had been given special permission to be with his tribesman for the final showdown with their Pashtun enemies.

The pilot eased back on the engine as Brigadier General Greg Leroux jumped from the aircraft down to the ground. He turned and grabbed a rucksack and an M16 rifle from an accommodating crewman. Then two more men joined him, each receiving field gear from the same sailor after unassing the aircraft. The trio swung the loads over their shoulders and walked toward the informal reception committee as the Super Stallion rose back to flying altitude.

Leroux, grinning happily, walked up in long strides with his companions following. He returned the salutes of the naval officers, then offered his hand to each man. "How're you boys doing?" he asked. He looked around. "Good God Almighty! It's fucking wonderful to be back in the field!" Then he gestured to his companions. "Let me introduce these two guys, who are going to be real important in the days to come. The first is Spencer Caldwell from our vaunted CIA, and his buddy there is Major Firdaus Khumar of Tajik Army Intelligence. Now with those preliminaries taken care of, let's get down to business."

The visitors were escorted back to the bivouac where the four fire teams and headquarters were formed up. Senior Chief Buford Dawkins bawled the order that brought the Brigands to attention.

"Knock it off!" Leroux yelled. "This is no place for that bullshit. Dismiss the formation and tell me where we can drop our fucking gear."

"Over there, sir," Dawkins said. "That's our command post."

Leroux, without breaking stride, went directly to the spot with his fellow travelers and the SEAL officers hurrying after him. The general spotted the picket line of horses. "Look at that, will you? It's a scene from the past." He dropped the rucksack by a campfire while Caldwell and Khumar followed his example. "It's colder'n shit out here."

"Welcome to the Pranistay Steppes, sir," Brannigan said.

"Thanks. Where the hell is Malachenko? Get his ass over here."

The terse command set up a bit of scurrying, and almost immediately Andy Malachenko reported in. He nodded to Caldwell. "Nice to see you again, Spence."

"Same here, Andy," Caldwell replied. He introduced Khumar, who had been fully informed of the SEAL's undercover mission in Tajikistan.

Leroux was impatient to get things rolling as he spoke to Andy. "Do you remember where that Russian town is?"

"Yes, sir," Andy replied. "That's something I ain't likely to forget." He pointed, saying, "Northeast, sir. Almost direct."

"Alright," Leroux said. "That's good." He switched his glance to Brannigan. "Here's the skinny, Brannigan. We got permission from the Tajik government to attack and occupy that place." His eyes snapped back to Andy. "What's the name of it again?"

"Logovishchyeh, sir."

"Yeah," Leroux said. "Logo-whataya-call-it."

"It means 'lair' in Russian," Andy explained.

"Whatever," Leroux commented. "When we get done with the place, the name will mean 'pile of shit.'" He reached in his pocket and pulled out a piece of paper. "Listen up, everybody! This is a copy of the map Malachenko had in his AAR when he came back from that undercover assignment. G-Two at Station Bravo sent it over to me. We need to work out an OPORD for the operation. It might be tricky since it looks like we got to penetrate a little deeper into Tajikistan than I want to. We'll have to follow the highway to get to Logo, er, whatever."

"Negative, sir," Andy said. "I know a more direct route straight up into the mountains. I reconned it while I was there. The Russians don't know about it."

"By God, Malachenko, you did a hell of a job," Leroux said. "If you were in the Army, I'd promote you right here on the spot. Give you a fucking medal too. How many of them Russkis were there, did you say?"

"Close to a hundred, sir."

Leroux looked at Brannigan. "And how many of them bastards did you kill or wound?"

"We counted seventy-four," Brannigan answered.

"Then that leaves about twenty-six still over there," Leroux said. "And you guys number twenty-four as I recall. With the element of surprise, that should give you odds of about three to two."

"We can call for Pashtun volunteers if you want to sweeten the advantage," Brannigan said.

"No can do," Leroux said. "The Tajiks said they didn't

want any native folks in on this. They'll only allow you guys into their sovereign territory, and they don't want you to be there very long. That's what Major Khumar is here for."

Brannigan looked at Caldwell. "What's the CIA's interest in all this?"

"Just consider me an interested observer," Caldwell said.

"Exactly," Leroux agreed, reaching in his pocket and pulling out a notebook and ballpoint pen. "Okay. Let's write up our cunning plans, shall we? You guys sit down."

The three SEALs immediately obeyed, retrieving their own writing implements to take notes. Spencer Caldwell and Major Firdaus Khumar stood off to one side and listened.

MAHSUD MAIN VILLAGE

THE principal group sitting outside the village was made up of four important persons. The Yousafzai tribe was represented by Awalmir Khan and Shamroz, the tribal clergy. Quajeer, the *malik*, and Ghairat, the war leader, acted for the Janoons. Behind them in a roughly formed semicircle stood the nearly 300 warriors of both clans. All had their *pukhoors* pulled tightly around their bodies because of the cold, but their eyes blazed with a fiery hatred.

Mohambar, the elderly *malik* of the Mahsuds, walked from the village toward the assemblage with two men close behind him. These were both *spinzhire*; one from the Kharotis and one from the Bhittanis. The Ghilzai tribe had no representation because all their mujahideen had been killed in the fighting at the Janoon village the day before. The three were weaponless as they approached the waiting enemy. When they reached the spot, all fell to the ground, touching their foreheads to the earth. After a moment old Mohambar raised his face to look directly at Awalmir and Quajeer.

"*Nonwatai!*" he cried piteously. "*Nonwatai!*"

ARTILLERY IMPACT AREA
TAJIKISTAN

THE driver kept the old Soviet military truck at a low
speed, keeping his eye out for unexploded shells that dotted
the area. The locale was littered with deadly duds from hundreds of Tajik Army firing exercises carried out with extremely aged and unstable Russian ammunition. Some of it
had been created prior to the German invasion of the Soviet
Union during World War II.

As the vehicle chugged along, an officer sat beside the
driver while six other men were in the back. Three of these
were armed soldiers and the others were miserable men with
their hands bound behind their backs with plastic strips. The
truck continued on its cautious way until they reached a
ravine. At that point the squeaky, unreliable brakes were applied and it came to a slow stop. The driver got out and
walked around to lower the tailgate while the officer went
around the opposite side to the back.

The soldiers jumped to the ground first, followed by two
of the men. One stayed aboard the vehicle. He was an extremely fat individual, refusing to budge. A disgusted soldier
angrily climbed into the back, and gave him a sharp hori-
zontal butt stroke that slammed into a pudgy arm. The man
cried out and scrambled awkwardly over to the edge of the
truck. An impatient soldier grabbed him and pulled him out,
causing him to fall to the ground.

Aleksander Akloschenko blubbered and begged. "Please!
Please! I have much money I can give you. Let me go!
Please! I can make you rich! All of you!"

The other two men, Pavel Marvesky and Andrei Rogorov,
waited while the fat man was hauled to his feet, still offering
wild bribes. All were marched over to the edge of the ravine
and told to face inward and drop to their knees. Akloschenko
did not move, continuing to weep loudly while promising
great rewards for setting him free. Marvesky was frightened,
but controlled himself the best he could. His lips quivered
and tears dribbled down his cheeks, as he struggled to keep
his dignity. However, Rogorov, the bodyguard/chauffeur,

showed no emotion whatsoever. He had known all along what was about to happen after their hands were bound with the plastic bands. Handcuffs would have to be taken off the corpses after execution, but the strips were cheap reliable substitutes that cause no inconvenience after death. They were not biodegradable, and would remain intact for eons after the corpses had decomposed into slush.

Finally Akloschenko was on his knees, still crying out for mercy. The officer made sure a rifleman was stationed behind each prisoner, then kept the incident informal without any ceremony. Rather than utter the proper order, he asked, *"Baroi chi sabr kard?* What are you waiting for?"

Triggers were pulled and skulls exploded an instant before two of the corpses tumbled down to the bottom of the gulch. The fat man's body had to be rolled over the side. Then the officer took his pistol and fired down at their heads to administer the coups de grace as custom prescribed. It took him eight shots to make the three hits.

Practice firing on the range was not done often in the Tajik Army.

LOGOVISHCHYEH
6 DECEMBER
0530 HOURS

THE SEALs, with Leroux, Spencer Caldwell, and Firdaus Khumar, had come up Andy Malachenko's trail the night before. They left the horses back at the bivouac, and made the ascent on foot to maintain noise discipline. Senior Chief Buford Dawkins and Frank Gomez were ordered to stay behind to keep an eye on the animals Both chaffed under the decision, but that was part of being a headquarters weenie, even in the OA.

The darkness was still prevalent as Brannigan, Leroux, and Andy Malachenko looked down on the settlement from the surrounding higher country. The rest of the detachment was nearby, waiting for the order to deploy for the attack. By then a few lights had begun to appear in windows, showing that the residents were starting their day's activities. Leroux, speaking in a whisper, commented, "Those buildings down there seem to be solidly built."

"They are, sir," Andy said. "One thing Russians can do is good construction. Those places are double-walled with dirt in between for insulation. You can bet those folks are cozy and warm inside."

Suddenly Leroux put his binoculars to his eyes. "What the fuck is that? A woman! Are there women down there?"

"Yes, sir," Andy said. "And kids too. Some of those guys had families."

Leroux chuckled. "Where did those reprobates go to meet girls?"

"They kidnapped them during raids onto the Pranistay Steppes," Brannigan explained. "The women can never go back to their families because they're considered shameful from having sex with men other than their husbands."

"Oh, yeah," Leroux remarked. "Those Islamic laws are kind of rough on the womenfolk, aren't they?" He continued to scan the area as the daylight increased. "I see some kids now. Doing chores, it looks like."

"There's no running water," Andy explained. "They have to draw it from wells."

"Well, guys," Leroux said, returning his binoculars to their case, "those females and offspring are an unexpected complication. I want to talk to Spence and his buddy Khumar."

The three edged back, then stood up and walked twenty-five meters down the slope where the rest of the detachment waited. When they arrived, Andy went off to join his fire team while Brannigan and Leroux settled down with the two outsiders. The general informed them of the women and children. He also took his copy of the recently written OPORD and tore it up. "I'm not real keen on collateral damages when it comes to noncombatants."

Spencer Caldwell was thoughtful for a moment before speaking. "There aren't many survivors among the Russians down there. Maybe a surrender could be negotiated." He looked at Khumar. "What about it?"

"I do not think my government would have any objections

to that," the major said. "We will no doubt deport them to Russia."

"I understand from Andy that several of them would face execution back in their homeland," Brannigan remarked.

Khumar grinned. "What's that you Americans say? 'Shit happens'?"

Caldwell had another angle on the situation. "What will be the final disposition on those women and kids? If you send the women back to their home villages, they will be killed by their male relatives. The kids would be outcasts and probably left to fend for themselves in the wild."

"I've been in that situation before," Brannigan said. "It happened during our first operation as a detachment. A warlord had forced some women into prostitution and when we liberated them, they faced the same fate. It would have been murder to send them home, so we turned them over to the UN. They have a place where such women and children can be taken as refugees. The females are protected and the kids get some pretty good schooling. The same outfit that took care of that previous case is now on the Pranistay Steppes. I'm sure they'll look after these women and kids from Logovishchyeh."

"I'm familiar with who you're talking about," Caldwell said. "That would be Dr. Pierre Couchier, would it not?"

"That's him," Brannigan said.

"Well, gentlemen," Leroux said, "in that case, I suggest we set up some negotiations with those Russian assholes." He glanced at Khumar. "I have a suggestion, Major, since we don't want any disturbances. Don't tell 'em they're gonna be sent home. Give them the impression they'll be interned for a short while, then allowed to settle in Tajikistan."

"You mean we lie to them, sir?" Khumar asked.

"I think that sums it up pretty good," Leroux said. "Let's get Malachenko back over here. He's going to have to interpret for us in this mess."

CHAPTER 27

THE four Russians—Valentin Danielovich Surov, Aleksei Ivanovich Barkyev, Fedor Zakharovich Grabvosky, and Timofei Yosifovich Dagorov—sat in a row with the fireplace to their left. Four other men—Lieutenant William Brannigan, U.S. Navy; Brigadier General Gregory Leroux, U.S. Army; Spencer Caldwell, CIA; and Major Firdaus Khumar, Tajik Army—were arranged similarly, facing the Russians. Petty Officer Second Class Andrei Malachenko stood to their rear to translate for the two American officers. Spencer and Khumar were both fluent in the Russian language.

Not in attendance, but waiting at the entrance to the settlement, were Brannigan's Brigands and a Tajik police squad. Also nearby, but gathered in the barracks, were a couple of dozen Russian survivors who had been ordered into the building. Twenty Pashtun women and thirty-two children of Pashtun-Russian ethnicity waited in a couple of houses near Surov's residence. All were frightened and expecting the worst from the awful situation that had come to pass.

The spokesman at the meeting was Major Khumar, who acted as an official representative of the Tajik government. Thus, he addressed the small assembly from a position of strength. If, at any time, he felt the talks with the Russians were proving futile, he had the right to order in both the SEALs and the Tajik cops to deal with the situation with extreme prejudice.

No refreshments had been served at the conference, and Khumar opened the affair with an announcement in Russian. "The Tajik government has made a magnanimous decision to show all the ex-convicts of the former Soviet military prison extraordinary consideration. If you agree to surrender to the authority of said government, you will be interned for a short period of time while your final disposition is determined."

Andy Malachenko leaned down with his head close to Brannigan and Leroux, whispering what was being said in English.

Khumar continued, "Those of you who wish to return to the Russian Federation will be allowed to petition for repatriation."

Surov spoke up, saying, "I wish to take advantage of that, but there are others of us who have no desire to go back to the Motherland."

"In those cases, the Tajik government will seriously consider granting political asylum," Khumar informed him. "And, of course, if there are other countries some desire to go to, arrangements can be made to accommodate those wishes."

Grabvosky, the little bookish man who had been an underboss under Luka Yarkov, raised his hand. "What are the chances of remaining in Tajikistan? I am qualified as a bookkeeper and wish to seek such a position in this country."

"There is no problem with that," Khumar said. "You or anybody else with like desires will be allowed to search for employment. You could even apply for Tajik citizenship after you meet the qualifications."

Burly Aleksei Barkyev had another concern. "What about our women and children?"

"You will have to forget them," Khumar said. "The women were taken by force from their homes in criminal acts. Because of religion and custom, they would be slain if returned to their families. Arrangements have already been made with a UN mission to have them taken somewhere to live in safety. The children they bore must go with them."

Surov grinned sardonically. "We really have no choice, do we?"

"Are the options you have so awful?" Khumar asked. "You have a chance to return to decent society and rebuild your miserable lives. One would hope you would demonstrate the intelligence and will to become useful citizens somewhere."

Dagorov was a bit stubborn. "What if my woman wants to go with me?"

"Forget your woman," Khumar said sternly. "She is gone from your life forever."

"Where will the UN send them?"

"You need not concern yourself with that," Khumar said. "We want your answer now."

The Russians looked at each other, then all shrugged. Surov continued as their spokesman. "We will accept your terms. My comrades and I will go to the barracks to prepare our men to be taken into custody."

"We will give you fifteen minutes," Khumar said. The quartet of ex-Soviet soldiers stood up and went to the door. As soon as they had left, the Tajik major glanced at Caldwell, speaking in English so Brannigan and Leroux could understand. "This is your last chance. Do you desire to have any of them serve your government in some capacity?"

"They're all useless bastards," Caldwell replied.

Khumar smiled. "How unfortunate for them."

1300 HOURS

A Tajik army bus was parked with its diesel engine idling as the Pashtun women and children walked toward it. Dr.

Pierre Couchier and a pair of female UN officials stood by the vehicle, offering cordial greetings to the refugees as they ushered them aboard. They would be taken to the airport in Khorugh to begin the long flight to a sanctuary on the island of Cyprus.

An hour and a half earlier, the twenty-four Russian survivors were formed into a column of twos by Tajik policeman and marched up to the entrance to the settlement where transportation awaited them.

Each prisoner's wrists were bound with a plastic strip.

SEALs BIVOUAC
THE PRANISTAY STEPPES
9 DECEMBER
1330 HOURS

THREE C-130 aircraft had landed in the area used as an LZ. One was from the United States Air Force, while two belonged to the Pakistani Air Force. The two journalists, Dirk Wallenger and Eddie Krafton, had come in on the American aircraft from Shelor Field. They were rather miffed about having to wait almost a week after they did the taping of the feature on Randy Tooley. When Wallenger made an angry inquiry about the delay, Brannigan told him that since nothing special was going on, there was really no rush in having them return. Wallenger's journalistic instincts told him this was an outright falsehood, but it would do him no good to protest.

The Pakistani airplanes were harbingers of very sad news for the Brigands. They had come to pick up the horses for transport back to Sharif Garrison in Pakistan. It was a time of misery for the tough SEALs. But it was Bruno Puglisi who broke into tears when he made his good-bye to Ralph. He leaned over the animal's muzzle and wept like a baby, unable to speak through his sobbing. Ralph, for his part, sensed something was wrong, and he nuzzled his human buddy in an equine show of sympathy and caring. After the horses were put aboard the aircraft, Puglisi turned and walked away. He went a couple of kilometers out onto the steppes, keeping his eyes turned from the sight of the departure.

None of the Brigands paid much attention to him. They each had their own grief to deal with.

EPILOGUE

THE Brigands returned to the USS *Dan Daly* to resume their between-mission routines. They arrived on the flight deck via a CH-53 chopper from the local CVBG, and disembarked dirty, tired, and ready to go back to the excellent meals provided by the ship's galley crew, as well as sleeping between clean sheets and showering regularly.

· The one previous activity the SEALs enjoyed the most while stationed aboard the *Daly* was now forbidden them by the ship's captain. That was their volleyball league, noted for its lack of rules, decorum, and human decency. A better name for the Brigands' version of the popular sport would have been volley brawl. The punching, kicking, and tackling was more of a riot than an athletic event. The noise and disturbance of the games disrupted the crew's routine to the extent that Captain Jackson Fletcher issued a written order to Lieutenant William Brannigan that his men would cease and desist conducting the games. The captain ended the missive with a serious suggestion that they take up chess. Two other alternatives he recommended were stamp collecting and raising hamsters, although he admitted he was a bit reluctant about the latter hobby. He stated that the SEALs would probably eat them.

But the first few days after their return were spent in maintenance and repair of gear and weaponry before settling down to a routine of PT on the deck under the exuberant supervision of Senior Chief Petty Officer Buford Dawkins. Of course, the usual classes on mandatory military and naval subjects were scheduled for the afternoons. Evenings were spent in card games, consuming beer, and attempts at seducing various female members of the ship's crew.

THE broadcast efforts of Dirk Wallenger paid off handsomely for the journalist. After his and the cameraman Eddie Krafton's return to the States, Wallenger was the toast of the TV airways because of his reports titled "Somewhere in the War." He appeared on all the major talk shows while broadcasting nightly on the GNB network. Eddie received very little credit for his part in the presentations, but like most people who did the taping, he was used to a dearth of accolades.

THE warmth of Florida suited Luka Yarkov and Igor Tchaikurov. They were placed into the U.S. government's Witness Protection Program with new identities. They were able to move in smoothly with the new and growing population of Russian émigrés in the Miami area to build new lives for themselves.

Yarkov had a rough time since he had to learn to speak English before being able to find decent employment. While studying the language at night, he worked the counter of a meat market dealing with mostly Russian customers. Although Tchaikurov had the advantage of possessing a reasonable working knowledge of English, he could find no better employment than that as a security guard on a bank armored delivery truck. He worked for minimum wage, but liked being able to pack a pistol and wear a proper uniform.

He almost felt like he was back in the Russian Army, and the pay was better.

THE tradition of *nonwatai* was practiced faithfully by both the Yousafzai and Janoon tribes. The Mahsuds et al. humbled themselves before them in a public display of apology and regret. Consequently, instead of being slaughtered, the victorious clans offered no punishment other than for the losers having to pay a hefty retribution out their shares of the coming opium poppy harvest.

ZAID Aburrani was sent from Barri Prison in Bahrain to an unnamed detention center in the south of Poland. He was scheduled for further examination before being returned to Afghanistan for final disposition. The Coalition Forces knew he would go unpunished by his own authorities. All crooked politicians and bureaucrats have enough dirt on their associates that they get no more than slaps on the wrist after being eased back into corrupt systems. It's never long before they are once again playing sleazy games.

GLOSSARY

2IC: Second in Command
2-Shop: Intelligence Section of the staff
3-Shop: Operations and Training Section of the staff
4-Shop: Logistics Section of the staff
AA: Anti-Aircraft
AAR: After-Action Report
ACV: Air Cushion Vehicle (hovercraft)
Afghan: Currency of Afghanistan—43.83 = $1
AFSOC: Air Force Special Operations Command
AGL: Above Ground Level
AK-47: 7.62-millimeter Russian Assault Rifle
AKA: Also Known As
AKS-74: 5.45-millimeter Russian Assault Rifle
Angel: A thousand feet above ground level, e.g., Angels Two
    is two thousand feet.
AP: Armor Piercing or Air Police
APC: Armored Personnel Carrier
ARG: Amphibious Ready Group
AS-50: .50-caliber semiautomatic sniper rifle with scope
ASAP: As Soon As Possible

ASL: Above Sea Level

Asset: An individual who has certain knowledge or experiences that make him helpful to individuals or units about to be deployed into operational areas.

AT: Anti-Tank

AT-4: Antiarmor rocket launchers

Attack Board (also Compass Board): A board with a compass, watch, and depth gauge used by subsurface swimmers.

ATV: All Terrain Vehicle

AWACS: Airborne Warning and Control System

AWOL: Away Without Leave; i.e., absent from one's unit without permission, AKA French leave.

Bastion: Part of a fortification or fortified position that juts outward.

BBC: British Broadcasting Corporation

BDU: Battle Dress Uniform

Blighty: British slang for their home nation.

Boot: A rookie or recruit.

Boot Camp: Navy or Marine Corps "basic training"

BOQ: Bachelor Officers' Quarters

Briefback: A briefing given to staff by a SEAL platoon regarding their assigned mission. This must be approved before it is implemented.

BUD/S: Basic Underwater Demolition SEAL training course

Bushido: The philosophy and code of conduct of Japanese samurai warriors.

BX: Base Exchange, a military store with good prices for service people. AKA **PX** in the Army for Post Exchange.

C4: Plastic explosive

CAR-15: Compact model of the M16 rifle

CAS: Close Air Support

CATF: Commander, Amphibious Task Force

CDC: Combat Direction Center aboard a ship

CG: Commanding General

Chickenshit: An adjective that describes a person or a situation as being particularly draconian, overly strict, unfair or malicious.

CHP: California Highway Patrol

CLU: Command launch unit for the Javelin AT missile

CNO: Chief of Naval Operations

CO: Commanding Officer

Cover: Hat, headgear

CP: Command Post

CPU: Computer Processing Unit

CPX: Command Post Exercise

CRRC: Combat Rubber Raiding Craft

CRT: Cathode Ray Tube

CS: Tear gas

CSAR: Combat Search and Rescue

CTT: Combat Training Tank—swimming pool at BUD/S

CVBG: Carrier Battle Group

Dashika: Slang name for the Soviet DShK 12.7-millimeter heavy machine gun

DDG: Guided-Missile Destroyer

DEA: Drug Enforcement Agency

Det Cord: Detonating Cord

DJMS: Defense Joint Military Pay System

DPV: Desert Patrol Vehicle

Draeger Mk V: Underwater air supply equipment

DZ: Drop Zone

E&E: Escape and Evasion

Enfilade Fire: Gunfire that sweeps along an enemy formation

EPW: Enemy Prisoner of War

ER: Emergency Room (hospital)

ERP: Enroute Rally Point. A rally point that a patrol leader chooses while moving to or from the objective.

ESP: Extra Sensory Perception

ETS: End of Term of Service

FLIR: Forward-Looking Infrared Radar

Four-Shop: Logistics Section of the staff

French Leave: See AWOL

FRH: Flameless Ration Heater

Front Leaning Rest: The position assumed to begin push-ups. It is customary to place malfeasants or clumsy personnel in the front leaning rest for punishment since it is anything but a "rest."

FSB: Russian acronym for the Federal Security Service, the organization that was the successor to the KGB after the fall of the Soviet Union.

FTX: Field Training Exercise

G-3: The training and operations staff section of a unit commanded by a general officer.

GHQ: General Headquarters

GI: Government Issue

GPS: Global Positioning System

Gunny: Marine Corps for the rank of Gunnery Sergeant E-7

HAHO: High Altitude High Opening parachute jump

HALO: High Altitude Low Opening parachute jump

Hamas: Palestinian terrorist organization that has been voted into office in Palestine. Their charter calls for the destruction of Israel.

HE: High Explosive

Head: Navy and Marine Corps term for toilet; called a latrine in the Army

HEAT: High Explosive Anti-Tank

Heel-and-toe: See Watch-and-watch

Hell Week: The fifth week of BUD/S that is five-plus days of continuous activity and training with little or no sleep.

Hezbollah: A militant Islamic terrorist organization located in Lebanon. It was organized in response to the Israeli occupation, and is still active.

H&K MP-5: Heckler & Koch MP-5 submachine gun

Hootch: A simple shelter structure one generally must crawl into. They are usually covered by extra ponchos or tarpaulins, and used as a basic shelter in the boondocks. This is a corruption of the word "hutch" such as would inhabited by a rabbit.

Hors de combat: Out of the battle (expression in French)

HSB: High Speed Boat

IFV: Infantry Fighting Vehicle

Immediate Action: A quick, sometimes temporary fix to a mechanical problem

INTREP: Intelligence Report

INTSUM: Intelligence Summary

IR: Infrared

IRP: Initial Rally Point. A place within friendly lines where a patrol assembles prior to moving out on the mission.

Island: The superstructure of an aircraft carrier or assault ship

JCOS: Joint Chiefs of Staff

JSOC: Joint Special Operation Command

K-Bar: A brand of knives manufactured for military and camping purposes

KD Range: Known Distance Firing Range

Keffiyeh: Arab headdress (what Yasser Arafat wore)

KGB: Russian organization of security, espionage and intelligence left over from the old Soviet Union, eventually succeeded by the FSB

KIA: Killed In Action

KISS: Keep It Simple, Stupid—or more politely, Keep It Simple, Sweetheart

LBE: Load-Bearing Equipment

Light Sticks: Flexible plastic tubes that illuminate

Limpet Mine: An explosive mine that is attached to the hulls of vessels

Locked Heels: When a serviceman is getting a severe vocal reprimand, it is said he is having his "heels locked," i.e., standing at attention while someone is bellowing in his face.

LSO: Landing Signal Officer

LSPO: Landing Signal Petty Officer

LSSC: Light SEAL Support Craft

LZ: Landing Zone

M-18 Claymore Mine: A mine fired electrically with a blasting cap

M-60 E3: A compact model of the M-60 machine gun

M-67: An antipersonnel grenade

M-203: A single-shot 40-millimeter grenade launcher

MATC: a fast river support craft

MC: Medical Corps

MCPO: Master Chief Petty Officer

Mecca: The city located in Saudi Arabia that is the destination of Islamic pilgrimages

Medevac: Medical Evacuation

MI-5: United Kingdom Intelligence and Security Agency

Mk 138 Satchel Charge: Canvas container filled with explosive

MLR: Main Line of Resistance

Mossad: Israeli Intelligence Agency (*ha-Mossad le-Modiin ule-Tafkidim Meyuhadim*—Institute for Intelligence and Special Tasks)

MRE: Meal, Ready to Eat

MSSC: Medium SEAL Support Craft

Murphy's Law: An assumption that if something can go wrong, it most certainly will.

N1: Manpower and Personnel Staff

N2: Intelligence Staff

N3: Operations Staff

NAS: Naval Air Station

NAVSPECWAR: Naval Special Warfare

NCO: Noncommissioned Officers, e.g., corporals and sergeants

NCP: Navy College Program

NFL: National Football League

NROTC: Naval Reserve Officer Training Corps

NVB: Night-Vision Binoculars

NVG: Night-Vision Goggles

NVS: Night-Vision Sight

OA: Operational Area

OCONUS: Outside the Continental United States

OCS: Officers Candidate School

OER: Officer's Efficiency Report

OP: Observation Post

OPLAN: Operations Plan. This is the preliminary form of an OPORD.

OPORD: Operations Order. This is the directive derived from the OPLAN of how an operation is to be carried out. It's pretty much etched in stone.

ORP: Objective Rally Point. A location chosen before or after reaching the objective. Here a patrol can send out recon on the objective, make final preparations, reestablish the chain of command, and other activities necessary either before or right after action.

PBL: Patrol Boat, Light

PC: Patrol Coastal vessel

PDQ: Pretty Damn Quick

PIA: Pakistan International Airline

PLF: Parachute Landing Fall

PM: Preventive Maintenance

PMC: Private Military Company. These are businesses that supply bodyguards, security personnel, and mercenary civilian fighting men to persons or organizations wanting to hire them.

PO: Petty Officer (e.g., PO1C is Petty Officer First Class)

Poop: News or information

POV: Privately Owned Vehicle

P.P.P.P.: Piss Poor Prior Planning

PT: Physical Training

RAPS: Ram Air Parachute System; parachute and gear for free-fall jumps

RHIP: Rank Has Its Privileges

RIB: Rigid Inflatable Boat

RIO: Radar Intercept Officer

RON: Remain Over Night. Generally refers to patrols.

RPG: Rocket-Propelled Grenade

RPM: Revolutions Per Minute

R and R: Rest and Relaxation, Rest and Recuperation, and a few other things used by the troops to describe short liberties or furloughs to kick back and enjoy themselves.

RRP: Reentry Rally Point. A site outside the range of friendly lines to pause and prepare for reentry.

RTO: Radio Telephone Operator

Run-flat tires: Solid-rubber inserts that allow the vehicle to run even when the tires have been punctured.

SAS: Special Air Services—an extremely deadly and super-efficient special operations unit of the British Army

SAW: Squad Automatic Weapon—M249 5.56-millimeter magazine- or clip-fed machine gun

SCPO: Senior Chief Petty Officer

SCUBA: Self-Contained Underwater Breathing Apparatus

SDV: SEAL Delivery Vehicle

SERE: Survival, Escape, Resistance, and Evasion

SF: Special Forces
SFOB: Special Forces Operational Base
Shahid: Arabian word for martyr (plural is *Shahiden*)
Shiites: A branch of Islam; in serious conflict with the Sunnis
SITREP: Situation Report
SNAFU: Situation Normal, All Fucked Up
Snap-to: The act of quickly and sharply assuming the position of attention with chin up, shoulders back, thumbs along the seams of the trousers, and heels locked with toes at a 45-degree angle.
SOCOM: Special Operations Command
SOF: Special Operations Force
SOI: Signal Operating Instructions
SOLS: Special Operations Liaison Staff
Somoni: Currency of Tajikistan—2.79 = $1
SOP: Standard Operating Procedures
SPA: Self-Propelled Artillery
Special Boat Squadrons: Units that participate in SEAL missions
SPECOPS: Special Operations
SPECWARCOM: Special Warfare Command
Spetsnaz: Russian Special Forces unit of various branches
Stand-to: Being on watch or at a fighting position
Sunnis: A branch of Islam; in serious conflict with the Shiites
Superstructure: The part of the ship above the main deck
T-10 Parachute: Basic static-line-activated personnel parachute of the United States Armed Forces. Primarily designed for mass tactical parachute jumps.
Tail-End-Charlie: Brigand terminology for the last man in an operation, e.g., the final guy getting off a vehicle, jumping from an aircraft, rear guard on a patrol, etc.
Taliban: Militant, anti-West Muslims with extreme religious views; in serious conflict with Shiites
TDy: Temporary Duty
Three-Shop: Operations and Training Section of the staff
TO: Table of Organization
TOA: Table of Allowances
TO&E: Table of Organization and Equipment
Two-Shop: Intelligence Section of the staff

U.K.: The United Kingdom (England, Wales, Scotland, and Northern Ireland)

UN: United Nations

Unass: To jump out of or off something

UNREO: United Nations Relief and Education Organization

USAF: United States Air Force

USASFC: United States Army Special Forces Command

USSR: Union of Soviet Social Republics—Russia before the fall of Communism

VTOL: Vertical Take Off and Landing

WARNO: Warning Order. An informal alert, either written or oral, that informs personnel of an upcoming operation or activity

Watch-and-watch: This is a watch bill that requires personnel to be off only one watch before going back on again. This is used as a punishment or when a shortage of personnel requires such scheduling. AKA heel-and-toe.

Watch Bill: A list of personnel and stations for the watch

Waypoint: A location programmed into navigational instrumentation that directs aircraft, vehicles, and/or vessels to a specific spot on the planet

Whaler Boat: Small craft loosely based on the types of boats used in whaling. They are generally carried aboard naval and merchant vessels and are diesel-powered.

WIA: Wounded in Action

WMD: Weapons of Mass Destruction: nuclear, biological, etc.

Yeoman: Sailors who perform clerical and secretarial duties

PASHTUN LANGUAGE GLOSSARY

Note: Speakers of Pashtun employ suffixes and prefixes to indicate verbal conjunction; gender and plurality of nouns, adjectives; adverbs; etc. In most cases, the words listed here are the roots.

Amrika: America
Aweshtel: To turn
Awredel: To listen, to hear
Badal: Pashtun code of vengeance
Barcha: Bayonet
Chapatti: Unleavened wheat flatbread, also a colloquialism for sandals
Chiku: A type of fruit with the taste of date and the texture of kiwi
Chorkey: Dagger
Hamla kawel: To charge
Ho: Yes
Kartus: Cartridge
Khan: Warlord, owner of much land
Khayr ose: Response to "Welcome"

Khuday pea man: Response to "See you later" or "See you tomorrow"

Lar sha!: "Go!"

Lasi Bam: Grenade

Malik: Tribal chief, headman

Mana: Apple

Manana: Thank you

Mashindar: Machine gun

Melmastia: Pashtun code of hospitality

Molla: Cleric

Na: No

Nonwatai: Pashtun code of submission to a victorious enemy; a plea for mercy and/or forgiveness that must be granted

Oleme: Judge

Pakora: Vegetables dipped in flour and then deep-fried

Payra: Patrol

Pe khayr raghle: Welcome

Pohedel: To understand

Puhtee: Beret-like cap that can be rolled and arranged into various shapes and styles

Pukhoor: A serape-type covering

Raket Lenchar: Rocket launcher

Qaze: Judge

Salamat osey: Response to "Hello" from a man

Samosa: Deep-fried pastry triangle filled with vegetables

Shal: Scarf, kerchief, shawl

Spinzhire: "Gray-beard," i.e., village elder (slang term)

Stari me shey: "Hello" to a group

Tayara: Airplane

Temancha: Pistol

Topak: Rifle

Tsapley: Sandals

Wazhel: To murder, to kill